Margaret Daley, an award-winning author of ninety books (five million sold worldwide), has been married for over forty years and is a firm believer in romance and love. When she isn't traveling, she's writing love stories, often with a suspense thread, and corralling her three cats, who think they rule her household. To find out more about Margaret, visit her website at margaretdaley.com.

A seventh-generation Texan, **Jolene Navarro** fills her life with family, faith and life's beautiful messiness. She knows that as much as the world changes, people stay the same: vow-keepers and heartbreakers. Jolene married a vow-keeper who shows her holding hands never gets old. When not writing, Jolene teaches art to inner-city teens and hangs out with her own four almost-grown kids. Find Jolene on Facebook or her blog, jolenenavarrowriter.com.

Her Holiday Hero

Margaret Daley

&

Lone Star Holiday

Jolene Navarro

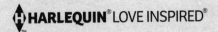 **HARLEQUIN**® LOVE INSPIRED®

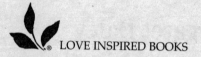 LOVE INSPIRED BOOKS

Recycling programs
for this product may
not exist in your area.

ISBN-13: 978-1-335-44815-6

Her Holiday Hero and Lone Star Holiday

Copyright © 2018 by Harlequin Books S.A.

The publisher acknowledges the copyright holders
of the individual works as follows:

Her Holiday Hero
Copyright © 2013 by Margaret Daley

Lone Star Holiday
Copyright © 2013 by Jolene Navarro

www.Harlequin.com

Printed in U.S.A.

CONTENTS

HER HOLIDAY HERO

Margaret Daley

To all our brave soldiers
who have kept this country safe.

God is our refuge and strength,
a very present help in trouble.
—*Psalms* 46:1

Chapter One

◆

Jake Tanner had pulled out the desk chair in his home office and started to sit when the front doorbell chimed in the blissful quiet. He would never take silence for granted again. A long breath swooshed from his lungs as he straightened and gripped his cane, then limped toward the foyer. Through the long, narrow window with beveled glass, he could make out his neighbor standing on the porch.

Marcella Kime found a reason to see him at least a couple of times a week. He'd become her mission since he'd returned home to Cimarron City from serving in the military overseas. A few days earlier she'd jokingly told him she missed her grandson, and he would do just fine taking his place. He still wasn't sure what to make of that statement. He had returned to Cimarron City, a town he'd lived in for a while and visited often to see his grandma. Dealing with family, especially his father, the general, had been too much for him three months ago when he'd been released from the military hospital.

He swung the door open to reveal Marcella, probably no more than five feet tall, if that, with her hands full. "Good morning." She smiled as she juggled a large box and a plate of pastries. He reached for the parcel.

"The Fed Ex guy left this late yesterday afternoon. I meant to bring it over sooner, but then I had to go to church to help with the pancake supper. You're always home so I was surprised he couldn't deliver the package."

"Went to the VA hospital in Oklahoma City."

"Oh, good. You went out." She presented the plate of goodies. "I baked extra ones this morning because I know how much you enjoy my cinnamon rolls. I'm going to put those pounds you lost back on in no time. I imagine all those K rations aren't too tasty."

"I haven't had MREs—meals ready to eat—in six months, and no, they aren't tasty. In the hospital I was fed regular meals." But he hadn't wanted to eat much. He was working out again and building up his muscles at least.

"Oh, my. *K rations* certainly dates me. That's what they were called when my older brother was in the army."

His seventy-five-year-old neighbor with stark white hair never was at a loss for words. After she left, his head would throb from all the words tumbling around inside. He wanted to tell her again that she didn't need to worry about him, that in time his full appetite would return, but she continued before he could open his mouth.

"I'd come in, but I have to leave. Saturday is my day to get my hair washed and fixed. It needs it. Can't miss that." She thrust the plate toward him. "I'll come back later and get my dish."

After placing the parcel on the table nearby, he took

the cinnamon rolls from his neighbor, their scent teasing that less than robust appetite. "Thanks, Miss Kime."

"Tsk. Tsk. Didn't I tell you to call me Marcella, young man? Your grandma and me were good friends. I miss her."

"So do I, Miss—I mean, Marcella."

When she had traversed the four steps to his sidewalk, Jake closed his front door, shutting out the world. With a sigh, he scanned his living room, the familiar surroundings where he controlled his environment, knew what to expect. Even Marcella's visits weren't surprises anymore.

Jake balanced the plate on the box, carried it into his office and set it on the desk to open later. It was from his father and his new wife—a care package as they'd promised in their last call. Finally, they weren't trying to talk him into coming to live with them in Florida anymore. He needed his space, and he certainly didn't want to be reminded daily that he'd let down the general—he wouldn't follow in his father's footsteps. He needed a sense of what this house had given when he was growing up—peace.

He snatched a cinnamon roll as he sat in front of his laptop, his coffee cup already on his right on a coaster. While he woke up his computer, he bit into the roll and closed his eyes, savoring the delectable pastry. Marcella sure could bake. Before getting started in his course work for his Ph.D. in psychology, he clicked on his email, expecting one from his doctor at the VA about some test results.

Only one email that wasn't junk popped up. He recognized the name, a message from the wife of a soldier who had served under him in Afghanistan. His heartbeat picked up speed. He should open it, but after an email a couple of weeks prior where he discovered one of his men had died from his injuries in an ambush, he didn't know if he could.

His chest constricted. But the woman's name taunted him. With a fortifying breath, he clicked on the message. As their commanding officer, it was his duty to know what happened to his men, even if he couldn't do anything about it.

His comrade was going in for another operation to repair the damage from a bomb explosion. Her words whisked Jake back to that day six months ago that had changed his life. The sound of the blast rocked his mind as though he were in the middle of the melee all over again.

Sweat beaded on his forehead and rolled down his face. His hands shook as he closed the laptop, hoping that would stop the flood of memories. He never wanted to remember that day. Ever. The walls of his home office began to close in on him, mocking what peace he felt in his familiar surroundings. He surged to his feet and hobbled around the room, dragging in breaths that didn't satisfy his need for oxygen.

I'm in Cimarron City. In my house. Safe.

In the midst of the terror that day in the mountain village, he'd grasped on to the Lord and held tight as He guided him through the rubble and smoke to save whomever he could. But where was God now when he needed Him? He felt abandoned, left to piece his life together. Alone.

He paced the room, glancing back at the computer a couple of times until he forced himself to look away. Lightheaded, he stopped at the window, leaning on his cane, and focused on his front lawn. Reconnoitering the area. Old habits didn't die easily.

He started to turn away when something out of the corner of his eye caught his attention. He swung back and homed in on a group of kids across the street—two boys beating up a smaller child.

Anger clenched his gut. He balled his hands as another kid jumped in on the lopsided fight. That clinched it for Jake. He couldn't stand by and watch a child being hurt. Adrenaline began pumping through him as though he were going into battle, pushing his earlier panic into the background. He rushed toward the front door. But out on his porch, anxiety slammed into his chest, rooting him to the spot.

Jake's gaze latched on to the three boys against the one, taking turns punching the child. All his thoughts centered on the defenseless kid, trying to protect himself. Heart pounding, Jake took one step, then another. His whole body felt primed to fight as it had when as a soldier he vied with the other part of him—sweat coating his skin, hands trembling, gut churning.

No choice.

Furiously he increased his pace until he half ran and half limped toward the group, pain zipping up his injured leg. The boys were too intent on their prey to notice him. When he came to a halt, dropping his cane, he jerked first one then another off the child on the ground. He tried holding on to the one he pegged as the leader while reaching for the third kid, but the boy yanked free and raced deeper into the park with the second one hurrying after him.

"What's your name?" Pain radiating up his bad leg, Jake blocked it as much as he could from his mind and clasped the arm of the last child, smaller than the other two who'd fled and more the size of the boy on the ground.

The assailant glared at him, his mouth pinched in a hard line.

The downed kid still lay huddled in a tight ball. As much as Jake wanted to interrogate the bully he held, he needed to see to the hurt child. He memorized the features of the third attacker then released him. As expected, the third attacker fled in the same direction as his cohorts.

That was okay. Jake could identify him. He wouldn't get off scot-free.

Adrenaline still surging, Jake knelt by the boy. That sent another sharp streak of pain up his thigh. But over the months he'd learned that if he concentrated hard enough, he could ignore the aches his injury still caused. "You're safe now. Can I help you? Where do you hurt?"

For a long moment the child didn't say anything. Didn't move.

Concern flooded Jake. He settled his hand on the boy's shoulder. "Where do you live? Can you make it home?" Should he call 911? Had the bullies done worse damage than he realized?

Slowly, the child uncurled his body. He winced as he turned and looked up. Jake took in the cut lip and cheek, blood oozing from the wounds, the eye that would blacken by tomorrow, the torn shirt.

"Let me help you home."

Wariness entered the kid's blue eyes. "I'm fine." He swiped his dirty sleeve across his mouth, smearing the blood.

"Who were those guys?"

The child clamped his lips together, cringing, but keeping his mouth closed.

"The least I can do is make sure you get home without those kids bothering you again."

The boy's eyes widened.

"Okay?"

The child nodded once then tried to stand. Halfway up, his legs gave out, and he sank to the ground.

Jake moved closer. "Let me help." He steadied himself with his cane.

When the boy stood with Jake's assistance, he wobbled but remained on his feet.

"I've been in a few fights. I know you have to get your bearings before doing too much."

The child tilted his head back and looked up at Jake, pain reflected in his eyes. "Did ya win?"

"Sometimes. Can you walk home? If you don't think you can, I'll call your parents." He dug into his pocket and pulled out his cell phone.

"No, I can walk." The child glanced over his shoulder. "Do you think they'll come back?"

"Not if they know what's good for them. I won't let them hurt you again."

"I wish that was true," the boy, probably no more than ten, mumbled, his head dropping. His body language shouted defeat.

"It's getting worse," Jake heard the kid mumble to himself. That again aroused the protective instinct in him.

"C'mon. Show me where you live. Is it far?" He looked back to check for the trio who had jumped the child. A male jogger and a couple, hands clasped, were the only people he saw in the park. "I'm Jake. What's your name?" With his injured leg throbbing, he used his cane to support more of his weight than usual.

"Josh." The boy dragged his feet as they turned the corner onto Sooner Road.

"Why were those kids bothering you?" The question came out before Jake could censor himself. He didn't want to get involved. Yet, the second he took the first step toward the fight, he had become involved, knowing firsthand what the boy was going through.

Josh mumbled something again, but Jake could hear only the words, "like to fight."

"Have those guys bullied you before?"

The boy's pace slowed until he came to a stop in front of a one-story, redbrick house with a long porch across the front. "Yeah. The big one has since he moved here," he said, his head still hanging.

"Do your parents know?" Jake studied the top of the child's head, some blood clotted in the brown hair. The urge to check the wound inundated him. He started to bring his hand up.

Josh jerked his chin up, anger carved into his features while his eyes glistened. "I don't have a dad. I don't want my mom knowing. You can't tell her." He took a step back. His hands fisted at his sides as if he were ready to defend that statement.

"I won't."

The taut set of the child's shoulders relaxed some, his fingers flexed.

"But *you* will."

"No, I won't. I can take care of this myself. Mom will just get all upset and worried."

"She'll know something is wrong with one look at

you." Jake gestured toward the house with a neatly trimmed yard, mums in full bloom in the flower bed and an inviting porch with white wicker furniture, perfect for enjoying a fall evening. Idyllic, as if part of the world wasn't falling apart with people battling each other. "Is this where you live?"

Josh stuck his lower lip out and crossed his arms, wearing a defiant expression.

Instantly, Jake flashed back to an incident with a captive prisoner who gave him that same look. His heartbeat raced. His breathing became shallow. His world shrank to that small hut in the mountains as he faced an enemy who had been responsible for killing civilians and soldiers the day before. He felt the shaking start in his hands. Jake fought to shut down the helplessness before it took over.

"Josh, what's going on?" A female voice penetrated the haze of memories.

Jake blinked and looked toward the porch. A tall woman, a few inches shy of six feet, with long blond hair pulled back in a ponytail that swished, marched down the steps toward them, distress stamped on her features.

"What happened to you?" Stooping in front of the boy, the lady grasped Josh's arms. When he didn't say anything, she peered up at Jake. "What happened?"

"Is Josh your son?"

"Yes." The anxiety in her blue eyes, the same crystalline color as the boy's, pleaded for him to answer the question.

Jake shifted. He'd done what he said he would do. He'd delivered the child safely home. It was time to leave Josh and his mother to hash out what had occurred in the park. He backed away, his grip on the cane like a clamp. He spied the imploring look in Josh's eyes. "Your son needs to tell you," he said.

She turned back to the boy. "You're bleeding, your eye is red and your clothes are a mess. Did you get in a fight?"

The boy nodded.

"Why? That's not you, Josh."

The kid yanked away from his mom and yelled, "Yeah! That's the problem!" He stormed toward the house.

Jake took another step back.

She whirled toward him, her face full of a mother's wrath. "What's going on?"

"He was in a fight."

"I got that much from him."

"I broke it up and walked him home." Jake could barely manage his own life. He didn't want to get in the middle of someone else's, but the appeal in Josh's mother's eyes demanded he say something. "Three boys were beating up Josh."

"Why?"

"That you have to ask him. I came in after it started, and he wasn't forthcoming about what was going on."

"But something is. I get the feeling this wasn't the first time."

"A good assumption."

"I'm Emma Langford." She paused, waiting for him to supply his name.

He clamped his teeth down hard for a few seconds before he muttered, "Jake Tanner. I live around the corner, across from the park." Why did he add the last?

Because there was something in her expression that softened the armor around his heart.

The woman glanced up and down the street, kneading her fingertips into her temple. "I don't know what to do. It sounds like they ganged up on Josh. Have you seen them around?"

"No, but I know what they look like, especially one of them close to Josh's size. The other two were bigger than him. Maybe older." He could understand a mother's concern and the need to defend her child. He'd often felt the same way about the men under his command.

"So my child is being bullied." Weariness dripped from each word.

Jake moved closer, an urge to comfort assailing him. Taking him by surprise. For months he'd been trying to shut off his emotions. Hopelessness and fear were what had him in his current condition: unable to function the way he had before his last tour of duty.

"He never said a word to me, but I should have known," she said in a thick voice. "No wonder he's been so angry and withdrawn these past few months."

"That would be a good reason. Chances are he doesn't know how to handle it, either."

"Do you think they live in the neighborhood?" She panned the houses around her as if she could spot where the bullies lived.

"Maybe. They were in the park when the fight occurred."

"I need to find out who's bullying my son and put a stop to it."

"How?" Jake could remember being bullied in school when he was in the sixth grade.

"I don't know. Confront them. Have a conversation with their parents."

"Often that makes the situation worse. It did for me when I was a child." The reply came out before he could stop the words.

"But maybe it would put a stop to it. Make a difference for my son." Her forehead creased, she glanced back at the house. "I want to thank you for what you did for Josh. Would you like some tea or lemonade?"

He hesitated. He needed to say no, but he couldn't, not after glimpsing the lost look in the lady's eyes.

"Please. I make freshly squeezed lemonade." She started toward her house. "We can enjoy it outside on the porch."

Part of him wanted to follow her, to help her—the old Jake—but that guy was gone, left in the mountains where some of his men had died.

She slowed and glanced back, anxiety shadowing her eyes. "I'm at a loss about what to do. Tell me what happened to you when you were bullied. That is, if you don't mind. It may help me figure out what to do about Josh."

It was just her porch. He wouldn't be confined. He could escape easily.

He took a step toward her, then another, but with each pace closer to the house, his legs became heavier. By the time he mounted the stairs, he could barely lift them. He paused several feet from the front door and glanced at the white wicker furniture, a swing hanging from the ceiling at the far end. Thoughts of his mother's parents' farmhouse where he'd spent time every summer came to mind. For a moment peace descended. He tried to hold on to that feeling, but it evaporated in seconds at the sound of an engine revving and then a car speeding down the street.

The sudden loudness of the noise made him start to duck behind a wicker chair a couple of feet away. He stopped himself, but not before anger and frustration swamped him. His heartbeat revved like the vehicle, and the shakes accosted him. He clasped his hands on the knob of his cane and pressed it down into the wooden slat of the porch.

What was he thinking? He should never have accepted her invitation.

"I'm sorry. I can't. I have stuff to do at home." He pivoted so fast he nearly lost his balance and had to bring his cane down quickly to prevent it.

"Thank you for your help today with my son," Emma quickly got out.

Sweat popped out on his forehead and ran down his face, into his eyes. He concentrated on the stinging sensation to take his mind off everything rushing toward him. As fast as his injured leg would let him, he hurried toward his house and the familiar surroundings where he knew what to expect. The trembling in his hands had spread throughout his body by the time he arrived in his yard.

Once inside his home, he fell back against the door and closed his eyes, trying to slow his stampeding heartbeat. His chest rose and fell rapidly as he gulped air. He slid down the length of the door and sat on the tiled foyer floor, blocking the deep ache that emanated from his recent injury.

Rage at himself, at his situation swamped him, and he slammed his fist into his palm. Pain shot up his arm.

He didn't care. It wasn't anything compared to how he hated what was happening to him.

What are You doing, God? I want a normal life. Not be a slave to these panic attacks. Why aren't You answering my prayers?

Chapter Two

From the front porch, Emma watched Jake Tanner limp down the sidewalk toward the corner at Park Avenue. Mr. Tanner had saved her son from getting hurt worse than he already was. Had the situation with Josh brought back bad memories of the man's childhood? Was that why he'd left so quickly? Why there was a poignant look in his dark brown eyes? She guessed she shouldn't have asked him about what happened to him when he was bullied. That couldn't be easy for anyone to remember.

Mr. Tanner rounded the corner and disappeared from her view. From what she'd seen of the man, it certainly appeared he could take care of himself, even with his injured leg. She was five feet ten inches, and he had to be a good half a foot taller. He might be limping but clearly that didn't stop him from doing some kind of physical exercise. Dressed in tight jeans and a black T-shirt, he looked well built with a hard, muscular body—a little leaner than he was probably accustomed to.

"Jake Tanner" rolled off her tongue as if she'd said it before. Why did it sound familiar to her? Where had she heard his name? Had she run into him somewhere in town? She wasn't from Cimarron City but had lived here for years. But then he would be a hard man to forget with his striking good looks.

Had he hurt himself recently? Was the injury to his left leg permanent? Questions began to flood her mind until she shook her head.

No. He made it clear he'd helped Josh, but that was all. Besides, she had her hands full with a child who was angry all the time. And there were her two jobs—one as a veterinary assistant at Harris Animal Hospital and the other as a trainer for service dogs with the Caring Canines Foundation with Abbey Winters, her best friend. Abbey had founded the organization that placed service and therapy dogs with people who needed them. Emma didn't want any more complications in her life, and she certainly wasn't interested in dating, even though it had been three years since her husband died, leaving her widowed at twenty-nine with a son.

Who is my top priority—Josh.

Emma threw one last glance at the corner of Sooner and Park, then headed inside and toward Josh's bedroom. They needed to have a conversation about what had happened today whether her son wanted to talk or not. Her child would not be used as a punching bag. The very thought tightened her chest and made breathing difficult.

She halted outside his closed door, drew air into her lungs until her nerves settled and then knocked. She half expected Josh to ignore her, but thirty seconds later, he swung open the door. A scowl puckered his face, and he clenched his jaw so tightly, a muscle in his cheek twitched, underscoring his anger. He left her standing in the entrance, trudged to his bed and flung himself on his back onto his navy blue coverlet.

"I'm not telling you who those guys are."

"Why not?" She moved into his room and sat at the end of the bed, facing him.

"You'll say something to them or their parents."

"Are you being bothered at school? Is that why you haven't wanted to go these past six weeks since school started?"

He clamped his lips together until his mouth was a thin, tight line.

"I'm going to talk to your teacher whether you say anything or not. I can't sit by and let someone, or in this case, several boys bully you."

"Don't, Mom. I'll take care of this. It's *my* problem."

The sheen in Josh's eyes, the plea in his voice tore at her composure. She wanted to pull him into her arms and never let go—to keep him safe with her. *Sam, I need you. This is what a dad handles with a son. What do I do?*

She'd never felt so alone as at this moment, staring at Josh fighting the tears welling in his eyes. "I know Mrs. Alexander would want to know. Every child should be safe at school. This is not negotiable. I can't force you to tell me, but I need to know who is doing this to you."

"I'm not a snitch. That's what they'll call me. I'll never live it down."

"So what's your plan? Let them keep beating you up? What if Mr. Tanner hadn't seen them and stopped them? What do you think would have happened?"

Josh shrugged, turned away from her and lay on his bed.

Emma remembered Jake Tanner's words about how

talking with the bullies' parents sometimes only made the situation worse. Then what should she do? What could Josh do? "At least make sure you have friends around you. Don't go anywhere alone. It's obvious now you can't go to Craig's house through the park. I'll have to drive you to and from your friends' houses. I'll pick you up from school and take you in the morning. I'll talk to Dr. Harris and figure out a way to do that with my work schedule. If I can't, I'll see if Abbey will. She takes Madi to and from school." As she listed what she would do, she realized all those precautions weren't really a solution.

Then in the meantime, she'd talk to the school about the bullying. She had to do something to end this. The thought of her son hurting, physically and emotionally, stiffened her resolve to help him somehow whether he liked it or not. She hated that bullies were almost holding her son hostage.

"Don't say anything to Mrs. Alexander, Mom."

Emma rose and hovered over Josh. "I have to. It's my job as your parent. I can't ignore what happened."

He glared at her. "I hate you. You're going to make my life miserable."

The words hurt, but she understood where they came from—fear and anger at his situation. She knew those feelings well, having experienced them after Sam passed away. "I love you, Josh, and your life right now with these bullies isn't what you want or deserve."

Her son buried his head under his pillow.

"I need to check your cuts and clean them."

"Go away."

"I'm not leaving. You aren't alone."

He tossed the pillow toward the end of the bed. "I

wish Mr. Tanner hadn't interfered. Then you wouldn't be making such a big deal out of this."

"Thankfully he did, and believe me, I would have made a big deal out of it when I saw you in this condition whether he'd stepped in or not. I'll be right back with the first-aid kit."

Josh grumbled something she couldn't hear.

As she gathered up what she needed, a picture of Jake Tanner flashed into her mind. Short, dark hair—military style like her brother's... Emma snapped her fingers. That was it. Ben had mentioned a Jake Tanner on several occasions because he was the army captain Ben had served under in his Special Forces Unit. Could this be the same man?

After she patched up an uncooperative Josh, she left him in his bedroom to pout. When she really thought about Josh's angry behavior and keeping to himself, she realized it had begun during the summer. She'd hoped his mood would improve when school started and he saw his friends more. But it hadn't. She'd tried talking to him. He'd been closemouthed and dismissive of her concerns. Why hadn't she seen it earlier?

She made her way to the kitchen to start lunch but first decided to call her brother. She knew it would nag her not to know whether the Jake Tanner she'd met was Ben's company's commanding officer. She remembered Ben's commenting they both had lived in Oklahoma so it was possible.

She called his cell phone number. "Hi, bro. Do you have a moment to appease my curiosity?" Emma leaned against the kitchen counter, staring out the window over the sink at the leaves beginning to change colors.

"For you, always. What's going on?"

"Josh was in the park and some boys jumped him and beat him up. Apparently, this wasn't the first time they'd approached him."

"How's Josh?"

"Some cuts and bruises but I think his self-confidence is more damaged than anything."

"I wish I didn't live so far away. I could help him. With my new job I'm working weekends, so that doesn't leave a lot of time to even drive to Cimarron City when Josh isn't in school."

She didn't want Ben to feel this was his problem. He lived in Tulsa and was just getting his life back. "I'm going to talk to the school on Monday about it. But that's not what I wanted to speak with you about. A man named Jake Tanner broke up the fight and brought Josh home. He lives across the street from where it happened on Park Avenue. Could he be your captain? You said something about his living around here once. Am I crazy to even think it could be the same guy?" And why in the world did it make a difference, except that it would bug her until she found out?

"So that's where he is. Some of my buddies from the old company who made it back were wondering where he went when he was let out of the army hospital a few months ago. He has an email address but hasn't said where he is when he's corresponded with any of the guys. I've been worried. I should have thought about Cimarron City. He lived there for a while when his father was stationed at the army base nearby. And he used to visit his grandmother there in the summer. I think his grandmother died last year, but I thought since his father is stationed in Florida, that might be where he went."

"What happened to him?"

"I was stateside when my old company was ambushed and about a quarter of the men were killed, many others injured. Captain Tanner was one of them. A bullet in his left leg. Tore it up. I hear he almost lost it."

She recalled how emotionally messed up Ben had been last year when he was first released from the military hospital and honorably discharged from the army. He didn't have a job then—couldn't hold one down—and lived with their parents in Tulsa.

"How did he seem to you?"

"He couldn't get away fast enough. I invited him to share a drink for rescuing Josh, and he backed away as if I was contagious."

"What did you say to him?" Half amusement, half concern came over the line from her brother.

"Nothing. He wasn't mad at me. He was—" she searched her mind for a word to describe the earlier encounter "—vulnerable. Something was wrong. Maybe his leg was hurting or something like that. I did see his hands shaking. He tried to hide it, and he was breathing hard, sweating. That didn't start really until he'd been talking to me for a while. Do you think it could be…" She wasn't a doctor and had no business diagnosing a person.

"Post traumatic stress disorder?"

Ben had recovered from his physical injuries within months of returning stateside, but what had lingered and brought her brother to his knees was PTSD. Last year she'd trained her first service dog to help her brother deal with the effects of the disorder. "How's Butch doing?"

"He's great. You don't know how much he changed my life for the better."

Yes, she did. She saw her brother go from almost retreating totally from life to now holding down a job and functioning normally. He still lived with their parents, but she'd heard from her mom he was looking for his own apartment. "Are you having any problems?"

"Yes, occasionally, but Butch is right there for me. I can't thank you enough for him. Do you think you could pay Captain Tanner a visit? See how he is? I know what happened to him was bad, and as tough as he was, I wouldn't be surprised if he's dealing with PTSD. It can take out the strongest people."

Like Ben. He'd been a sergeant with an Army Special Forces Unit with lethal skills she couldn't even imagine. Yet none of that mattered in the end.

"Please, sis. I owe Captain Tanner my life. He pulled me out of the firefight that took me down. If he hadn't, I would have died."

"What if it isn't your Captain Tanner?"

"Was the person six and a half feet, dark brown hair, built like a tank, solid, with dark eyes—almost black?"

"That's him." She thought of the man she'd met today and realized she owed him, too. Not only for Ben but Josh. "I'll go see him. What do you want me to do?"

As her brother told her, she visualized Jake Tanner. The glimpse of anguish she'd seen in those dark eyes haunted her. He'd been quick to disguise it until the end when he started backing away from her. That black gaze pierced straight through her heart, and she doubted he even realized what he'd telegraphed to her—he was a man in pain.

* * *

The following Tuesday, Emma brought a terrier on a leash into the back room of the Harris Animal Hospital where she worked for Dr. Harris, the father of her best friend, Abbey Winters. "I think this gal will be great to train as a service dog. She's smart and eager."

"Even tempered?" Abbey, her partner in the Caring Canines Foundation, asked as she looked at the medium-size dog with fur that was various shades of brown.

"Surprisingly calm. That combined with this breed's determination and devotion can make a good service dog."

"I'll take her out to Caring Canines since you're working with the German shepherd at your house." The kennel and training facilities of the organization were housed at Winter Haven Ranch where Abbey lived with her husband, Dominic.

"Shep will make a good service dog, too. I've even got a possible owner for him. You know I've been doing the same training with Shep as I did with Butch."

"How is your brother?"

"Doing so much better. I talked to Ben twice this past weekend."

Abbey's eyebrows lifted. "That's unusual. Doesn't your brother hate talking on the phone?"

"Yeah, he prefers video chatting where he can see a person's face, and the second time that's what we did. I got to see Butch. Ben looks better each time I see him. Butch has been good for my brother, and if what Ben thinks is true, Shep will be good for Captain Tanner."

"Another soldier? Is it a physical injury? PTSD?"

"Both. When those kids I told you about yesterday

jumped Josh, Captain Tanner was the man who rescued him. After he left my house Saturday, I couldn't shake the feeling I'd heard that name somewhere. I finally remembered Ben served under a Captain Jake Tanner."

"So you called your brother to find out. I know how you are when you get something in your head. You don't give up until you find out the truth."

Emma laughed. "You've nailed me. I called him to see. Ben did some checking around after we talked on Saturday and found out that Captain Tanner has basically withdrawn into his house. Ben has a few connections, and one thought the captain was suffering from PTSD, although he doesn't seem to be participating in any therapy groups through the VA."

"How does Captain Tanner feel about having a service dog?"

"I don't know. I only talked to him that one time. I plan on taking him some brownies as a thank-you for helping Josh. Shep will go with me. I'll introduce him to the idea of a service dog slowly."

She wasn't sure if Jake Tanner would even open the door. She'd use the excuse she needed more information about the three boys who attacked Josh. Not only did she want to help the captain if he was suffering from PTSD, but she did need descriptions of the boys to give her an idea who could be bullying Josh. His teacher had requested any information to help her with the situation at school.

"Shep could help him, but he needs counseling, too. Maybe he's getting private therapy."

"Possibly, but Ben doesn't think so from what he's hearing from his army buddies in the area. Do you have room in your PTSD group?" Though Emma's best friend ran the Caring Canines Foundation, she still conducted a few counseling groups.

"If he'll come, I'll make room. The members are there to support each other, and talking about it has helped them. But there aren't any soldiers in the group."

"Maybe you should start one for people who have been bullied." Josh was dealing with some of the same symptoms as someone with PTSD—anger, anxiety and depression.

"If I only had more time in the day. Even quitting work at the hospital hasn't changed much because I'm training more dogs now. There is such a demand for them. So you didn't get any answers about who's bullying Josh from your meeting with Mrs. Alexander yesterday?"

"She hasn't seen anything, and since I didn't know the bullies' names and couldn't describe them, there wasn't much she could do but keep an eye out for any trouble. Most of the boys in his class are bigger than Josh, so the bullies could be in Mrs. Alexander's room. Or from the other fifth-grade classes."

"They could even be sixth-graders. It was a good idea to get him off the bus. It's hard for the driver to keep an eye on the road and what students are doing at the same time." Abbey leaned down and stroked the terrier. "Did Dad give his okay on this dog?"

Emma nodded. "Your father checked her over and she's medically sound. It's Madi's turn to name the dog. Let me know what she chooses." Madi was Abbey's ten-year-old sister-in-law whom she and Dominic were raising.

"Madi takes her job as name giver very seriously. She'll stew on it for days," Abbey said with a chuckle.

"Not too long. I want to start right away and a name helps. Now that I'm winding down with Shep, I have a slot open." Since she still worked full-time at the animal hospital, she could train only one dog at a time.

Abbey took the leash from Emma. "Good. Before long we're going to need another trainer, or you're going to have to quit your job here."

"Your father might have something to say about that. I'm going to look at training more than one dog. Hopefully that will help."

"I know, but the requests for free service dogs have increased over the past few months, especially now that veterans have heard about our foundation and the VA has stopped paying for service dogs. Many of the veterans can't afford an animal from the agencies that charge for them."

"How are the donations coming?" Emma leaned against the exam table, the terrier rubbing against her leg.

"They're increasing. My husband is very good at helping to raise money for Caring Canines. Dominic can attest to the good a dog can bring to a person after how Madi responded to Cottonball following her surgery to help her walk again."

Emma smiled. "And now Madi is running everywhere. You wouldn't know she had been in a plane crash twenty months ago."

"She's telling me she wants to learn to train dogs. I'm having her shadow me."

"A trainer in the making. There was a time I thought Josh would want to train dogs, but lately nothing interests him."

A frown slashed across Abbey's face. "Because he's too busy dodging the bullies after him."

"I know God wants me to forgive the boys, but I'm not sure I can. Josh has already had to deal with losing his dad. They were very close."

"Madi needed a woman's influence, and I suspect Josh could benefit from a male being in his life."

"He has Ben when he comes to visit."

"You don't want to get married again?" Abbey started for the reception area of the animal hospital, leading the terrier on a leash.

Emma followed her down the hallway. "I know you found love with Dominic, but Sam gave me everything I needed. I've had my time." Abbey had loved her husband so much that when he'd died, it had left a big hole in her heart she didn't think any man could fill.

"That's wonderful, but he's been gone for three years. I realized when I met and fell in love with Dominic that we could have second chances, and they can work out beautifully."

"Says a lady madly in love with her husband. When am I going to fit a man into my life with work, training dogs and raising Josh?"

"When your heart is ready," Abbey said. They stood at the entrance into the reception area where a client waited with her cat. Abbey winked at Emma and started toward the main door. "See you later at the ranch."

"I'll be there today, but tomorrow I'm going to be busy baking brownies and scouting out the situation with Captain Tanner. At the very least, my brother wants a report he's okay. And if Captain Tanner needs Shep, I'll do my best to persuade him of the benefits of a service dog."

At the door Abbey turned back and answered, "He may need more than Shep. Animal companionship is great but so is human companionship." She gave a saucy grin then left.

Emma faced the receptionist and lady in the waiting room. "Ignore what that woman said. She doesn't know what she's talking about." Emma turned and headed for exam room one to prepare it for the next client. The sound of chuckles followed her down the hallway, and heat reddened her cheeks.

On Wednesday, Jake's hand shook as he reread the letter from the army. He was being awarded the Distinguished Service Medal for his heroic actions in the mountains in Afghanistan.

Why? I'm no hero. Not everyone came home. Those left behind are the true heroes.

Guilt mingled with despair as he fought to keep the memories locked away. The bombs exploding. The peppering of gunfire. The screams and cries. The stench of death and gunpowder.

The letter slipped from his hand and floated to the floor. He couldn't protect all his men. He'd tried. But he'd lost too many. Friends. Battle buddies.

He hung his head and his gaze latched on to the letter. Squeezing his eyes shut, he still heard in his mind the words General Hatchback would say when he gave him the medal during the Veterans Day Ceremony—six weeks away. And no doubt, his father would be there.

No, he wouldn't go. He didn't deserve it. He'd done his duty. He didn't want a medal for that. He just wanted to be left alone.

The doorbell chimed, startling him. He jerked his head up and looked toward the foyer. He went to the window and saw the delivery guy from the grocery store. Using his cane, he covered the distance to the door at a quick pace and let the young man in.

"Hi, Mr. Tanner. I'll put these on the counter in your kitchen."

While Morgan took the sacks into that room, Jake retrieved his wallet from his bedroom and pulled out some money for a tip then met the guy in the foyer. "Thanks. See you a week from tomorrow."

"I'm off next Thursday. A big game at school. Got to support our Trojans."

"When will you be working next week?" Jake handed him the tip.

"Friday afternoon and evening." Morgan stuffed the money into his pocket.

"Then I'll call my order in for that day."

"You don't have to. Steve delivers when I don't."

Jake put his hand on the knob. "That's okay. Friday is fine. I'll have enough to tide me over until then." He was used to Morgan. The young man did a good job, even putting his meat and milk into the refrigerator for him. He didn't want a stranger here. Jake swung the front door open for Morgan to leave.

"Sure, if that's what you want." The teen left.

When Jake moved to close the door behind Morgan, he caught sight of Emma and a black and brown German shepherd coming up the sidewalk. He couldn't very well act as if he wasn't home, and there was no way he would hurt her by ignoring the bell since she'd seen him. But company was not what he wanted to deal with at the moment.

Then his gaze caught the smile that encompassed her face, dimpling her cheeks and adding sparkle to her sky-blue eyes as though a light shone through them. He couldn't tell her to go home. He'd see her for a few minutes then plead work, which was true. He had a paper due for his doctorate program.

"Hi. How are you doing today?" Emma stopped in front of him, presenting him with a plate covered with aluminum foil. "I brought a thank-you gift. Brownies—the thick, chewy kind. I hope you like chocolate."

"Love it. How did you know?"

"Most people do, so I thought it was a safe dessert to make for you. I love to bake and this is one of my specialties."

"Thanks. You and my neighbor ought to get together. Marcella is always baking," he said, with the corners of his mouth twitching into a grin, her own smile affecting him.

"And bringing you some of it?"

"Yes." He stared into her cheerful expression and wanted to shout there was nothing to be upbeat about, but something nipped his negative thoughts—at least temporarily. Her bright gaze captured him and held him in its grasp.

Since Saturday, he'd been plagued with memories of their meeting that day. He'd even considered going to her house and seeing how Josh was. He only got a couple of feet from his porch before he turned around. They were strangers, and she didn't need to be saddled with a man—even as a friend—who was crippled physically and emotionally.

Jake stepped away from the entrance. "Come in. I have to put away the rest of my groceries." For a few seconds, panic unfolded deep inside him. He was out of practice carrying on a normal conversation with a civilian after so many years in war-conflicted areas. Sucking in a deep breath, he shoved the anxiety down.

As she passed him, a whiff of her flowery scent wafted to him—lavender. His mother used to wear it. For a few seconds he was thrust into the past. He remembered coming into the kitchen when his mom took a pan of brownies out of the oven. The aromas of chocolate and lavender competed for dominance in his thoughts, and a sense of comfort engulfed him.

Emma turned toward him with that smile still gracing her full mouth. It drew him toward her, stirring other feelings in him. He'd had so little joy in his life lately. That had to be the reason he responded to a simple grin.

"It's this way." He limped ahead of her through the dining room and into the kitchen.

"I like this." Emma put the plate on the center island counter. "It's cozy and warm. Do you cook?"

"No, unless you call *cooking* opening a can and heating up whatever is in it. My meals aren't elaborate. A lot of frozen dinners." Jake's gaze landed on the German shepherd. *Beautiful dog to go with a beautiful woman, but why did she bring the animal with her?* Had his strange behavior the other day scared her somehow? When a panic attack took hold of him, it was hard for him to do much about it, which only made the situation worse.

"That's a shame. You need to come to my house one evening. I love to cook when I have the time."

"What keeps you so busy you can't cook very often?" Jake asked, resolved to stay away from any topic about him as he began emptying the sacks on the countertop. Focus on her. A much safer subject to discuss.

"Training dogs, working a full-time job at the animal hospital and trying to raise a child who's giving me fits."

"Things aren't any better?"

"No. The Cold War has been declared at my house. He didn't appreciate my talking to his teacher."

Jake whistled. "Yep, that will do it."

"Are you taking his side? Are you saying I shouldn't have talked with his teacher about his being bullied?"

Jake threw up his hands, palms outward. "Hold it right there. I am not taking anyone's side. That's between you and your son."

"I could use your help with this situation."

He scanned the room, looking for a way out of the kitchen and this conversation. He didn't want to be in the middle between a mother and son. "I don't know the boys who ganged up on Josh."

"But you saw them. Can you describe the culprits? Even one of them?"

"Maybe the smallest kid. Brown hair, brown eyes."

"Good. Do you have a piece of paper and a pencil?"

"Yes, but..." Staring at the determination in Emma's expression, he realized the quickest way to get rid of her was to give her what she wanted—at least the little he knew. He crossed to the desk under the wall phone and withdrew the items requested.

Emma took them. "I love to draw. If you tell me what he looks like, I'll try to sketch a portrait of him. Brown hair and eyes as well as a small frame fit a lot of kids in Cimarron City. So let's start with what shape his face is—oval, oblong, heart shaped? Is his jaw square, pointy, round?"

Staring at the dog sitting near the back door, Jake rubbed his day-old beard stubble. He'd forgotten to shave this morning. He was doing that more lately. When he glanced down at his attire, he winced at the shabby T-shirt and jeans with several holes in them. If someone who didn't know him walked in right now, that person would think Jake was close to living on the street. Suddenly he saw himself through Emma's eyes. And he didn't like the picture.

The military had taught him always to be prepared and to keep himself presentable. Lately he'd forgotten his training. The least he could do was change clothing. He wouldn't shave because her visit was impromptu, and he didn't want to give her the wrong impression— that he cared. He knew better than to care, not with the upheaval in his life.

"Your visit has taken me by surprise. I'll be back in a minute." He gestured to the kitchen. "Make yourself at home. I have a large, fenced backyard if you want to put your pet outside. A big dog like that probably requires a lot of exercise." He wanted to add: *I won't hurt you. I'm only hurting myself.*

"That's great."

As she walked to the back door, Jake slipped out of the kitchen and hurried to his bedroom. He felt encouraged she wasn't afraid of him since she was putting her German shepherd outside. Somehow he would beat what he was going through…but he didn't think he could by the time of the medal ceremony on Veterans Day.

After rummaging in his closet for something nicer to wear, he began to change. He caught sight of himself in the full-length mirror on the back of the door and froze. He didn't know the man staring back at him in the reflection. He sank onto his bed and plowed his fingers through his unruly hair.

I just want some hope, Lord.

Chapter Three

Jake hadn't kicked her out of his house yet. That was a good sign. Emma knew how much control meant to him right now because Ben had gone through a period where he tried to manage everything around him. He needed to know what was going to happen next. The trouble was life wasn't predictable, and that was where Ben had problems. He'd lost his patience and laid-back attitude, but in the past nine months he was getting them back. He was realizing finally that God was the one in control and He was always there to help him through. Did Jake believe in God?

After letting Shep out into Jake's backyard, Emma glanced around the neat kitchen, an olive-green-and-gold decor—no doubt his grandmother's touch when she lived in the house. She'd asked Marcella Kime, who went to her church, about Jake and this place. His grandmother had lived here until she died last year. The family hadn't sold it yet, so Jake must have decided to move in.

One sack of groceries was left on the counter. While she waited for Jake to return, she emptied the bag of food, then prowled the room. Maybe he skipped out the front door. When she heard a bark at the back one, she let Shep into the house.

She knelt and rubbed her hands along his thick black and brown fur. "I think the man is trying to send me a message," she whispered near the German shepherd's ear. "He doesn't know yet that I'm relentless when on a mission. He needs help and you. He's the reason Ben is alive. I owe Jake."

She nuzzled Shep, relishing the calmness that came from loving on the dog. In her house, there was always a dog she was training. With her full-time job, bringing a trainee home helped her to be around more if her son needed her. But the animal would eventually move on to another person. She'd found it easier not to have her own dog in case there were territorial issues when a new canine came for training. But maybe one day....

"Did he decide not to stay outside?"

Jake's question startled her, and she gasped. She swiveled around. "I didn't hear you come in."

"Sorry. I've learned to move quietly."

Emma straightened. "My husband made enough noise to alert the neighbors. Josh is just like his dad."

"What happened to your husband?"

"He died three years ago. He had epilepsy. It got worse over the years, and then he had a seizure he never recovered from." While on a ladder putting up Christmas lights because she had mentioned she wanted some. She'd intended for the teen next door to do the chore—not Sam. Guilt nibbled at her composure, and she shut it down. She was here to help Jake and possibly get some information concerning the kids bullying Josh.

"I'm sorry."

"Life has a way of changing and throwing you a curve when you least expect it."

He flinched. "Yeah, I know what you mean."

For a few heartbeats her gaze connected with his, and her stomach flip-flopped. The intensity in his look weakened her knees. She grasped the countertop.

As Jake moved to put away the canned goods and boxes from the last sack, she noted his change in clothing, trying to keep her attention somewhere besides those dark, compelling eyes. He still wore jeans but without any holes and a navy blue polo shirt. She saw his actions as a good sign. He wanted to look nicer for her, and that gave her hope.

"We can go into the living room, and I'll try to describe that last child I caught bullying Josh."

Emma retrieved the pad and pencil. "I appreciate it. I'm not sure what I'll do when I find out who the bullies are, but I need to know, if for no other reason than to help my son deal with the situation."

She went first toward the living area off the foyer. Shep walked beside her. Inside the room, she headed toward the couch. Her foot stepped on something, and she peered down. A sheet of paper—a letter? She picked it up as Jake entered. Her gaze lit upon the subject of the letter.

She swept around. "You're being awarded the Distinguished Service Medal. Congratulations!"

Jake stiffened. A thunderous expression descended over his features. He limped toward her and plucked the letter from her hands. "No reason to congratulate me because I survived when many didn't."

She eased onto the couch behind her, Shep sitting at her feet, close enough that she could stroke the back of his head and neck. She looked up into Jake's warring gaze as he skimmed the contents of the letter, then balled it up, crossed to the trash can and tossed it.

"They don't give the Distinguished Service Medal for being wounded. That's for serving your country above and beyond your normal duties. It's awarded for meritorious and heroic behavior. It's an honor you no doubt deserved."

"How would you know?"

She winced at his reproachful tone. "Because my brother, Ben Spencer, told me what you did for him. You saved his life so I'm not surprised you're receiving the medal, one of the highest awarded by the government."

The color drained from his face. "You're Ben's sister?"

She nodded.

"How is he? I haven't had a chance to touch base…" The words faded into the quiet. Jake stared at his clasped hands. "I meant to see how he was once I was better."

"He's doing all right. His injuries are healed, and he's been coping with his PTSD. Making progress."

Jake lifted his head and gave her a searing look. "So what I heard is true? How's he dealing with it?"

She couldn't have asked for a better opening to talk about Shep. *Lord, give me the right words to say. This man is hurting.*

"Ben has a PTSD counseling group he attends in Tulsa, but he also has a service dog I trained for him. Butch has made a big difference in Ben's being able to go out and to participate in life without having so many panic attacks."

His eyebrows crunched together. "He's cured?"

"No, but the incidences he has are few, especially

lately, and he's been able to work his way through them."

"I'm glad. He was a good soldier. I missed him when he returned home. Is he working?"

"Yes, at Gordon Matthews Industries as a computer programmer."

"Does he like it?"

"Yes, he's really enjoying it."

"That's good to hear. Sometimes it's hard to go back. A lot of men's lives have been messed up." Jake stared at the floor for a long moment, lost in thought.

Most likely remembering. The rigid set of Jake's shoulders made Emma wonder about his particular story. Each soldier had his own, some more traumatic than others. Ben had been flown back to the States eight months earlier due to his encounter with a land mine that had blown up a few feet from him in a field where one of his friends died. He lost part of his left arm while several other soldiers were also injured. But Ben kept in touch with many of the ones still in his old unit—there to help if they needed it. Jake wasn't staying in touch. Emma nudged Shep, giving him the signal to bark. He did.

Jake lifted his head, turning his attention toward the German shepherd. "He's a beautiful dog. How long have you had him?"

"Almost nine months. I've been training Shep to be a service dog. His specialty is working with people with PTSD." She watched Jake for a reaction.

He looked at her, a frown pulling his eyebrows down. "Why did you bring him today?"

"Because I like to take him out for a walk when I

can and—" she swallowed to coat her dry throat "—I wanted you to meet him."

His eyes narrowed. "Why?"

Her gaze caught his. "Because I think you need a dog like Shep."

He rose, grappling for his cane. "I have work to do. Thank you for bringing the brownies." His hard expression shouted, *But don't ever come back!*

She didn't move. "Please. Let me explain."

He started to say something but pressed his lips together.

She took his silence as an okay. "I want to help you. I know what my brother went through when he came home. He couldn't hold down a job, even a simple one. He lived with our parents and didn't leave the house hardly at all—often holing himself up in his old bedroom. He got angry at the least little thing. He had the shakes and would shut down if something even little went wrong. He had nightmares and didn't want to sleep. When I gave him Butch, I saw how effective the dog was with him. Still is. Butch has a way of calming him down and centering him."

"That's your brother, not me." Jake took his seat again.

From checking with a few of his neighbors, Emma knew Jake rarely left his house. Jake Tanner was hiding out. Easier to stay home than go out in crowds where he had little control of what would happen around him. Ben had been like that at first. Butch had made the difference.

"I can help you if you'll just give Shep a chance."

"I'm capable of dealing with my problems. Healing takes time."

"A service dog can help that along."

"How? My injury was my leg. I'm up and about. I can walk now."

"There are other injuries that aren't so visible. A dog can help with those."

"What? Emotional ones?" He clasped his cane between his legs with both hands and leaned forward slightly.

"Yes. Dogs can sense when a problem is going to occur and intervene before it becomes worse."

His grip tightened around the ivory knob on the end of his cane until his knuckles whitened. "I've heard of other soldiers using service dogs. I don't want to have to care for an animal. I'm barely—" He snapped his mouth closed.

"What? Barely holding it together?" Emma asked, returning his unwavering gaze. She hadn't given up on Ben. Though they were virtual strangers, she could tell Jake needed help. She had promised her brother she would do what she could for his former commanding officer and she would, somehow.

Jake stiffened. "I have work to do."

She sighed. "Sometimes I can be too blunt. I'm sorry if I've upset you."

"I respect a person who speaks her mind, but that doesn't change the fact I don't need a service dog. I'm coping."

"That's good because Ben wasn't."

"It hasn't been that long since I came home. Recovery takes time." Jake's voice didn't sound as convincing as the man probably wanted.

"Time *and* help. I agree."

His gaze pinned her down. "I'm receiving help from my doctor."

Emma resisted the urge to squirm under his intense glare. "Is he here when you have panic attacks, flashbacks, nightmares?"

Jake winced, a mask falling into place as if he were shutting down all emotions.

The problem was a person couldn't block his feelings forever. They were there in the background, ready to strike when he least expected. Emma said, "A service dog can help a person with those kinds of things. When someone has a panic attack, the dog's trained to calm him. The animal can be trained to wake up a person who's having a nightmare. Flashbacks often lead to panic attacks or at the very least, emotional upheavals. A dog can be there at all hours to console, be a companion. Not to mention they're great listeners."

A tic twitched in his hardened jaw. "Does he talk back?"

Emma grinned. "I can do a lot with the dogs I train, but I haven't accomplished that yet. But they can understand a lot of commands, if properly taught. Shep has been trained in all those areas."

Jake stood. "Thanks for coming."

Jake's polite words and neutral expression didn't totally cover a hopelessness in his eyes. Emma could identify; she remembered how, when her husband died, she'd struggled to pay off his debts. She was still paying the hospital bill every month from the last time Sam was admitted.

Emma followed Jake from the living room. Shep trotted next to her. Ben's captain opened the front door and moved to the side to allow her to leave.

She stepped outside and pivoted. "Where did the boys attack Josh?"

He took two steps out onto the porch and pointed to the right near the wooded area. "There, and they fled into the trees. You didn't get around to doing the sketch of the small one."

"I've got another idea if you're willing."

His forehead wrinkled, wariness in his eyes. "What?"

"Josh has a yearbook from last year. Would you be willing to look through it and see if you recognize any of the kids?"

"I'll try."

She smiled. "Great. I can bring it by tomorrow after work if that's okay."

He nodded, a solemn expression on his face.

"Then I'll see you around six."

She had started down the steps when he called out, "Tell Ben I'll be okay."

With a glance over her shoulder, she said, "You should call him and tell him yourself."

"I don't have his number."

"I can give it to you."

"Maybe tomorrow." He turned back into his house and shut the door.

As Emma walked home, she couldn't get Jake Tanner out of her mind. That haunted look in his dark eyes when she had talked about Ben's problems, and later what a service dog could be trained to do only reinforced in her mind that he needed help. Her brother had tried to deny it, too, and it had made things worse. She prayed Jake wouldn't. Tomorrow she had another chance to persuade him to try Shep.

* * *

The enemy surrounded Jake and what men he had left in the small mountain village, gunfire pelting them from all sides. The terrorists were closing in. He was trapped.

He signaled to his men to fall back into a house. He covered them as they made their way inside the shelter, then zigzagged toward it, seeking cover wherever he could. But as he ran toward the hut, it moved farther away from him. Escape taunted him. A safe haven just out of reach.

Someone lobbed a grenade that fell a few yards in front of him. He dived to the side, the explosion rocking him.

Crash!

Arms flailing, Jake shot straight up on the couch, blinking his eyes. He couldn't get enough air in his lungs. They burned. Everything before him twirled and swayed. He scrubbed his shaky hands down his sweat-drenched face, then drew in one deep inhalation then another. He folded in on himself, his arms hugging his chest, his head bent forward. Afraid even to close his eyes, he stared at his lap until his rapid heartbeat slowed. When the quaking eased, he looked up at his living room in Cimarron City. Not in a tent or hut in Afghanistan.

Safe. Quiet.

His gaze fell upon a lamp on the floor, shattered, along with a broken vase his grandma had cherished as a gift from his granddad. The sight of it destroyed what was left of his composure. His hands began to tremble more. Cold burrowed deep into his bones. He stuck them under his armpits.

Focus on the here and now. Not then. He shuffled through images in his mind until he latched on to one: Emma Langford, Ben's sister. He zeroed in on her light blue eyes, as bright as sunshine. He shifted his attention to her dazzling smile. He couldn't look away. The warmth of her expression chased away the chill.

He finally relaxed against the couch cushion. He couldn't believe he'd invited her back today. That realization earlier had driven him to take a short nap before she arrived since he hadn't slept much the night before. For that matter, since the nightmares began a couple of months ago, he slept only a few hours here and there.

He couldn't keep going like this, or he would stop functioning altogether. The very idea appalled him. In the army he'd been a leader of men who went into tough situations to protect and defend. Now he couldn't even leave his house without fearing he would have a panic attack and appear weak.

Lord, why? You brought me home to this—living in fear? How am I supposed to get better? What do I do?

His gaze returned to the mess on the floor, then trekked to the end table where the lamp and vase had been. He pushed to his feet to clean up the shattered pieces.

The chimes from the grandfather clock in the foyer pealed six times. Emma would be here soon. He hobbled toward the kitchen and retrieved the broom and dustpan. The glass lamp was beyond repair. He swept the shards and tossed them into the trash can.

Then he turned his attention to the vase. His granddad had created pottery bowls and vases in his spare time. This was one of the few left. He picked up each piece and laid it on the end table, trying to decide if he could fix the vase with glue. Maybe it was possible with time and a steady hand.

The doorbell sounded, jolting his heartbeat to a quicker tempo. Emma. *She can't see this,* he thought, as though it were a symbol of his weakness. He opened the drawer on the end table and hurried to place what was left of the vase inside, then closed it.

It took him a minute to limp toward the foyer. Maybe she'd left. He hoped not, and that surprised him. When he opened the door, she stood on the porch with that warm smile and her hands full with a slender book and a plastic container.

"I'm sorry it took me so long to get to the door," was all he could think to say.

"I figured it would. You're still recovering from a leg injury. It might be a while before you're up for a jog." She stepped through his entrance. "I hope you don't mind, but I made beef stew this morning in the Crock-Pot and had plenty to share with you." She lifted the lid for him to see.

His stomach rumbled. The aroma filled his nostrils and made his mouth water. He'd had breakfast but skipped lunch. "How did you know I haven't eaten much today?"

"A lucky guess. I'll put this in your refrigerator, and you can heat it up when you feel like it." She walked toward his kitchen. Pausing at the entrance to his dining room, she looked back at him. "Then I'll show you the yearbook."

He started to follow her into the kitchen but decided not to and headed for the living room. "I'll be in here when you're through." He wanted to make sure there were no remnants of the broken vase or lamp on the floor.

After searching around the couch, he walked lamely to the leather chair with an ottoman. His left leg ached. He must have wrenched it when coming out of his nightmare. As he laid his cane on the floor by him, Emma came into the room. He lifted his leg onto the upholstered stool.

She took the couch, sitting at the end closest to him. "I'd heat it up in the microwave for about six minutes on high. I put bread in to bake, but it wasn't done when I left."

"You make your own bread?" Jake remembered his grandmother baking bread once a week, a good memory. "I used to love that smell when I was a kid and came to see Grandma."

"I'm not a coffee drinker, but I love to smell a pot percolating. As well as bacon frying and bread baking." She snapped her fingers. "Oh, the best smell I remember from my childhood is my mother baking a cherry pie. I loved to eat it with vanilla ice cream."

"If I wasn't hungry before you came, I am now."

"Good, you'll enjoy my stew." She rose and covered the short space between them. "This is the yearbook I was talking about."

He reached up to take it. Their fingers briefly touched, and his breath caught. He held it for a few extra seconds then released it slowly. Their gazes connected, and Emma paused as though not sure what to do.

He grinned, trying to dismiss the bond that sprang up between them for a moment. "Where's your German shepherd? I thought you'd bring him again."

She laughed, letting go of the yearbook, then sat on

the couch. "I'll never force a dog on anyone, even when I think it would be good for him. Besides, Josh was throwing the Frisbee in the backyard for Shep, complaining that he was stuck at home and not at a friend's."

"Any problems with Josh in the past few days?"

"Nothing I can pin down. He tells me nothing more has happened, but he comes home from school angry and silent. I have to drag what little I can out of him."

"I remember those days when Mom tried to get me to tell her about my day at school, especially when the bullying was going on in the sixth grade."

"How did you handle it?"

"My mom found out and told my dad, who paid the parents of the instigator a visit. Tom Adams's parents didn't do anything to him, but Tom was furious at me. I won't ever forget his name. I did learn one thing. I learned to defend myself if I had to and to let others know I could take care of myself. Also, I made sure I was always with a group of friends. That way it was hard for Tom and his buddies to find me alone. They only attacked when I was by myself."

"Kids shouldn't have to worry about this. Did you have trouble at school?"

"Yes, especially at recess."

"Josh has been misbehaving so he doesn't go out for recess."

"Then it's probably happening at school. Some bullies can be very sneaky. They might even have a lookout."

Emma frowned. "When did the bullying stop?"

"Not until we moved here when I became a seventh grader." He quirked a grin. "I also started growing over the summer and began to lift weights. I wanted to go out for football." He flipped open the yearbook. "How old is Josh?"

"Eleven."

"He's small for his age. I was, too."

Her eyes grew round. "But you're what, six-four or five now?"

"Yes. I shot up not long after I was Josh's age and used my size to help others who were bullied. Lifting weights helped me to bulk up. That's what I mean by looking as if I could take care of myself. My dad taught me some self-defense but stressed I should only use it if it was absolutely necessary. Telling Tom's parents didn't work at all. I think his dad was actually proud of his son for being big and tough."

"How can a parent…" Her tight voice trailed off into silence.

"I'm telling you what happened to me, so you'll be aware there could be a backlash. That course of action doesn't always take care of the problem."

Her shoulders slumped, and she stared at her lap. "This is when I wish my brother or father lived nearer."

"Maybe Ben can teach Josh some self-defense."

"You mean to fight back?"

"Not exactly. There are techniques he can use to protect himself from getting as hurt when he's outnumbered. One's to run as fast as he can. He needs to know it's okay to do that, and if he makes that decision, to do it right away or the first chance he gets. He needs to know he isn't a coward for running but smart for protecting himself. Also, a child who knows he can defend himself is more self-assured."

"My brother's going to be on the road for his job for

the next month or so. And my father wouldn't know how. Not to mention he's frail."

Jake didn't have a reply to that. He didn't want to commit himself, not with the way his life was going. "You'll think of something," he said finally, realizing how lame that sounded. "Many bullies fight because they have low self-esteem. Make sure Josh knows that, and build him up. Bullies try to tear down others. It makes them feel superior. If Josh lets them know they can't do that, it might help."

She glanced up at him with that look that sent warm currents through him. "Will you have a talk with Josh and explain some of this to him? He won't listen to me."

Chapter Four

The seconds crawled by as Emma held her breath, waiting for Jake's answer.

His expression went blank, and he stared at his leg propped up on an ottoman. "All I can tell him is how I handled it. I don't know if that would work for him or not."

"I'll have you to dinner and you can talk to him. Anything you can tell him is better than nothing. He shuts me out. I don't know what else to do." She hated the desperate tone in her words.

"I can't come to your house for dinner. I don't want you going—"

"How about I bring the dinner here? I'll throw in fresh-baked bread, too."

Shaking his head, he chuckled. "You don't give up, do you?"

"No, stubborn is one of the traits I need to work on. When would you like me to bring dinner?"

He pressed his lips together, forming a tight, thin line, then said, "Do you work on Saturday?"

Hope flared in Emma. "I work at the Caring Canines

Foundation until the early afternoon. Saturday night would be good for me. How about six-thirty?"

He nodded, then began looking through the pages of the yearbook. Halfway through the book, he tapped a picture. "That's the smallest one of the three."

Emma moved to glance over his shoulder at the photo. "Carson McNeil. He was in the same class last year with Josh. I don't think they're in the same one this year. His family goes to my church. Josh and Carson were friends at one time. I can't believe he's part of the group."

"Let me see if I can recognize the other two." Jake continued turning the pages and scanning each child until he pointed to another one in sixth grade.

She leaned forward to read the boy's name. "Sean Phillips. I haven't heard of him." She got a whiff of Jake's lime aftershave and pulled back, realizing how close she was to him. Her heart raced.

She retook her seat while he continued his search for the third kid. Catching herself staring at him, she dragged her attention away and scanned the living room, taking in the decor. Focusing on anything but the man across from her. As in the kitchen she saw his grandmother's touches in the knickknacks, a quilt thrown over the back of the couch and a myriad of pictures on the wall. She didn't see anything of Jake other than a photo of him on the wall in his dress uniform with his arm around his petite, white-haired grandma. Was this a place he would recuperate then move on?

The sound of Jake closing the book drew her away from her survey and back to him. "The third one wasn't in there?"

"Not that I could tell, but then I didn't get a good look at him. He was the first to run off."

"With Sean and Carson's names, I have something to go on."

"What do you plan to do?"

"I'm not sure. I guess I need to talk with these boys' parents, then see what happens." When his eyes darkened, she asked, "What would you do?"

He stiffened. All emotions fled his face.

"Never mind. I shouldn't have asked you. This isn't your problem." She started to rise.

Sighing, he waved her down. "Since you know Carson's family, I would start with him. But Josh needs to know what you're doing."

"I know. That's the part I dread more than talking to the parents. Why not Sean's? He's more likely the one behind the attack."

"I noticed he's older, in the sixth grade. You're probably right. That means either he or the unknown boy is the leader. Not Carson. You have a better chance of getting something from Carson, and since you go to the same church and know his parents, they may step in." Jake massaged his left thigh above the knee.

"I think so. Sandy McNeil and I are friends. We've lost touch these past couple of years since Carson and Josh aren't playing together the way they used to, but I can't imagine her condoning what her son's doing."

"But you can't say that about the other parents. Start with the known first."

A clock somewhere in the house chimed seven times. Emma glanced at her watch and bolted to her feet. "I've overstayed my visit. I need to get dinner on the table."

"I'm sure I'll enjoy my supper. It beats opening a can of soup." Scooping up his cane, he struggled to stand.

As she watched him, she forced herself to remain still and not try to assist him. That would be the last thing this man wanted. He needed to feel he could do it on his own. But that didn't make the urge to help any less strong. She was here because of Ben, but she would stay because she wanted to.

At the front door, Emma waited until he came nearer before saying, "Thanks for looking at the photos. The more I know about what Josh is going through, the better I'm equipped to help him."

His features softened as he looked at her. "I hope everything goes okay when you talk to Josh about Carson and Sean. I doubt he'll be too happy."

"No, he'll be angry at me. But I'm his mother, and I'll do what I have to to protect him."

"He'll appreciate it one day."

"Just not today," Emma said with a grin. "We'll see you Saturday night." She turned to open the door but paused. "Oh, what do you like to eat?"

His eyes gleamed. "Surprise me."

"Then no big dislikes or allergies?"

"Nope. I do have one request."

Hand on knob, she glanced at him. "What?"

"Bring Shep with you."

Emma's mouth dropped open. Her large blue eyes fixed on Jake. Surprise flitted across her face. "You're going to take Shep?"

"I don't know. I'd like to see if we can get along first. If that's okay with you."

She grinned. "Sure. If you two don't connect, then

he can't do his job. But I know you will. You won't regret it."

The sparkle in her gaze lured him toward her. "I have my doubts, but I hope you prove me wrong." After the last nightmare in a string of many, Jake had to do something. Here at home he could control a lot of his environment, but when he went to sleep, he couldn't choose his dreams. If a service dog could help him with that, great. If not, then at least he tried.

Sliding her hand into the pocket of her light jacket, Emma looked up. "I almost forgot. I've written Ben's number on this card for you. He wants you to call him when you're ready, and if you have any questions about a service dog, you can ask me or him."

Jake took the phone number, not sure if he would. "Thanks. See you Saturday."

"If you change your mind about picking something special to eat, my number's on the card, too. I won't shop until early Saturday afternoon."

He clasped the edge of the door as she moved out onto the porch. Her lavender scent lingered in the air. For a second he didn't want her to leave. She descended the steps and strolled down the sidewalk, stopping to wave to him. He waved back.

As he closed his door, he decided he wouldn't call Ben. It was one thing to admit he had a problem, but totally different to talk with someone about it. He wasn't there yet. Wasn't sure if he ever would be. He couldn't put what was happening to him in words, so how could he talk to anyone about it?

He was committed only to spending some time on Saturday night with the German shepherd, Emma and Josh. No more than that. Other than Marcella from next door and a few delivery people, no one else had been in this house until Emma. In less than a week, he'd seen her more than anyone lately.

He should keep his distance. He was in no condition to get involved with anyone, even as a friend. But while he didn't have much to give another, the thought of not seeing Emma on Saturday churned his gut.

On Saturday morning, Emma stood at the back door at the Caring Canines Foundation facilities and watched her son and Madi play with a few of the dogs in the fenced-in recreation area. A beautiful fall day still held a chill in the air, but the sun beamed down and would soon burn off the last of the fog rolling over Winter Haven Ranch.

"Josh is so good with the animals," Abbey said as she came up behind Emma.

"So is Madi. Maybe when we get old and gray, they'll take over the foundation."

"Don't forget Nicholas. He may be only a couple of months old, but he's already responding to the animals."

Abbey's son is such a happy baby. It made Emma want another child.

"Dominic and I have been talking about having another child soon so they'll be close in age. I want a little girl."

Emma hugged her best friend. "That would be great. I know how much you miss your daughter." Lisa, her daughter by her first marriage, had died at five.

"You know how scared I was when I was pregnant with Nicholas. Maybe I shouldn't risk having another."

Emma held up her hand. "Shh. You aren't to think

like that. Turn this over to God and don't worry. It doesn't do you any good."

"I know." Abbey sighed. "Let's talk about you for a while. What are you preparing for Jake tonight?"

Emma shrugged. "I don't know. He was no help at all. What if I fix something he doesn't like?"

Laughing, Abbey shook her forefinger. "No. No. Didn't you just tell me not to worry?"

Emma's cheeks burned. "I didn't say I always follow my own advice."

"You cook what you and Josh will enjoy. I have a feeling Jake will like it, too. If not, he had his chance to get what he wanted. What I really want to know is did you say anything to Josh last night about Carson and Sean?"

Emma lowered her gaze. Yesterday she'd rehearsed with Abbey how she was going to tell Josh. "No. The right time didn't present itself."

"You chickened out."

"No, he came home from school in a bad mood. I didn't want to make it worse."

"Shh. Here come Josh and Madi. You better say something before this evening." Abbey lowered her voice. "Isn't the point of the dinner with Jake—to have him help Josh? That won't happen if Josh doesn't know what's going on."

"I know."

It was one reason for seeing Jake again. But equally important, she wanted Jake to work with Shep. There was something about the man that caused her to think of him at odd moments throughout the day. Last night she had even dreamed about him. They were in the park throwing a ball for Shep to fetch. Then she remembered why she'd awakened suddenly. Her son had been there grinning, happy. The scene gave her a feeling of family. She mentally shook herself. She would help Jake, but she wasn't looking for anything beyond friendship.

"Are you ready to go? I'm supposed to be at Craig's in half an hour," Josh said, stopping in front of her.

"Yes, I have to go to the grocery store and then start dinner."

"Do I hafta go tonight? I'm sure I could stay with Craig."

"I'd hoped you'd help me convince Mr. Tanner to take Shep."

"Okay. I guess I can since he helped me last Saturday." Josh headed inside with Madi, the two talking about the new terrier.

"Smooth. He has no idea what you're really doing," Abbey whispered close to Emma's ear.

"Hush," Emma said, then louder she called out to the little girl, "Hey, Madi. What's the terrier's name? I'll start training her next week."

Abbey's sister-in-law turned around. "Buttons. Josh and me decided that today."

"See you all tomorrow at church." Emma followed her son out to her gray PT Cruiser. If she was going to say anything to him, she had to now while she could focus on the conversation rather than driving. Inside her car, she shifted to face Josh in the front passenger seat. "I've discovered the names of two of the boys who attacked you last weekend."

He grew rigid. "Who?"

"Carson O'Neil and Sean Phillips. It's only a matter of time before I find out who the third guy is. You might as well tell me."

His blue eyes became big and round, fear inching into them. "No. I can't. And you can't say anything to anyone about Carson and Sean. Promise me, Mom."

"They really have you scared. How? Why?"

"Because they're mean."

"Carson? He used to be a friend of yours."

"Well, he's not anymore. He thinks Sean and..." His eyes bored into her. "Oh, never mind. You don't care about me. If you say anything to their parents or them, it'll only get worse for me. Is that what you want?"

Conflicting emotions crammed her throat, making it impossible to reply. Her stomach roiled with frustration and her own fear she wouldn't be able to help her son with this problem. But Josh's anguish pierced her. She felt so inadequate to make everything all right for him. He and his father had had such a close relationship. Sam would have known the right thing to do in this situation.

She straightened behind the steering wheel and started the engine. "I'm friends with Carson's mother. I'll start there, and if there's any backlash, I want to know about it." As she pulled away from Caring Canines, she glanced at Josh.

Turned away from her, he stared out the side window, his left hand opening and closing.

"Josh?"

"Sure. Why don't you follow me around? That oughta work and alert everyone in school my mother fights my battles."

"If I could to protect you, I would. I know you have to learn to deal with these boys, but you may need help."

With his back still to her, he ran his hands through his brown hair. "How did ya find out their names?"

"I have my resources."

"Which friend snitched?"

She didn't want to tell him Jake identified the two in the yearbook, but she didn't want her child angry at his friends. He needed them. For a few seconds, she thought of lying, but that never worked and would only make the situation worse. "Mr. Tanner."

Josh twisted around. "How? He didn't know their names."

"I brought him your yearbook, and he found them in it."

Silence reigned the rest of the way to Craig's house, and the frosty atmosphere underscored how mad her son was. The second she stopped, Josh thrust open the door and hurried toward his friend's place.

"I'll pick you up at six-twenty," Emma yelled. She would call Craig's mother and let her know.

Now more than ever she needed Jake to help her son cope with the bullying. If her son would even talk to him.

Saturday night, carrying a cardboard box full of the food for dinner, Emma approached Jake's house with her son shuffling his feet at least three yards behind her. She set the meal down on the porch and waited for Josh who led Shep on a leash. Other than telling her again he didn't want to come to Mr. Tanner's, he said nothing in the car when she picked him up at Craig's.

"I expect you to use appropriate behavior tonight."

Josh's bottom lip stuck out farther. "It's none of his business."

"The minute he stepped in and helped you it became his business. It's like a person witnessing a crime. He has an obligation to come forward and report it. That's the right thing to do. And beating up someone, especially three to one is wrong. If adults do that to one another, they are charged with a crime and jailed."

"Can't you trust me to handle my own problems? I don't butt in with yours."

"Guess what? I'm your mom and that's part of my duty as a parent." She rang the doorbell then scooped up the box. She was beginning to think it was a bad idea including Josh, but she wanted Jake to help her son.

When Jake let them inside, Emma fixed a bright smile on her face, determined to go ahead with her plans, even if her son wasn't cooperating. In the past Josh rarely held a grudge long, but lately he'd changed so she had no idea how he would act with Jake.

"It's nice to see you again, Josh," Jake said as he closed the front door, his back to them.

Which was a good thing because her son scowled. Emma clasped his shoulder and squeezed gently. Josh's expression morphed into a neutral one.

Jake swung around. "I've been anticipating a home-cooked meal all day."

Emma smiled, hoping it would cover the fact her child wasn't being too friendly. "I'm going to put this enchilada casserole in your oven to reheat. Josh, why don't you show Mr. Tanner some of the things Shep does in the backyard?"

Displeased by that suggestion, her son huffed and headed to the back door with Shep in tow.

As Emma put the salad bowl in the refrigerator, Jake moved to her and waited until the back door clicked closed. "He knows I pointed out the boys in the yearbook?"

Emma nodded, her throat thick.

"Did something happen between Josh and them?"

She faced him, just a few inches of space between them. Her heartbeat kicked up a notch. "No, not that I know of. I haven't done anything about the two boys yet. I'm going to talk to Carson's mother tomorrow. I thought I would see her after church. Find out what she thinks, especially about Sean. I wanted Josh to know before I did it."

"And he wanted to know how you found out?" No emotions indicated what Jake was feeling.

"Yes, I'm sorry. I didn't want him to know, but I can't lie to my son. If you want us to go home, I'll leave the food and we'll take off."

"No. You went to a lot of trouble to cook a meal for us. Besides, it's time I have a talk with your son if you still want me to. Avoiding this won't solve any problems, either."

"You don't mind?" She inhaled a deep breath, laced with his lime aftershave.

"Your son needs help. The second I decided to break up the fight I made that decision. Bullies shouldn't be tolerated. If something isn't done now, it'll only get worse." He started for the back door.

"Jake," she said. When he glanced at her, she continued, "I didn't think you wanted to get involved. What changed your mind?"

His gaze was riveted to hers. Intense. Compelling. "You."

There was so much feeling behind that one word. She attempted a laugh that came out shaky. "You mean I wore you down?"

"Not exactly. But the compassion you've shown me,

even when I tried to reject it, reminded me how beneficial it is to help others. Maybe then I won't think about my own problems all the time."

She grinned. "So you're taking Shep?"

"Maybe. If we're a good fit. I've been reading up on service dogs, and I talked with Ben this afternoon."

"You did? I didn't think you would call him."

"Can't a guy change his mind?"

"Sure." She shooed him outside. "Then go see Shep."

His chuckles lingered in the air as he left. The sound warmed her. She closed her eyes for a moment, immediately picturing the laugh lines at the corners of his eyes deepening and the edges of his mouth tilting up. The image sent goose bumps spreading over her. She rubbed her hands up and down her arms as though she could erase his effect on her.

In his backyard Jake slowly eased himself down on the step next to Josh. The boy stiffened but didn't move away. Instead, he lobbed a tennis ball for Shep to retrieve.

"Does he like to do that a lot?" Jake asked, not sure how to approach an angry eleven-year-old to deal with a problem he probably thought was unsolvable. He could remember feeling that way on more than one occasion.

For a long moment Josh's mouth remained clamped. "Yeah," he said finally.

"That's good to know."

When Shep trotted back to Josh, he dropped the ball in the child's lap, then sat waiting. Jake petted the German shepherd while the dog's attention was on the boy's hand. Josh didn't toss the ball but instead squeezed it over and over.

"I know you aren't happy that your mom wants to talk with Carson's mother or that I pointed out the two boys in the yearbook to her," Jake said, hoping to get a reaction out of Josh and a chance to approach the subject of bullying.

A frown descended on Josh's face, the quiet lengthening. Jake searched for another way to start a conversation. He'd led men into battle, but this wasn't an area of expertise for him. About the only qualification he had for this was that he had been a boy once.

"Why did you show her their pictures? I thought you weren't going to tell her." Disappointment leaked into Josh's voice and expression.

And that bothered Jake more than the child's anger. "I told you that I wouldn't say anything about the fight because you were going to. Some things you can't hide from a mother, and being beaten up like you were is one of them. What did you expect her to do? Not to care and let it keep happening? Do you think that's realistic, knowing your mother?"

Josh shook his head. "I was going to hide from her until I looked better."

"That would be days, possibly a couple of weeks. Do you think that would have worked?"

"She's doing exactly what I knew she would: interfering."

"Because she's acting like a typical mother. You should have seen my mom when I was first beaten up by some bullies."

Josh twisted around and pressed his back against the wooden railing on the stairs and the decking, his focus on Jake's arms. His muscles were evident since he was wearing a short-sleeved shirt. "You were bullied? You're *huge*."

"I was small when I was your age." The subject still bothered Jake. He'd been taught by his father never to show weakness. As stress began to blanket him, he continued to stroke Shep. "It seemed like everyone was bigger than I was. In sixth grade one boy was determined to make my life miserable. When my mother found out and told my dad, he went to the other guy's parents."

Hope brightened Josh's blue eyes. "He left you alone after that?"

"No, he didn't. His dad even looked the other way. Later I found out that his dad behaved that way and didn't see anything wrong with it. He got his way by intimidating others."

The boy's shoulders slumped. "So you kept having trouble."

"Yes, I kept having trouble, but my attitude began changing. I was determined not to be a victim. I started exercising and making myself as strong and capable as I could. I was small at that time, but that didn't mean I couldn't use my wits. I found out other kids were being bullied by these boys, too. We stuck together and helped each other. A lot can happen when you realize you aren't alone."

Josh moved down a step closer to Shep and hugged the dog. "I told the lady who supervises recess at lunch about Sean and the other guys last week. They got me alone at the side of the building and took my money then pushed me down in the mud. She didn't do anything."

"Why not?"

"She didn't see it. They said I was lying, but I had mud all over my clothes. That's why they beat me up in the park the next day. To teach me a lesson." Josh rubbed his face against Shep's neck, and some of the tension dissolved from his features.

Watching the interaction between the dog and the boy reinforced what Jake had heard and read about service dogs for people with PTSD. "If one person at school doesn't do anything about it, go to another. Find someone who'll listen to you. From what your mother's told me, your teacher seems sympathetic. Start with her."

"But they'll come after me."

"Possibly. I can teach you a few self-defense moves when you're cornered, but try to outsmart them. Don't put yourself in a place where they can get you alone. Have friends around you. If you see them, get to a safe place where others are."

"But they'll call me a chicken."

"For defending yourself any way you can? I call that smart. Even the United States Armed Forces use defensive moves to protect themselves."

Josh straightened on the step, his shoulders back. "Yeah." Shep barked a couple of times, nudging Josh's hand with the ball. "Do you want to throw it for him?"

"Sure." Jake took the ball and hurled it so far it ended up at the back of the fence on the one-acre piece of property.

"Wow!" Eyes wide, Josh looked at him. "Did ya play baseball or something?"

"In college I was on the baseball team."

"Where?"

"Oklahoma University. I got my degree in psychology."

"I want to go there. My dad did."

When Shep returned, he released the ball at Jake's feet. Jake snatched it up and gave it to Josh. "Your turn."

"I can't do what you did."

"I wouldn't expect you to. I played the sport for years and practiced a lot. I also lift weights to keep my muscles in my arms strong."

"When did you start playing?"

"When I was ten. Are you on a team?"

"I thought about it last spring, but I didn't try out. I'm not very good. Maybe next spring if I can get better."

"When you throw the ball, put your whole body into it, not just the arm you're using."

Josh rose and tried to do what Jake had said. The ball flew a couple of yards farther.

"That's better. With practice you'll improve. It's a good way to build up your body." Jake heard the screen door open and close behind him. The hairs on his nape tingled as if Emma were staring at him. "If you want, we can practice a couple of times a week. I'll also teach you those defensive techniques." He looked behind him. "That is, if it's okay with your mom."

Josh whirled around. "Is it? Did ya see him throw the ball? He's *good*."

"If Mr. Tanner doesn't mind, that's fine with me." Emma's eyes glinted with a smile—aimed at Jake.

"I don't. We can use my backyard. It's big enough even to work on batting, at least at the beginning. But we'll need a fielder since I'm not ready to do too much running after the ball." Jake turned his attention to Emma, who was wearing a look that had power to slice through the barriers he'd erected. "Do you know anyone who can do that?"

Pink tinted her cheeks. She lowered her eyelids, veiling her expression. "If you can be patient, I will. I got hit with a baseball when I was a kid and can't say that I'm very good at putting myself in the way of one. My first instinct is to run from it."

Laughter welled up in Jake, and its release felt good. Even better, Josh and Emma joined in.

"Josh, you need to go wash your hands. Then please get the salad and dressing out of the refrigerator and set the table with the paper goods I brought."

When the boy disappeared inside, Jake used the wooden railing to hoist himself to his feet and faced Emma at the top of the steps. "We had a good conversation. He wasn't very happy with me at first, but he listened to my explanation."

"I'm so glad you volunteered to help. You should see me throwing a ball. Not a pretty picture. I have never been athletic. Actually, as you heard, I'm pretty much a wimp."

"A cute one."

Her blush deepened. She looked down for a few seconds before lifting her head. "Are you sure you want to do this? I know a lot is going on in your life and I don't want to add—"

"Stop right there. I wouldn't have offered if I didn't mean it. Josh reminds me of when I was young. When I struggled with bullies, I had a father to help me. Josh doesn't." When Shep planted himself next to him, he stroked the dog's head as though he'd been doing it for a long time.

"How are you and Shep getting along?"

"Fine."

"He can stay the night if you like."

"You're one determined lady. I don't have anything for a dog."

"I've fed him already today. I could come pick him up tomorrow morning before going to church. It would give you a chance to bond with him without doing the day-to-day care. Then if you want to try longer, I can help you get what you need and show you how to work with Shep."

"Ben warned me about you. You did the same thing to him." Jake mounted the steps. "You do know that Josh is attached to Shep?"

"Yes. He's that way with every dog I bring home to train."

"He needs his own dog. I saw that earlier when we were talking about being bullied."

"He talked to you about that?"

"Yes, after I told him what happened to me. Maybe Shep should stay with you and Josh."

"No, I'm bringing home a new dog that would fit Josh better. I've seen him with Buttons at Caring Canines. She responds with him already. I could involve him in Buttons's training."

Leaning on his cane, Jake opened the back door, and Emma went inside ahead of him. The aroma from the dinner reheating filled his kitchen and enticed his taste buds. He hadn't been eating as well as he should, but this evening he planned on having a second helping, and he hadn't tasted the dish yet. But anything that smelled this good had to be delicious.

"Take a seat, guys. I'll get the casserole out of the oven, and then we're ready to eat."

Both Josh and Jake washed their hands, then Josh sat while Jake remained standing and waited until Emma had placed the casserole on a trivet in the center of the table. He pulled out a chair for her. She flashed him a surprised look but eased down onto it. Then he took his seat.

"Do you mind if we pray?" Emma asked, reaching across the table to take Josh's hand, then offering hers to Jake.

He clasped it, and the feel of her small one surrounded by his larger grasp seemed so right to him. Astounded by that sensation, he almost released it.

But Emma bowed her head and said a prayer over the food, concluding with, "Please, Lord, put a wall of protection around Josh and Jake. Amen." She squeezed his hand then let it go.

Stunned, Jake couldn't think of anything to say. To be included in the prayer with her son spoke of her depth of caring. The gesture touched his heart as nothing else had in months. Somehow he would return her kindness by aiding Josh with his problem.

Chapter Five

Later, in Jake's living room, Emma sat on one end of the couch while Josh curled up at the other and fell asleep. After dinner he had asked Jake to show him a self-defense move, and they had practiced while Emma and Shep watched. Jake demonstrated how Josh could use his arms to form a triangle to block certain punches. Josh had wanted to go over the move again and again until finally Emma called a halt.

Fatigue lined Jake's face, and yet he stayed right there trying to help her son. She didn't like the idea of Josh fighting, but she understood he needed to defend himself, especially when she remembered her child's injuries. The cuts and bruises were healing, but Josh's self-esteem was damaged.

"Thank you for working with Josh. I hope he never has to use any of those moves, but at least he knows them." Emma had wanted to smooth the tired lines from Jake's face, but instead she curled her hands at her sides.

"He'll need to practice them until they become second nature."

She winced. "He's eleven. This isn't something he should have to know."

"Like you, I hope he doesn't have to use them. I know how to snap a man's neck and kill him, but that doesn't mean I ever want to use that skill. If someone were trying to kill me, though, I'd protect myself. Those boys could have done a lot worse damage to Josh. They could have injured his eye, broken his nose, caused a concussion just to name a few things."

Emma's stomach knotted. "I get it. You don't have to convince me. But isn't there a peaceful way to take care of this problem?" Was that too much to ask a warrior?

"When people decide they aren't going to tolerate bullying, then yes. When others stand up and say no, that makes a difference. No tolerance is the best policy, but it takes a majority of people pitching in to make that work."

"Maybe I can get other mothers to help fight the bullying."

"There are probably organizations out there. Check and see what they're doing."

"I will. I'll do an internet search when I get home." She rose and stretched her stiff muscles. It had been a long, tiring week. "So what have you decided about keeping Shep overnight?"

Shep lay at Jake's feet. The dog's ears perked forward, and he sat up. Jake patted Shep then ran his fingers through the German shepherd's fur. "I'd like to give it a try." Standing, he gripped his cane. "Where does he usually sleep?"

"In his crate. I didn't want him to get too used to sleeping somewhere special in my house since he wouldn't be there long."

"Should I have the crate, then?"

"Try without it. You can fix up a bed with a blanket on the floor. I'd suggest in your bedroom. That'll strengthen your bond. If there's a problem, give me a call—anytime."

As they talked, Emma realized they kept stepping closer to each other. To her surprise, she wanted to touch him, reassure him this would work. Still, she kept her arms by her sides. "Okay?"

"I can't ask Josh to help himself if I won't at least give this a try. He's a smart kid. He'll figure that out. I'll be fine."

"I know you will. Shep's a good service dog. When I've had a particularly bad day, he's sensed that and is right next to me, rubbing against my leg or nudging my hand to pet him."

"That's a good reason for Josh to have one. As I said before, I don't want to take anything away from your son."

Without thinking, she started to place two fingers against his lips but stopped herself inches away from him. "Not another word." The feel of his breath against her fingertips tickled, and she dropped her arm back to her side. "I'll involve Josh in the new dog's training, and if Josh wants to keep her, we will."

Jake's eyes shone as they roamed over her facial features. "You have your hands full working two jobs. Do you have to work so hard?"

"I'm still paying off my husband's medical bills. The hospital is patient, but I want the debt paid off this year. Then I might be able to cut my hours at Harris Animal Hospital and devote more time to training. The demand for service and therapy dogs is growing."

He lifted his hands but dropped them back to his sides, a hesitance entering his expression. "It sounds like you need to relax."

She attempted a smile. "I watched my parents struggle with debt, and it nearly destroyed their marriage. I worked hard never to have any until Sam went into the hospital. Then it was like the floor fell from beneath me. My life changed in an instant."

He stepped back. "I know that feeling firsthand."

"I know there are no guarantees in life, but it seems I take one step forward, then two back." In his eyes she saw a reflection of her concerns. He was going through the same thing for different reasons. In that moment she experienced a kinship with him she hadn't felt with anyone but her husband. The realization left her speechless.

Sounds of her son waking up propelled her back a few paces. When she turned toward him on the couch, he opened his eyes slowly and looked from her to Jake.

"What did I miss?" Sleepiness coated his words.

"Not much, kiddo," said Jake. "I've agreed to take Shep tonight and see how it works."

For a fleeting moment, a frown skittered across Josh's face.

"This way we can concentrate on making Buttons feel at home her first night at our house," Emma said, glad to see Josh looking more relaxed. "I was thinking of letting her stay in your room at night if you think that's okay."

He perked up and scooted to a sitting position. "Sure. She'll probably be lonely without the other dogs at Caring Canines."

"That's what I was thinking."

Josh rubbed his eyes then peered at Jake. "Can I come visit Shep sometime?"

"Yes. Don't forget we'll be working on your baseball skills and self-defense. There'll be plenty of time for you to see Shep."

The boy grinned. "Yeah, right." He hopped to his feet, started for the foyer but paused a moment to pat Shep and say goodbye, then continued his trek toward the front door.

Emma laughed. "I guess we're leaving." She turned to follow Josh. "Call if you need me."

"Okay." He waited until Josh went onto the porch, then lowered his voice. "I hope your conversation with Carson's mother goes well tomorrow."

For a short time tonight she'd forgotten what she needed to do. She prayed Sandy would be receptive. It wasn't a conversation she was looking forward to. "Can I ask you a favor?"

One of his eyebrows rose. "Yes, you can ask, but I won't guarantee I'll do it." One side of his mouth turned up.

"I have an idea. I'd like to drop Josh off at two then go see Sandy at her house where it's more private. I don't think it'll take long. But if you'd rather not watch Josh, just say so. I'll understand."

Jake glanced over her shoulder at the boy. "No problem. We can practice the moves he learned today."

The urge to hug Jake swamped her. Instead, she murmured, "Thanks," then scratched Shep behind his ears and left. Josh knelt next to Shep and rubbed his hand down the length of his back. "Goodbye, boy."

As her son descended the porch steps, he said, "You know, Mr. Tanner isn't so bad. I'm not mad at him anymore for showing you those guys' pictures. I've been thinking. If Dad had been alive, I'd probably have told him who they were. He'd have understood."

"And you don't think I would?"

"You're a girl. Girls freak out about fighting."

She stopped on the sidewalk, blocking her son's path. "I don't condone fighting, but I want you to be able to protect yourself long enough to get away."

"Sure, Mom."

"Self-defense is one thing. Being aggressive is totally different. Understood?"

"Yeah. I'd be stupid to pick a fight with them. They're bigger than me, except for Carson."

"I'm glad we understand each other." She draped her arm over his shoulder and began walking.

Jake sat in his bedroom that night staring at Shep, who was sitting on his makeshift bed. The German shepherd had scratched and walked around in circles then finally settled onto the two blankets.

"I'm not sure how this is going to work, but if you're willing to give this a chance, I am, too."

Shep cocked his head, his ears sticking up.

"I still don't see how you can really help. I hope you prove me wrong."

Jake switched off his light and lay on his bed, tired from lack of sleep and overextending himself with Josh. Still, he felt as if he had made a difference. For a long time he kept his eyes open and stared up, the digital clock on his radio throwing shadows on the ceiling. But slowly his eyelids grew heavy and slid closed, whisking him into a world of dreams he would avoid if he could....

*The noise of gunfire cracked the air around him.
Boom, boom rocked the ground beneath him. He lunged
for shelter, screaming to his men to do likewise.*

Something wet and rough scraped across his cheek,
followed by a loud sound. Barking? Jake's eyes popped
open to find Shep propped up on his hind legs against
Jake's bed. The dog's tongue swept him again. Jake
fumbled for the light and turned it on. Shep nosed Jake's
nearest hand, and he began petting the dog.

Had he screamed out loud? Awakened the dog? Or
had Shep sensed something wasn't right? Either way,
Shep had managed to stop his nightmare before it became full-fledged. That the German shepherd could
do exactly what Emma had described amazed Jake. He
scooted over and patted the top of his coverlet. Shep
jumped up on the bed and stretched out beside Jake.

With the light off again and one hand on the dog,
Jake went to sleep, feeling hope for the first time in
months.

On Sunday afternoon Sandy O'Neil gestured toward
a wingback in her living room. "Have a seat, Emma.
You sounded serious at church today. Is something
wrong?"

Emma's heartbeat tapped out a fast tempo against
her rib cage. All the way to Sandy's house she'd practiced what she would say to her friend, and every word
she'd come up with fled her mind.

"Emma?"

She swallowed then said, "Last weekend Josh was
jumped by three boys in the park. As you could see
today, he has bruises, a cut on his lip and above his eye."

"I wondered about that, but I figured if you wanted

to tell me about it you'd say something. I asked Carson on the ride home if he knew what happened. He told me Josh was in a fight."

"Yes, one that was completely lopsided and not of his choosing."

"I'm sorry to hear that."

Emma gripped her hands, rubbing her thumb into her palm. "Thankfully, a man who lived near the park saw what was happening and broke it up before Josh was hurt worse. Two of the boys were bigger than my son. I know one was older. I'm not sure about the third kid."

Sandy covered her mouth with her fingers. "Oh, no. Do you know who did it?"

"Two of the boys and I thought Carson could help me with the third one."

"Josh doesn't know who he is?"

"Yes, but he's scared to say anything."

Sandy pushed to her feet. "Carson's out back. I'll call him in and see if he and Josh talked. They aren't in the same class this year so they might not have."

"Wait before you ask Carson to join us. The reason I know Carson can tell me the name of the third boy is because your son was one of the three beating up Josh."

Sandy collapsed onto the couch across from Emma, the color washing from her face. "Not Carson. He doesn't know how to fight. Josh told you he did?"

"No, but I asked Jake Tanner, the man who stopped it, to look at the yearbook from last spring and see if he could find any of the boys. He picked out Carson and Sean Phillips. Then I talked to Josh, and he admitted it. My son is afraid of retaliation, so he didn't want me to know who's bullying him."

Sandy cringed. "My son? A bully? I don't see that. I didn't raise him like that."

"I know. That's why I'm here talking to you. Carson and Josh were friends once. I know they drifted apart but…" Emma's throat jammed with helplessness and frustration.

"They had a falling-out, and Carson would never say why."

"Neither would Josh."

"I'll be right back. We need to get to the bottom of this." Sandy shot to her feet and marched toward the back of the house.

Emma took a deep breath, then another, but her lungs still didn't feel as if they had enough oxygen. The whole affair left her sick to her stomach. She heard Sandy call Carson inside, and the boy stomped toward the living room, denying he did anything wrong.

Lord, please guide me with what to do. Let the truth come out.

When Carson entered, he saw Emma and immediately lowered his head and pinched his lips together.

"Hi, Carson. I haven't seen you much but occasionally at church. I've missed you coming over to the house."

Sandy nudged her child farther into the room. "Sit. We need to talk to you." While her son obeyed, she continued, "Did you take part in beating up Josh last weekend in the park?"

Seconds ticked away without an answer, then finally Carson raised his head, tears in his eyes. "Yes. But I had to."

"Why?" His mother sat next to him.

"If I didn't, they'd have done it to me. I was scared."
Carson's lower lip quivered.

Emma's heart cracked at the sight of Carson's fear—
much like Josh's when he wasn't trying to mask it.
"Who are they? Sean Phillips. Who else?"

Carson blinked rapidly. "Josh told you about Sean?"

"No. The man who caught you fighting identified
Sean and you. Who's the third boy?"

"If he thought I said anything, I'd..." His voice faded,
replaced with crying, tears running down Carson's face.

Emma looked at Sandy. Her face reflected shock that
slowly transformed into anger. Emma sat back in her
chair, forcing her tight muscles to relax. She needed to
let Sandy deal with Carson. She knew her friend would
do the right thing.

Sandy wound her arms around her son and brought
him against her while he sobbed. "Emma, we'll talk,
and I'll call you later with the third boy's name. Then
all four of us need to talk. This can't continue."

"I agree. Bullies in our neighborhood and school
can't be tolerated." Emma rose. "I can see myself out.
Thank you, Sandy. Goodbye, Carson."

"I should be thanking you for bringing this problem
to my attention."

Emma left the O'Neils' house. Hope seeded in her
heart, and she prayed it would grow. That they would
come up with a solution to help their sons and others.

Emma drove to Jake's place in ten minutes and
parked in the driveway. Josh had wanted to bring Buttons over to see Jake and Shep, but she'd told him maybe
some other time. When she'd gone in to wake her son
for church, Buttons had been sleeping right next to Josh,
his arms lying over the terrier. This was one animal she

decided she wouldn't train for Caring Canines, and she knew Abbey would understand, especially with what was going on in her son's life right now.

The sounds of her son and Jake talking came from the backyard. She headed for the gate and let herself in. When she rounded the corner of the house, Josh hurled a baseball the farthest she had ever seen and Shep ran to fetch it.

Emma approached Josh and Jake by the deck. "I don't think you're going to need me to be a fielder. Shep's doing a great job."

"He loves to get the ball, Mom. I'll teach Buttons to do the same thing."

"So I can leave and come back when you're through?"

Jake shook his head and smiled. "You can be the cheerleader."

For the next half hour Jake patiently worked with her son to show him the correct way of throwing a baseball. As she cheered on Josh, she watched Jake and saw the traits of a good leader—he provided honesty when Josh needed instruction, support even when he didn't quite get the move right, confidence as they practiced again and again.

When Jake sat on the deck steps, Josh plopped down next to him, breathing hard from his exertion. Shep joined the pair and lay down on the grass nearby.

"I'm changing hats. I'm going to be the water girl. You all look like you could use some."

Jake leaned back, bracing himself with his elbows. "Sounds good. How about you, Josh?"

Her son followed suit, relaxing against the stair behind him. "Yep, with lots of ice."

Emma mounted the steps between the two and went

inside the kitchen. After serving and cleaning up the night before, she was familiar with Jake's setup and in no time found the glasses and a bowl for Shep. She filled a pitcher with ice and water, put everything on a tray, then returned to the deck.

"How did the self-defense lesson go?" After passing the drinks to everyone, including the dog, she sat down behind her son at the top of the stairs.

Jake slid her a glance. "Good, but it's not easy to practice with Josh when I'm so much taller. Maybe I can show you a few moves, and you two can go through them. It wouldn't hurt for you to know these in case you're ever attacked."

Josh's eyes grew round and his body tensed.

Emma hurriedly said to her son, "That's nothing for you to worry about. It never hurts to be prepared. Just as a precaution, hon."

"Mom's still a lot taller than me." Josh's stiff posture eased, and he gulped down most of the water in his glass.

"Jake, are you back here?" Marcella Kime came around the corner with a basket. She smiled. "I thought I heard you."

Out of the corner of his mouth, Jake murmured, "Sunday afternoon is always one of her days to bring some food to fatten me up. She thinks I've lost too much weight."

"I heard that, and I'm right." Marcella set the basket down on the step then bent over to pet Shep. "He's adorable. It's about time you got some companionship." His neighbor's gaze flitted from the dog to Emma. "Nice to see you here. Jake is way too introverted. That's my vocabulary word for today."

"What's it mean?" Josh peeked into the basket, licking his lips.

"You can have one, kiddo. She brings enough to feed an army. I'll let Miss Kime explain since it's her word."

"Introverted means someone who likes to be alone. Jake, all my goodies can be put in the freezer to enjoy another day. Dig in, Josh. It's my cookies with both white-and-milk chocolate chips and walnuts." Marcella lifted the basket for Emma's son.

"Mmm. Thanks, Miss Kime. This is great," Josh said with his mouth full.

"Josh." Emma gave him "the look" to remember his manners, then took a bite of a cookie, savoring its rich taste. "I hope I can get this recipe. These are delicious."

Marcella nodded. "I have all these great recipes and no children to pass them on to. Come by one day and you can take what you want and make a copy of it."

"Love to. I'll give you a call."

Marcella set her hand on her waist and peered at Jake. "What do you think?"

"Since I'm an introvert, I thought I should keep quiet." He grinned and popped the last bit of his cookie into his mouth and chewed it. "Perfect as always."

Marcella beamed. "Music to my ears. That's why I bake. I love hearing how much people enjoy what I make." She started for the gate. "Share with your friends. I'll make you some more tomorrow." As she went around the side of the house, she waved.

Reaching for another cookie, Jake laughed. "I'm not sure there are going to be any left to share."

Josh looked from Jake to Emma. "I worked up an appetite. I should have asked Miss Kime to help me demonstrate my moves." He hopped up. "Maybe I should ask her—"

"No," both Emma and Jake said at the same time.

Emma looked at Jake who added, "She may be the right height, but if you accidentally broke one of her bones, you would feel awful."

"Older people have more brittle bones and aren't in as good shape as—"

Marcella popped her head around the corner of the house. "I heard that. I may be having trouble with the lock that keeps sticking on your gate, but I have strong bones and would love to help."

Josh stood to his full four feet ten inches. "I don't want to hurt you."

"You aren't going to hurt me. I'm in tip-top shape." The older woman strolled back to the group. "What have you learned?"

The boy swung his gaze to Emma then Jake, mouthing the words, *Help me.*

Jake pulled himself up and with his cane approached Marcella, gesturing for Josh to join them. "I showed him how to block some punches by forming a triangle with his arms. Since it's such a large discrepancy between my height and his, it's easier for him to practice with a person closer to his height."

The petite neighbor, still wearing her church clothes—a flowery dress, a hat and one-inch high heels—said, "I'm ready and willing. What do you want me to do?"

"Grab the front of his T-shirt near the collar." Jake demonstrated.

Marcella rubbed her palms together, her eyes gleaming. When she made her move toward Josh, his expression was wary. Marcella clutched the cotton by his neck and moved in closer. Leaning back, he brought his arms up as though to ward her off and crossed one over to clasp his forearm, then brought the locked move down on his "attacker."

"Good, Josh!" Jake said. "You broke the hold. Depending on the circumstances you can go for various vulnerable spots or hopefully, since you're already leaning back, you can turn and run. Get to a place where there are people."

Emma watched as Jake put Josh and Marcella through a couple of different scenarios using the triangle hold. Her son's attention stayed totally focused on Jake.

At the end, Marcella stroked her chin. "You know, I have some friends who would love to learn how to protect themselves. Me, for one. Then there is Bertha, Florence and—"

Jake's expression went blank. "I don't mind your participating when I work with Josh. You two are close in size. But I don't have time to do classes. I…" His voice sputtered to a halt. He pivoted and started for the deck stairs. "Thank you, Miss Kime, for helping us. I'm afraid all of this activity has tired me out."

"Remember, call me Marcella."

"Josh, go with Miss Kime and help her with the gate and make sure she gets home all right. I'll meet you out front by the car." Emma gestured toward the side yard.

Josh's forehead creased. "Okay." He watched Jake who was opening the back door, Shep on his heels. Josh went to Emma and whispered, "Is he okay?"

"Yes. You know how Uncle Ben would get when he was recovering from his injuries. He may have overdone it today. I'm going to check with him about Shep then I'll be out front."

As her son and Marcella left, Emma snatched up the pitcher with the three glasses and hurried after Jake before he closed the door and locked her out. Worry nibbled at her. The sight of him shutting down reminded her of Ben. She didn't give up on her brother; she wouldn't on Jake, either.

Chapter Six

Emma stepped through the entrance into the kitchen as Jake was swinging the door closed, stopping him in midmotion.

He frowned. "I'm really tired."

"I won't keep you but a few minutes. I wanted to put these in your dishwasher and check with you about Shep."

Jake glanced at the dog, noticing he'd followed him into the house. "I want to keep him. But would you do me a favor?"

"Sure, anything. Josh has really responded to what you're teaching him."

"So did Marcella—too much." The thought of going somewhere and teaching self-defense had sent a bolt of panic through him. It was one thing to help Josh with a few moves, but he didn't want to be responsible for instructing others—not when he'd been unable to save his men from walking into an ambush. Their deaths felt like a bombed building crushing him beneath the rubble.

Emma put the pitcher and glasses in the dishwasher, then faced Jake. "What do you need me to do?"

He dug his wallet out of his back jean pocket and gave her some money. "If you'll get me everything that Shep needs, I'd appreciate it. You know what he's used to. Any toys. Treats. Food."

"We'll go after we leave here. Do you need anything for his bedding?"

"No, that's been taken care of." He remembered waking up this morning with Shep stretched out inches from him on top of the cover. His fingers instinctively went to stroke the dog's fur, and he'd known in that instant he didn't want to return Shep. A calmness flowed through him as he petted the German shepherd. If there had been any doubt left, Shep's eyes, conveying instant affection for Jake, would have erased it. The dog had low crawled what space had been between them and placed his head on Jake's chest, forging a bond that went straight to his heart.

Emotions swelled in his throat, and he turned away from Emma. "I'm going to take a nap so if you'll leave the items on the porch, I'll get them later. Please lock the door as you leave. Thanks for your help." He limped down the hall toward the living room.

From the foyer Emma said, "Bye. Thanks for helping Josh." Then the sound of the front door closing echoed through the house.

Total quiet, finally. Today the level of noise had strained Jake's nerves, yet working with Josh had made him feel good about himself, as if even with the shape he was in, he could still help someone. When he felt tension begin to take hold of him, he put his hand on Shep and the stress melted away.

Then the sight of Emma when she returned from seeing Carson's mother lifted his spirits. Her bright smile and twinkling eyes reminded him of the sunrays peeking through a bank of storm clouds.

He stretched out on the long couch, and Shep lay down on the carpet near him within reach. "I wonder how Emma's meeting with Sandy O'Neil went. Maybe I'll call her later and find out," he said to the dog, who cocked his head as he listened. "She's a special lady. Too bad we met at this time in my life."

All the way home from work, Emma tried to think of a way to check on Jake. It had been two days since she'd seen him. She had been Shep's trainer, so she should see how he was doing with the dog. *Yeah, right.* That wasn't the main reason she wanted to see or at least talk to him. She cared. The last look he had given her before hobbling out of the kitchen was a resigned one, as though he had come to the conclusion he would fight panic attacks for the rest of his life, that he wouldn't be able to deal with change easily or crowds. But that wasn't the case. People worked their way through PTSD. It wasn't easy, but it could be done, especially if he had a support system—people who cared. He had isolated himself.

At home Emma paced her kitchen, holding her cell and deliberating between calling Jake and putting her phone in her pocket. Josh would be home soon from Craig's. She'd stayed longer than usual at work, and Craig's mother had picked both boys up at school and taken them back to her house to work on a project for science. She appreciated her network of friends and parishioners who would help her if she needed it.

Jake was alone. Did he even turn to the Lord for guidance and strength? She couldn't have made it through Sam's death without God.

Staring down at her cell, she recited Jake's phone number, surprised she could remember it. Usually she had trouble recalling one unless she used it a lot. She'd only called him twice in the ten days she'd known him. She started to punch in a nine when the doorbell rang.

Odd. Josh had a key and would let himself into the house. Maybe it was Jake. She had no reason to believe that, but she hurried toward the entry hall, peered out the peephole and frowned.

When she swung the front door open, concern surged to the forefront. "Sandy, what's wrong?"

Her friend's swollen eyes indicated she'd been crying and right behind her was Carson, sniffling. One of his eyes would be black-and-blue by tomorrow.

Emma stepped to the side to allow them in. "Let's go into the living room, and you can tell me what happened."

Sandy sank onto the couch with Carson right next to her, his head hanging down. "I had a long talk with Carson last night about what we discussed on Sunday and told him he needed to apologize to Josh today at school for what he did. I also told him I'd better never hear that he's done that to anyone again."

As Sandy talked, her son's shoulders slumped, his chin now resting on his chest.

"I appreciate that, Sandy. Carson, why are you hurt?" The thought set alarm bells off in her mind.

"Tell her what happened at school, Carson."

The child started crying.

Sandy's forehead pinched into a frown. "That isn't going to help. You should never have become involved with Sean Phillips and Liam Rogers." She looked at Emma. "That's the third boy and the leader. He moved here this summer and should be in sixth grade but was held back. He is in Josh's class." She stopped for a few seconds, drawing in a deep breath.

Emma used that pause to say to Carson in a gentle voice, "Tell me about today. I haven't seen Josh yet. He's at Craig's house and should be home soon. Please help me to understand what's going on."

Carson sniffed and lifted his tear-streaked face. "I found Josh at recess and told him I was sorry about what happened in the park. I didn't want to hurt him, but if I hadn't, they would have turned on me. Liam likes to pick on smaller guys. When he didn't with me, I couldn't believe he wanted to be friends. Then he started going after Josh. I tried to back off. Liam said I was either on his side or against him."

"How can one or two boys have so much power over you all?" Emma knew Sean was about four or five inches taller than Josh, but Craig, her son's best friend, was almost that much taller, too.

"It's not just Liam and Sean. There are two others, both sixth-graders. They've got lots of kids scared. It's getting bad. They said no one better rat on them. They saw me talking with Josh and heard I told him I was sorry. They didn't like that. They paid me a visit." He touched the area by his eye and winced. "This was my warning."

"This has got to stop for your son and mine," Sandy said, twisting her hands together. She shook her head. "But I don't know what we can do. I'll talk with his teacher as well as the principal tomorrow about Liam."

Fear gripped Carson's face. "No, don't, Mom. *Please.*"

"That's what Josh kept telling me. But we can't stand

by and let boys like Liam get away with what they're doing."

The sound of the front door being unlocked then opened announced Josh's arrival. Emma wasn't sure if she was glad for his timing or not. She wished Jake were here to help her with the situation. He might have some more insight that would aid them.

When Josh came into the living room, he stopped a few feet inside and stared at Carson. Her son's face went pale. "What happened?"

"Liam," Carson mumbled, and lowered his head again.

Thunder darkened her son's expression. "We need to take our school back."

Emma's mouth dropped open. His fierce tone shocked her. "What do you have in mind?"

"We've got to stand up to Liam and his buddies."

Carson shot a look at Josh. "How? They're bigger."

"I have a friend that's teaching me how to defend myself. Mom, do you think Mr. Tanner would help Carson and Craig? I talked to Craig about it."

"Honey, I don't know." *Especially after his reaction to Marcella's request.*

"Can you ask him?" Sandy inquired, all three of them staring at Emma.

She gulped. "I will."

After Carson and Sandy left, Josh turned to his mom. "Do you think Mr. Tanner will help us?"

"I don't know. Do you want to fight the bullies physically?" She still felt bothered about having Josh learn moves, even self-defense ones.

"No, there are better ways to settle disagreements. Mr. Tanner told me that. But I like knowing I can take care of myself. I've got some homework to do, but let me know when you talk with Mr. Tanner."

Josh left and Emma paced. This wasn't something she could talk about over the phone with him, and yet it was better not to surprise Jake by just showing up. She withdrew her cell from her pocket and punched in his number. Still, it would be good for him to be involved and give him something to think about other than what had occurred in Afghanistan.

"Shep and I are doing fine," Jake said in a husky voice, as though he hadn't used it a lot in the past few days.

The sound of it made her shiver, and an image of the man occupied every inch of her mind. His hand-some features—

"Emma?"

She blinked away the vision of him and said, "I need to see you. Can I come over?"

"You don't need to worry about Shep. You trained him well, and you've shown me the signals he responds to. We're doing fine."

"Please."

Jake held the phone to his ear while massaging his temple with his free hand. "Fine, I'm not going anywhere."

"Thanks. I'll be there in ten minutes."

When Emma hung up, Jake stood in his kitchen listening to the dial tone for a moment before disconnecting. The urgency in her voice spoke to the protector in him—something he hadn't tapped into much since his days in Afghanistan. Yet part of him was broken and lay in fear of the slightest loud noise, anything unexpected, the press of people, especially strangers.

Something was wrong. That much was clear from the tone of Emma's voice. Six months ago, before his world blew up around him, he would have been charging over to her house to fix whatever had her so concerned. She was Ben's little sister with no immediate family nearby.

It was bad enough that she haunted his waking hours. Often when he looked at Shep, he thought about the time she must have put in to train the German shepherd. But whatever she needed—what if he couldn't do it? He'd already turned down Marcella's perfectly reasonable request. He was just so scared to have people begin to rely on him. Half his men were killed or wounded that day in the mountains. He'd let them down. He hadn't been able to bring them all out alive.

When he sat at his table to finish the frozen dinner he had microwaved, Shep came over and positioned himself next to Jake, laying his head in Jake's lap. Jake took his last bite, then stroked the dog, inhaling deep breaths to keep the anxiety at bay.

I can't fix everything. I can't control everything. He said those sentences over and over to himself while he ran his fingers through Shep's fur. *But the Lord can. Then why aren't You? Haven't I suffered enough?*

When the doorbell rang five minutes later, he was still seated at the table, petting Shep. He wanted to ignore the summons to answer, but he also felt the draw to help Emma as she was trying to help him.

"C'mon, Shep. Let's see what she needs." Jake shoved back his chair and strode toward the foyer. The thought that he might actually be able to do some good lifted his spirits.

With his dog by his side, he opened the door, his heartbeat increasing at the sight of Emma—beautiful, caring and in need. That was evident in the tiny lines wrinkling her forehead, the absence of a sparkle in her blue eyes.

"Come in. Let's go into the living room." He limped across the entry hall.

"You aren't using your cane."

"My physical therapist wants me to go without it as much as possible." He eased onto the couch. "He said I was using it more than I should. He's probably right." At least he could do without the physical crutch. Now if only he could get his life in order.

"How often do you go see him?" Emma took a seat at the other end of the sofa.

"He comes here twice a week." He saw the lines deepen on her forehead. "I do go out occasionally."

"When? No, forget I asked that. It isn't any of my business. But Shep can help you leave the house more."

He didn't want to talk about his problems. He was tired of dwelling on what he couldn't do anymore without fear of a panic attack. "Is this what you came to talk to me about? It sounded urgent on the phone."

"You know I talked to Sandy on Sunday about Carson. She insisted that he apologize to Josh. Carson did at school today and later Liam Rogers, the third bully, made it clear he wouldn't tolerate that with Carson and punched him a few times. He'll have a black eye like Josh did."

"In other words, they're coercing Carson to be one of their followers."

"Yes, or at least not be a friend to Josh."

"Why are they targeting Josh?"

"Liam Rogers is in Josh's class. He was held back this year. Josh has always been well liked. Maybe Liam resents that. That's just a conjecture, but whatever the reason, he wants to make my son's life miserable."

Rage at the situation simmered in Jake's gut. He worked to tamp it down. "And you want me to do what?"

"Josh hoped you would work with Carson and Craig, his best friend, teaching them some of the self-defense moves. He feels if they can protect themselves they won't be so fearful all the time. It'll give them some self-confidence. Right now even Carson feels like a victim."

Was that the way he felt about himself—that he was a victim? Jake's first urge was to say no, but then he looked into Emma's hopeful face and the denial wouldn't form. Instead, he said determinedly, "On two conditions: it'll be done here, and there should be a fourth boy. That way I can pair them off to practice. But no more than four." Four might even be too many. He'd taught self-defense and fighting skills to men— not children.

"That's great. Josh has another good friend named Zach. I'll talk with his parents and him to see if they'll agree. When can we start?"

Emma was like a dog that smelled a buried bone and would keep digging until it found the prize. "I figured that would be your next question," he said with a laugh. "Thursday. We'll work an hour Saturday, Tuesday and Thursday. Weekdays right after school and Saturday in the morning at ten. Okay?"

"It is with me. I'll check with the other parents and

get back to you. If it is, I'll be here on Thursday to introduce you to everyone involved and to help if you need it."

He knew what she was doing. Since this would be a new situation, she wasn't sure if he would have a panic attack. The fact he couldn't reassure her he wouldn't frustrated him. Just another example of what little control he really had in his life.

"I'll call you tomorrow evening." Instead of rising to leave, Emma shifted to face him squarely. "So how are you and Shep getting along? Do you have any questions about his training?"

"In other words, what has he done for me?"

"Yes. He's capable of a lot."

"Every night he wakes me up before I get too far into my recurring nightmare about the ambush. During the day, he senses when I need to calm down. I haven't gone anywhere since he came to live with me. We'll find out how that is at the first of next week when I go back to my doctor."

"How has it been in the past?"

"Not easy, but necessary. I have the first appointment in the morning and that helps, but I battle anxiety. I'm determined to overcome it." Amazed that he had admitted his fear to Emma, he realized in a short time he'd come to trust her. That surprised him even more.

"You should practice with short trips to different places. Shep will be able to help you with your anxiety before it really gets started."

"Can he stop panic attacks?"

"Possibly. It depends on what triggers an attack and how fast it comes on. I've got a proposition for you."

He tensed, not sure he wanted to hear it.

"You came to my house when you brought Josh home that first day. I could tell that was hard for you. What if you and Shep came to dinner tomorrow night? Since I'm just around the corner, it'd be a short trip."

"Then what?"

"Maybe the park or the ranch where I can show you the facilities for Caring Canines and then after that a store."

"All by Monday?"

"We can if you want, or do some after Monday."

Listening to her plan to help him with his panic attacks with crowds and unexpected situations, he felt anger mushroom inside him. He was an invalid and that didn't sit well. He swallowed what pride he had left and said, "Ben mentioned that your friend Abbey is a counselor and has a group for people who suffer with PTSD."

"Yes. No one in it is a veteran, so it might not be the right one for you. From what I understand, the vets in this area have to go to Oklahoma City for a PTSD therapy group. Abbey only started it a few months ago."

"Oklahoma City is two hours away."

"I know. Abbey's good. Try her group. The cause of the PTSD may be different from the others', but you all are still going through the same problems. I was glad Ben was in Tulsa where he had one for vets nearby. He never regretted attending."

Jake scrubbed his hands down his face, feeling the stubble of his beard. He'd forgotten to shave again this morning. "Do you know when the group meets?"

"Monday evenings. She has an office and room she uses at the ranch. She used to work at the hospital, but with the foundation growing, she quit that job to run Caring Canines. Still, she didn't want to give up some of the groups she'd started at the hospital. I'll give you her number. Let her know you're interested." Emma dug into her purse and withdrew a card. "Here's her number."

He took it from her, the brief brush of their fingers like an instant connection leaping between them. He didn't know if he could go to a therapy group and discuss his problems, but he had to do something. He didn't like what was happening, and it wasn't getting better with time. He needed more.

"I'll call her tomorrow, but with the doctor appointment on Monday, I'd rather push it to next week. I can start the group session the following Monday."

She smiled, those blue eyes light like the sea. "I hope you like pizza."

"Sure, but I can order that and bring it."

"No, this is homemade pizza. Josh and I usually have it on Wednesday night." She rose. "I'd better get back. I don't like to leave Josh too long by himself, even though he complains he's eleven. He thinks I baby him."

"You've been here awhile."

"I know but I'm only a block away and Buttons is becoming quite the watch dog. Not to mention I have a great neighbor."

The other day with Marcella, his neighbor, still bothered him. "I let Marcella down, but I'm not ready to do what she asked."

"What if this group with the four boys works out? Maybe then you can consider having the ladies over to your house. You could start with a small group and see what happens."

"I don't know. I don't want to commit to too much."

He didn't want to let down any more people than he already had.

Jake walked Emma to the door and said good-night. When she left, he felt lonely. She brought an energy into his house that teased him with future possibilities—that he could have a normal life again.

"You could open a pizzeria. That was delicious." Jake sat next to Emma on her porch swing the next evening, darkness blanketing the landscape beyond the security light by the front door. Shep lay stretched out nearby with his eyes trained on Jake.

"With my son monopolizing your time from the minute you came into the house, I never got to ask you how the walk over here went. I didn't have you over to answer a hundred questions and practice baseball with him."

"Then why did you have me to dinner?" A strand of her blond hair had worked its way out of her ponytail and enticed him to smooth it behind her ear. He balled his hands to keep from following through on that impulse.

"To help you get out more and feel like you won't have a panic attack. But also to have food other than from a can or a frozen box."

"I'm not starving. I do have a list of places that deliver food when I get tired of frozen dinners." He couldn't resist the temptation any longer. He brushed the stray lock behind her ear. The silken feel of her hair sliding over his fingertips made his stomach quiver, his breath catch.

Her gaze was riveted to his and for a long moment they looked at each other. She finally broke the silence, saying, "I love to cook." Her voice quavered, and she paused, glancing away. "My husband enjoyed my cooking. I miss that. Josh only wants a simple meal like pizza, spaghetti, macaroni and cheese. I don't get to experiment with new recipes the way I did when Sam was alive."

"You can experiment on me anytime. I know it's a tough job, but I think I can handle being your taster."

"Then you have a standing invitation to come to dinner Sunday night when Josh is at the youth group at church. That way I won't subject him to any of my fancy gourmet dishes."

"I can't let you do that."

"You'd be doing me a favor. I'd be elated to spend some quality time in the kitchen."

The thought that he could give her joy made him smile. There was so little of that in his life lately. "Then I'll be here. Same time as tonight?"

"Yes. Craig's mom is driving the boys to church on Sunday so I'll have plenty of time to wow you with my culinary skills."

"After the food I've eaten in the army and here, it won't take much. I used to appreciate good food, but I'm more like Josh lately. Just something simple that doesn't require a lot of thought or work on my part."

"But that's the beauty of this invitation. You won't do either. I will and I'll enjoy doing it. There's something creative about coming up with a dish that is delicious and different from the usual."

"If you feel that way, why didn't you train to be a chef? Why a veterinary assistant?"

"Because I love animals more. There was a time I contemplated being a veterinarian, but I got married between my second and third year in college and had Josh about a year later. With my husband having to finish his last year to get his engineering degree, we didn't have the money." She stared at her lap, her hands clasped together. "After that, there never seemed to be a good time to go back to school, especially with Sam's seizures becoming worse."

Jake couldn't see her expression well with her eyes glued to her lap, but he heard the pain in her voice and saw the stiff set of her body. Laying his hand over hers, he wished he could take her hurt away. "I'm sorry. I shouldn't have asked. It's none of my business."

She shook her head. "No, I consider you a friend. What I was going to add is that I've found something I really love doing, training dogs to help others. I'm not sure I was cut out to be a vet like Dr. Harris. He's a great boss and handles the bad things that happen to animals so much better than I do." When she lifted her head and peered at him, she was calmer, her expression neutral. "How about you? What made you go into the army? Josh told me you went to college and got a degree in psychology?"

"My father was a career military officer. I thought I would work on my master's and possibly my Ph.D. while I was moving up the ranks in the army. Then when I retired, I would have a profession. All my life that was what was expected of me: to follow my father into the army."

"And you regret now that you can't?"

"No, but I'm not the person I was. That's one of the reasons I didn't want to live in Florida where my father and his second wife are. He sees me one way, and that Jake died the day of the ambush."

"That's understandable when you have a major trauma occur. Ben feels a lot like that."

He didn't look at Emma. He couldn't. When he'd been with his father the last time, he'd seen the disappointment in the general's expression. Jake was being discharged because of his injuries, and he didn't fight leaving the army. In the general's book, he was giving up.

"Maybe your parents were more understanding about what Ben was going through. My dad wasn't. He never said it, but I think he thought I was weak. A man in the Army Special Forces is supposed to get patched up and keep going, return to the field and fight another battle."

Emma touched his hand, stroking it before she curled her fingers around it. "I'm sorry. How did he expect you to keep going with your leg like it is?"

"I was supposed to take a desk job in Washington until I was fully recovered. The general has a lot of pull. If I had wanted, it would have happened, however long it would have taken for me to get back the full use of my leg."

Using her forefinger, she turned his head so he looked right at her. "You answer to yourself and God. Not anyone else. You have to ask yourself what you want. Not your father. Not anyone else but you."

His eyes slid closed for a few seconds. "I've never said any of this out loud. How do you do it—get me to talk about something I'd just as soon forget?"

"One of my many talents." One corner of her mouth tipped up. "Seriously, people do need to talk to someone about what's bothering them or often it makes the situation worse. Not speaking about it doesn't make it go away, no matter how much we wish it did."

"You sound like you know this firsthand."

"Yes, but I haven't taken it as far as you have."

"You haven't said anything to anyone? You've kept something painful to yourself?"

She nodded, slipping her hand to his upper arm to keep the physical connection in place.

"Forget about the mess I'm in. I do have a master's degree in psychology. Maybe I can help you. At least I can listen."

She checked her watch. "Oh, look, it's getting late. I need to make sure Josh has finished his homework. It's nearing his bedtime."

In other words, she didn't trust him with what was bothering her. The thought hurt Jake after he'd revealed nearly everything to her. At least he didn't tell her how he felt he was pathetic; that part of what his father said was true. He should be able to bounce back and live a normal life, even if it was as a civilian.

He stood and signaled for Shep to do likewise. "We'll be going. Thanks again for a delicious meal. I'll see Josh tomorrow for his self-defense." He started for the porch steps.

"Jake."

He kept going as though she hadn't said his name in almost a plea for understanding. "Good night."

Even though it hurt his leg to move as fast as he did, he strode toward the sidewalk, holding Shep's leash, refusing to look back. Somehow he knew she was still watching him.

When he rounded the corner and walked down Park Avenue, at first he didn't see the front of his house, but as he grew closer, a chill flashed down his spine. In the glow of his porch light he saw that the large glass window in his living room was shattered.

Jake's gaze fastened on the destruction, and he flashed back to the village in the mountains with its windows and doors blasted out, debris and carnage lying everywhere. Fallen buddies. Civilians caught in the crossfire. Huts destroyed.

The sounds of gunfire inundated him. The moans and cries of suffering soldiers and villagers filled his mind.

He quaked, his heart racing. Sweat poured off his face. The noise of war all around him and even the scent of gunpowder assailed him.

Bark! Bark!

Something wet and cold nudged his hand over and over.

Another yelp, followed by more, demanded his attention.

Jake looked down and saw a large dog rubbing himself against his leg. No, his dog. Shep.

He blinked and knelt, putting his arms around the German shepherd. He clung to him as though his life depended on the dog.

Time passed. He had no idea how long he sat on the sidewalk in front of his house, holding Shep, feeling the dog's calm breathing, his warmth chasing away the cold that encased Jake.

Finally, when the trembling eased, Jake felt his thoughts clearing, bringing him back to Cimarron City. Safe. No enemy was waiting behind a building to shoot him. No more rocket launchers were annihilating buildings or transport vehicles.

Then he glanced toward his house and remembered

the window. Had someone broken in? If he went inside and found someone there, he didn't know what he would do. He dug his cell phone out of his pocket and called 911.

Chapter Seven

As Emma finished cleaning up the kitchen after Jake left, she reflected on what he had told her about his father. It had taken Ben months to start talking about what he was going through, and once he did he was more open to therapy to help with the PTSD. She hoped it was the same with Jake because...

What? I'm attracted to him? She didn't want to be. She'd dealt with her husband and his problems and was glad she could be there to help him, but in the end she was the reason he was on the ladder that he fell from. She couldn't be responsible for someone else that way. But she could be a friend to Jake and help him when he would let her.

The ringing of the phone startled her, and she gasped. She dried her hands and hurried to answer it.

"Emma, this is Marcella. I was going to bed when I saw a police car outside Jake's house. I thought I would let you know. I'm heading over to his house right now."

Emma wasn't sure what was going on, but Jake probably didn't need a lot of people showing up at his house.

"Let me check on him and Shep, then I'll give you a call."

"Promise. No matter how late."

"I will." When she hung up, she rushed to Josh's room to let him know where she was going. "The police are at Jake's house. I want to make sure he's okay."

Josh shut down his computer. "I'm coming with you."

"You'll need to stay out of the way. Maybe on his porch until I know what's going on." Emma began imagining all kinds of scenarios, causing her breathing to become shallow until she was panting as she headed out of her house.

A few minutes later, Emma approached Jake's place as the police officer was leaving. They passed on the sidewalk, her attention trained on Jake in the doorway with Shep right next to him. He looked all right. Relief flowed through her the closer she came to Jake, and she didn't see any signs of a panic attack.

"Mom, look at his window." Josh pointed toward the one in the living room that faced the street.

She mounted the stairs to the porch, her eyes returning to Jake's. Beneath his calm expression she spied a hard glitter in his eyes for a few seconds before he masked it. He was holding himself together, his hand on top of Shep's head.

"Marcella called to tell me the police were at your house. We were worried. I told her I would find out what happened then let her know."

"What happened?" Josh waved his hand toward the window. "Someone rob you?"

Jake stepped back. "Come in." As he walked toward the living room, he continued, "I couldn't find anything missing. The officer thinks it was a prank. There were several large rocks found on the floor. He took them to see if they could pull any prints from them. But he wasn't hopeful."

Entering, Emma peered at the glass all over the carpet, a cool breeze blowing in from the gaping hole. "I'll help you clean this up. What are you going to do about the window tonight?"

"I hadn't thought that far. Tomorrow I can get it replaced but I'm not sure…" Jake stared at the large, shattered pane.

"We've got two sheets of paneling in our garage we didn't use when redoing the den. They'll cover most of the window. Josh and I can go back home and bring them. They're pretty big so it might take two trips."

Jake looked at her son still taking in the destruction. "I can help. Maybe between the two of us, we can do it in one trip. What do you think, Josh?"

He nodded, his chest puffing out. "They aren't that big. We can do it together."

Emma looked at Jake. "Are you sure?"

"Yes, my trip home earlier went fine. But I'm leaving Shep here with you."

"No, I'll be fine."

"This isn't up for debate."

She started to argue with Jake, but the determination in his expression told her it would be useless. "Where's your vacuum cleaner?"

"In the hall closet." Jake put his hand on Josh's shoulder. "Come on, kiddo. You can even help me nail the boards up."

"Wait, here's my key." Emma passed it to Jake.

"Good thinking."

His chuckles sprinkled the air and made Emma

smile. She quickly called Marcella and told her what happened then retrieved the vacuum cleaner. After she picked up the large pieces of glass, she swept the carpet over and over and then straightened a metal lamp that had been hit.

Shep barked as the guys returned with both sheets of paneling. Josh's face beamed, and Jake seemed all right, his expression even. Then he focused on her, and a light gleamed in his eyes, warming her.

"I appreciate these panels. Otherwise, I might have had to sleep on the couch to make sure no one tried to come through the window." Jake greeted Shep, rubbing him behind the ears.

"Those jagged edges probably would be a deterrent for most rational people, but I have my doubts about anyone who goes around doing this." Emma wound the cord on the vacuum cleaner.

"Mom, I'm gonna help Jake put these up. Okay?"

She glanced at her watch. "Only if you agree to go right to bed when we get home."

"I can manage without—"

Emma waved her hand. "No, we're staying and both of us will help you. The job will go faster."

"Then I'll go get my nails. I think there are two hammers in the garage." He started toward the hallway, stopped and glanced at her. "Did you call Miss Kime?"

"Yes. Don't be surprised if she isn't over here first thing in the morning."

When he disappeared from view, Josh moved closer and asked quietly, "What if this is Liam and Sean getting back at Jake? He did stop the fight. Liam went to the principal's office at the end of class today. What if they do it to us, too?"

"Stop. You can't worry about what might happen. Worrying is wasted energy. If someone does something, we'll call the police and fix the window, just like Jake's doing."

Josh frowned. "Liam gets away with so much. He's sneaky."

"It'll catch up with him. Sandy and I are rallying the moms. And Mrs. Alexander and the principal are aware of the situation. They don't support any kind of bullying."

"Tomorrow Jake's gonna work with us."

In less than two weeks Jake had become important in their lives. But he had his own problems and didn't need to be burdened with theirs. She never wanted Jake to regret knowing them. She knew how fragile his world was.

Lord, if this is the work of Liam and his buddies, please bring them to justice. They need to be held accountable for their actions. Too many people have been hurt by them.

When Jake came back, carrying his supplies, quivers flashed up her spine. He had a commanding presence that kept drawing her to him.

"Here we go. Two hammers and enough nails to put these panels up. Who wants the extra hammer?" When Josh's arm went up, Jake gave him the tool. "You can nail the bottom part while I do the top."

"What do I do?" Emma asked as the guys walked out onto the porch, the lighting still bright enough to work.

Jake gave Josh a look that said they would tolerate her assistance. "Supervise."

"I can at least help hold it up until you get enough

nails in the panel, and if you need more nails, I can give them to you."

"Sure, Mom, that's a good job for you." Josh and Jake shared another look, accompanied by her son's rolling his eyes.

"On second thought, I think I'll take Shep out back. You two can do some male bonding."

Josh giggled.

Snorting, Jake started hammering.

In the backyard, Emma sat on the top step while Shep went around sniffing the ground. This was what she wanted, her son bonding with a man. There were times she couldn't help Josh the way a male could. But was this what Jake wanted? Having a young boy looking up to him, wanting his opinion? Was he willing to listen to Josh's problems while he was wrestling with his own serious issues?

Finally, Shep trotted to the stairs, mounted them and sprawled across the deck next to her. "Hey, boy, how are you liking your new home?"

In answer he rubbed against her then hopped to his feet and ambled to the back door. After a series of barks, Jake let him in. While Shep pranced in as though he owned the house, Jake locked looks with Emma.

He stepped back from the doorway and called out, "Be back in a minute. I need to talk to your mom."

She turned toward him and watched him shrink the distance between them in three long strides. His limp was more pronounced after a long day.

Clutching the railing, he lowered himself down next to her. "You've got a fine son. You've done a good job with him."

"I don't always feel that way." She shivered more

from the silky thread of his words than the cool breeze blowing.

"Cold?"

She nodded, not sure she could adequately explain she was but wasn't.

He slipped his arm around her and pulled her closer. "We talked about tomorrow with his friends coming over. He wanted to know if I was sure I wanted to do it. Did you tell him I am suffering from PTSD?"

"No, there isn't any reason to. But I'm sure he knows something is going on. He's a smart kid." She turned until their gazes linked, their faces only inches apart. "He knows about his uncle Ben, and it hasn't affected how he feels about him. You aren't less of a man because of it."

"I feel like I am."

She wanted to say that was nonsense, but he wouldn't believe her. Her brother hadn't. Once her husband had basically said the same thing after a severe seizure. Still, she went on, "PTSD isn't who you are. That doesn't change, not the core essence of you. The same was true of Sam with his seizures. They were something he had to deal with, but they didn't make him who he was."

Jake studied her face. "I appreciate what you're trying to do, but—"

She stopped his words with her fingertips pressed against his mouth. The physical contact with him captivated her, the softness of his lips in contrast with the day's growth of beard on his chin. Her throat went dry. Her pulse accelerated.

"I'm only telling you the truth," she murmured, his head bending closer.

She wound her arms around him, wanting him even

nearer. This was the first kiss she'd shared with a man since her husband died, and it felt so right. A scary thought. What was she doing? She wasn't ready for any kind of relationship with a man when she was the reason her husband died.

She pulled back. "I need to get Josh home. It's a school night. Sandy is bringing all the boys over tomorrow at four-thirty. I'll be here at five to help and then take them home later." She pushed to her feet, her legs shaking. "Is that all right? If not, what sounds good to you?" Her words flew out of her mouth so rapidly she could hardly follow herself.

All emotion fled his face as he rose and crossed to his back door, letting her go inside first. "Whatever works for you all. I'll be here."

She blocked his way into the hallway. "I won't ever tell Josh about your PTSD. If you want him to know, that'll have to come from you. In Josh's eyes his uncle Ben was the greatest before he was injured and still is now that he knows the problems Ben has."

"How did you explain Shep?"

"He thinks Shep helps with your leg. I train all kinds of dogs—service, therapy, companions. If I'm not needed at the animal hospital, I'm working with a dog. Dr. Harris is one of the supporters of Caring Canines." She made her way to the living room, feeling the drill of Jake's look as she walked ahead of him.

"Ready, Josh?"

Her son nodded, whispered something to Shep and rose from the floor. "I finished nailing that last piece of paneling. See ya tomorrow, Jake, Shep."

"Thanks, kiddo, for helping me."

Josh grinned and waved goodbye then headed down the porch steps.

Emma hung back, wanting to explain why she'd broken off the kiss. But the words wouldn't form in her mind. She couldn't tell him about her part in Sam's death. Instead, she mumbled, "Good night," then hurried after her son.

Jake watched Emma and Josh leave, replaying in his mind the sensation that had swirled through him when he'd kissed her. Then the feeling of rejection when she had yanked back as though he was damaged goods. And he was. He wasn't whole, no matter how much she tried to reassure him he was, that his PTSD had nothing to do with his masculinity.

It wasn't true. It controlled his life. He sometimes felt like a prisoner.

Anger surged through him. He slammed his door so hard, the pictures on the walls in the foyer shook.

I want to be whole. I want my life back. Lord, help me.

Chapter Eight

Saturday afternoon Emma wrote a check to the hospital, draining the last of their funds for the month, but at this rate she would have it paid off by the end of the year. That would be a good feeling, and her next payday was in a few days.

Josh came into the living room, beaming. "Mom, you should've seen us with Jake today. We were awesome. I learned two new moves."

Emma basked in the expression on her son's face. Since Jake had been working with Josh on his baseball skills and self-defense moves, she'd seen more smiles and joy in his eyes. "I was impressed when I saw you all on Thursday working with Jake."

"He told us today you aren't a snitch if you tell the authorities a crime's being committed. That we all need to stand up to someone who's doing something wrong. He told the guys about when he was bullied and what he learned from it."

"What was that?"

"Letting the bullies get away with it only encourages them to do more."

"True, but I don't want you starting any fights."

"He doesn't believe in that, either. He says as a group we should stand strong."

She imagined if Ben were here he would be telling her son the same thing. She was glad Josh had Jake to turn to. "He's going to be here any minute. Are you ready to go to the ranch?"

Josh's smile grew. "Yeah. I get to show him the dogs at Caring Canines. Can I take Buttons? Jake said Shep was going with him."

"Sure, but on a leash."

Josh whirled around and raced back to his room to get the leash then went to the backyard for his terrier.

Emma rose from the desk and rolled her head around, then stretched, trying to work the tightness out of her muscles. She hated balancing the checkbook, but at least it was done for the month. Now she intended to have a nice day at Winter Haven Ranch with Jake and Josh.

Glimpsing Jake pull into the driveway in a blue Ford Fusion made her heart seem to pause in her chest then begin pounding faster than normal. This was a first. He was driving her and Josh to the ranch. She knew he drove when he went to the doctor or a few other required places, but this trip was for fun. It was just an opportunity for Jake to get out more with Shep and spend some time with her and Josh.

Like a family popped into her mind, and she quickly brushed it aside. Jake was a client she was helping adjust to the service dog she'd trained. But in her heart she knew Jake and Shep had bonded and didn't really need any help from her.

"Josh, Jake's here. Let's go!" she yelled and grabbed her purse.

Her son hurried from the back of the house with Buttons on a leash. "Do you think he'll mind her going?"

The doorbell rang. "We'll ask him." Emma moved to open the door.

Seeing Jake standing on her porch rather than honking for them to come out sent her heart racing again. She imagined him in his dress uniform, and her legs went weak with the picture in her mind. He would have been impressive.

"Hi, we're ready," she said with a grin that matched his.

"Good. I've heard a lot about this place. It'll be nice to finally see it." Jake glanced at Josh. "Do you want to take Buttons?"

"Can I?"

"Sure. Let's go." He stood to the side while Emma and Josh left their house, then he followed them to his car, opening the front passenger door for Emma. "Josh, you can hop in with Shep in the back. I figure you can keep the dogs entertained. I hear you're good at working with them."

Josh blushed but drew himself up tall. "I wanna train them like Mom."

When Emma settled herself in the car, she glanced back to make sure Josh sat between the two dogs. Shep was thoroughly trained, but Buttons had only started. She lay down and placed her head on Josh's lap as if staking her claim to him.

"Josh was telling me the lesson this morning went well. I know the other parents are happy with what you're doing."

He glanced at her then backed out of her driveway.

"The boys are eager to learn." His gaze slid to her again, a gleam in his eyes. "I've been enjoying it."

"Did you ever hear anything back from the police about your window?"

"They managed to pull a print off one of the smooth rocks, but nothing turned up in their database."

"That's because it was Liam," Josh said from the backseat.

"What makes you think that?" Jake stopped at a red light, his knuckles white as he gripped the steering wheel.

"Because I heard him bragging about toilet-papering someone's house where he used to live. He likes to do stuff like that," Josh answered.

Emma twisted toward her son. "That's not the same thing. I don't want you saying anything without proof."

Josh tilted up his chin. "It was him. I know it."

Emma chanced a look toward Jake, trying to read his expression. Tension poured off him, but she wasn't sure whether it was because they were talking about the other night or the fact he was driving. She shouldn't have brought it up.

He'd warned her that driving for him was hard. Did a piece of trash in the road hide a bomb? Would stopping at a light invite a sniper's shot? He had to keep reassuring himself he was home and safe.

His chest rose as he dragged in a deep breath. Jake started across the intersection. "Josh, I'm pretty sure it was Liam or one of his friends, too. Since the police haven't found them, they'll start to get reckless and mess up. They'll be caught. Until then I wouldn't waste any energy thinking about it. I refuse to let someone like Liam ruin today."

"Okay," Josh said. "But when do ya think he'll get caught?"

"In time." His tight grip on the steering wheel loosening some, Jake turned onto the highway that led out of town. "So what are we going to do first?"

"Caring Canines," Emma and Josh said at the same time.

"Not the horses? I've heard that Dominic Winters is building up his herd."

"When I go to the ranch, Madi and me like to ride. Once we went to the factory Dominic built on part of the ranch."

Emma frowned. "You never told me. That's pretty far from the barn."

"We just went to the hill overlooking the factory. Chad went with us. I think Madi bugged him until he did."

"Who's Chad?" Jake drove through the gate to Winter Haven Ranch, the stiffness in his shoulders relaxing.

"The foreman. Madi has him wrapped around her finger. He lets her do a lot of things." Josh's forehead creased. "Maybe I should find out how from her."

"Maybe I should say something to Abbey," Emma said with a chuckle.

"Mom! You better not. Madi will get mad at me."

With laughter in his eyes, Jake looked at Emma. "So how old is this Madi you keep talking about?"

"Ten. She's not like most girls. She's cool."

When Jake parked in front of the building that housed Caring Canines, Josh grabbed Buttons and scooted out of the back of the car.

"He likes coming out here." Jake watched Josh hurrying into the building.

"Yeah. Madi and Josh have grown closer since Abbey and I have been working together to get this place going. Don't tell my son, but Abbey says that Madi has a crush on him."

"Probably a good idea. At that age, I didn't have any interest in girls."

She shifted toward him. "So, Jake Tanner, when did you acquire an interest in the opposite sex?"

"Oh, about eighth grade when the most popular girl asked me to the dance at the end of the year. How about you? When did you become interested in boys?"

"Ah, I remember it as if it were yesterday. Keith Chambers moved to Tulsa, and the first day he walked into my sixth-grade class, I thought it was love at first sight. Sadly, he didn't. We did become friends by the end of the year."

"See? Girls seem to be into that much earlier than boys."

"Because we figure out way before you all that love makes the world go around."

His laughter filled the car. It wrapped around her as though his arms embraced her.

"What a cliché."

"But true. I'm not just talking about a man and a woman. I'm talking about friendship, family, the Lord. Love is what it's all about. Even when I become attached to a pet, that's a form of love. I don't want to do anything halfheartedly."

"So you either love something or someone or what—hate? Isn't that the opposite of love?"

"I don't think there has to be an either/or. I look for ways to heighten my good feelings about something—someone." *Is that why my feelings for Jake are shifting?*

He leaned toward her, hooking a stray strand of hair behind her ear, then cupping her face. His brown eyes delved deep into hers, assessing, probing for answers. *Where do I stand with you?* Her heartbeat picked up speed.

"My grandma used to tell me that God is love and love is God." The rough pad of his thumb made circles on her cheek, sending chills through her.

She swallowed hard. "She's right. Marcella and your grandmother were good friends. I can remember when she died last year how heartbroken Marcella was."

"I didn't get the news of her death until a week later. I was on assignment behind enemy lines. The first thing I did when I came here to live was go to her grave site and say goodbye." He glanced away. "I fell apart when I saw it. She understood me and was always there to support my decisions. I refused to go to West Point the way my father, her son, wanted. My dad and I had a huge fight over it. That summer between high school and my first year in college I stayed with Grandma. My dad didn't speak to me for months. I wasn't sure if I wanted to go into the service. I was eighteen and needed more time to think about my future. In the end, after I completed my bachelor's degree, I did sign up but my father was always disappointed I didn't go to West Point."

"I'm so sorry. I know it's hard when parents have one vision for us and we have a different one. Mine didn't want me to quit college so I could work and put Sam through his last year. I don't regret doing that one bit, but they thought I was putting my dreams on hold." She covered his hand, and his look connected with hers. "I love what I'm doing, and I might never have stumbled across training dogs if it hadn't happened the way it did.

Now my parents understand, especially when they see how Ben is with his service dog."

"I wish I could say the general will understand one day. He won't. The army is his life, and he thinks one way or another it should be mine, even with this injury." His hand tensed under hers.

"What are you doing about the medal they want to give you? Veterans Day is only a couple of weeks away."

"I don't know if I can accept it. I…"

Someone banged on the window next to Emma and she jumped, swiveling around to find Abbey and Josh standing next to the car. "A lot of things can change by then. Give it some more time. I think we're being summoned." She pointed her thumb at the two. "I'd like to introduce you to my best friend."

When she started to open the door, he grasped her hand and stopped her. "Thank you. I appreciate what you've done for me."

I want more than gratitude. The words were on the tip of her tongue, and she swallowed them. Being friends was all that Jake could handle or want. She would have to settle for that, especially since she wasn't sure what she wanted anymore.

When she climbed from the Ford and Jake joined her, Emma made the introductions while Abbey and he shook hands. Then Josh grabbed him and tugged him toward Caring Canines.

Abbey gave a low whistle. "Good thing I already found my man, or you'd have competition."

"For what? We're friends."

"Girlfriend, what I saw on his face when I approached the car didn't look like friendship to me."

Emma blew a breath, lifting her bangs on her forehead. "No, it was only gratitude. Nothing else." Then she walked after her son and Jake before her best friend had them engaged and the wedding planned.

Jake watched Madi and Josh racing toward the black barn with a bichon and terrier right beside them. Josh wasn't going full speed probably in order to allow Madi to keep up. All around Jake were green pastures, black fences and horses. He spied a foal next to its mother nursing in the paddock next to him. There was something about the scene that calmed him.

"From what you've told me about Madi, she's doing remarkably well since the plane crash." Emma walked beside him, and Jake fought the urge to slip her hand in his. It would send the wrong message. All he could handle was the friendship she offered.

"Her injuries involved both of her legs. She had to really work to get where she is today, but she was determined. I have been amazed, but then I think a lot of it had to do with Cottonball, Abbey and Dominic."

"So that fluff ball of fur was her therapy dog?"

"Yeah, a stray Dr. Harris found. She hadn't been on her own long, thankfully. Madi fell in love with her and the rest is history."

"I see a black Lab at the barn. I think there are as many dogs here at the ranch as horses."

Emma chuckled. "Not quite but who knows in the future. Abbey has ambitious dreams about Caring Canines. She wants her dogs to help people not only around this area but all over the region."

A tall, dark-haired man came out to greet the children. "Is that Chad, the foreman?" Jake slowed his step, his leg aching from walking so much this afternoon, as well as the self-defense lesson in the morning. He wished he'd brought his cane.

"That's Abbey's husband, Dominic. She told me he'd meet us down here. She thought it would be fun for the kids to go riding."

"And us?"

Emma smiled. "Yes, unless you want to stay back."

His expression brightened. "I haven't ridden since I was a teenager, but I used to love it when I went to my grandparents' farm in Virginia."

"Your mother's parents?"

"Yes, my mom's father was an army man, too, but he was in only four years. Not like my dad's family who all made long careers in the military."

"Was your dad's father a general, too?"

"Yes." Jake came to a stop.

Emma stepped in front of him, and her gaze drew his. "You did your part for eight years. You did all you could. You've done nothing wrong. Isn't the army wanting to give you one of its highest awards an indication of that fact?"

Shep planted himself right next to Jake, his body pressing against him. Automatically, Jake's hand went to the top of Shep's head. His throat thickened. His eyes blurred when he peered into Emma's beautiful face. "Why was I one of the soldiers to survive? I rarely leave my house. I..." As usual, he couldn't completely express what he was wrestling with deep inside. Although it hurt his leg, Jake knelt to stroke Shep's back, relishing the calmness that washed over him when he did.

Emma stooped next to Jake, laying her hand on his arm. "You aren't the only one who feels guilty about surviving. Ben went through the same thing when the soldier he was with died. My husband should never have died. He shouldn't have been up on that ladder. He—" Emma clamped her lips together.

"He what?"

She closed her eyes for a second. "This conversation is about you. Not me."

Like Jake, she could share only so much before she shut the door on what was going on inside. But that didn't stop him from wishing she would say more.

"Mom, aren't you two coming?" Josh called from the entrance into the barn.

She rubbed her hand up and down his arm. "Are you up for riding?"

Jake glimpsed over Emma's shoulder the eagerness in the kids' eyes. "Actually, it'll be a relief not to walk for a while."

"Okay. I see Abbey coming." Emma rose.

"I'll be there in a moment." Jake watched her move away from him, the whole time his hand gliding over Shep, the soft feel of fur beneath his palm.

He cared for Emma. He needed to pull back emotionally from her. He didn't want to hurt her. He had nothing to give a woman, and she deserved so much.

He struggled to his feet as Abbey neared. He'd talked to her earlier about the PTSD therapy group but hadn't said he would do it. He was nervous. Accepting the dog was one thing but once he participated in a group specializing in PTSD, he was admitting out loud that he needed intensive help.

Abbey smiled at him and paused. "Are you going to ride with us?"

"Yes." He started toward the barn with her. "You have quite a nice training facility with Caring Canines."

"I couldn't have done all of it without Dominic, my father and Emma. They all helped me tremendously. Have you considered joining our group on Monday evenings?"

"I have and…" The word *no* wouldn't come out of his mouth. In that moment he realized he would deeply regret not going. Exhaling a deep breath, he murmured, "Yes, I want to."

"Great. Will you start this Monday night?"

"No, not until next week. This Monday is already full for me." He realized he should jump right in, but he couldn't go that far—not yet, but he hoped by next Monday evening he would be able to.

When Jake neared the barn with Abbey, Josh and Madi came out with their saddled horses, followed by Dominic, leading two others behind him.

He approached Jake and shook hands with him. "I'm Dominic Winters. Welcome to the ranch."

"I hear you're one of the driving forces behind Caring Canines." Jake took the reins of one of the geldings.

"I don't take any credit for it. That's Abbey and Emma and their hard work."

"Not according to the two ladies." Jake smiled.

Dominic threw a look at his wife, his eyes softening. "Supplying the money is the easy part. Josh said something about showing you the stream and woods. It's Madi's special place."

"Sounds nice." Jake caught sight of Abbey and Emma bringing their mounts out, their heads bent together as they talked.

He drew in a long breath, full of the scent of horse, earth and leather. What tension still lingered from driving to the ranch vanished.

Madi challenged Josh to a race, then both kids climbed onto their mares and spurred their horses forward. Dominic scrambled onto his gelding and hurried after the children.

Abbey laughed. "We'll spend the whole ride to the stream trying to keep up with the kids." Then Abbey mounted her horse and left with Jake and Emma still standing in front of the barn.

While Shep sat nearby, Jake swung up into the saddle and grinned. "I hope you know where this stream is."

"Yes, I've been there many times." Emma mounted her mare and came up beside him. "But I'd rather take it nice and easy."

By the time Jake and Emma arrived at the stream with Shep trotting alongside, Josh and Madi had rolled up their jeans and were walking in the water that came up to their calves. Dominic and Abbey had spread out a blanket under a large oak tree. For a few seconds Jake looked at the couple and envied their idyllic relationship. There had been a time when he'd wished to have what they had. At the moment that dream seemed unattainable.

He dismounted and tethered his horse to a branch, petted Shep for a few seconds, then made his way with Emma to the blanket. "You've got a beautiful place," he said as he eased down, using the trunk to help him. Shep stretched out near him. "Emma told me you're trimming your cattle herd and adding horses. How do you manage your ranch and a big business?"

Dominic exchanged a warm glance with Abbey. "I have a wife who looks the other way when I have to work long hours. But mostly I've got good people who work for me, which lets me grab time with my family now and then."

As Jake sat and listened to the others, their conversation occasionally sprinkled with laughter, his dream taunted him. It would never happen if he didn't admit to his problems and do something about them. Coming out to the ranch had shown him he couldn't remain hiding in his house if he wanted to get better.

"I had the best time today," Josh said from the backseat as Jake pulled out onto the highway leading into Cimarron City. "What about you, Jake?"

His headlights sliced through the darkness, making Jake realize he had stayed longer at the ranch than he had intended—and had enjoyed it. The quiet had appealed to him. "My favorite part was the ride. I'd forgotten how nice it was to be on the back of a horse."

"Yeah, I know what you mean. And the barbecue dinner was great." Josh yawned. "How about you, Mom?"

"I always love coming to the ranch. It was nice seeing Nicholas at dinner. He's growing so fast. Before Abbey knows it, he'll be one."

Jake looked at Emma. In the soft lighting she appeared content, relaxed, luring him to join her—let everything go and relish the moment. He sighed, loosening any tightness gripping him. Today he'd come the closest to feeling normal since the ambush. His hands gripped the steering wheel. The second he thought that word a picture of the mountain village crept into his mind. He shoved it away—not wanting to go down the path that led to memories.

"So what was your favorite part?" Jake asked to keep

the conversation going, his mind focused on the two in the car with him.

"The big slice of cherry pie with vanilla ice cream at the end of dinner," Emma said with a laugh. "I probably shouldn't have had it, but it was delicious."

"Yeah, that was good, but racing across the field was my favorite part." Josh's voice slurred with sleepiness.

"Mine was seeing where your mom worked and the different dogs being trained." When there was no response from Josh, Jake peered at him through the rearview mirror. "He's fallen asleep."

"That doesn't surprise me. He was up early practicing his self-defense moves and lifting those five-pound weights you gave him to use. He's taking this seriously. I usually have to drag him out of bed in the morning."

"I'm giving him a new exercise each lesson, and he's promised me he won't do it until I tell him he's got the right technique. I've been stressing that's more important than how much he lifts."

"I'm sure Josh will follow your directions, but it wouldn't hurt for me to see the exercises and the right techniques so I can keep an eye on it."

Jake came to a halt at the four-way stop sign and glanced at her, the way the streetlight angled across her features, throwing part of her face in the shadows, but not her eyes. They were trained on him. "That's a good suggestion. But not only how he does it, watch that he doesn't do it too much."

"Maybe I should take up weight lifting." She raised her arm and flexed her muscles. "I doubt you can feel much there."

He reached out and squeezed gently on her upper arm. "It wouldn't hurt."

"Is that your way of telling me I have no muscles in my arms?"

"There's a muscle somewhere in there." He chuckled. "If you didn't want me to tell the truth, you shouldn't have asked."

Headlights from the car behind flooded the Ford. Jake pressed his foot on the accelerator and went across the intersection. Two minutes later, he parked in Emma's driveway and started to get out of his car.

"You don't have to walk us to the door."

"Yes, I do."

"This isn't…"

"What?"

"A date."

"We didn't think we were going to be gone this late. Your porch light isn't on. I'm walking you to your door." Climbing from the vehicle, Jake began to skirt around the front of the Fusion when Emma hopped out and opened the back door.

A pungent, nauseating smell suffused the air. Rubbing his nose, Jake scanned the area.

"What's that smell?" Josh asked as he scooped up Buttons and trekked toward his house.

"Don't know. It seems to be coming from our…" Emma's words sputtered to a stop. Her hand clasped over her mouth and nose.

"Gross." Josh mounted the steps.

With his leg throbbing, Jake limped after Emma and Josh. "Stop, Josh."

The boy turned toward Jake.

"Let me check everything out first. Come stand by your mom." To Emma, Jake continued, "Give me the key to the house. I'll turn on the porch light. It's hard to see exactly what has happened."

Jake took the key from her trembling hand and headed toward the stairs, using the penlight he carried to scope out the area before him. Piles of trash and feces littered everywhere he shone the light. He gagged but kept moving forward to turn on the security lamp so he could inspect the damage.

Chapter Nine

Emma held her nose, trying to block the smell. Her stomach roiled. "Josh, go back to Jake's car with Buttons and stay there."

"But, Mom—"

"Please."

He stomped across the yard toward the Ford, mumbling.

As he slammed the car door, the security light flooded the porch. Jake came out of her house, surveying the porch area. A frown carved deep lines into his face, and he locked gazes with her. "Do you think Josh can go to your neighbor's while I clean this up?"

"You mean while *we* clean it up."

"In a war zone, I've smelled some pretty bad things before. After a while, it won't be as bad."

"I've changed diapers and cleaned up after my son got sick. We'll do it together."

"Where are your trash bags, shovel, rake, broom, dustpan and plastic gloves?"

After she told him the location of each item, she hurried to the car. "You're going to stay with Miss Baker for a while."

"This is Liam's doing."

"We'll talk about that later." She rang her neighbor's doorbell, and when Miss Baker answered, Emma explained to the older woman what had happened.

"You know I thought I heard some racket about half an hour ago—like dogs getting into my trash can when I leave it out, except that tomorrow isn't trash day so it wasn't out."

"Did you look and see anyone?"

Miss Baker shook her head. "I was watching my favorite TV show, and it was getting to the good part. Sorry." She stepped aside to let a pouting Josh into the house. "I baked some snicker doodles today. Want any?"

Josh looked back at Emma then said, "Yes, ma'am."

"It may be a while."

"Hon, don't worry about Josh and me. We'll be fine."

Emma rushed back to her house as Jake reappeared on the porch with all the cleaning items. The obnoxious smells bombarded Emma's senses, but the quicker they took care of this mess, the faster she could breathe clean air again. Jake took out his cell phone and shot some pictures of what had been done, then he placed a call to the police.

When he hung up, Emma scanned the piles of rotten food mixed in with what had to be a bag of manure dumped throughout the trash. "Someone went to a lot of trouble." On her porch wall, she spied words she wouldn't repeat spray-painted across it. That would be the next thing she dealt with.

"Yes. This isn't a prank but pure rage and intimidation."

"What are we going to do about Liam and his buddies?"

"Although we don't have any proof it was Liam, I'm going to tell the police about the boy and the motives he might have for vandalizing our houses."

"Should we wait for the police to come?"

"Yes. They'll be here shortly."

"I've run out of things to do about those boys." Frustration and anger overwhelmed her. She didn't like feeling that way, but she couldn't stop the emotions demanding release.

Jake took her hand and led her down the steps. "Let's put the dogs in your backyard. I could use some fresh air."

The feel of his fingers wrapped around hers soothed some of the fury building in her. As they crossed her front yard, the smells lessened.

Jake slipped his arm around her shoulders and pressed her against him. "We'll find a way to deal with the boys. I hope the officer will pay Liam and Sean a visit tonight to find out where they've been."

"They'll retaliate against Josh."

"They'll try, but I'm going to work with Josh and his friends. We aren't going to make it easy for Liam and Sean to get back at them, and every time they harass us, we'll call the police. I know a couple of officers I went to school with when I lived here. I'll involve them if I need to."

When he said *we* or *us,* her tension eased a little more. She wasn't by herself, trying to figure out what to do. And she also had the Lord. There were many times in history His people were harassed and threatened, and He came to their defense. *Please help us,*

God. Not just for us, but for Liam and Sean. It's time to turn their lives around.

Emma scooped Buttons into her arms while Shep walked beside Jake. At the gate to her backyard, she put Buttons down and the dog hurried away, but the German shepherd didn't want to leave Jake's side.

In the stream of light from her kitchen window, he smiled at her. "I guess he doesn't care that the place stinks."

"Think about those cadaver dogs who work with the police looking for dead bodies. If they don't mind that, the porch won't be a big deal for Shep."

Jake's laughter shivered down her—a wonderful sound she hoped to hear more and more. "And their sense of smell is much better than ours. To each his own, I guess."

His presence made her forget for a few minutes what they needed to clean up. He moved nearer and framed her face with his hands, the look in his eyes soft, appealing. "I had a nice time today. I wasn't sure how it would turn out, but I was comfortable at the ranch. I enjoyed meeting Abbey and Dominic. Madi and Josh are fun to see together, playing, kidding each other. Almost like brother and sister."

Warmth suffused her face from his caress as he brushed her hair back, his fingers combing through the strands. "I like to feel this," he said. "Until lately I didn't realize how calming a touch could be."

Neither had she. Emma wanted to melt against him, cling to him. Somehow she remained upright, but his nearness was quickly unraveling her composure. Her heartbeat hammered a mad staccato against her rib cage. Her breathing became shallow, her total focus on the man only inches from her. She wound her arms about him to steady herself.

Slowly, almost hesitantly he bent toward her mouth and claimed it in a kiss that rocked her. This man who had been a soldier, capable of taking care of her, protecting and defending, gently possessed her with just a touch of his lips against hers.

She didn't know how long she would have stayed there at the side of her house enfolded in his arms, enjoying the feel of his lips on hers if Shep hadn't barked. She blinked, dazed, trying to orient herself to the here and now.

Jake's arms slipped away from her. He leaned down and whispered, "The police are here." The words flowed over her cheek.

"Police?"

"Yes, Emma." He gave her a kiss on the forehead and began limping around to the front yard.

She watched him, reliving every second of the past ten minutes. Step by step. Touch by touch. She sagged against her house for a moment, composing herself before heading over to talk with the police. The trash on her porch didn't bother her nearly as much as before, not when she thought about the kiss Jake and she had shared.

Jake sat at Emma's kitchen table, needing to go home and take a long, hot shower to rid himself of the stench. He would when she came back from talking to Josh and making sure he went to bed. Nursing a cup of coffee, he replayed kissing Emma and wondered where in the world his brain had been. No good would come of starting that kind of relationship with her. She deserved a whole man. He wanted her friendship—and he wanted much more.

How would he back away from a woman who had come to mean so much to him? *Lord, any suggestions? One that won't hurt her.*

Nothing came to mind—except the touch of her mouth on his. If Shep hadn't barked, he would never have known the police had pulled up.

Although her footsteps were faint sounding, he heard her coming. He finished the coffee in one long swallow and rose.

"Did Josh finally go to sleep?" Jake asked when Emma came into the kitchen.

"Let's say he acted like he was, but I won't be surprised if he's still up. He had a hundred questions about what the police said, what to do about Liam and Sean. A few I could answer. Most I couldn't. I doubt the police can do much."

"At least the officer's going by both boys' houses to find out where they have been in the past few hours." Jake took his empty cup to the sink.

"I thought I would go around the neighborhood tomorrow and see if any of my neighbors saw something. I think from what Miss Baker said, I know what time this happened." Emma crossed the room and went into the garage.

Jake followed her and stood in the doorway, watching her kneel in front of a cabinet and search it until she found a can of paint and a brush. "What are you doing?"

She glanced up. "I'm going to paint the porch."

"Now?"

"I can't have people see what's written on the wall out there." She rose.

"Get another brush. I'll help you."

"You don't have to."

"No, but it's late. If I help, it'll be done twice as fast." Jake covered the space between them and took the can and brush. "I'll be out on the porch."

She started to reach for the items in his hands. He turned away. "Jake, please go home. You've done enough. I noticed how pronounced your limp is. You're tired."

He peered back at her. "And you aren't?"

"This is my house, not yours."

"You helped me. Let me do this for you." *I need to be needed* almost came out of his mouth, the thought taking him by surprise.

"Fine, but all we have to do is cover the offensive words. Josh and I can do a proper job tomorrow. I'll have to go to the store and get some more paint. We don't have enough left in that can to redo the whole porch."

Jake hobbled toward the foyer, still stunned by what he had almost said. True, in his former life that was one of the things that had driven him: to serve and protect. But after what happened to him, he'd buried that deep inside because that meant putting himself out there with people in situations he couldn't control. The thought sent shudders down his body.

At the front door, hand on the knob, he closed his eyes, tensing for what often followed—the shakes, the sweating, the fast heartbeat, the gasps for air. Shep rubbed against his good leg. Jake peered into the brown eyes of his service dog. He sat with his head cocked as if he needed Jake to pet him, when in reality it was the other way around.

Sticking the paintbrush into his pocket, Jake hooked the can's handle over the doorknob then bent over to pay some attention to his dog. When he finally rose, he snagged Emma's gaze as she stood back, watching and waiting. The kindness in her expression reached out and took hold of him as though they were embracing again.

All tension faded.

She came toward him. His throat closed at the inner beauty pouring from her. She made him want more than ever to be well. To be the man she deserved.

He opened his mouth to say something but no words formed in his mind. He just stared at her bridging the distance between them.

Emma smiled, radiating joy. "I appreciate your help. I don't know what I would have done if I'd come home and found this without you here. Thanks."

Still no words for her came into his thoughts.

"Jake, are you all right?"

He nodded.

Tiny lines creased her forehead. "Are you sure?"

"Yes. Sorry. I was just thinking about how beautiful you are."

"Me?" She glanced down at her jeans and shirt covered with filth from the cleanup.

"Yes." He released a long breath and pivoted to open the door before he kissed her again. "When you pick up some more paint, buy a couple of motion-activated security lights. I can install them for you tomorrow." He glanced back at her and grinned. "Let's get those words covered up so we can clean up ourselves."

Sunday afternoon when Emma saw Jake carry the ladder out of her garage, she froze in midmotion, painting the porch wall. She remembered driving up to the house and finding Sam on the ladder and before she could ask him to get down, watching him turn to see her pulling into the driveway. Then in the blink of an eye he was falling.

Emma squeezed her eyes shut, trying to wipe the memory from her mind forever. But she would never be able to because she had to live with the guilt. Why had she mentioned getting someone to put up Christmas lights?

The paintbrush slipped from her numb fingers and crashed onto the tarp-covered porch.

"Mom, you got paint all over you. And you thought I was gonna be messy." Josh laughed and continued working on his section.

She was thankful her son wasn't looking at her because her hands began to tremble. She clasped them together and marched toward Jake. "I want to put up the security lights."

"Do you know how?"

"No, but I'm sure I can figure it out."

Jake frowned. "Why should you when I do?"

"I don't want you to use the ladder." There, she said it. She couldn't tell him why; she wouldn't tell anyone.

"My leg is perfectly all right. I'm capable of climbing up and down this ladder."

She folded her arms over her chest. "I saw how you were limping after the long day yesterday."

He moved close to her—too close. "And I rested it last night and this morning. I'm fine," he said firmly.

"I don't think we need a light over the garage. We have one on the porch. That should be enough." She tilted up her chin and dared him to disagree.

"Its range doesn't cover this part of your yard. You need both of them. What's this really about?" His gaze drilled into her, straight to her heart. "I can do this, Emma."

She looked down. "These lights probably won't deter those boys, anyway."

"I'm asking again what's really..." Silence electrified the air for a few seconds. "This is about your husband falling off a ladder, isn't it?"

She nodded, finally reestablishing eye contact with him. "Please find another place to put up the security light besides over the garage."

He clasped her arm, his eyes soft. "I understand. I didn't think about that. You've got a small ladder. How about I put it on the side of the garage? I'll only be a few feet off the ground. That'll still cover your whole front yard."

"Okay. Thanks for understanding."

"Of course." Those soft eyes roamed over her face, lingering for a long second on her lips.

Instantly, the picture of her and Jake kissing yesterday replaced the one of her husband falling off the ladder. Heat flashed through her. She backed away. "I'd better get back to work so we can finish today." She still couldn't look away as she took another step toward the porch.

Finally, he did, picking up the tall ladder and going back into the garage.

Emma put her hands to her face, her cheeks hot beneath her palms. When she looked toward her son, she found him staring at her with a grin on his face. She hurried to occupy herself with completing the job and keeping her attention on her task—not Jake.

As she painted her side of the porch, Josh kept glancing at her until she asked, "What's the problem?"

He giggled. "Nothing. In fact, everything's great. Jake's a good man."

Emma averted her face, not wanting her son to see her shocked expression. "Yeah, he is."

"I know you were scared for him to get on the ladder because of what happened to Dad. He doesn't have seizures."

But he does have panic attacks. "I know."

"Then don't worry. He isn't walking around with his cane anymore. His leg's getting better."

She couldn't answer her son without revealing fears and concerns she didn't want to voice to him or Jake—or even to her best friend. To her relief her son didn't pursue the conversation.

An hour later Emma stood back at the porch to examine the finished paint job. The cream color managed to cover up the black spray paint effectively.

"Not a bad job, you two." Jake finished putting the last trash bags of the refuse from the night before in the trunks of their cars.

Josh grinned from ear to ear, highlighting the slash of cream color across his left cheek. "They aren't gonna win."

Jake settled his hand on Josh's shoulder. "That's right, kiddo. We can clean up messes and paint over graffiti."

The boy gave a thoughtful look. "We should return the trash to Liam and Sean."

Emma glanced at the PT Cruiser she would drive out to the landfill with Jake following her in his car. "I'll be glad when we don't have to smell those anymore, but we can't resort to what they do. When we do, we stoop to their low level."

"But, Mom, they deserve it."

"She's right. They'll get their due one day."

"I want it to be today."

"Yeah, it would be nice, but we have to learn patience. As a soldier, I often had to. Rushing to do something isn't always the answer."

Josh frowned. "I guess so." He peered at the road. "Mom, Carson and his mother are pulling up."

Emma swept around, greeting the two with a smile. Neither had been at church that day. She'd thought someone might be sick in the family. As they stepped from the car, she said, "Hi, what brings you by here?"

"I wanted to tell you our house got trashed last night," Sandy said. "We've been cleaning up today. I tried calling you earlier to let you know." Sandy scanned the front of Emma's house. "What have you been doing?"

"Cleaning up, too. We just got through with painting the porch to—"

"Cover up nasty words," Sandy interrupted Emma. She nodded. "Did you call the police?"

"We didn't see it until this morning and yes, we did."

"I did, too."

"Good. If enough people complain, something will be done about those boys."

"I'm going to call Craig's and Zach's mothers and see if anything happened to them and let them know to be on the lookout. We need to pray for Liam and his buddies. Something must be wrong for them to feel the need to do something like this."

"Mom," Josh said in a voice full of disbelief. "We should be praying they get caught and punished."

Carson said, "Yeah. They're mean."

Sandy placed her arm around Carson's shoulder. "I agree they aren't being nice, but Mrs. Langford's right. God wants us to forgive."

"How can we forget what they've done to us?" Josh scowled.

"You don't have to forget, hon. Forgiveness doesn't mean forgetting. Nor does it mean they shouldn't be held accountable."

Sandy headed toward her car, nodding toward Jake. "See you on Tuesday. Carson has been enjoying the self-defense classes."

When Sandy and Carson left, Josh went to Emma's side. "I don't know how I'll be able to forgive Liam. This all started when he moved here."

"I know it's hard, but I hope you'll try." *Can I forgive myself concerning Sam's accident? How can I expect my son to forgive if I can't?*

"Let's go out to the dump and get rid of the last of this," Jake said, cutting into her thoughts.

Josh ran toward Jake's car. "I'm riding with Jake and Shep."

"Is that okay? He'd asked me earlier and I forgot to ask you."

No, I don't want to be alone in the car with the direction of my thoughts lately. Emma faced Jake and couldn't say that. "Sure. You two just follow me." As she walked toward her car, she decided she would turn up her music loud to drown out anything threatening to invade her mind. Forgiving another was different from forgiving yourself.

Chapter Ten

"You've totally impressed me with this dinner." Sunday evening Jake relaxed in his chair in Emma's dining room. "I love pork chops, but they are even better stuffed with cranberries and apples."

"Did you get enough? I fixed extra in case you would like to take one home with you for later in the week." Emma relished the smile of satisfaction on his face. "This was the first time I prepared the side dish."

"What's in it? I know feta cheese, tomatoes and spinach but what else?"

"Orzo and pine nuts. It could be a meal by itself. A nice lunch."

"It went well with the meat, but I understand why Josh wouldn't necessarily want it."

Emma laughed. "Yeah, it isn't pizza, junk food or spaghetti."

"Best suggestion you made was asking me to Sunday dinner. I enjoyed last week's meal and this one is great, too."

"Since last Sunday we were cleaning up the porch, I had to throw something together."

"You call making chicken cordon bleu *throwing something together?* You could open your own restaurant."

"No, I couldn't. I don't have a head for the financial aspects that go with a business. I hold my breath each month, hoping that my checkbook will balance within a few dollars. If it does, then I'm happy." Emma put her cloth napkin on the table and rose.

"You don't look for the mistake so it reconciles with your bank statement?"

"Nope. I guess you do."

"Yep. It would drive me crazy if I was off."

"That doesn't surprise me. You like order." She took his plate and stacked it on hers.

"And you like chaos? I haven't seen that. Let me help you clear the table." He started to stand.

Emma waved him back. "I have crème brûlée. I don't always make dessert, but I had some extra time. I promised Josh I would save him some. This he does like. Stay right there. I'll be back in a minute."

She walked into the kitchen and scanned the room. Pans and pots were still sitting on the stove. Ingredients were left on the countertop. She'd even forgotten to shut a cabinet door.

"Is this what you mean by chaos?" Jake asked behind her, amusement sprinkling his words.

She gave him a smile over her shoulder. "You were supposed to stay seated then you would never find out about my deep, dark secret. It'll all get cleaned up afterward, but when I'm in my creative mode, I let everything go until later."

"Then the very least I can do is help you later."

She swung around and gently nudged him back into the dining room. "Sit."

Jake glanced at Shep nearby. "Is this how she trained you?"

The dog's ears perked forward, his tail wagging.

She closed the door between the kitchen and dining room, hurried toward the refrigerator and retrieved the dessert. After she presented the crème brûlée to Jake, she sat and waited for him to take a bite.

"Mmm. I think this is the best crème brûlée I've ever had."

"This is one of my specialties. I'm glad you like it."

"I can certainly understand why Josh wanted you to save him some. Smooth. Rich." When he'd finished half his dessert, he cleared his throat. "I have a favor to ask."

"I have some extra dessert you can take home, too."

"That's good, but that isn't the favor." He swallowed hard, his jaw line tensing. "It's about tomorrow evening. Is it possible you can go to Caring Canines when I go for the therapy group? I know I've been getting out more and driving some, but I don't know what to expect tomorrow night."

"Yes and I'll ask Miss Baker to watch Josh."

"In case there's a problem?"

"Yes. I know you don't want him to know about your PTSD. He'd figure it out if he went with us."

Jake exhaled a deep breath. "Thank you. I feel like I'm saying that to you all the time."

"It's a two-way street. This week has been quiet. Maybe the police visiting Sean and Liam was exactly what was needed to make them back off."

He slid the last bite of his dessert into his mouth, frowning.

"You don't think so?"

"Usually it isn't that easy."

"Josh heard that Sean was grounded for a week."

"How about Liam?" The frown remained on Jake's face.

"I don't know about him."

"He hasn't said anything to Josh at school?"

"I made Josh promise to tell me if he did, and I've asked every day. He said no. And there hasn't been any retaliation on Craig, Zach or Carson, either."

"Then we wait and see."

She loved hearing him say *we,* but she didn't want him to feel obligated to help them. He had enough to deal with, and she felt more and more indebted. It was harder to fight her growing feelings for Jake when she felt she owed him so much. Last week when she'd seen him with the ladder, she remembered all the reasons she could *not* fall in love with the man. "This really isn't your battle."

"Yes, it is. Remember the window. That makes it my business. I'm sure Liam and Sean aren't happy I'm working with the boys." Jake pushed to his feet. "Let's clean up."

Emma rinsed the dishes and he put them in the dishwasher. She passed him a plate. "Have you decided about the Veterans Day celebration?"

"Not yet. I haven't told them no, but I want to see how the therapy sessions go. I have to feel I can do it. If I don't, I won't."

"I understand. You've got some time."

"Not much. Dad phoned today and left a message about the ceremony and medal. I need to return his call soon."

"Would he come to the celebration?"

"I hope not. I don't want him to."

Emma realized that one of Jake's problems was his relationship with his father. The man should have supported him rather than act as if Jake should be able to overcome PTSD as quickly as snapping his fingers. The general should know better because Jake certainly wasn't the first soldier to come back from combat facing PTSD. Either way, she would back his decision.

Then a thought struck her. "Does your father know about the PTSD?"

"No. I don't want him to know."

"Why? He's a soldier. Surely he knows others dealing with it. Maybe he could help."

"You don't know the general. No good would come from his knowing." The finality in his voice declared the conversation over.

Emma's heart hurt for Jake. At least Ben had their mother and father supporting him. That only reinforced her determination to be there for Jake. He needed it.

Jake observed the four boys practicing, each pair trading turns throwing the punch and blocking it. "That's a great block, Craig. The more you do it the more natural it will feel, and you'll automatically block the hit before it lands on you. Okay, I want you all to do some curls and push-ups then cool down. Class is almost over."

"It can't have been an hour," Josh said as he lay on the hardwood floor in the dining room that Jake had turned into a minigym for the boys.

Jake glanced out the picture window. "Afraid so. I see your mom pulling up in front."

"She must be early." Josh worked on his tenth curl.

"Keep going. I have to get the door." Jake made his way to the foyer and let Emma into his house. "Why the frown? Something wrong?"

"I heard back from Craig's mother, Kim, about what the mechanic said was wrong with her car this morning. Sugar in the gas tank."

"Did it happen to anyone else's?"

"No. I called to check, but Kim's car sits out in the driveway at night. The others park theirs in the garage."

Jake hung back from the dining room and lowered his voice. "Did Kim report it to the police?"

"Yes and her suspicions about Liam and his buddies. But that's just it. That's all it is—conjecture."

"Has anything happened at Zach's house?"

"So far nothing. We're going to keep each other informed of what's going on and be on the lookout, especially at night."

He took her hands and pulled her close. "They'll mess up. They're getting bolder. That'll be their downfall."

"I hope before someone gets hurt."

He moved her a few steps out of view of the boys in the dining room. "Have I told you thank you for going with me to Caring Canines for the PTSD therapy group?"

"Yes. A couple of times last night. I'm glad your first session went well."

"Listening to what others are coping with makes me able to put my experiences in perspective. When it's happening to you, you think you're the only one dealing with it." When she started to say something, he grinned. "I know Ben and other soldiers have gone through PTSD. But knowing it and really believing it are two different things. Sometimes I think I'm the only one suffering from the same nightmare or getting a panic attack because something out of the blue reminds me of the ambush."

"Yesterday I was your chauffeur. That's all. You did all the hard work."

"I slept better last night than I have in weeks— months. Shep's getting so good at detecting when my nightmares begin and stopping them. I have you to thank for that, too." Sounds from the dining room indicated the boys were finished. Jake squeezed her hands gently. "I'm glad you're stubborn and talked me into taking Shep." He backed away as Josh and his friends appeared in the doorway. "Don't forget to practice between lessons."

They all nodded.

"Thanks, Jake." Emma smiled and left with the boys trailing after her.

Jake went out on the porch to watch them walk to Emma's car. He caught sight of three kids across the street in the park, standing around, their stares trained on Josh, Craig, Zach and Carson. Jake didn't know one of the guys, but the other two were Sean and Liam. Their body language and expressions shouted intimidation.

Jake moved to the top of his steps and crossed his arms, glaring at the trio standing in the park at the exact spot where they had beaten up Josh. For a few seconds Josh reacted—fear swept down his body. Josh glanced back at Jake. He nodded his encouragement. Josh straightened, his chin lifting, his stare directed at the three guys across the street.

Emma hustled the four boys into her car and stomped on the gas, leaving the trio behind. As much as Jake wanted to go back into his house, he stayed where he was with his feet apart, his muscled arms folded over his chest. In every line of his body he conveyed a warrior stance. They stayed for only a moment more then hurried away deep into the wooded area of the park.

Jake waited another couple of minutes, then with the release of a deep breath, relaxed his tense posture. He and Shep went back inside and strode to the dining room window to look out. No sign of the trio. He didn't like the bold gesture—a taunt, really—they'd made a while ago. This wasn't over.

Lord, I know what Josh is going through. Give me the right words to say to him, to help him deal with these bullies. I haven't felt You around much lately, but please answer this request for Josh's sake, not mine.

As Jake walked toward his bedroom, his phone rang. Thinking it might be Emma, he snatched up the receiver without looking at the caller's number on the display. When he heard the general's gruff voice, he fought the urge to slam the phone back into its cradle.

"Jake? Are you there?"

"Yes, sir." He sank onto his bed.

"Why haven't you returned my last few calls?"

"I've been busy."

"Doing what? Do you have a job now?" The skepticism in his father's voice came across loud and clear.

"I'm *working* on getting my Ph.D. I want to finish within the year."

There was a long silence on the other end, and Jake was tempted to hang up.

"I got a call from General Hatchback. You're going to accept the medal on Veterans Day."

"Yes, I called him this morning." After the improvement the past month, he felt he could do it with Shep's support and the fact he would accept the medal for every man in his unit.

"Then I'll be there. I can only stay overnight, but I want to attend."

"You don't have to. It isn't a big deal. General Hatchback will give me a medal, and I'll sit down."

"Not a big deal?!"

Jake pulled the receiver away from his ear and could still hear his father. "It's an honor few soldiers receive. I will be there. That's not up for discussion."

Jake grew taut as if he had been flash-frozen. His teeth dug into his lower lip until a metallic taste coated his tongue.

"You could have gone far, son. This medal is an indication of the type of soldier you were."

"I'll see you at the ceremony." *If I go.* "Goodbye, sir."

"Jake—"

He returned the phone to its resting place before he lost his temper. He'd been taught to honor and obey the man as his father and superior in the service, but right now all he could remember was the barrier that had been between himself and the general for his whole life.

Shep jumped up on the bed and nuzzled Jake's face and neck. He put his arms around the German shepherd and thought of a childhood memory. One time his father swung him around and around. When he'd stopped, Jake had giggled and staggered, trying to catch his dad. His dad had always let him. Where was that man now?

* * *

Hours later, after eating the rest of the dinner Emma had sent home with him Sunday night, Jake sat down at his desk to work on a paper for his doctoral program. Five minutes into his trying to come up with an introduction, the phone rang. He checked the caller ID this time before answering.

"Hi, what's up?" he asked Emma, remembering the worry that had knitted her brow as she climbed into her car with the trio in the park watching.

"I went into the garage to get something out of the backseat of my car and noticed I have a flat tire caused by a nail. I've tried changing it, but I can't budge the lug nuts. It's official now. I need to start lifting weights like my son."

He smiled, peering at the blank screen on his computer. *This'll be a nice distraction.* "I can come over and change it."

"I was hoping you'd say that. I don't have a car service."

"I'll be there shortly. Do you have everything you need to change a tire?"

"Yes. At least I have that. Can't do anything with it, though. I should have had my dad or brother teach me how."

"See you in a few." After he hung up, he looked down at Shep lying on the floor next to his chair. "Boy, we need to go rescue a damsel in distress. Emma."

At the mention of her name Shep stood, his ears perked forward. Jake felt as his dog did—eager to see her. Maybe talking with her would help him forget his phone conversation with the general.

Ten minutes later Emma opened her front door before he had reached the top porch step. The expression on her face stopped him for a second. Her eyes gleaming, she radiated warmth and relief that she had him to turn to. That feeling bolstered him.

She greeted Shep with a thorough petting. "He's really the reason I call you."

The twinkle in her gaze lightened his mood even more. "I aim to please, ma'am."

"I've put on some hot chocolate—made from scratch. With the chill in the air, I thought it might be nice before you go home."

"It is the first of November."

She walked through the kitchen. "Yes, I can't wait for the holidays. Thanksgiving and Christmas are the two times my family comes to my house. They know how I feel about cooking and let me have my way. Even Josh."

"For the past seven years I was usually in a war zone during the Christmas season."

She smiled. "Then you're invited to Thanksgiving and Christmas dinner. I go all out for the holidays. It's a time to celebrate."

"I hate to intrude on family—"

"Shh, Jake. You won't be intruding on my family. I won't let you celebrate alone. Please."

He laughed. "If I don't agree, I've got a feeling I won't hear the end of it."

Emma opened the door into the garage and gestured toward a mountain of plastic containers along the far wall. "That's where I store my decorations."

"You do have it bad." When he stepped through the doorway, Jake immediately saw the flat tire on the passenger side in the back. "Good thing you caught it tonight rather than tomorrow morning when you're trying to get Josh to school and you to work. By the way, where is Josh?"

"Doing his homework. He tried and couldn't budge it, either."

Jake set to work changing the tire. "Have you been driving through a construction area?"

"No, Josh thinks it was the work of Liam and his friends today while I was at your house. Maybe that was why they were watching us leave your place."

"This kind of leak would have taken a little time. I think they were trying to intimidate the boys."

"You mean trying to tell them that no matter how much they practice their self-defense moves it won't make a difference in the long run?"

"Something like that."

"You're probably right."

"Always."

She chuckled. "I'll remember that at least until you finish changing the tire. Then, who knows?"

Every part of him hummed with awareness of the woman standing a few feet behind him, observing him. Not one ounce of him felt uncomfortable. Actually, he liked her watching but he knew he shouldn't. He needed to be careful. He couldn't let his feelings keep developing for Emma. Not while he was dealing with PTSD.

Finished, he rose. "Where do you want me to put the flat?"

"In my trunk. I hope it can be patched. I don't have the money to buy a new one right now."

"I think it can be."

"If it was Liam, I'm glad he didn't slash my tire. That probably couldn't be fixed." She headed toward the door into the house. "You can wash up in the kitchen. I'm going to get Josh. He wanted a cup of the hot chocolate."

While she was gone, he scrubbed the dirt from his hands and tried to compose himself. He couldn't ignore his feelings for Emma. *Why, Lord? Why now when I can't do anything about it?*

He heard Emma and Josh coming and shook the questions from his mind, busying himself getting mugs down from her cabinet and pouring the hot chocolate. "Anyone want a couple of marshmallows?"

"Me. Cover the top with them." Josh took his cup and sat at the table, with Buttons lying on the floor nearby.

"Not me," Emma said with a chuckle. "There are already enough calories in the hot chocolate. I don't need to add more."

"I'm with Josh. The more marshmallows, the better." Jake took the chair across from the boy with Shep settling beside Jake.

She set her mug down then went back to a cabinet. "I've got something for Shep. It wouldn't be fair if we're enjoying our drinks and he doesn't get anything." After she gave him a treat shaped like a bone, she eased into the chair between him and Josh.

Josh took a large swallow of his hot chocolate, a brown mustache above his upper lip. "What do you think, Jake? Was it Liam and his guys that put the nail in the tire?"

"Don't know and without proof there isn't anything we can do about it."

"I just hate that they're getting away with everything." Josh took another gulp.

"In this country a person is innocent until proven

guilty. We have to respect that, but that doesn't mean we don't take steps like we're doing to protect ourselves."

Josh blew a frustrated breath out. "I can't wait until the Veterans Day celebration. Craig told me his mom said you're getting a medal for bravery."

Jake clutched his mug until his fingers ached. "How does she know?"

"There was something in the Sunday newspaper about it," Josh replied, reaching down and petting Buttons.

Jake exchanged a look with Emma, feeling trapped into attending the ceremony whether he wanted to or not.

Emma gave him a sympathetic look. "I don't get the paper. I didn't know that." She turned to her son. "How's your homework coming? It's time for bed."

"Mom, I'm old enough to stay up past ten. I still have a little."

"Then take your drink to your room and finish your work. Then to bed."

Josh grumbled the whole way out of the kitchen with Buttons trotting after him, but Emma waited until he was gone before asking, "You decided to do the ceremony?"

"I told General Hatchback I would at the end of last week as long as it was clear I was accepting for the whole unit." And before he had talked to his father or he would have said no. He would call his dad and tell him he wouldn't accept if he came. The ceremony would be stressful enough without the general there watching.

"Good. I'm glad you're doing it. I'll be in the front row, cheering you on, and I imagine the kids you're working with will be, too. And Marcella."

An extra hundred pounds seemed to weigh him down at the thought of an audience. He'd always been a private person, and this went against everything in his comfort zone. "Do many people attend the celebration?"

"I've never gone. I'm usually working, but I'm taking the day off. I want to be there to support you. You deserve this."

"No, I don't just because I made it out alive."

"That's not true. Ben told me what you did. The ones who survived did so because of you and your quick action. You're a hero. All you have to do is ask those men and their families."

Hero? He didn't feel like one. He was a man barely holding the pieces of his life together. "I still don't know about this. What if I have a panic attack during the ceremony?" The very thought sent a bolt of tension through him.

"Shep will be there. I'll be there. We'll help you leave afterward as fast as possible."

"I don't want Josh to know or the other boys."

"That you're human? That you can suffer like anyone else?"

He blinked rapidly and scooted his chair back. He started to rise when she grasped his hand and held it tight. "It'll help if my dad doesn't come."

"Will he honor your wishes?"

"I don't know. The general does what he wants. Always has and he doesn't like it when someone tries to mess with his plans. He didn't when I went to OU, and he didn't when I took the honorable discharge. I've heard him talk about PTSD before. I don't think he believes so many soldiers have it."

"Was he ever on the front line in a war zone?"

"Not that I know of. He graduated from West Point as the Vietnam War was coming to an end and by the time the Gulf War erupted he was promoted to colonel and assigned to headquarters. I know he was in Bosnia for a while before he moved to the Middle East, but again, I don't think he was involved in the actual fighting. Then he made general. Mom died and he returned to the States to be the head of a couple of different bases over the years."

She tilted her head to the side, her hand still over his, warm, comforting. "Then he doesn't know what it's like?"

"I can't say. He never talked about his job at home."

"Maybe you should ask him about his experiences."

"Don't you think I've tried? He's always managed to avoid the subject."

"That sounds like a man who hasn't dealt with something."

Jake paused to inhale composing breaths, trying to ease the tension wrapped around him. "I know. When I was getting my degree in psychology that's what I thought. I asked him about it. He accused me of psychoanalyzing him and stalked out of the room."

"When my husband died and so much hit me at once, I learned to take each moment as it came. Don't worry about the future until it's the present and happening to you."

"Isn't there something in the Bible about that?"

"God wants us to trust Him, not put all our trust in ourselves. We can't do it alone."

"I'd like to go to church with you and Josh next Sunday. I'm going to need prayers to get through the ceremony on the following day." He turned his hand over and clasped hers, then stood, tugging her to her feet. "Walk me to the door. I need to leave. You have to get up early for work."

"While you're a man of leisure, treasure each moment," she said with a grin.

"I don't want to be. I enjoy work."

She stopped in the foyer and placed her hands on his shoulders. "I understand. That's the way I'd be. I get pleasure from a job well done. When you get your doctorate, think of the people you can help, especially ones with PTSD because you have been through it."

"As this town grows, we sure could use more services for the vets here."

"Then that could be your mission."

He drew her close. "Like yours is to help provide service dogs to the people who need them."

She ran her tongue over her lips. "Yes, exactly," she said softly.

His gaze fixed on her mouth, he bent his head toward her. He wanted to kiss her again. And again. No! As much as he would enjoy every second, he would regret it later. It wasn't fair to her. He brushed his lips across her forehead, set her away from him and strode toward the door.

"Good night, Emma."

The whole way home, thoughts flew through his mind. *What were you thinking? Where is your discipline?* Now his actions probably left her more confused than ever. They sure did for him.

As he neared his place, someone wearing a dark hoodie and black pants darted across his yard, lobbing something at his house. Jake froze.

Chapter Eleven

A grenade flashed into his mind, and Jake automatically dived for cover while his heartbeat slammed against his chest. A crashing sound followed by another invaded his thoughts, zipping him back to the noise of the first explosion in the village that took out three of his men. Quaking, he felt paralyzed, trying to crawl for the shelter of a hedge. Searing pain shot through his body as he tried to breathe and couldn't.

Shep stood over him licking him, nuzzling against him—focusing him on the calming techniques he'd learned.

Then suddenly a low growl came from his dog. Jake looked up in time to see another boy running past him, wearing a dark hoodie and black sweats. In the glow from his motion-sensitive light, Jake saw Liam slow and glance back at the hedge where he lay. The boy increased his speed and disappeared around the corner.

Sweat drenching him, Jake visualized a beach with gentle waves lapping against the shore. Their rhythmic sounds soothed him as he stroked Shep.

When he was composed enough, having used some

techniques he'd started learning from Abbey, he dialed the police then struggled to his feet, his legs still shaky. If he hadn't become panicky, thinking he was under attack, he could have caught the pair red-handed. Anger gripped him—more at himself than anyone else. He limped toward his house to see what damage the duo had done.

To his amazement Marcella stood in the middle of the sidewalk leading to his house, her arms crossed over her chest, a fierce expression on her face. She spied him and relaxed some of the stiffness in her posture, but her arms remained in place as did the narrow-eyed look.

She marched toward him. "I called the police. I saw two boys throw something into your house. I think they're stink bombs from what I smelled."

"Stay here, Marcella." As he neared his house to get a closer look, he smelled the noxious odor of rotten eggs coming from a hole in the new window in the living room and one in the dining room.

Putting his hand over his mouth and nose, he checked to make sure the only damage was the windows and the smell. Satisfied that was all, Jake returned to wait for the police with his neighbor.

"Did you happen to see what they looked like?" Jake moved farther away from his house and the smell.

"Yes, I did. After the problems you and Emma have had, I've been extra vigilant. Never know when this kind of behavior will spread to others in the neighborhood. I saw your light go on and went out on my porch with my video camera in case it wasn't you returning home."

"You knew I was gone?"

"Yes, sirree. Like I say, I've been watching. I've positioned my chair to keep an eye on the front of my house and part of yours."

"Where's your camera?"

She pulled it out of her pocket and gave it to Jake.

When he replayed it, he grinned. "Gotcha. Between this and my testimony, Liam and Sean will have some explaining to do with the police tonight."

"They should have to clean up the mess they made in your house."

"A great suggestion, Marcella." Jake leaned close and kissed her on the cheek. "Thank you for keeping watch." He was relieved. He hadn't been sure his identification would have been enough because he didn't actually see the face of the person who lobbed the first stink bomb.

On Veterans Day, Emma mounted the stairs to Jake's porch. The door opened. Her steps slowing, she drew a deep breath at the sight of Jake in his uniform. Wearing his dress blues, he stood in the entrance, looking every bit a soldier—distinguished, capable of protecting. But when her eyes connected with his, vulnerability lurked in the brown depths.

Since last week when Liam and Sean were arrested for vandalizing Jake's home, he'd had a couple of private counseling sessions with Abbey, who was working with Jake's doctor on a treatment plan.

Jake was determined to accept the medal for the men in his unit and make it through the ceremony without incident. He'd told Abbey about his reaction when he'd seen Liam lob something at his house, and if it hadn't been for Marcella, the boys might not have been held accountable for their actions. Until that moment she didn't think Jake fully embraced that he was dealing with PTSD. But he did now and was determined to overcome it.

"I'd whistle, but I can't very well," Emma finally said when the silence had stretched for a long moment.

"I didn't think I'd be wearing this uniform again."

"Are you and Shep ready to leave?" She had offered to drive him so he didn't have to deal with that, too.

"Shep is. I'm not sure about myself." Jake moved out onto the porch with his service dog wearing a dark blue harness with a leash attached.

"You both look nice."

"You're certainly good for a man's ego."

"I aim to please, sir."

As they got into Emma's car, Jake asked, "Are the guys coming?"

"Yes. Since I'm going early, I'm saving seats in the front row. Actually, probably the whole row since Abbey, Dominic and Madi are coming as well as Sandy, who is bringing the boys."

Red crept into his cheeks. "I'm not comfortable with all this attention."

"In two hours it will be over."

"It may not sound like a long time to you, but to me it does."

"Then let's change the subject." Emma backed out of the driveway and drove toward city hall and the park across from it where the celebration was taking place. "I understand Liam and Sean will be doing community service and going to counseling."

"Sean's parents were livid about their son's behavior and grounded him again. They're making him do chores to earn money to pay me back for the two windows. Whereas Liam's dad, with no mom around, doesn't care."

"Josh has several more boys who want to come to your class."

"Yeah, he told me yesterday at church. I'll have to think about it."

"It appears others are stepping forward to complain at school about Liam and Sean."

"If the majority won't accept bullying, it can't prevail. A few bullies against many in the end won't succeed."

Emma pulled into a parking space near city hall and the park. Because of Jake, her son wasn't as angry as before. He was smiling and laughing, not complaining about going to school. "Sandy and I have a mom's group organized and we're working with the school on an anti-bully program. After Thanksgiving they're going to have a 'Stand Up Against Bullies' day."

Jake stared out the windshield at the platform erected for the ceremony.

"Ready?"

"No. I'd like to sit here for a while. Okay?"

"Of course." She took his hand and held it, feeling his slight tremor. "I'm ready when you are. Use the relaxation techniques Abbey showed you. Keep Shep next to you. And remember you aren't alone. I'm here to support you. The Lord is with you."

More people began to arrive. The day was beautiful, the sky clear and the temperature in the low fifties. Slowly, the quiver she'd felt in him melted away, and he turned toward her.

"Why don't you go ahead and grab those seats you need? I'll be along in a few minutes."

"Are you sure?"

"Very."

Emma climbed from her car, part of her wanting to stay whether he agreed or not. But ultimately Jake would have to learn to handle his PTSD when it flared up. After crossing the street, she glanced back at him. With his eyes closed, he sat perfectly still. Was he praying? After going to church with her and Josh yesterday, he'd told her he would like to attend again.

God, he's in Your hands.

Shep, wearing his service dog vest, walked next to Jake, who took a seat on stage, scanning the large crowd. As promised, Emma sat in the front row with the four boys he worked with and her friends. He stroked the top of his dog's head while taking in fortifying breaths and visualizing himself on that beach with the calming sounds of the waves.

He'd asked to be on the program first when he had agreed. An older man slipped in behind Emma and tapped her on the shoulder. She threw her arms around him. Then Jake spied Ben coming up the aisle and sitting next to the person Emma had greeted. That must be her father. She mentioned once that Ben hoped to come to the ceremony but then hadn't said anything else. He nodded once at Ben as the high school band played "The Star-Spangled Banner." Along with Jake, everyone stood.

The mayor approached the podium to lead the crowd in the Pledge of Allegiance. When the audience retook their seats, the mayor said a few words about honoring the veterans who helped preserve the citizens' freedoms. "It is my great pleasure to have a two-star general here to give our very own hero the Distinguished Medal of Honor. Please welcome General Tanner, former Captain Jake Tanner's father, to present the award to his son."

Jake heard the words, their sound growing further away the more the mayor spoke. His heartbeat pulsated against his rib cage, increasing its thumping when he glimpsed his dad climbing the stairs to the platform. He should have known his father wouldn't honor the wishes he'd made very clear a few days ago.

As his dad joined the mayor at the podium, the world around Jake faded, noise assailing his ears but with no meaning. Beads of sweat popped out on his forehead. Shep moved closer, nosing his hand. Jake went through the calming techniques Abbey had shown him, his focus on Emma. He didn't want to have a problem in front of Josh and the other boys.

Emma smiled and rose, clapping. It took a few seconds for it to register that he was supposed to go up to the podium. He pushed to his feet, his gaze trained on Emma, his hand clutching Shep's leash. Slowly, he moved toward his father, the sound of the applause echoing through his head.

When he swung his attention to the general, his vision narrowed into a laser point. He watched his dad speak but didn't hear the words. Stopping at the general's side, Jake stood at attention while his father pinned the medal on him.

The short speech he'd written fled his mind as the crowd cheered.

"Don't you have some words to say?" his father whispered through the haze that surrounded Jake.

Jake swallowed twice then leaned toward the mike.

"I'm accepting this Distinguished Service Medal in the name of the men who served under me in the Night Hawk Company." His throat swelled, cutting off any other words. He stepped back, saluted his father, then did an about-face and walked to his chair.

It took all his willpower not to keep going until he'd left the platform. Instead, he sank onto his seat. Shep placed his head in Jake's lap, and he scratched his German shepherd behind his ears, the action soothing his taut nerves.

He hadn't fallen apart—even with his father here at the ceremony. Even with the park full of people—most strangers.

The rest of the ceremony passed in a blur with Jake keeping Emma in his line of vision. She anchored him. She believed in him. He didn't want to let her down or make a fool of himself. But he wouldn't appear on stage before a crowd again anytime soon.

When the throng dissipated, Josh flew toward his end of the platform with the other three boys following. Emma hurried after them.

"Can I see it? Can I see it?" Josh and his friends crowded Jake, cutting off his view of Emma.

Carson cocked his head. "What's that in the middle of the circle?"

"The United States Coat of Arms. That's a bald eagle," Jake said, pointing at it. "And it's clutching thirteen arrows for the original thirteen states in one talon and in the other an olive branch."

Josh's forehead creased. "War and peace?"

"Yes," Emma said, putting her hand on his shoulder and moving him back to give Jake more breathing space.

"Cool." Zach's eyes grew round. "And you got this."

"Not just me. All the men in the company."

"Are they going to get a medal like this?" Craig asked.

"No, I'm keeping it safe for them." Jake looked at Emma. "Let's get out of here."

"I've got a spread set up at my house to celebrate Veterans Day. Ben and Dad are heading over there and getting the food out on the table."

When Jake saw his father disengage from a reporter and the mayor, he took Emma's elbow, moving toward the stairs. Leaning toward her, he whispered, "Who else?"

"The kids, Sandy, Abbey and Dominic. If that's too many, I can make some excuse."

"No, I'm used to them."

She glanced over her shoulder. "Should I say anything to your father?"

"No. If I know my dad, he'll be waiting for me at my house."

"Outside?" Tiny lines puckered her brow.

"No, he has a key. The house belongs to both of us." Maybe he'd outwait his father if he stayed at Emma's.

When he heard his name being called, he hurried his pace, causing his leg to ache. But he couldn't deal with the general after the ceremony. He could do only so much and keep it together. If he had his preference, he'd go home and lock the world out.

"Mom, I'm coming with you. Carson's mother will bring the other kids." Josh fell into step beside Jake.

"Uncle Ben told me that medal you got is a big deal."

Jake remained quiet, not sure what to say to Josh. The medal declared to the world that he performed heroically, but he didn't feel like a hero. He felt like a man barely holding his life together and beginning to care about someone he shouldn't.

At Emma's house, Jake hugged Ben and clapped him on the back. "It was good to see you today. Are you staying for a while?"

"Dad and I are driving back in a couple of hours. I got today off but not tomorrow." Ben smiled. "We'll be back for Thanksgiving. You haven't had a holiday meal until you've been to Emma's."

"She's had me to dinner a few times, so I know what a great cook she is."

Ben edged him away from the doorway as others began to arrive. "How's it going? It looked like Shep was helping."

"Was I that obvious?"

"I know the signs. Remember I've felt all of the symptoms." Ben moved into the dining room. "I don't know about you but I'm hungry. Hey, I thought General Hatchback was giving you the medal."

"He was."

"It was nice seeing your father give it to you. I can imagine how proud he is. Is your dad coming to the party?"

"No, but I'm sure I'll see him later."

Ben assessed his expression. "You're not on good terms with your dad?"

"No. He doesn't see why I left the military."

Ben blinked, his eyes wide. "He wanted you to stay in with a bum leg?"

"When I was hurt, his dream of my following in his footsteps vanished. Now he has a crippled son who would rather stay in his house."

"He said that to you?"

"Not exactly, but I know him. He'd go to work even when he was ill. He once said to Mom pain is part of a soldier's life. It comes with the job. He never had patience for anyone who got sick."

Ben shook his head. "Hey, man. I'm sorry. You're one of the toughest men I know."

Emma appeared in the dining room. "I figured I would find my brother hanging around the food."

"That's because I'm starved." Ben grabbed a paper plate and began piling seven-layer dip on it followed by tortilla chips.

Emma enclosed her hand around Jake's. "I want you to meet my dad. Okay?"

"I'd love to," Jake said, realizing he looked forward to being introduced to Emma's father. He'd been stationed so much of his time in war zones the past few years that he'd forgotten what it was like to live a "normal" life.

As Jake neared his house, his body tensed more with each step. Maybe his dad had had to go back to Florida immediately. But when he came in view of his place, his stomach plummeted. An unfamiliar car sat in his driveway. As he approached the porch stairs, his pace slowed.

He wasn't ready to face the general. Taking a seat on the top step, he petted Shep and stared at the park across the street. He'd enjoyed the surprise celebration at Emma's. Even with his dad's appearance at the ceremony, he'd dealt with the day's activities well. When he'd talked with Abbey at the party, she'd been pleased. Although he had not been in the midst of the crowd in the downtown park, but up on the platform, he'd been able to handle so many people in one place. And he didn't flash back once to that time in the packed marketplace in Afghanistan's capital when a bomb exploded, killing and hurting a lot of innocent people. Then not three days later, his company left for the mountains.

At the sound of the front door opening, Jake shuddered. As much as he'd prefer to stay outside in the crisp evening air, he didn't want to have a conversation with the general that the whole neighborhood might overhear. Weary, he pushed to his feet, using the railing to steady himself.

The dreaded words came out of his dad's mouth: "We need to talk."

With a sigh, Jake pivoted and made his way into his house.

"Where have you been? You can't avoid me forever."

Jake stopped in the entrance into the living room and faced the general. "A friend threw me a surprise party." When his dad flinched, he continued. "I didn't know about it until we were driving away from the ceremony."

One of his father's thick eyebrows arched. "And you didn't think I'd be here? I didn't come all this way just to give you a medal."

Jake cringed at the barb. "Since the last time I talked to you I asked you not to come, I didn't anticipate your being at the ceremony."

"That's one of the reasons we need to talk. Why didn't you want me at the ceremony?"

As much as he wished he didn't have to, Jake limped toward the couch and sank down. All his life he'd tried never to show any kind of weakness in front of the general.

"I see your leg is healing nicely. You're not using

your cane." Dressed in his uniform, his father remained in the doorway into the living room, his hands clasped behind his back. He looked every bit a two-star general in the U.S. Army—tough, distinguished, unrelenting.

"I've been using it less over the past few weeks."

"I see you have a dog."

"Yes, a service dog. Shep."

"Why do you need a service dog if your leg is getting better?" His father finally traversed the distance between them and took the chair across from Jake.

For a long moment he couldn't say anything to the general. He could still remember when he'd been harassed by that bully in sixth grade. No sympathy or understanding came from his father. Instead, his father worked with him every spare moment, building his muscles and teaching him to fight and protect himself. If his dad could have added inches to Jake's height, he would have done that, too.

"You're not one of those soldiers who thinks having a dog will make everything better?"

Anger flashed through Jake. His willpower stretched to its limit, he remained seated when all he wanted to do was leave. He raised his chin. "Yes. I am, sir."

"How can you say that?"

"Because I've seen it work for myself and a soldier in my company. It's not the only thing I'm doing to deal with my trauma, but it is one that I will continue. If it hadn't been for Shep, I doubt I would have stayed at the ceremony when I saw you coming up onto the platform."

The general scowled but behind that expression Jake saw something else—susceptibility to being hurt by another—him. "How did we get to this place?"

Jake ground his teeth, waiting before he answered. "You wanted to make all my decisions. I'm thirty and perfectly capable of deciding what's best. I can't fulfill your dream for me because it isn't mine."

"All I've wanted is for you to succeed."

"Yes, in the army. I used to think that was what I wanted, but for the past couple of years I've been dissatisfied. I didn't know how to approach you about it. Now it's a moot point because I'll always have some problems with my leg when I overextend myself. A soldier needs to be at the top of his game. I've accepted I can't be."

"With that dog by your side, I'm guessing you think you have PTSD. You don't need a service dog for your leg injury."

Is that contempt in his words? Jake couldn't tell for sure. "When you've walked in my shoes, then you have a right to say what you think of PTSD. But I don't think I have it—I *know* I have it."

His father's mouth dropped open, his eyes wide.

"I've heard you say before you think it's just an excuse a lot of people use. It isn't." Jake rose before he said more. "Now if you'll excuse me, I'm going to bed."

"But it's only nine."

"That doesn't change the fact I'm tired, sir."

"I have an early flight in the morning."

"Then goodbye. Have a safe trip," Jake said in a monotone, needing the space between him and his father. Nothing would ever make a difference. He had to face it. He wasn't the son his dad wanted.

After removing his coat and shoes, Jake collapsed onto his bed, exhaustion filling every part of him. Without changing out of his uniform pants and shirt, he stretched out to relax a while…

Through the haze of gunfire, Jake spied the young boy crying, no more than four or five, coming toward him. All he could think about was the child getting killed. He rushed toward him, scooped him into his arms and hurried back to the hut he'd been using as a shelter. After he put the boy on the floor, Jake returned to the window and scouted his surroundings. With a quick glance back to check if the boy was all right, he saw the child playing with a grenade.

Jake screamed, "No! Put that down!"

In slow motion the child pulled the pin.

Nooo!

Mixed in with the sounds of the explosion were—barks?

Something scraped across his cheek. He twisted then rolled away. Suddenly he fell, hitting something hard.

His eyes bolted open as his door slammed against the wall.

Next to him Shep continued to bark while his father charged into Jake's bedroom, fear carved into his features.

"Son, are you all right?"

Jake ached from landing on his left side. Crashing against the hardwood floor sent a shaft of pain up his leg. But that didn't dominate his thoughts. He couldn't shake the picture in his mind of the little boy playing with the grenade.

"Where did it come from? The child didn't have it on him. I would have felt it."

"Jake!" his dad shouted, kneeling next to him, grasping his arms. "What are you talking about?"

His heart racing, Jake inhaled then exhaled, the room spinning. The words describing his nightmare came out haltingly, but somehow he got to the end or at least the part he remembered.

"It didn't happen exactly like that."

"How do you know? You weren't there."

"You forget the camera on your helmet. I viewed all the footage of what was recovered from the ambush. You were wounded but giving one of your men cover as he darted toward the hut, carrying a young crying boy. When your sergeant put the child down in the hut and took his place at the other window, he left his backpack on the floor. You turned, saw the boy with the grenade and as he pulled the pin, you dived for him, grabbed the grenade and threw it out the window. It exploded a few seconds later. The aftershocks knocked you back and that was when you blacked out."

"There was a child? He didn't die?"

"No."

Relieved, Jake sagged back against his bed frame, holding on to Shep.

His dad sat next to him, and he felt the general's stare as he patted Shep. The feel of the dog's fur as he ran his fingers through it soothed something deep inside Jake, grounding him in the here and now—not the past.

"He really helps you," his father said in wonder.

"Yes. He reminds me of the present. He can sense when I'm troubled and only wants to help me. I've had him a month and yet it seems like we've been together forever."

"You always were a dog lover."

How would you know? You were gone half my childhood. But he couldn't voice that. For some reason his dad was sitting by him and something was different. "That's not it. I'm learning various calming techniques from my therapist. Shep is one of the tools I use. I don't want to be debilitated with these panic attacks, afraid to do things because I'm scared I'll have a flashback. I want my life back."

When his dad didn't say anything, Jake turned toward him. His father's head hung down, his eyes closed. He clenched his hands then flexed them, over and over.

"Dad?"

"I never wanted you to go through what I did. I've never been wounded, except in here." He tapped his temple. "I was sent to Vietnam at the end—not long before we pulled out."

"I never knew that."

"Because I never talk about it. I was so young, right out of West Point. I thought I knew what to expect in a war situation." He shook his head. "I had no idea what was in store for me. It was brutal, and I was never the same. I had nightmares and flashbacks for years." When he looked into Jake's face, his eyes glistened. "Not many for the past fifteen years. I thank God for that every day."

"You never said anything. You always seemed so together, in control."

"Because I worked hard to present that facade, especially at home, around others. I had to climb the ranks to general like my father before me. I'd been groomed for that all my life. You think I was tough on you. My father was the toughest man I've ever known. You were never to show any weakness around him. It wasn't acceptable."

Jake felt the shudder snake down his dad's body—a man who was always together. Just like his own father.

"I thought my reaction to what I'd seen meant I was

cowardly, not whole, so I didn't let anyone know. I never talked it over with anyone. I wanted to but then that would have marked me as a weak man."

Jake thought about his own journey to this point. The feelings of being weak, not whole. The denial that anything emotional was wrong with him. Then he met Emma and things changed. He couldn't deny it any longer, but he still felt weak, not whole.

"When I saw you after your return, you never said anything about what was really going on other than with your leg injury. I wish you had."

"How could I when I knew I wasn't doing what you wanted me to do?" Jake's hard stare bore into his father. "You should know since you never told anyone."

"But you had the courage to. You're getting help. I didn't and the price I paid was isolating myself from my family and friends. I pushed you and your mother away. I…" His Adam's apple bobbed. "I failed you and her."

Jake never thought he would hear his dad admit he failed at something. For the first time he didn't seem larger than life, untouchable. Using the bedpost, Jake pulled himself to his feet then offered his dad a hand. "I don't know about you, but I doubt I'll get any more sleep tonight. Want to put on a pot of coffee and talk?"

His eyes softened as his dad grasped his hand and rose. "Sounds like a good plan."

Maybe we can repair our relationship—actually build one. Jake had enough to deal with. He didn't want to continue pushing his father away.

Chapter Twelve

"Now tell me why Josh isn't helping you with this?" Jake followed Emma with a grocery cart while the sound of Christmas music filled the store.

Emma grinned. "Because I thought it was about time you went grocery shopping and I needed someone to push the second cart." She paused and tilted her head. "Don't you just love the sound of Christmas music? I could listen to it all year long." She leaned toward him and lowered her voice. "Don't tell anyone but I do listen to it. Usually around April and August I need to for a week or so."

Jake laid his palm over her forehead. "You really have it bad."

"Yep, I love what Christmas stands for. Hope." During the next weeks she wanted to share that with him.

Jake scanned the aisle, crammed with other shoppers. "Why does everyone wait till the last minute to get food for Thanksgiving? Look at all the people here."

"It's like Christmas shopping at the last minute. A habit. I shop right up to the last minute for Christmas."

"I didn't take you for someone who would wait like this."

"Are you kidding? This is my second trip. I came yesterday, but my menu keeps growing. I figured you could take leftovers home with you tomorrow. Besides, I thought you could get your own groceries, too."

His eyebrow hiked. "You did?"

Jake pulled up right behind her as she searched the shelves for the spices she needed. The smile on his face caused her pulse to pick up speed. He could do that so easily to her—make her react to his presence. She was falling for him yet trying not to. If he knew he'd run the other way because he had so much to handle right now in his life. A girlfriend wasn't something he needed.

Emma waved her hand toward his cart. "You haven't chosen much for yourself."

"Dog food."

"For yourself to eat."

"I thought you were going to send home leftovers with me tomorrow."

"I am but you still need other things to eat."

He tossed a container of salt into his cart. "There."

"I hope that isn't all."

"I'll get a few other items," he said with a chuckle.

Emma moved to the next aisle, not as crowded as the last one. "You'll be bringing Marcella with you tomorrow morning?"

"Yes. Anything else I can do?"

"Nope."

Someone bumped into Jake's back. He stiffened and pivoted, stepping back. His chest rose and fell with a deep breath, then another.

The young mom with two small kids murmured, "Sorry" and rushed past him.

Jake watched her for a moment, blinked then focused on Emma.

"Okay?"

"Sure. I have to expect that in a crowded store the day before Thanksgiving. Just don't make me fight over the last turkey."

She laughed. "I've got the turkey and the ingredients for the dressing already. Now all I need is everything else."

"I'm sure my stepmom has their dinner already cooked or at least what she can do ahead of time. Priscilla is one organized woman. Like my dad. That's probably why they get along so well. Did I tell you Dad asked me to come for Thanksgiving when we talked this past weekend?"

"What did you say?"

"I'm not ready to deal with that yet—not us being together but flying on a plane. Giving control to another—the pilot."

"Haven't you figured it out yet? We don't really have control. God does." She smiled at him.

In the fresh vegetable and fruit section with more room, he pushed his cart next to hers. "Right now I get through best when I feel I have some control, some say in what happens. I know the Lord is in control of the universe, but I'm just one of billions. I doubt He's much interested in my day-to-day life."

"Why not? You're His son and He loves you."

"I know."

"Do you?"

Jake frowned. "Of course."

But the way he looked and spoke made her doubt it. She changed tactics before Jake decided to cut their trip short. "So how's it going with your father since he was here Veterans Day?" They had talked several times, but Jake hadn't said a lot about the visit.

"Awkward at first but this last call was better. It's been thirty years one way and it isn't going to change overnight, but at least now I have hope it'll improve. Just knowing he dealt with issues after Vietnam gives us a place to start."

"I'm so glad for you. A person with PTSD needs all the support he can get." Emma gathered up some sweet potatoes, then moved on to the celery and onions.

"Is that what you're doing for me? Because of Ben?"

Emma swept around, his look trapping her. "That's the way it started."

He took a step toward her. "And now?"

"We're friends. I'm doing it because of that."

"Anything else?" His earnestness charged the air.

It was as if no one else were in the grocery store. The intensity emitting from him enticed her closer. "Well, there's what you did for Josh. He's getting to be his old self thanks to your assistance. Oh, and the times you helped me to change that tire and to clean up the trash on the porch." She stared at him—couldn't look away.

"Why, Jake Tanner, it's so good to see you out and about," Marcella said, coming up and almost planting herself between them. "I'll be ready at ten tomorrow morning."

"Yes, ma'am. I'll be there to escort you."

Marcella waved her hand in front of her face as though the temperature in the store had soared. "Escort. I like that. See you then. Don't forget we need to discuss those self-defense classes for me and some of my friends." She returned to her cart. "I'm bringing the cinnamon rolls to hold everyone over until dinner is served. See you, Emma, Jake."

Emma watched the older lady wheel her basket of food around the corner before glancing at Jake. The humor in his eyes infected her, and she burst out laughing.

"I think Marcella Kime has a crush on you."

Thanksgiving Day Jake lounged in his chair at the dining room table with seven squeezed around it. Right across from him sat Emma, who had jumped up more times than he could count. This dinner had been a big deal to her—and absolutely delicious from her crunchy sweet potato casserole, moist cornbread stuffing with mushrooms and corn, lemon and herb slow-roasted turkey to his favorite— artichokes au gratin.

Ben patted his stomach. "I think I have some room for dessert. What is it?"

"I thought we'd have pumpkin ice cream." Emma pressed her lips together.

Ben's eyebrows slashed down. "What! Pumpkin and ice cream don't go together."

She chuckled, the sound light and sweet. "No, we're having something a little bit more traditional—white chocolate pumpkin cheesecake topped with shaved almonds."

"What happened to the pecan pie you have every year?" Robert, Emma's father, asked.

"I made that, too. Just for you, Dad."

"Can we have a slice of both of them?" Josh glanced from his granddad to his mom. "I'm still hungry."

"Probably because you didn't eat everything on your plate." Emma rose and gathered the plates near her.

"'Cause I was saving room for the dessert. Like Jake."

Emma started for the kitchen. "But he ate his dinner."

Jake stood, picking up the rest of the plates. "I'll help you."

"Jake, make sure my pieces are big. I'm a growing boy," Josh said as Jake left the room.

He couldn't remember having such a nice Thanksgiving—informal, full of laughter and relaxation. "What do you think of going to the park after we eat and working off some of this wonderful food?"

Emma took the cheesecake out of the refrigerator. "Doing what?"

"It's time for Josh to work on his batting. He's got throwing down pretty good. Batting isn't something we should do in your yard. We need more space. Ben, Robert and I were talking before dinner about doing something so we don't all end up falling asleep in your living room."

She swept around to face him. "You guys can help Mom and me with cleaning up."

Jake trapped her against the counter, his arms on either side of her. "Today's gorgeous for this time of year. Let's play in the park then I'll come back and help you clean up. There's no rule that says it has to be done right after we eat."

Her eyebrows shot up. "What about the leftover food?"

"We'll take care of it before we leave."

"We? You and I?"

"Yep. I may not cook well, but I can wrap food in foil and put it in containers. So what do you say?" He inched closer, her scent of lavender mingling with the lingering aromas of the dishes.

"You're not going to expect me to chase the ball, are you?"

"No, we have Ben and your dad as well as Shep and Butch."

"We have a leash law in Cimarron City."

"Then you and your mom can hold their leashes and cheer."

She cocked her head. "What's this really about?"

He shouldn't have gotten so near her. All he could do was stare at her lips with their hint of red lipstick.

"Jake?"

He averted his gaze for a few seconds. "Josh mentioned he used to enjoy playing in the park but hasn't for a while, even when a group of his friends were doing something. I think it's because of what Liam and his buddies did."

"They've been behaving lately."

"Yes, but when he thinks of the park he thinks of what happened there last. I don't want him to be afraid and stay away because of that fear."

She lifted her hand and stroked it down his jawline. "You've been so good for Josh. Yes, we'll go. I didn't realize he was avoiding the park with his friends. They used to play there a lot. I don't want what happened with Liam to taint those memories."

"Hey, you two, what's taking so long? We're starved!" Ben yelled from the dining room.

"We're coming. I think there's some turkey and dressing left. Munch on that." Emma turned toward the counter. "We'll do the park after dinner but on one condition. You'll join us this evening to decorate my Christmas tree. We always do it on Thanksgiving. Okay?"

"You drive a hard bargain, but I'll help clean up *and* decorate your tree."

He and Emma worked as a team getting the desserts and clearing the rest of the dishes from the table while her mom, Nancy, sliced and served the pie and cheesecake.

Before returning to the dining room to eat his helping, Jake captured Emma's hand and tugged her to him. "Have I told you how wonderful the meal was?"

She cuddled against him. "Yes, while you were eating, but I don't mind hearing it again."

"Well, it was. Thanks for inviting me to share your Thanksgiving. I had a frozen turkey dinner in my freezer for the occasion. I'm glad I didn't have to eat it today." In eight weeks this woman had changed the direction he was going and given him hope. His arms surrounded her and pressed her against him, and the feel of her in his embrace soothed his soul.

"Since you came this morning, you've been in a cheerful mood. Should I thank Marcella? Her cinnamon rolls?"

He smiled. "It was all you and the fact that I finished a big project for my doctorate. And one other small detail. I didn't have a nightmare last night for the first time in months."

"It was all those groceries you brought into my house yesterday. It wore you out."

"Before I know it—" he clasped her hand, enjoying touching her "—you'll be having me running laps around the park with you."

"Nope. You never have to worry about that. I don't jog or run. Maybe walk."

When they reentered the dining room, the pecan pie and cheesecake were gone except for one thin slice of each.

Emma placed her hand on her hip. "Did you all forget the cook hasn't had her dessert yet?"

"Neither has her assistant," Jake added with a laugh.

Robert looked up from eating. "You have to be quick in this family to get the goodies." Then he went back to finishing his pie.

Marcella took her last bite, pushed her plate away and patted her stomach. "That was the best cheesecake."

Jake's stomach rumbled.

Laughter echoed through the room.

Nancy scooted her chair back and walked toward the foyer. When she came back, she held two plates, laden with large pieces of both desserts. "Do you really think we would do that to the cook and her assistant? Although that is a dubious title for a certain person." Emma's mom looked at Jake and gave him his dessert with a smile. "Weren't you in the living room with Robert, Ben and Josh watching the game?"

"I helped yesterday with the shopping." He snatched his plate and took his seat. "That qualifies."

Ben snorted while Marcella snickered.

As Jake dug into the cheesecake, he relished the moment. *Thank You, Lord, for showing me what it can be like. My family was never like this.*

Emma stood on the sidelines of an impromptu baseball game at the park's ball field with Jake as the pitcher while Ben played catcher and the outfielders were

Craig's dad and Sandy. Emma's dad, Kim and Nancy positioned themselves at the bases. Josh, Carson and Craig each took a turn at bat.

"Josh is loving all this attention," Marcella said as she grasped Buttons's leash while Emma held Butch's and Shep's.

"All three boys are going to try out for baseball this spring. Craig played last year. Between his and Jake's help, Josh has been really improving in the past month."

"I still haven't gotten Jake to agree to teach a self-defense class at church, but I think I'm wearing him down, especially since he's started attending the Sunday service. That's what he did when he visited his grandma." Marcella turned her attention to Emma. "When he first came back here, I knew he was home, but when I went over to his house, he didn't answer the door. Finally, one day I caught him while the teen was delivering his groceries to him and barreled my way into his house. Normally I wouldn't have done that, but his grandma was my best friend. I owed her that much."

"I'm glad you did."

"He was in a bad place. At that time, he was still using crutches. I know he's dealing with more than his leg but that's none of my business. I'm just glad you're part of his life now. He needs someone to make him care again."

Emma watched Josh take a swing at the ball and miss. The next one, though, he hit and it sailed through the air. Her son ran to first base then kept going while Sandy scooped up the ball and threw it to Emma's mom. Nancy bobbled her catch, and Josh raced past her for home plate. Emma and everyone cheered him on. When Josh reached it, he pumped his arm in the air and beamed as though he were playing in the major league and had won the game for his team.

Jake limped toward Josh and gave him a high five. "That's the way to hit the ball. You're a fast learner."

"Josh needs a good man in his life," Emma said as Craig stepped up to bat.

"Jake is that, even with what he's going through," Marcella said.

"I agree." In that moment as Jake stood again on the pitcher mound, Emma knew she loved him. She hadn't wanted to fall in love, not after Sam. But in spite of the guilt she felt for her husband's death, she had.

"Are you going to the Christmas tree lighting next weekend at the park downtown?"

"Yes, do you want to go with us?" Emma asked, remembering that Marcella drove only during the daylight hours.

She winked at Emma. "I thought you would never ask."

"You know you're always welcome."

"I didn't know if you had a date or not."

"A date? With my son?"

"No. With Jake. I know last year your son went with Craig's family so I thought this would be a great opportunity for you and Jake to go out."

"I haven't even said anything to Jake about the Christmas tree lighting. It's gotten awfully big in the past several years." She wasn't sure Jake would like it, but after how things had been going in the past couple of weeks, maybe he would.

"Ask him, and if you want to make it a twosome, just let me know. I can catch a ride with another neighbor."

Emma combed her fingers through her hair. "I will say something to him but you're going with us."

"I've already got my presents bought and wrapped. How about you?"

"Not totally. I'm not that organized." Since her money was limited, it wouldn't take long to finish her short list. The fall had flown by and before long it would be winter—and the possibility of snow and ice. "I love Christmas, but I could do without the cold temperatures."

"Me and these old bones feel the same way."

Emma turned her attention again to the game. She scanned the baseball field and caught a glimpse of Sean, standing next to one of the dugouts watching them play. Even from a distance she could see a look of yearning on his face. The expression made her wonder what was going on with the boy lately. Josh hadn't said much to her about him. She hoped he wasn't here to make trouble or waiting for Liam and his buddies to come. Then Emma remembered all the adults surrounding her son, keeping him safe.

Josh made it to second base before he was tagged out. Jogging back toward home plate, her son passed close to Jake who said something to Josh. He swung around, saw Sean and detoured toward him. Emma tensed and began to make her way toward the pair. She couldn't see her son's face but surprise flitted across Sean's. Then the older boy nodded and disappeared behind the dugout. A few seconds later he came into view and out onto the field.

Jake stopped his windup and kept an eye on Josh and Sean as they walked to where the boys were waiting for their turn at bat. Jake headed toward the group at the same time Emma did, still holding the leashes for Butch and Shep.

As she approached, Jake said, "As long as you agree to play by the rules, we'd love to have you join us. Wouldn't we?"

Sean looked in each boy's eyes as he nodded, then said, "Yes, sir."

Emma's throat filled with emotion as the boys played for another half hour, including Sean as a friend would. Jake was worth fighting for. He was teaching her son the right way to handle problems.

The soft sounds of "What Child Is This" played in the background while Jake, seated near the eight-foot pine, handed Emma and Josh Christmas ornaments. His leg ached from pitching at the baseball game earlier then helping Ben string the lights on the artificial tree. But he didn't mind the dull pain. Today was worth it.

Emma glanced back at him. "Do you see any spots that need more decorations?"

"Are you kidding? I can't see the tree now," Jake said with a chuckle, the song ending and "Joy to the World" starting.

"It's there, under memories of my past." Emma held up a cutout from an egg carton transformed into a bell with glitter, paint and a pipe cleaner used as a hook. "Josh made this when he was three. I have a set of six."

They were all prominently displayed, Jake noted as his gaze went from one to the other. "Well spaced on the tree."

She gave him a narrow-eyed look. "Are you making fun of me?"

He held up his hands, shaking his head. "No way. I know better."

Stretched out by the chair, Shep looked up at Jake then settled back with his head resting on his front paws.

Josh giggled. "Mom never throws away an ornament until it totally falls apart or smashes. Didn't you notice Grandma, Grandpa and Uncle Ben left before she brought out the rest of the balls to put on the tree?"

Emma put her hand on her waist. "Hold it right there, you two. I warned you I had a lot. Besides, my parents and brother had to get back to Tulsa. Ben has to work tomorrow." The teasing gleam in her eyes brightened then, the sparkle competing with the lights on the tree.

Her look transfixed Jake. "About those extra boxes. I thought you told me your decorations were all out in the garage. Where did these five come from?"

"These are my special ones."

"Yeah, mostly made by me or ones from her childhood." Josh took an ornament from Jake and loaded a branch with another ball.

"Time for a break," Marcella said, carrying in a tray with mugs of hot chocolate.

Emma took it from her and placed it on the coffee table. "We only have a couple more, then we're finished."

Jake struggled to his feet, ignoring the ache in his leg, and hung two of the last five ornaments while Josh put the others on the pine. "Done. Your timing, Marcella, is perfect." He limped toward the couch and sank onto the cushion at one end, Shep settling at his feet.

"But we still have the garland to put up." Emma opened the last box over in the corner and showed the group the shiny red strings.

"That will cover up your beautiful ornaments." Jake reached for a mug of hot chocolate, steam wafting from it.

Emma stood back from the tree and cocked her head. "You're right. Except for this one." She pulled out a length of homemade red-and-green paper rings. "Josh made this in first grade."

The child's cheeks turned a rosy tint. "Mom, do you hafta put that up?"

Emma studied the pine again then scanned the room. "No. You are right. The tree has enough, but—" she headed to the mantel and hung the paper garland along its edge "—this will be a nice addition here where it won't get lost among the ornaments."

Josh looked at Jake. "I'll never make another decoration again."

Jake laughed and handed the boy a mug, then raised his. "That's moms for you."

"Yeah, but mine goes overboard."

"I hear you, Josh." Emma finally took a seat at the other end of the couch and grabbed her drink.

Marcella leaned back in her chair across from Jake and sipped her hot chocolate. "I want to thank you, Emma, for inviting me to share your Thanksgiving dinner and meet your family. This was a treat."

"I second that." Jake lifted his mug again and tapped it against Emma's then Josh's and Marcella's. "This was a wonderful Thanksgiving, and I'm looking forward to Christmas for the first time in years." As he said those words, he realized the holidays hadn't meant much to him in the past but Emma's enthusiasm was contagious.

Emma rose and bowed. "I've done my job. I've spread my joy of the Christmas season to others. Finish your drink and then all we have to do is put away the empty boxes."

Jake groaned along with Josh and Marcella. When Emma gave each one of them a mockingly stunned look, Jake laughed. Josh joined him, followed by Marcella and Emma. Both Shep and Buttons began barking.

"You're a hard taskmaster, but since I helped make the mess, I'll help clean it up." Jake turned to Josh. "You game?"

The boy nodded.

Thirty minutes later with Shep by his side, Jake stood in the entrance to the living room, surveying his work. With all the lamps turned off, the tree dominated the area, the hundreds of lights shining. Emma came up behind him and touched his arm as she moved beside him. Her lavender scent vied with the pine aroma from a lit candle on the mantel.

She glanced toward him and took his hand. "Thanks for going along with me today."

"That was easy to do. It was fun." *I almost felt normal today.* But one good day didn't mean everything would be all right tomorrow or the following ones. He would cherish, though, the time spent today with Emma and her family.

Clear lights were strung everywhere—in the trees and on the bushes—in the downtown park across from the city hall. As Jake, with Shep by his side, strolled with Emma toward where the Christmas-tree ceremony would take place, he slipped his arm around her, their steps slowing. Marcella and Josh hurried ahead of the couple, wanting to find a good spot from which to watch. One of the town's celebrities—a pro baseball player—was throwing the switch to light the fifteen-foot pine. Josh wanted to get his autograph afterward.

Coming to a stop, Emma looked up at Jake. "This looks like a fairyland. I always love walking through here at this time of year. It's even prettier when it has snowed."

"I don't remember this ceremony being as festive and big when I was here at Christmas as a child."

"It's grown each year. Afterward, all the stores and restaurants stay open late and people linger downtown. I was hoping we could. I need to do some Christmas shopping. After the ceremony, Josh is going home with Craig to spend the night."

"How about Marcella?"

"When she heard about Josh, she told me she was grabbing a ride home with a neighbor. They were meeting at the café across the street for some dessert."

Laughter welled up in him. He clasped Emma against him. "That means we have the evening to ourselves. Interesting how those two maneuvered that."

"You think? I don't think it crossed Josh's mind, but Marcella, yes, she could have. Are we still on for decorating a tree at your house tomorrow?"

"Just because you put yours up Thanksgiving night, doesn't mean I have to have one."

"Yes, it does. When I look at mine, I think of all the past Christmases. The ornaments from friends and family bring back fond memories, but they also make me realize why we celebrate Christmas. With Christ's birth, the world changed forever. He gives me hope. Sometimes I need that reminder."

He did more than ever. Somewhere along the way Jake had lost hope. God and Emma were teaching him how to find it again. "Put that way, how can I refuse?"

"You can't. Besides, all those ornaments your grandma kept will be put to good use."

He brushed his hand through her hair, loving the feel of it sliding through his fingers. "Thanks for helping me to get them down from the attic. It's still hard for me to climb all those steps to the third floor, and with the amount she had I would have had to do it several times."

She smiled, her eyes sparkling like the lights all around them. "Anytime."

As people headed for the ceremony, they skirted around Jake and Emma on the path. He pulled her off the trail to allow everyone to pass and for a little privacy. He wasn't in any hurry to be with a crowd.

"You're beautiful, Emma, inside and out."

"You ain't too bad to look at yourself! But I can't thank you enough for what you've done to help Josh. Since Thanksgiving and the baseball game, Josh told me Sean has talked to him at school as a friend. Sean doesn't seem to be involved with Liam much anymore."

"Liam has a lot of anger inside him. I hope he gets the help he needs."

"See what I mean. You're a fine man."

He smiled, slowly lowering his head toward hers. The few kisses they'd shared only left him wanting more, and with his better outlook lately, maybe they had a chance for being more than just friends.

"I know we need to get to the ceremony before Josh comes looking for us, but I can't resist..." He whispered the words over her parted lips and bridged the gap.

Pop! Pop! Pop!

The sound of gunfire sent him in motion. He was suddenly back in the mountain village. He dived for the ground and cover, taking Emma with him, shielding her as best as he could.

Chapter Thirteen

As Emma lay plastered against the cold ground, Jake's body over hers, she felt him shaking, his heartbeat hammering against his chest.

The popping sound of the firecrackers resonated through the chilly air, the noise similar to rapid gunfire. She wiggled out from under a paralyzed Jake, frozen in probably a flashback, sweat drenching his face.

As she freed herself, she noticed a crowd forming around them, Josh's eyes huge, fear on his face. "Please get back," she said to the people, then turned toward Jake, Shep nudging him and barking.

In her calmest voice, Emma said, "Jake. Jake. You're in Cimarron City at the park. Those were firecrackers going off. Probably some kids."

He stared at her, but she didn't think he was really seeing her. Her concern mounted, especially with the crowd still pressing close.

She stood, gesturing with her hands to move back. Someone said, "Should I call 911?"

"No, that's not necessary." That was the last thing Jake would want.

An older man plowed through the people. "I'm a doctor. Can I help? Is he having a seizure?"

"No, a panic attack," Emma said as quietly as she could but several people heard her, including her son. Josh's face went pale.

When the onlookers began to disperse, Josh stepped back but didn't leave.

Emma went back to Jake, not touching him but near if he needed her. "Let's breathe deeply on my count. Inhale one, two. Exhale one, two." She continued until she reached the count of four.

Jake's stiff body began to relax. His awareness of his surroundings came back, and he scanned the area. His gaze latched on to Josh, then Marcella, who came up behind him.

"Shep's here to help," Emma said to pull his attention from Josh. "Everything's all right."

"What was that sound?" Jake finally asked.

"Firecrackers." When he seemed calm, no longer shaking or sweating, she asked, "Do you want to go to the ceremony?"

His eyes widened. "No. Home."

"Fine. Let me tell Josh and Marcella." As she approached them, Jake struggled to his feet, still stroking the top of Shep's head.

"What happened, Mom? What's a panic attack?"

Emma glanced at Jake to make sure he hadn't heard her son. "He thought the firecrackers were a gun going off."

"He's like Uncle Ben?"

"Yes, hon. Marcella, will you make sure Josh connects with Craig and his parents?"

"I will. Come on, Josh. We don't want to miss the ceremony and your chance to get an autograph."

The boy peered back as he walked away, his brow knitted, uncertainty making him hesitate.

"See you tomorrow at church, hon."

"He knows about me?" His voice bleak, Jake stood right behind her.

"Yes. Let's go."

"I want you to drop me off and then you can come back here. I know you wanted to do some shopping. I don't want this to stop you."

She didn't answer. She decided to give him some time and distance from the incident. But she wasn't dropping him off and leaving him alone. She loved him and wanted to be near if he needed help.

At his house, a familiar environment where firecrackers wouldn't send him into a panic, thinking he was back in Afghanistan being shot at, Jake finally released the last bit of tension gripping him. He turned in the foyer and spread his arms wide. "See. I'm fine. You can leave now."

"No, I'd rather stay with you."

"But I don't want you to."

Hurt darkened Emma's blue eyes, and her shoulders sagged slightly. "Because of what happened at the park? I've seen panic attacks. What happened to you is nothing new. You had one. It's over. Move on."

Her tough, matter-of-fact words hit him as though she'd slapped him. "I tackled you to the ground. Aren't you just a little embarrassed?"

"If that had been a real gun going off, you could have saved my life. You reacted to a noise that was similar.

You have been trained to react quickly. Firecrackers aren't supposed to go off in the city limits so it was an unexpected sound."

"Quit trying to rationalize something that isn't rational."

"Don't start feeling sorry for yourself. You're improving, but that won't happen overnight. Ben still has some problems. Acknowledge the panic attacks, deal with them then let them go. Don't let them rule your life."

"You don't know what you're talking about. You haven't dealt with panic attacks."

"No, but I lived with a husband who had epilepsy for most of our marriage. His seizures would happen unexpectedly, and we had to deal with them. We knew what to do, what not to do…" Her voice disappeared as she gulped.

There was that look she got when talking about her husband. Regrets she'd married a person with epilepsy—deeply flawed the way he was? A seizure led to his death. "What aren't you telling me? Every time we start to talk about your husband, you put a distance between us. I've told you about my relationship with my father, about my panic attacks."

She averted her gaze, staring into the living room. Her teeth bit into her lower lip. Her hands balled. "My husband died because of me."

He'd expected her to say a lot of things but not that. "He fell off a ladder. How are you responsible?"

When she peered at him, sadness dulled her eyes. "Josh and I were talking about decorating the outside of the house with lights the way we'd decorated the inside. My husband overheard, and before I told him I was hiring the teenage boy next door to put them up, he was doing it. He shouldn't have been up that high, especially without someone there and with concrete below him."

"And you blame yourself?"

"Yes. I knew that Sam thought he could do everything like a normal person—that he didn't have to keep in mind his seizure disorder. He hated that I had to drive him everywhere. I should never have said anything to Josh with my husband in the house."

"Your husband is responsible for his own actions. He knew he shouldn't get up on a ladder like that. You're not at fault. It was an accident."

"I should have been able to protect him. He had epilepsy. I needed to be there for him."

"Smothering him?"

"I—I didn't think so. I always looked at it as though we were in it together." She closed the space between them. "I can't turn my back on someone I care about. Someone I love." She swallowed hard. "Like you."

He wanted to pretend he hadn't heard what she'd said, but he couldn't. He could never ask her to tie herself to a man who was damaged and needed fixing. What if he never got better? He thought he was, and then he'd had a full-blown attack in public—for Josh to see. "You're a caregiver. That isn't love. Go back to the ceremony. Enjoy yourself."

"I don't want to leave. We need to deal with this together."

"Why? So you can manage my life? I don't want that. I want to be cured. I want to be normal."

"What's normal for one isn't what is for another."

"I should have known those were firecrackers. I've heard them before. I used to set them off as a kid. I couldn't stop the panic attack. Please leave." He strode to the door and opened it. "Thanks for bringing me home." He stared into space, avoiding meeting her eyes. He might give in and try to hold on to her when it wasn't fair to Emma to saddle her with another man like her husband—broken.

Surrounded by all her Christmas decorations with the pine tree full of ornaments in front of the picture window in the living room—the one Jake had helped her put up—Emma paced while Abbey sat on the couch and watched her. "I don't know what to do. Jake isn't answering the door or his phone. Last Sunday Josh and I left the Christmas tree we were going to decorate together on his porch. I know he's there because the tree's gone. It's been four days since what happened Saturday night at the lighting of the Christmas tree ceremony. He's gone back to being a hermit."

"He did come to Monday night's session. We don't have our private one until tomorrow. I could go by today and see if he'll talk to me."

"Please try to get him to talk about Saturday night. He told me he wanted to be normal. He wouldn't believe me when I said normalcy is relative. I think he feels like he's beaten, may always be that way."

"I'll try my best. The good news is he came on Monday night so he hasn't given up. He's just frustrated."

Stopping her pacing, Emma intertwined her fingers, clasping them together until her knuckles whitened. "I told him I loved him Saturday. He said what I'm feeling isn't love." She connected visually with Abbey. "I love him. His having PTSD doesn't change how I feel. Sam's having epilepsy didn't change how I felt about him."

"Give him time to get a grasp on what he's dealing with. He's gone through a lot in the past eight months."

"I know. I didn't set out to fall in love, and I didn't mean to say it to him, especially right after a panic attack."

"I'm working with him on some techniques, but they will take time to become automatic and feel natural to him. What he said just came out."

Emma's eyes blurred with unshed tears. She'd cried for the past few nights, wishing they hadn't gone to the ceremony. But that panic attack in such a public place could have happened at another time. Not going wouldn't have necessarily changed the end result. "I told him about feeling guilty concerning Sam's death." Since she hadn't told anyone but Jake, she explained to Abbey.

"Did he tell you it wasn't your fault?"

Emma nodded.

"He's right. People are responsible for their own actions. You can't control everything. When Sam died, you felt your life do an about-face. Suddenly, you were going in a different direction—a single mom with a debt to pay off. Don't put more burdens on yourself by feeling guilty. God has a wonderful way of forgiving anyone who repents and asks for forgiveness. If you need to, ask him to forgive you and then let it go. Give control over to the Lord. He'll take you on a wild and exciting ride." Abbey stood, rolling her shoulders.

Emma closed the space between them and hugged her. "Thanks. I should have told you when Sam died how I was feeling, but I was afraid of what you would think of me."

"The only thing you should care about is what God

thinks of you. When you have Him in your corner, everything else falls into place."

Emma thought about what Abbey had said about guilt and control. She needed to let both of them go. Whether or not Jake wanted to continue one day in a relationship, she needed to say goodbye to the past.

Jake stared at the Christmas tree Emma and Josh had delivered on Sunday, bare of any decorations. A box of four ornaments—homemade by Emma and Josh—sat next to the live pine, its scent permeating the room. They still were in the carton. He couldn't put them or the boxes of ornaments that were his grandma's on the branches.

When the doorbell rang, he considered ignoring whoever was there, but he couldn't keep doing that. Marcella had left him some cinnamon rolls yesterday, and the worried look on her face had almost made him answer the door.

When the chimes filled the air again, he rose and plodded toward the foyer. When he saw Abbey, he hesitated then realized this couldn't keep going on. He might not be able to have the type of relationship with Emma he wanted, but he had to get on with his life. Abbey could help him.

He let her in. "Our next session isn't until tomorrow."

"Yes, but I thought we could talk today, too. Except for the Monday night group, have you left this house since Saturday night?"

"No, but that was only four days ago. Not that unusual for me."

"I would agree if we were talking about a month ago. Let's talk." Abbey marched into his living room and took a seat in a chair. "I have some material for you. I would like you to read it today, and then we'll discuss it tomorrow. It's a method to help you overcome your panic attacks beyond what you're doing. It's reprogramming how you think about the attacks when they begin."

He sank down on the couch across from her, his gaze momentarily lingering on the Christmas tree behind Abbey.

"You need to accept this will take time and that's okay. You've come a long way in the past two months, and you'll go further, but not overnight."

"In other words, I shouldn't become a recluse because of what happened Saturday night in front of a crowd."

"Exactly."

"Have you seen Emma?" He didn't want to ask but couldn't stop himself.

"I saw her this morning before she left for work, and she's worried about you. You canceled the self-defense class for Tuesday. You aren't answering her calls or the door. She gets it—you don't want to talk to her. But you didn't answer for Marcella or Sandy when they came by, either."

"I made a fool of myself in front of so many people. In front of Josh."

"He knows you have PTSD and understands. His uncle does, and he loves Ben. Emma talked to Josh on Sunday. To him it doesn't mean anything. You are his hero."

"I'm no one's hero."

"Because you survived when some of your men didn't?"

He nodded.

"God has special plans for you, and you can't argue with the Lord. So what are you going to do about it?"

He stared at the material she'd placed on the coffee table. "I'll start by reading this, then I'll meet with you tomorrow."

Abbey pushed to her feet. "Then I'll leave you to get started."

After she was gone, he began reading what she had brought him. When he finished, he looked up and caught sight of the Christmas tree. He remembered what Emma said about seeing hers and feeling hope. He rose and went to the box with the four ornaments in it. He took each one out and put it on the pine.

The next day Jake faced the four boys in his workout room with Sandy off to the side. She'd brought them, and he'd asked her to stay for a few minutes. He scanned the face of each one, and all he saw in their expressions was respect—nothing different from before. His chest tightened.

He cleared his throat. "I'm sorry I canceled Tuesday afternoon, but after what happened Saturday, I had some thinking to do. I have panic attacks occasionally. In the case of Saturday night the sound of firecrackers going off caused me to react as though I was under fire. I'm working to deal with my panic attacks, but it'll take time. I'll understand if you don't want to continue with the self-defense classes."

Josh's face screwed up in a puzzled look. "What does that have to do with our class?"

"Yeah, I want to keep learning," Craig said with the other guys nodding.

Sandy moved between the children and Jake. "We have faith in you. These boys look forward to these classes. You have made them feel like they can handle anything. They feel better about themselves, not to mention you took care of the bullying."

The constriction in his chest eased as he swept his gaze from one child to the next. *Sandy has it wrong. These guys have made me feel better about myself.* "Then let's get going. We have a lot to do today. First, let's stretch."

An hour later Jake realized how important these sessions with the four had been for him, too. They had looked to him for guidance and help, and he'd been able to give it to them. Maybe he would be able to deal with his own problems.

When Emma showed up to take the boys home, he didn't know what to say to her. She deserved more than he could give her. He didn't know how long it would take for him to overcome his PTSD.

Emma said, "Josh, you and the guys go on out to the car. I'll be there in a minute."

Then Emma turned to Jake with a neutral expression. Slowly, hurt invaded her eyes. "I wanted to thank you for doing this for them. Josh was so disappointed not to be able to come on Tuesday, but he understood you needed time and so did I." Her voice became husky. "My feelings are the same whether you have a panic attack or not. That doesn't define you as a person in my mind." She waited a moment for him to say something and, when he didn't, she swung around and left.

He knew he loved her as he watched her walk away, but no words came to mind to say to her. He couldn't come to her the way he was now.

* * *

In the pitch dark Jake woke up to the sound of ice pelting his bedroom window. He tried his lamp on the nightstand but nothing happened. His battery-operated clock read six o'clock. The chill in the air indicated the electricity had been off for hours.

The predicted ice storm must have moved in last night. He needed to get up and check outside. If it didn't look as if the electricity was coming on anytime soon, he would use the generator he'd bought for an emergency like this. But the warmth under his covers enticed him to stay in bed until it was light enough to see rather than make his way to the kitchen in the dark to get his flashlight.

The continual bombarding of the ice against his house set off alarm bells in his mind. He hadn't been in an ice storm in years, but it could leave a town crippled if it lasted long. Did Emma have a generator to warm at least part of her house? The temperature high for the next few days was only supposed to be in the mid-twenties. Maybe in the morning he'd try calling her if the phones still worked and find out if she was all right. He'd feel better—

The blare of his phone startled him. His heartbeat accelerated as he fumbled for it on the bedside table. "Hello."

"Jake, a tree fell on our house. Mom's trapped in her bedroom." Tears laced Josh's urgent words.

"I'll be right there, Josh. Is she hurt?"

"She says no but she can't get out and the ice is falling on her. I called 911, but they can't get here for a while."

Throwing back the covers, Jake swung his legs over

the side of the bed, then rose. "Don't go in there. Tell her I'm coming."

"Hurry. I'm scared."

In the dark Jake searched for the jeans and sweatshirt he'd tossed toward the chair last night. When he found them, he dressed quickly, telling himself over and over Emma and Josh were okay. He would get them and bring them back here. But his heart pounded against his rib cage, and his chest felt tight.

Feeling his way to the kitchen, he went through his mental routine to keep him focused on getting to Emma's without having a panic attack. After he retrieved the large flashlight, he looked for a saw in his toolbox, then started for the front door.

The sky a dark gray, Jake paused on his porch to figure the best way to go while he swept his flashlight in a wide arc over the terrain. Ice coated everything at least an inch thick, glittering when his light hit it. Although the landscape was beautiful to behold, to be out in it was dangerous. Fortunately, snow was beginning to fall and would allow him to walk better.

Bundled up, Jake descended the steps, gripping the railing, then headed out into the mixture of falling snow and ice. *Lord, please keep Emma and Josh safe. Help me to get there before any harm is done.*

The silence was eerie until a loud noise like the crack of a rifle reverberated in the air. Adrenaline pumped through him. Instead of tensing, he breathed from the diaphragm, slow, deep inhalations. He began to relax, even when another cracking noise—louder, nearer— echoed through the quiet. A limb on Marcella's oak in the front snapped and crashed to the ground. When

Emma and Josh were safe back at his house, he would check on his neighbor.

As Jake crept toward the middle of the street where there were no overhead branches to break off and fall on him, he kept taking in and releasing those deep breaths while acknowledging he was having a panic attack. "I'm okay. This gives me a chance to prove to myself I can cope. There's nothing to be afraid of. The sounds aren't gunfire but limbs breaking off trees."

He headed toward Emma's as fast as he could, praying the whole way. With each step he took he felt more capable of handling his panic attack, even though he continued to hear branches snapping off nearby as well as in the distance. The rapid beat of his heart slowed. The trembling faded.

In the distance he saw a light flash in the sky and a loud boom resonated through the air. *Just a transformer going. That's all. I'm okay.*

By the time he reached Emma's block, all signs of a panic attack were gone, although the loud noises still sounded in the biting, cold wind. When he'd had an attack before, he'd always gotten upset, making it worse. Abbey had been working with him to accept what was happening to him, and then move on.

And he had. He smiled. *Thank You, Lord.*

Then he spied Emma's house two down from the corner. A large elm tree had split and fallen on the right side of her place—where her bedroom was. He tried increasing his pace, but he slipped and went down on the knee of his good leg. Catching himself by clutching a mailbox, he used it to pull himself up then slowed his steps. *With the Lord and patience, I'll make it.*

Dressed in a heavy coat, sweats and gloves, Josh

opened the door before Jake made it halfway up the sidewalk to the porch. Worry lined the boy's face.

When he started to come outside, Jake said, "Don't. Close the door. I'll be there in a minute," then he proceeded at his slow pace.

When he made it inside Emma's house, he heard the whistle of the wind coming from the hallway to the right. "How's your mom?"

"She says okay, but I can hear her teeth chattering."

Jake covered the distance to the hallway and started down it, noticing the bedroom door was closed.

"Mom made me shut it to keep as much heat in the house as possible."

"Good thinking." Jake swung the door open, saying, "Stay here. If I need you, I'll call you," then he closed himself in the room with Emma, assessing the situation.

"I'm sorry you had to get out in this. I asked Josh to call 911. He did, but they won't be here for a while since I'm not hurt. I told him I could wait. Instead, he called you."

"As I told him a few seconds ago, good thinking."

Jake examined the split half of the elm, a large branch falling across Emma's bed, several smaller limbs trapping her. A coverlet blanketed her but so did a layer of ice and now snow. Her face pale, she shivered, her lips turning blue.

Jake set down his flashlight so it shone on what he needed to cut. "Do you have something plastic I can cover you with? It'll keep the snow and ice off while I saw you out of there."

"A raincoat...oh, and I have a plastic tablecloth. It's bigger than the raincoat. It's in the cabinet in the utility room."

Jake climbed over the branches between him and the one he needed to remove. "Josh." When the boy came into the room, Jake said, "I need you to fetch a plastic tablecloth." After Jake told him where it was, Josh left, and Jake started sawing the biggest limb.

When Josh returned, he wiggled through the limbs and handed Jake the tablecloth. "I wanna stay and help."

Emma said, "I want you to stay out—"

Jake interrupted, "Sure. I need you to hold the flashlight." As the child grabbed it, Jake whispered to Emma, "He needs to know you're okay."

Emma attempted a smile that stayed a few seconds. "I know but it's so cold."

"I'm fine, Mom."

With snow swirling on the wind coming through the hole, Jake spread the plastic over Emma to protect her then returned to sawing. He put all his strength into it, and minutes later he caught the first branch before it fell on Emma. Adrenaline still surging through him, he heaved it over to the side and let it go, then began on the second limb.

Soon he severed that branch from the split trunk and tossed it to the right. "Do you think you can crawl out now?" he asked, but Emma, dressed in sweats, was already wiggling out from under the coverlet.

Jake clasped her arm and tugged her the rest of the way loose, then assisted her over the limbs. When he got a good hold of her, he swung her up into his arms and followed Josh from the room. The boy slammed the door, cutting off the wind, but the temperature was probably thirty-five in the hallway.

Clasping Emma against him, Jake strode toward the living room. "Josh, get some blankets for your mom."

qqsmaller live Christmas tree and studied the display she, Josh, Jake and Marcella had worked on for the past hour. The sound of Christmas music filled the room from a battery-powered radio.

After Emma had been rescued from her house, Jake had made his way to Marcella's and brought her over because she had no generator. Then they had been busy consolidating what they would need into a couple of rooms on the first floor that would be heated with the generator and fireplace.

Jake had wanted to talk with Emma, but they'd been busy. Now that she had stopped and sat next to Marcella on his couch, exhaustion began to weave its way through her. From the tired lines on Marcella's face, Jake could tell she was also bone-weary.

"Josh, you said you wanted to put the star on top of the tree." Jake presented him with a beautiful glittered and sequined ornament.

Josh grinned, climbed up on the step stool and placed the last decoration on the pine. "Perfect."

First Shep barked then Buttons, as though to give their approval.

"I agree. Now to turn on the lights." Jake plugged them in.

The soft glow from the tree along with the blaze in the fireplace illuminated the room.

"I know we're two weeks late decorating your tree, but I think we did good." Emma leaned forward to gather up the mugs they had hot apple cider in. "Time to clean up the mess we made."

Jake looked at Josh. "Is your mom always like this?"

"Yep."

"I've still got to clean up from dinner, so the least you all could do is put the empty ornament boxes away."

"I'm not climbing those stairs again today. We'll store them in my bedroom. Wanna help me, Josh?"

The boy started picking up some to carry down the hallway.

"I'll help you, Emma." Marcella began to rise from the couch.

"No, you stay in here and relax. It's been a long day," Emma said then hurried away before Marcella protested.

The furnace, refrigerator, stove, hot water heater and a few lights were running on Jake's generator stored in the garage. With some conservation of electrical usage, the generator kept the house comfortable for them. While listening to the radio, Emma washed the dishes in hot water, a luxury she wouldn't take for granted again. "Silent Night" came on the station, and Emma began singing the song.

When she finished, applause sounded behind her. She whirled around to find Jake standing in the entrance, lounging against the doorjamb. Her pulse rate kicked up a notch.

"The news on the radio doesn't sound promising for getting our electricity anytime soon," Emma said, drying her hands, her throat tight with emotion. Peace and joy filled her.

His gaze roped hers, and he moved toward her. "Towns all around us are affected. They're going to have to bring people in from other areas to help."

"I've never heard ice breaking limbs like that—almost nonstop as we walked here."

"It sounded like a war zone."

She hadn't wanted to use that analogy, but he was right. "You were okay."

"I was—even when I had an attack on the way over to your house. I've been working on changing my attitude about my panic attacks. I'm not going to let them control my life anymore."

She threw her arms around his neck and drew him against her. "Mmm. You're warm. I never thought I would thaw out this morning, but your house became toasty in a few hours. I know I've thanked you for—"

He claimed her mouth in a deep kiss she felt down to the tips of her toes. "I love you."

He said the words she'd dreamed he would but she didn't want to misread what he meant. "I love you, too, but you know that. I want more from you. A life together as a family." Emma cuddled closer.

Leaning back slightly, he looked deep into her eyes with a half smile on his face. "It won't always be easy, but would you be interested in a guy with a slight problem?"

"Who doesn't have a problem?" Her embrace tightened. She never wanted to let go. "What changed your mind?"

"You, Josh and Abbey. She has been working double-time to get me to a place where I don't let the panic attacks overwhelm me before I have a chance to deal with them. I'm learning to ride them out and lessen their effects. It won't be perfect, but far better than it was. Today demonstrated that to me. A month ago that cracking noise would have sent me into a full-blown attack, like the one I had at the Christmas-tree lighting ceremony. The crack-pop sounds so close to gunfire in a battle."

"I love you, Jake. I want it all. Marriage. A family. Josh looks up to you, even after witnessing that attack. That didn't change his mind and it certainly didn't mine." She watched for any negative reaction from him.

Instead, an expression full of happiness graced his face. "I was embarrassed and scared. I reacted by pushing everyone away. As a soldier I've learned not to show my weaknesses, but I have them."

"Like everyone else. God made us with strengths and weaknesses and loves us, anyway."

"I know that now. It took some soul searching and some conversations with Him to finally figure that out."

She slid her hands to his face, framing it. "If I ever gave you the idea that Sam's seizures made me regret marrying him, then I'm here to correct that impression. When I married him, it was for better or worse, and in every marriage you have both."

"Have you forgiven yourself for his accident?" Jake closed the inches separating them and feathered his mouth across hers.

"Yes, both you and Abbey helped me to see it wasn't my fault."

"I'm looking forward to the future. I want to help others the way you and Abbey do. Once I earn my doctorate, I'm thinking of working with veterans, especially ones with PTSD. Who better than someone who's dealt with it?"

"Perfect." Emma slanted her head to the side and kissed him with all the love she felt in her heart.

Epilogue

One year later on Christmas Eve...

Emma snuggled closer to her husband of three months on the couch in front of the fireplace, adorned with a combination of her and his decorations. "I loved the service at church this evening, especially since we missed last year's because of the ice storm."

Jake laughed. "We did have a white Christmas last year. This one is going to be a balmy fifty-eight if the weatherman is right."

Emma's glance strayed to the Christmas tree, so loaded down with the ornaments, she worried it would collapse under the weight. "I'm surprised Josh could get to sleep. Good idea about you two going to the park earlier and jogging."

"That's because I wanted you all to myself tonight. Tomorrow your parents, Ben, my dad and stepmother will be here for dinner and the opening of the presents."

"Your father and his wife should have stayed here."

Jake kissed first one corner of her mouth then the

other. "We're newlyweds, and they wanted us to have some privacy."

"With a twelve-year-old here. Some privacy."

"As a family." His mouth touched hers.

When he leaned back, Emma grinned. "I thought last Christmas was perfect even with the ice storm, but this one is going to beat it hands down."

"I want to give you my gift now."

"I get to go first. I've been dying to ever since I got it this week." Emma hopped up and went to the Christmas tree set before the front window, its lights blazing, and dug around the packages under it until she pulled the wrapped gift out from the back. "I hid it so a certain person who will remain nameless didn't try to discover what it is." She laid a gold-foiled square box in his lap.

He tore into it and slowly lifted up baby booties, staring at them for a long moment.

"Just in case you haven't figured it out, I'm pregnant. Eight weeks."

An awed expression descended over his features. "I don't think I'll ever get a better gift than this for Christmas."

"So you like it?"

"Like, no. Love, yes." He planted a kiss on her mouth, all his love poured into it. "My gift pales in comparison to yours."

"I'll cherish anything you give me."

Jake pulled out the drawer of the end table next to him and gave her a small, wrapped present in red-and-green paper.

She had it open in two seconds. Her gaze glued to the beautiful gold heart locket, she held it up, dangling from her fingers. "Perfect."

He took it and showed her the two pictures inside—one of him and the other of Josh.

She twisted around and lifted her hair off her neck. "Please put it on."

After he did, he took her hand and kissed it. She'd captured the heart of a hero.

* * * * *

Dear Reader,

Her Holiday Hero is the second book in the Caring Canines series. I've had many dogs in my life, and more recently three cats. They have brought much joy and laughter to me and my family. They're so accepting and give us unconditional love. When it's been a stressful day, I like to hold my cat, hear him purring. How has having a pet made a difference in your life? Drop me a line and let me know.

I also wanted to show how a service dog trained to help someone suffering from post traumatic stress disorder can be so valuable. Remember, PTSD doesn't happen just to soldiers, but to anyone who has had a traumatic experience. And these wonderful dogs help people get back to a semblance of a normal life.

I love hearing from readers. You can contact me at margaretdaley@gmail.com or at 1316 S. Peoria Ave., Tulsa, OK 74120. You can also learn more about my books at www.margaretdaley.com. I have a quarterly newsletter that you can sign up for on my website.

Best wishes,

Margaret Daley

LONE STAR HOLIDAY

Jolene Navarro

Come to me, all you who are weary and burdened,
and I will give you rest.

—*Matthew* 11:28

Chapter One

Lorrie Ann's sports car hugged the curves of the country road. Fence posts and cattle flew past her window as she ran back to the small town she fled twelve years ago. No one had warned her that in the pursuit of fame and fortune she could become emotionally and spiritually bankrupt. She glanced at the Bible with the purple tattered note sticking out of it. Well, her aunt might have, but she had been too stubborn to listen.

On the soft leather seat, next to the Bible, her cell vibrated again. Brent's face filled the screen. How did she ever find her now-ex-fiancé's grin charming? For two years she had ignored his behavior—until yesterday. Their last fight had escalated to the point where he'd hit her. When had she become her mother? Relationships were not her thing, and the situation with Brent proved her right.

That was the moment she took a long hard look at her life and didn't like what she saw. She had no one to turn to. They shared the same friends. He played the drums for the band she managed.

She hadn't taken a vacation in three years. With the

holidays coming up she'd called the lead singer of the band she managed and told her she was heading home. Where was home? With nowhere to go, she headed to the only place she had family—her aunt's pecan farm in Clear Water, Texas. She couldn't imagine anyplace more different than Los Angeles.

The phone went quiet only to start chiming again a moment later. Teeth gritted, she shifted gears and picked up speed. She didn't want to hear his apologies.

A burst of anger had her grabbing the phone and throwing it out the window. She dashed past the green sign that said Clear Water was eight miles. She turned up the music and pushed down on the gas pedal only to have the engine sputter and jerk. The steering wheel became stiff under her hands. With all her muscle she forced the BMW to the side of the road.

She checked the gauges and sighed. No gas, no phone, and she only had herself to blame.

One moment of temper had caused her to chuck her phone out of her car. Now she could walk the eight miles to town or walk back to find her phone—and hope that it still worked.

She needed to make the call she had been avoiding anyway, so she started the hike to find her phone.

Lorrie Ann fought to keep her balance as she walked back up the hill she had just driven down. Her five-inch-heel boots, designed for flat city life, didn't take well to the rocky hike across the uneven ground.

The cool breeze whispered over her shoulders. She adjusted her brown felt fedora and glanced around the vast landscape of the Texas Hill Country. The Black Angus cows stopped chewing and silently watched her stumble along the fence. With one hand on the rough cedar post, she stared back. "What are you looking at?"

Great—less than a day back in Texas and she was talking to cattle. Closing her eyes, she took a deep breath. "Dear God, I know for the last twelve years I put You in the backseat, and now I'm asking for help every time I turn around. Please, just give me the peace to know You're in control and I'm doing the right thing." Peace. She doubted she'd recognize it if it turned out to be a rattlesnake about to bite her.

A loud engine broke the endless silence of rolling hills. Lorrie Ann swung around, fearful for a moment of being so alone in the middle of nowhere without her phone.

A blue work-worn truck appeared over the hill. Coming straight at her, the black deer guard on the front looked menacing. The driver slowed down and pulled off the road.

Swallowing, she started praying for it to be a friendly stranger. The door swung open, displaying the Childress quarter-horse logo. Her heartbeat settled. She remembered the Childress family.

From behind the door stepped a walking Hollywood version of the American Cowboy. Tall and lean, his work-faded jeans rode low over slim hips. The dark T-shirt hugged his broad shoulders under a waist-length denim jacket. His fit body looked shaped by hours of working outdoors, instead of designed by a personal trainer. He must be one of the hired ranch hands.

He stepped across the road with confidence and walked in a way that might tempt a girl to give up her plans. Each stride of his long legs moved him closer to her. Her heart flip-flopped. She bit her lip. *Stupid heart.*

She had returned to Clear Water, Texas, to reconnect with God and to refill her spiritual bank, *not* to get tangled up in another relationship. Having her mom's defective gene for picking men, her best option would be to remain male free.

A welcoming smile eased across his face. Lines creased the corners of golden-brown eyes and ran down his well-formed cheeks. One lone dimple appeared on the left side. Her mouth went dry.

"Are you lost?"

His deep Texas drawl washed over her. Lorrie Ann shook her head and searched for words.

"No, but I'm sure that depends on who you ask." A nervous laugh ran away from her lips. She looked at the ground. *Ugh, let me count the ways to sound like an idiot.* Raising her gaze, she flashed her best smile. In California it never failed her.

Instead, he glanced off into the pasture, at the cows. "Is that your car up ahead?"

She sighed. Apparently, Texas cowboys were a completely different breed from the men she had been working with in Los Angeles.

"Yeah, I ran out of gas."

Bringing his gaze back to her, he looked puzzled. "Town is about eight miles that way." His long fingers pointed in the opposite direction she faced.

"I know, but my phone is somewhere over here." She waved toward the pasture, and her collection of bracelets jingled.

On cue, the phone rang somewhere on the other side of the barbed-wire fence. At least Brent was good for something. "Oh, it still works." She tried to climb between two strands of wire, but a barb snagged her long silk shirt, and her sunglasses hit the ground. When she turned to free the blouse, the top wire caught her hat, causing her hair to fall forward. The thick waves covered her face, blinding her.

"Hold still." The cowboy's voice emitted assurance. Gently his hands freed the corner of her shirt and held the wires farther apart so she could easily step through.

When she stood on the other side, she pushed her hair back. She reached for her oversize shades and shoved them over her eyes. Ouch! She'd forgotten the bruise. Her skin throbbed with a dull ache.

"Are you sure you're okay?" He leaned over the fence, handing her the hat.

Lorrie Ann didn't like the look she read in the cowboy's eyes. At best, it was concern, at worst, pity. Her nails cut into her palms. She hated pity.

"Anyone I can call for you?"

"No, no. Really, as soon as I get my phone, I'm good."

He turned that devastating smile back on her. "How your phone ended up in a cow pasture is bound to be an interesting story." He held his hand out to her, the fence still between them. "I'm John Levi."

The phone sounded off again. Forgetting his hand, she spun around to locate the device. In a tall clump of gold grass, it vibrated. "I found it!" She lifted it high.

He smiled. "Now we just need to get you some gas, and you'll be on your way. Where're you headed?"

"Can you believe my destination is Clear Water?"

Lorrie Ann smiled back at him, a genuine smile this time. It felt good. The past couple years anything real had been hard to find, especially any type of happiness or joy.

"Come on." He chuckled. "Let's get you back on this side of the fence before the herd gets too curious." He stepped on the bottom wire and held the top one up, leaving a large opening.

"Thanks." With one hand on her hat, she stepped through without a problem this time.

"I'll drive you to your car. I have some gas in a can in the back. Not sure your boots could make it down the hill." She had forgotten cowboys always stayed prepared for anything. He held out his arm, like a gentleman from an old movie.

Her fingers wrapped around his denim sleeve. Masculine strength seeped through the sturdy material, warming her skin. "Thank you for helping." Her shoulders rose and fell with a heavy sigh. "I can't believe I ran out of gas this close to arriving home."

"Home? You're a local?" A deep chuckle rumbled from his chest. "I should know better than to judge by appearances or license plates."

"Oh, I'm probably everything you thought. I'm sure if you ask anyone in town, they'll give you all the gory details."

"In order to ask them, I'd have to know your name."

She looked up at him, assessing his expression. "Hmm…that's true." Fear of what they would say tightened her muscles. She had left town in a swirl of lies started by the homecoming queen.

He waited a moment with eyebrows lifted. He finally grinned and closed her door. The cowboy walked around to the driver's side. Climbing into the cab, he continued to grin.

His eyes stayed focused ahead as he eased them

back onto the road. "So what brings you back to Clear Water?"

"My aunt. Maggie Schultz."

"You're Maggie's niece, Lorrie Ann Ortega? She didn't say anything about you coming home."

She shouldn't be surprised he knew her. Her aunt volunteered on about every committee in the small town and had always helped anyone that needed something, including her. "She doesn't know."

"She's going to be thrilled."

Lorrie played with the rip in her shirt. He obviously didn't know the whole story. "I'm not so sure about that. It's been a long time."

"She's been waiting for you." He flashed her a quick glance accompanied by a grin. "Trust me. She'll be very excited to see you."

"How do you know her?"

He gave a casual shrug and smiled. "We're at the same church."

The big truck pulled up behind her small BMW. "Go open your tank. I'll get the gas." With a quick motion, he jumped out of the cab and went to the bed of his truck.

Leaping down from the side step, Lorrie Ann made her way to the silver BMW. She glanced into her car and cringed. With the top tucked away on her convertible, he would see the mess she had made in her twenty-five-hour run from California—the candy wrappers, huge plastic cups and haphazard packing that littered the backseat.

Yeah, it pretty much represented her life with Brent in L.A., all pretty and shiny on the outside and chaos on the inside. Now with no gas, the expensive machine sat on the side of the road, useless.

She leaned inside and picked up the Bible. The hand-written note from Aunt Maggie stuck out, purple and tattered around the edges. She didn't need to read the words as they were etched in her memory. *Matthew 11:28, Come to me, all you who are weary and burdened, and I will give you rest.*

Those words had brought her back to Texas, to the closest place she had ever called home. She had been working so hard to prove herself, but somewhere along the way she had lost sight of the big picture.

"You have a note from Maggie." He nodded toward her Bible. "Which verse did she send you? I have a full collection."

Unaware he had approached, Lorrie Ann blinked to clear her thoughts. Did Aunt Maggie send these notes to everyone? Not sure how that made her feel, she laid the Bible back in the car. "She's always looking for ways to help."

He nodded. "She's a prayer warrior. We're blessed to have her."

This all felt very surreal. In the world she just left, no one spoke of God and prayer, let alone Bible verses. And if you did, they'd only laugh and make some witty cut-down.

She pulled in a deep breath. "I need to be going. Thanks so much for your help."

"I'll follow you into town. The closest gas station is the mercantile. We can stop there and get you filled up then head out to Bill and Maggie's farm."

"Oh, no. You've done enough."

"It's on my way. I can't look your uncle and aunt

in the eye if I don't make sure you're delivered safe and sound." He winked at her. "See you in town." He stepped back and walked to his truck.

Okay, then. Her knight in denim remained on the job. She shouldn't like the idea. Slipping into her car, Lorrie Ann turned the key and pulled back onto the road. With a glance at her rearview mirror, she watched John follow her.

Scolding herself, she muttered, "Remember, Lorrie Ann, your short-term goal is to get your life back in order and get back to work. A boyfriend's not even on the long-term list."

John Levi turned on the radio. Music he had shut out five years ago filled the cabin of his truck. His fingers tipped the guitar pick hanging from the rearview mirror. Carol, his wife, had given it to him when they were still dating. He watched the heart she had drawn on it swing back and forth. It was the only piece of his music career he kept after her death. The pick reminded him of what he had taken for granted.

The sporty car in front of him pulled out, and he followed. Lorrie Ann Ortega was a surprise, and any pull he felt had to do with her needing help. Through her aunt and mother, he knew her past, and now he saw the wounded look in her eyes. She needed encouragement and support. He could do that for her.

He tapped his fingers along the cracked steering wheel.

Holding the phone in her hand, Lorrie Ann wavered calling Aunt Maggie. What if she didn't want her? Her mother hadn't wanted her. Now that she was an adult, her aunt and uncle had no responsibility to help her.

As she came into town, she eased on the brake. A burst of purple and silver stretched across Main Street and covered every storefront window, each proudly supporting the Fighting Angoras football team.

Homecoming week. The day after graduation, she'd made sure to tell everyone that she would never be back. How ironic that she return the week of the homecoming game. Some rituals never changed. Lorrie smiled. An unexpected comfort washed over her. Not a single fast-food or chain-store logo cluttered the skyline.

Her phone vibrated. With clenched teeth, she battled the urge to throw the phone out of the car again. She imagined running over it until nothing but dust clung to her tires.

She wanted to leave everything in Los Angeles behind, long enough to figure out her life, anyway. The band had taken the holidays off. Could she develop a new-life action plan in less than four weeks?

Pulling next to the aged gas pumps, Lorrie Ann pushed the button to roll the top back over the car. She took a deep breath, slid out of the car and straightened her spine.

Her hands shook slightly as she adjusted the oversize shades. Lorrie Ann ran a manicured finger over the convertible top of her Z4 BMW. Definitely not the hand-me-down Dodge she had driven away in as a scared teenager.

She took a slow surveillance of the single-street town. A group of old ranchers still sat in front of the feed store. Their never-ending game of dominoes was as much a part of the landscape as the giant oaks.

John parked his truck on the other side of her. "Here, let me fill her up for you."

She was not used to men offering to do things for her unless they wanted something. It made her a bit uncomfortable. She noticed new construction at the end of the street, an unheard-of occurrence in Clear Water. She gestured to the site, causing her bracelets to jingle. "What's being built? Looks like a regular building boom for Clear Water."

He nodded and smiled at her as he held the gas nozzle to her car. "The churches have banded together to build a new youth building."

A gleam came to his eyes, reminding her of a proud parent. Bringing his gaze back to hers, he continued, "There's still some fundraising that needs to be done, but enough has been raised to get the building started."

"Wow, I'm impressed." She cut a glance toward him again. He turned his gaze on her, started to say something and then looked away.

The silence stretched and got awkward. She bit her lip. *Say something, girl.*

"Um…so are you involved in the project?"

"It's my goal to see it done before summer." Nodding, he stepped back and replaced the nozzle. "Well, your steed is fed. I'll walk you to the store."

She couldn't hold in the giggle. Did she just actually giggle? Lorrie Ann took a moment to savor the joy.

"Thank you." She slid a glance to the old ranchers, now openly staring at her and the cowboy. She waved at them. "Hi, boys." Swinging back to her knight in faded denim, she winked. "Think they appreciated the show?"

He laughed. A real laugh not measured or managed.

"They enjoy anything new to talk about. Are you good? I could wait."

"No, I'm fine. I need to pick up a few items, then I'll make my escape to the pecan farm." Yep, she had become very skilled at running. "Thank you for the escort."

He looked right into her eyes, and for a second she forgot to breathe. She had the sensation he saw past the makeup and fashion to the real her.

"It's a true pleasure meeting you, Lorrie Ann Ortega. Welcome back." He tipped his hat and pulled open one of the glass double doors to the mercantile for her. A little bell made a sweet musical sound.

He gave her one last wink. "I'm sure we'll see each other again. Can't hide in a town this small."

The door closed, and she turned and watched through the large storefront windows as he walked away. Once he disappeared from sight, she noticed the flyers in an array of colors taped everywhere, announcing cabins for rent, hunting leases available and horses for sale. Well, she was back.

A loud squeal filled the air followed by a high-pitched voice. "L.A.? Lorrie Ann. Oh, my, it is you!"

Lorrie Ann cringed at her old nickname. No one had called her L.A. for years. She found herself ambushed in a tight hug by a tall woman with big blond hair. Knocked off balance, Lorrie Ann grabbed the girl's arms. A death grip kept her from moving back. The overzealous greeter yelled over her shoulder, "Vickie, hurry out here. L.A. is back in Clear Water!"

"Katy? Katy Norton?" Relief flooded Lorrie as she greeted one of the few girls she trusted from high school.

"I didn't recognize you till you came in. You sure look fancy. I hear you hang with rock stars now. Your aunt says you're getting married to the drummer of Burn White." Katy leaned back, but her hands remained clasped around Lorrie's forearm. "Maggie didn't say anything about you coming for a visit."

"She doesn't know. How are you?" Lorrie Ann glanced around the grocery store. From the hundred-year-old wooden floor to the meat counter in the back, all appeared the same as it did in her memories. "You work at the mercantile?"

"I married Rhody. We manage the store for his parents now."

"You married Rhody Buchanan?" Lorrie Ann forced her eyebrows back down. "He picked on you in high school."

Katy smirked and playfully slapped Lorrie Ann on the shoulder. "Well, I came to find out it was just his way of flirting. We have four boys now."

"You and Rhody have four kids...together?" Her forehead went up again.

Before Katy could answer, Vickie Lawson, the conductor of Lorrie Ann's high-school nightmare, ambled from the deer-corn aisle.

"Well, well, well, if it isn't big-city girl L.A." Vickie's stare slowly moved up and down. "Thought you were never coming back to our town."

"Honestly, I'm as surprised as you are to find myself here. I came to visit Aunt Maggie for the holidays." Lorrie Ann's gaze darted around the store.

Katy hugged her again. "She's been waiting for you. We've all prayed for you to come home." She threw her arms wide. "And lookie, you're here, an answered prayer. You'll have to tell me all about your exciting adventures in L.A." Katy sighed.

Lorrie Ann could hear the expectation of glamorous stories about life in Los Angeles.

Vickie crossed her arms and leaned against the counter, face pulled tight. "Where's your boyfriend? Waitin' in the car? Probably thinks he's too good for the likes of us."

Lorrie Ann drew a deep breath and smiled the smile she used to close deals with in L.A. "No, he's not here. We broke up." She turned to Katy with a genuine smile. "Once I get settled, we can have lunch or something."

"Ooh, just like in the movies!" Katy tilted her head. "Will you be at church for our Wednesday-night prayer meeting?" She nudged Lorrie Ann's shoulder. "Looks like you already know Pastor John."

A frown replaced the smile when the word *pastor* sank into Lorrie Ann's brain. Only one other person had spoken to her. That good-looking cowboy couldn't have been a…

"That cowboy is a preacher?" Her jaw dropped, and she closed her eyes. Horror stomped out the shock. She had flirted with a man of God.

Katy's smile went wider as her eyes sparkled. "Yes! He seemed to really like you."

Vickie gave a loud snort and narrowed her glare. "You've always tried taking men who aren't yours. He *will* see right through you."

Katy punched Vickie's arm and laughed. "Oh, stop it! Lorrie Ann just got into town. We don't need to bring up what happened in the past. Anyway, Pastor John has not dated anyone since the horrible accident five years ago. I think it's about time he left his daughters at home and went out for some fun."

"Whatever." With a shrug, Vickie turned and walked to the back of the store.

Lorrie Ann's chin went up. No longer was she the pathetic girl abandoned by her mother. Now she made big deals and managed bands in her daily life. She controlled her destiny. Not some…

A warm hand on her arm brought her around.

"Don't let her get under your skin. She's always been jealous of you." Katy waved her hand in the air and lowered her voice. "And since the divorce, she's just gotten downright bitter. She should have never married Tommy. Poor thing, her life is a mess right now. Let's get your stuff so you can go home."

Katy's soft gaze brought a knot to Lorrie Ann's throat. Well, she could relate to a messy life. "I always thought her and Jake were an item. She hated my friendship with him."

"Yeah, now they are both back in town and avoiding each other—sad, really." Katy shook her head. "Come on. Let's get your things so you can surprise Maggie."

Purchases in hand, Lorrie Ann stepped out of the store and spotted the Ford truck still parked outside the mercantile. She groaned. Less than thirty minutes in town, and she had already been flirting with the town pastor right on Main Street. The gossips would have a field day with that tidbit.

Chapter Two

"Aunt Maggie? It's—"

"Oh, *mija,* it's so good to hear from you!" A slight pause came through the line. "Is everything okay?"

The love and concern in the older woman's voice wrapped itself around Lorrie Ann's heart. Eyes closed briefly, she eased a smile across her face.

"Yeah, I'm good. I'm actually in Clear Water heading to the farm." As the silence lingered, her stomach knotted.

"What? Oh, my, Lorrie Ann Ortega! What do you mean you're in Clear Water? Why are you just now calling me?" Lorrie could almost hear her aunt's thoughts processing. "Oh, sweetheart, what happened?"

"Nothing.... I just need a place to rest, get my thoughts together. Is it okay that I came to the farm? I don't know Mom's latest location." Nerves hit her stomach hard. "It's just for a couple weeks while I figure things out. I can rent one of the cabins."

"You hush about paying. This is your home. Your room's always ready for you."

Lorrie pulled in her lips and bit down. The need to

cry burned her eyes. She pulled a deep breath through her nose before she dared speak again. "Thank you, Aunt Maggie. I'm at Second Crossing now, so I'll—"

A deer darted across the road. Her phone slid to the floorboard as she grabbed the steering wheel with both hands. Hitting the brake, she pulled her car to the side of the road.

The deer's hooves slid on the pavement, fighting to regain control. The white of the doe's eyes flashed, and in a frenzied twist it turned back the way it had come and ran behind her.

In Lorrie Ann's rearview mirror, she tracked the animal as it scurried right in front of a yellow Jeep. Eyes wide, Lorrie Ann watched the events as if in slow motion. Horror filled her mind as the deer collided with the grille of the oncoming vehicle. The deer flew over the hood into the windshield, and the Jeep lost control. It slid in the loose gravel and rolled toward the river. Frozen in her seat, Lorrie Ann stared as a group of cedar trees stopped the rolling car.

"Lorrie! Lorrie Ann, answer me!" Her aunt's frantic voice brought her back to herself. White fingers had a death grip around the leather of her steering wheel. As she reached for the phone between her feet, her hands shook. She took a deep breath. The dark shades fell to the floorboard, and she didn't bother picking them up.

"I'm here. I'm fine, but there's been an accident. I have to call 911." Without waiting to hear her aunt's response, she ended the call and hit the emergency button. She stepped out of her car and jogged along the shoulder of the road, her heels clicking across the asphalt. Breath held tight, she approached the flipped vehicle.

When she heard crying, relief eased her muscles a small bit, proof of life.

She knelt to look in the cab, her heart pounding at the thought of what she might see. A young girl hung upside down by her seat belt in the backseat.

A sob muffled her words. "Rachel! Rachel!"

Her weeping broke Lorrie's heart. "Sweetheart, my name's Lorrie Ann. I called the ambulance."

The voice on the line demanded her attention, asking for details. "There has been a car accident at Second Crossing. Oh, I'm Lorrie Ann Ortega. There's a girl about five or six in the backseat. She is awake and suspended by her seat belt."

Lorrie scanned the cab, noticing two more girls up front. Broken glass covered the roof, but the roll bars had done their job and created a pocket for them.

The passenger in the front seat appeared to be around ten or twelve. "There are two girls in the front, both strapped in their seats. The driver has blood on her face. She looks unconscious." A deep sigh of relief escaped. "But breathing."

The young girl in front started twisting against her shoulder strap. "Celeste? Celeste, where are you?" A frantic tone edged her voice.

"Rachel! I'm...I'm scared." The smaller one in the backseat reached forward.

"Don't be scared. Stop crying! It won't help." Her voice sounded more mature than her age.

Lorrie Ann couldn't help being impressed. "Girls, help is on the way. Are you sisters?" Their matching ponytails bobbed as they nodded their heads. "It's Rachel and Celeste, right?"

"Yes." The older girl in the front spoke, moving both

hands to rub at her face. "Amy's our babysitter. Oh, Daddy's going to be so mad."

"I'm sure your father just wants you safe."

"Oh! My leg is stuck. I can't move it." Rachel sounded calm, though her voice pitched higher at the last word.

Lorrie Ann narrowed her gaze on Rachel's right leg surrounded by metal. It looked as if a piece of the engine had pushed through.

The driver groaned.

"Amy, Amy, wake up!" Rachel reached across and touched her shoulder.

"What happened?" Amy pushed back her hair. "Oh, no!" She sucked in deep breaths, and her eyes went wide. "Rachel? Celeste? Please, please tell me you're all right!" She cried out in pain, hugging herself and moaning.

"Easy. Don't hurt yourself." Lorrie Ann pressed a hand to the older girl's shoulder. "I hear the sirens. Help's almost here. Just hang on, girls, and try to stay still."

Lorrie Ann turned from the crumbled metal and watched as an ambulance arrived.

A state trooper pulled in from the other direction. He quickly stepped from his car and made his way to the wreckage. Lorrie Ann squinted against the sun to get a better look at him and then hung her head.

He hunched next to her, scanning the inside of the car. "Hang tight, Amy. Girls, we'll have you out soon." He turned until she saw her reflection in his aviators. "Lorrie Ann Ortega? What in the world are you doing here?"

She stared into the face of another ghost from her

past. Even with the dark shades masking most of his face, she knew who hovered over her.

"Jake Torres, I'm trying to help three scared girls here."

He nodded. Bracing a hand on the door as he peered back inside, he spoke again, his voice softened. "We're here to help you girls. So breathe and stay calm."

He glanced back at Lorrie Ann over his shoulder. "Girl, you sure know how to make an entrance back to town."

Making his way to the post office, John could not stop the urge to whistle a sweet tune as he waved to the cars slowly passing by. The plans for his day had fallen apart when Dub called, needing help with a renegade horse.

He smiled, remembering his frustration when the church secretary, JoAnn, called right after with a problem at the construction site. Both unscheduled events put Maggie's niece right in his path.

It had been a long time since he allowed himself to enjoy the company of a female. He should have fully introduced himself, but he suspected the easy camaraderie would have ended. As soon as someone found out he was a pastor, they started acting differently around him. Ordinarily the attitude didn't bother him, but today, he just wanted to be a normal man getting to know another person. Another person who happened to be a woman.

That thought gave him pause. He tilted his face toward the sky, trying to recall how long it had been. Time had a way of slipping past unnoticed.

The tiny, dark-haired female had boldly gotten his attention. He grinned. Knee-high boots were not his style, but something about her had radiated past her appearance. He shook his head and started walking again. He needed to get back to the task at hand. Guilt roared at him. He had no right to flirt with anyone.

With a quick flip of his wrist, he checked the time. In order to make his lunch date, he had to get in and out of the post office undetected by any well-meaning parishioners.

With a slow pull on the glass door to ensure the bells remained silent, John slipped into the small post office and held his breath. With a swift glance to his left, he found the room clear.

Today he would not break his promise to the girls. He would be home by noon. A grin pulled at the corners of his mouth as he thought of all the whispering and giggling involved in planning a surprise picnic for him. He never seemed to spend enough time with them.

Small-town life had become much more complicated than he'd imagined when he'd accepted the job as senior pastor four years ago.

He pulled the envelopes from the square compartment and gently closed the long brass door to box 1, feeling like a CIA spy behind enemy lines…almost free.

"Oh, Pastor John, what a pleasant surprise. What brings you into the post office so early?"

Caught. For a split second, his shoulders sagged, and he closed his eyes.

"Pastor John? Is everything okay? I have the cranberry-oatmeal cookies you love so much." Postmistress for the past thirty years, Emily Martin spoke around her daily chicken-salad sandwich. "They're in the back."

Relaxing tight muscles, John put on his welcoming

smile and glanced down at the tiny woman who made him feel taller than his six-foot frame.

"No, thanks. The girls are waiting for me." He glanced at his escape route. Fondness for the sweet lady won over. "How are you today, Miss Emily?"

"Oh, those babies—that oldest looks just like her momma, poor thing. Well, my sister is pestering me again about Momma's house and my knee is bothering me, which I hope means we'll be getting some rain—the ground's so dry—but other than that, I can't complain." She swallowed her last bite. "It's all in God's hands, right, Pastor John?"

"Yes, it is." John glanced behind Emily again, to the door only five feet away. So close yet so far. "Well, I've got to be going. You have a nice day."

Behind his smile, John gritted his back teeth. Utter defeat consumed him as he watched Elva De La Soto, another elder member of his church, open the door. She rushed in wearing the familiar expression of tragedy on her face.

"Pastor John! I'm so glad you're here. There's been an accident at Second Crossing. It's the Campbell girl's Jeep. Is she babysitting your girls today?"

John ran to his truck and drove toward the pecan farm without a conscious thought. Fear and faith clashed in John's brain. His phone started buzzing. Recalling the phone call about his wife's accident, he froze. He stared at the unfamiliar number. If he didn't answer he could stay ignorant of any bad news. He prayed with every fiber of his being for his girls' safety.

Why had they been in the babysitter's car? They weren't allowed to travel with anyone without his permission. Amy knew his rules. His mind numb and his knuckles gripping the steering wheel, John turned onto Highway 83.

Faith would enable him to handle whatever waited for him. With a firm move, he accepted the call.

"This is John." His own voice sounded foreign.

"Daddy?" a small tentative voice came over the line.

Relief flooded his body, and his hands began to shake. John cleared his dry throat. "Hey, sweet girl. Are you okay?"

"I'm...I'm a little scared, but Rachel told me not to be. The car is upside down. A deer ran into us. Ms. Amy and Rachel are in the ambulance. Rachel told me not to cry, and Lorrie Ann said everything'll be okay." She sniffled. "Daddy, please come get me."

Amy's yellow Jeep came into view. He swallowed back the bile that rose from his stomach. Reality and memories tangled in his vision. Flashes of his wife's crumbled silver Focus clouded his eyesight. The accident had been his fault. Shaking his head, he forced himself to focus on today.

All four wheels faced the clear sky. The driver's side was smashed against a cedar break. The trees had stopped the Jeep's free fall into the river below. At the sight, his body stiffened; he could no longer feel his limbs.

His two little girls had been in that jumbled piece of metal.

John pulled his truck to an abrupt stop on the side of the highway, the loose gravel crunching under his tires. His gaze scanned the area.

The trooper's red and blue lights reflected over the people starting to mill around the crushed car. His six-year-old daughter sat on the front seat of a little BMW, her bare feet dangling in front of Lorrie Ann.

His throat closed up, and for a minute, he couldn't breathe. *Thank You, God! Thank You!*

"I'm right behind you, baby. I'm here. I'm going to hang up now, okay?"

His youngest daughter's head whipped around, searching for him. Before his boots left the old truck, she had started running to him. In a few strides, he had her pulled up close against his heart.

Her thin arms tightened around his neck, threatening to cut off his air. One hand cradled the back of her head; the other scooped up her bottom. Her legs wrapped around his torso.

"Hey, monkey. It's all right. I'm here. I've got you." He whispered into her ear, taking in the smell of her apple shampoo. He closed his eyes and for a moment focused on her heartbeat. The warmth of her tiny body absorbed into his.

Thank You, God.

He opened his eyes and found Lorrie Ann staring up at him.

"Hello again." She reached out and patted Celeste's back. "I was first on the scene. Amy and Rachel are with the EMTs. They'll be fine—just a bit more banged up." Her voice remained calm, and the softness in her eyes soothed him with the compassion he saw.

He glanced to the open doors of the ambulance. Fear slammed its way through his gut. Celeste wiggled under his tightened grip. He closed his eyes, sent a quick prayer and relaxed his muscles.

"You can take Celeste with you. I promise it's not

bad." Her smile reassured him she understood his hesitation of taking Celeste to the ambulance.

What she couldn't see? The images flashing in his mind of his wife's accident. He swallowed hard and pressed his lips against Celeste's forehead. With another prayer, he hurried across the street to his oldest daughter while carting his six-year-old on his hip.

"Rachel?" He poked his head around the door only to find Amy, his seventeen-year-old babysitter, on the stretcher. "Hello, Amy."

She wouldn't meet his gaze. "Pastor Levi, I'm so sorry. I know I wasn't supposed to take them, but they wanted apples for the chicken salad. They said it was your favorite. I'm so sorry."

"I just want y'all to be safe."

From the far side, he heard voices.

"Daddy? Are you there?" Ducking around the ambulance, he found Rachel. His stress lightened a bit at the sight of Brenda Castillo, in her blue EMT uniform, bent over his daughter's leg.

"Hello, Pastor John." Brenda smiled at Rachel. "See, I told you he would get here before we left."

"Daddy, I'm so sorry." Huge tears spilled out of her eyes. "I'm so sorry."

His chest clenched at the sight. "Oh, princess, there's nothing for you to apologize for. It was an accident." He went to bend down, but with Celeste still in his arms, he almost lost his balance.

"Here, let me help." The soft voice surprised him.

Lorrie Ann had followed them over. Before he could do anything, a pink zebra-print golf cart drew everyone's attention as it charged onto the highway. Dust flew as the small woman, Margarita Schultz, set a determined course straight at them.

"Aunt Maggie!" his daughters and Lorrie Ann yelled as one voice.

The cart threw pebbles as it slid to a stop. Without slowing down, Maggie jumped from the seat. Short black-and-silver-streaked hair flew around her face. Large dark eyes flashed with worry as she hurried over. "What is going on here, *mija?* You scared me to death with that call, young lady." She looked around, and her hand went to her chest. "Oh, no, Amy's Jeep is…" She went to her heels beside Rachel. "Oh, *mija,* are you all right?" She glanced at Brenda and then to John. "Is she going to be all right?"

"Her leg needs to be x-rayed." Brenda spoke to John. "We have it stabilized. You can take Rachel to the hospital yourself. Steve and I are taking Amy to Uvalde."

Maggie turned back to John. "You take Rachel." She put a hand out to rub the slim back of John's youngest daughter. "We'll take care of Celeste. You won't feel right until you have Rachel all safe and sound. I'll start the prayer chain."

"Are you sure, Maggie?" Torn, he pushed his daughter's loose curls behind her ear, hesitating. "Maybe I should take Celeste with me."

"You don't know how long you'll be there. We'll make sure she eats lunch. I'd get you something to eat, too, but I know you won't touch a thing until you see for yourself Rachel is fine. So go on with you."

"Thank you, Maggie." With a finger under her little pointed chin, John lifted his tiny daughter's face up to his. "Do you want to stay with Aunt Maggie?"

She nodded slowly and, to his surprise, reached for

Lorrie Ann. Maggie's niece extended her arms, pulling the little precious body from him. He reluctantly let her go.

In truth, he wanted to hold on to her forever, but he needed to get to Rachel and focus on her. "Lorrie Ann, thanks for being here and staying with them."

"I'm glad I could help."

Her smile held him mesmerized for a moment, until he heard Maggie's gasp. She had noticed the bruise under Lorrie Ann's eye.

"Were you hurt, too?"

"No. It's just a bump. Go on," she said to him. "You need to get Rachel to the doctor."

As a pastor, he had gotten good at spotting a guilty face, and Lorrie Ann's screamed guilt as she sliced a look back from him to her aunt. They both knew the bruise had been there before the accident.

With a last kiss on Celeste's forehead, he promised to return soon.

Lorrie Ann watched as John carried his injured daughter across the street. Her heart ached at the careful tenderness he used to settle her in the cab of his old Ford.

She wondered what it felt like to be cherished that way. With a shake of her head, she forced her attention back to the child and Aunt Maggie. "Well, ladies, ready to go to the house?"

"I want to ride in the zebra car."

"No, you go on with Lorrie Ann. I'm going to speak to a few people." Maggie turned and cut off a small crowd heading their way, sacrificing herself to the persistent string of questions. Lorrie Ann gratefully dodged the mob and hurried to her BMW.

She buckled her new friend in and headed for the ranch house up the hill.

"Do you live close by, Celeste?"

Celeste twisted and stretched from her seat belt, looking out the window. Her blond curls bounced with each bob of her head.

"Yes, ma'am, we live in the big cabin there—the one behind Aunt Maggie's house." She pointed and turned back to Lorrie with a grin.

Lorrie fought the urge to bang her head against the steering wheel. Of course they did. Where else would he live, other than the cabin a few steps from her aunt's back door?

Chapter Three

Lorrie Ann paused at the wrought-iron gate that led to the terra-cotta-paved courtyard. Wisteria and roses climbed the white stucco walls. The large ranch house rambled off both sides of the patio. Lorrie Ann smiled at the turquoise door.

All the hours and years she'd spent waiting for her mother to come back rushed in and filled her mind.

"Are we waiting for Aunt Maggie?"

The child's voice pulled her back to the present. She smiled down at the rumpled-looking doll and took the small hand in hers.

"No, just caught up in some memories." Pulling air through her nose and slowly releasing her breath, she took one step forward. "Let's go to the kitchen door. I bet she has something we can heat up for lunch."

Obviously familiar with the home, Celeste headed to the breezeway. The traffic-worn stones gave testimony that family and friends went straight to the back door.

Stepping into the kitchen, Lorrie Ann had the unexpected urge to cry. Spices from all the meals cooked over the years lingered in the air. The clay bean pot and flat cast-iron griddle sat on the old white stove.

"Did you live here when you were a little girl?" Celeste asked as she twirled in the middle of the large open kitchen. "I want tortillas. Do you think she has some *papas?*"

"Now, that is a word I have not heard in a while." Lorrie Ann opened the refrigerator door and dug around until she found an old margarine tub with cubed potatoes that had been panfried. "Here we go—*papas!*"

"And tortillas!" Celeste held a wicker basket of tortillas like a trophy. "But I'm not allowed to touch the stove."

Lorrie Ann turned on the burner and adjusted the flame.

"After school, my cousin, Yolanda, and I would race in here to fight over the first tortilla." Maggie's daughter always argued that since she was younger by four years and it was her mother who made them that she should get the first one.

At the counter that separated the kitchen from the dining room, Celeste jumped on a stool and started spinning in circles. "Is Aunt Maggie your real aunt? Did your mom and dad live here, too?"

"Maggie is my mom's older sister. My mom traveled, so I just stayed here." The story slipped from her lips naturally as she flipped the tortilla.

"What about your dad?" The child spun the chair in the opposite direction.

"My father?" A good question her mother never answered. "Um…well. He's gone."

"He's dead?"

Lorrie Ann gasped. "Oh, no." What had she done?

"Oh, oh, no. I mean...I don't know. No, uh..." How did she get out of this?

"You don't know? I'll ask Daddy to pray for him. Rachel says he has the most important job in the world."

Lorrie Ann scooped the potatoes into the warm tortilla. She glanced at the door. "Aunt Maggie should be here any minute." With plate in hand, she turned away from the stove to face the child.

Celeste's head popped up over a pyramid made of red cups. Her tongue stuck out between rows of tiny white teeth.

Lorrie Ann froze. "Oh, my...you...um...you need to sit down."

"I just need to add the last guard to my castle." She balanced the spoon against the side of the top cup, but as she pulled away, the whole structure collapsed.

Heart in her throat, Lorrie Ann dropped the plate on the counter and rushed to grab Celeste before she fell. "I think it would be better if you didn't stand on a swivel chair." With a heavy sigh, she started picking up the cups.

Celeste joined her. "I'm sorry, Miss Lorrie Ann. My sister says I need to learn to sit still." Her voice sounded subdued.

With a forced smile, she faced the little girl. "No harm done." She patted her on the head. "It's okay, rug rat." They put the last cup back on the counter. "See, everything's back in place and nothing broken. But I would suggest not standing on moving chairs." She patted the seat. "Cool tower, by the way."

"Thanks." The smile beamed again.

"Here you go. Time to eat." She scanned her brain for a safe topic. "I think I saw grapes. Do you want some?"

She went back to the refrigerator and pulled out a clear bag full of the fruit. While washing them, she glanced out the big picture window, hoping to see her aunt. She sighed at the empty driveway and tore off a small bunch of grapes for Celeste.

"Oh, I can't eat whole grapes. Daddy says they have to be cut in half so I don't choke. Hot dogs, too." She tossed a cubed potato in her mouth. "Why do they call the purple crayon *grape* when grapes are green? Will you please cut them? Daddy won't let me use a knife."

"Sure." She pulled a small knife from the same drawer they had been in twelve years ago.

"I tell Daddy that only babies eat cut grapes, but he says I'll always be his baby." She stuck out her tongue and scrunched her little nose.

"In Los Angeles, cut grapes are gourmet food. I only eat sliced grapes myself." She pulled a white plastic knife from the drawer and handed it over to Celeste. "Here, you can use a plastic knife."

Together they sliced the grapes. Lorrie Ann tossed one up to catch in her mouth, but it bounced off her chin, causing the sweetest giggle to come from the other side of the counter. She closed one eye and looked at the little girl with the other. "Hey! Are you laughing at me?"

Celeste sat up straight. Her ponytail swung with the shake of her head while her shoulders trembled as she failed to hold down her laughter.

Both turned at the sound of the screen door opening.

"Aunt Maggie, look! Miss Lorrie Ann taught me how to make gourmet grapes."

"She has always been very creative." She smiled at them then headed to the red wall phone. "Give me a minute. I need to start the prayer chain and call your grandpa."

"He's at the five hundred pasture today, Aunt Maggie."

Maggie ran her finger down a list of names. "Well, then, I'll just leave him a message." She pushed the buttons on the phone. Bare spots on the twisted ten-foot cord exposed colored cables.

Lorrie Ann smiled. "Do you ever think about getting a cordless?"

"Oh, Yolanda bought me one of those, but I lose it all the time. This one works just fine." As she listened to the rings on the other end, she glanced around the kitchen. "Where'd Celeste go?"

With a gasp, Lorrie Ann turned to the empty chair the little girl had been sitting on, and her heart froze in her chest. How did she lose one little person? "Celeste?"

She moved through the large archway that led to the family room. "Celeste?" Behind her, she heard muffled giggling. Shooting her aunt a questioning look, she only received a smile and shrug. Aunt Maggie turned to finish her phone call.

So, she was on her own again with the small creature. "Celeste, where are you?" She started scanning the floor and under the counter.

Huddled in a ball under the ten-foot pine table, Celeste giggled again.

Lorrie Ann went to the floor. "May I ask why you're hiding in the chair legs?"

"I'm a rabbit and this is my home."

"How about a movie?" Aunt Maggie asked from across the room.

Celeste wiggled her nose. "Okay." She started hopping out then stopped. "You'll stay with me?"

The same golden-brown eyes Lorrie Ann had looked into this morning pierced her heart. What would it be like to see your own features in a child? She doubted she'd ever know.

"Sure."

Less than fifteen minutes into some princess movie, Celeste fell asleep, curled up like a kitten with her head resting on Lorrie Ann's thigh. She closed her eyes and tilted her head back on the overstuffed leather sofa.

Aunt Maggie walked into the living room. "I figured she'd go to sleep." One click of the remote and the princess's song went silent. "Now, Lorrie Ann Ortega, you will tell me what happened that brought you home."

Lorrie Ann kept her eyes closed and wondered how long she could fake sleep.

"I know you aren't asleep."

Apparently less than a minute. With a heavy sigh, she opened her eyes.

"I needed to get away. Once I was on IH 10, coming here just felt right." She rubbed her arms and studied the sleeping child in her lap. "I really don't want to talk about it right now. I have the holidays off, so here I am. After Christmas I'll go back to L.A. recharged and ready to take on the world again."

"Is it your fiancé?" Her aunt's voice turned quiet. "Does it have anything to do with that bruise?"

"Now that I'm here I'm fine." *As long as I don't become my mother.* "You don't need to worry about Brent. That's definitely off, no regrets, no maybes about it. We are over."

"Okay, then." She reached over and picked up her

quilting hoop. "This is your home. I'm glad you're here." She placed her purple reading glasses low on her nose and contemplated the stitching in her hands. "We can throw a party."

Lorrie Ann groaned and ran her hands through her hair. Ugh, she needed a shower. She rested her head on the back of the sofa. "There are people who won't be happy I'm back." The one thing she regretted most was bringing shame to Aunt Maggie and Uncle Billy. "You know I didn't leave on the best of terms."

Aunt Maggie slipped off her glasses and moved to sit next to Lorrie Ann. Reaching past Celeste, she put her hand on Lorrie Ann's shoulder. "*Mija,* I have prayed every day that God brings you back to your family." A soft smile eased its way across her milk-chocolate skin. She pushed a piece of hair away from Lorrie Ann's face. "Let the petty high-school drama go."

At her aunt's soft touch, Lorrie Ann felt like a little girl again.

"When you're ready, you can talk to me." She gently squeezed her shoulder. "But know this...you sitting here is an answer to many, many prayers."

Uncomfortable with the love in her aunt's gaze, Lorrie Ann turned her head and closed her eyes to block the feelings of guilt. Instead, she focused on the heartbeat of the sleeping child in her lap.

Maggie stood and placed her quilting hoop back in the basket. "I need to call around to make sure Amy's parents have meals."

Lorrie Ann relaxed and closed her eyes again but couldn't shut off her brain.

Her hand moved to stroke the silky blond hair of

the little person in her lap. She smiled, thinking of Celeste's father.

Her gaze fell across the family pictures on the bookshelf. Smiling faces of her many aunts and uncles along with all the cousins crowded together in mismatched frames. She lingered over the only picture of her with her mother. Blue-and-purple icing smeared on both their faces at her tenth birthday, the last birthday she'd spent with her mom. Happiness filled the face of the little girl she had been, thinking her mother would stay.

She realized returning to the farm, she wanted to find the family she never really knew and the only place she had felt God.

The image of John holding his daughters crossed her mind and melted her heart. What would it have been like to have that kind of father? Her mother had refused to say her father's name. Lorrie Ann had eventually stopped asking.

She watched her manicured nail make little circles on Celeste's shirt. John's life reflected God. Hers? Not so much.

She rested her cheek on her other hand supported by the arm of the sofa. Even though she shouldn't want to see more of his dream-changing smiles, she found herself listening for an old blue truck's tires on the gravel driveway.

Chapter Four

John turned the key and shut the engine off. Sitting in the silence, he watched the full moon reflect over the river below. Rachel had fallen asleep on the way home, her leg now in a black stabilizer from ankle to the top of her thigh. In a few days when the swelling went down, he'd have to take her back for the cast. Her apologies had run nonstop. Several times, he reassured her it would be fine, but his preteen seemed to pick up his doubts.

All the problems bounced around his brain. With his eyes closed, he pressed his forehead against the cracked steering wheel.

"God, I know worry is a sin. Please show me how I can be the pastor people need and the father my girls deserve."

The to-do list started clicking off in his head. The youth building still needed funds, his house sat gutted and Dub needed help with the ranch. The big annual Christmas pageant loomed around the corner, with no one to direct it. He sighed. Now Rachel required extra help, and his babysitter, Amy, was out while she recovered.

Deep in thought, he jumped when a hand pounded on his window. He opened the door, but before he could move, Celeste had climbed into his lap. Her small hands framed his face.

"Hello, Daddy."

He smiled and covered her precious fingers with his hands. "Hey, monkey. How are you?" He turned to Lorrie Ann, Celeste's late-night escort, and grinned. Was it only this morning they'd first met? "Did she cause you any problems?"

She shook her head. "No, we had fun."

"Daddy, I was good, and Miss Lorrie Ann let me use a knife."

He shot a heated glare to the woman who had kept creeping into his mind all day. "You let a five-year-old use a *knife?*"

"No, no, it was a plastic knife. You know, the small picnic ones."

"Daddy, I'm six now. I turned six at the football game. I could cut my own grapes." She rested her head on his shoulder, facing her sister. "What's wrong with her leg?"

"It's broken. I need to get her into the house."

"Come here, rug rat. Let your dad out of the truck, and we can get you all settled in the cabin."

His daughter giggled as she reached for Lorrie Ann's hand.

"She calls me rug rat, Daddy, because they're cute, real smart and are always moving around." She swung her arm back and forth. "Right, Miss Lorrie Ann?"

"Yes, ma'am." Lorrie Ann brought her face back to his. "Aunt Maggie sent some dinner over." With her free hand, she lifted a foil-covered plate.

Celeste led Lorrie Ann toward the porch. The security light automatically flooded the area as they reached the steps.

"It's unlocked." They went inside as he made his way around the truck feeling much older than his thirty-one years.

He opened the passenger door and slipped his arms under Rachel. Careful of her leg, he pulled her to him. She was eleven now. For a moment, he pulled her closer and closed his eyes. When was the last time he had carried her from the car? So many moments in life just slipped past without thought or fanfare.

Headlights came up the driveway and parked behind his truck. His head slumped for a minute as he hoped it was not some concerned member of his congregation, but then he prayed for forgiveness and patience.

"Are our girls all right?"

Relief relaxed his shoulders as his father-in-law's baritone voice came from the dark. He should have known a phone call wouldn't be enough.

"Hey, Dub. Celeste doesn't have a scratch on her. Rachel has a broken leg. Amy has the most injuries, with a broken collarbone and concussion. They kept her overnight."

"Daddy?" Rachel's head lifted.

"Hey, sweetheart, we're home. And look, Grandpa's here."

"Hi, Grandpa." Her head went back to his chest.

Dub followed, carrying the silver crutches and closing all the doors behind them.

John scanned the open living room and kitchen area. He grimaced at the shoes, books and crayons scattered on the area rug. The kitchen had a stack of dirty dishes in the sink, and it looked as if the girls had been making sandwiches before they left for town.

"Grandpa!" Celeste flew down the wrought-iron spiral staircase.

"Celeste Rebecca Levi, slow down." She froze midstride, and he noticed Lorrie Ann's eyes go wide. He must have managed to use his best angry-dad voice. Somewhere in the past couple hours, he'd switched to autopilot. He felt empty. He eased Rachel to one side of the large L-shaped sofa and moved a cushion under her leg.

"Sorry, Daddy. I wanted to show Miss Lorrie Ann my room." With a hand on the railing, she took one slow step down. Dub went to the stairs and picked her up, swinging her above his head.

"Higher, Grandpa, higher!" Her laughter filled the cabin.

"Dub, you're not helping." John went to the kitchen to retrieve a bag of frozen peas.

"Humph." He pulled his granddaughter close and tickled her before he looked up at Lorrie Ann. "Hello, I'm Dub Childress." Celeste wrapped herself around his barrel chest and pushed his gray felt hat back, kissing his cheek.

"Grandpa, this is Miss Lorrie Ann. She's my new friend. She let me cut my own grapes."

"Maggie and Billy's girl? I remember you. Weren't you a few grades behind Carol?"

"Yes, sir. Carol Childress? Oh, she… I'm sorry."

John watched as awareness then pity filled her gray eyes. He knew what would come next. On cue, she became awkward as she looked around the room, moving to the double glass doors.

"This is not what I expected when I heard they had added cabins to the farm. It's beautiful and comfortable." She ran her fingers along the rock edge of the fireplace, stopping in front of the family picture he had on the mantel. She quickly turned.

"I thought they were summer rentals. I didn't know they had them rented for living."

"Maggie was nice enough to take us in when we had nowhere to go." John adjusted the frozen bag on Rachel's leg. "Dub gave us the old homestead to live in, but it needed to be gutted and made livable, so we are here until I can get that finished."

Lorrie Ann hurried past him. "Oh, Maggie said to make sure you ate dinner."

In the kitchen, she started making beeping noises with the microwave.

He'd grown accustomed to women trying to feed him, but it was a first for one to take over his kitchen.

"You don't need to heat that up for me."

"Have you eaten?"

"No."

"Well, then, you're getting a warm meal. I promised Aunt Maggie."

Dub chuckled and John shot him a glare. Dub's bushy gray brows shot up but he remained silent.

Celeste's head jerked and her eyes popped open.

"Thank you for taking care of Celeste." John watched his baby girl fight sleep and smiled.

Dub stood. "She can be a handful. That's for sure." With those words, he laid Celeste in the wingback chair. "Well, I just wanted to see the little bits and make sure they were okay." He moved to the entryway and paused.

"If you need anything, John, call me. I'm heading to Houston tomorrow, but I can cancel."

"Dub, go on to Houston. We're fine." He pushed Rachel's hair back from her face.

"Nice seeing you again, Mr. Childress." Lorrie Ann had moved to the sink and started running water.

"Please call me Dub. And welcome back. I know your aunt must sure be happy."

"Lorrie Ann, you're not washing the dishes." John tried to make his voice sound firm.

"Um…yes, I am."

Dub chuckled again and headed out the door.

"Really, Lorrie Ann, you don't have to do the dishes."

The microwave went off, and she turned to get the food out. Setting the plate on the counter, she dug around for some silverware.

"The girls are asleep. Come eat or Aunt Maggie will get mad at both of us."

He sat and attempted to give her a smile, but it felt more like a halfhearted contortion.

"Anything else I can do for you tonight?" She looked around the small kitchen.

"No, we're good, and you can report back that I ate." He saluted her with his fork before taking a bite.

After a few more mouthfuls, he set the fork down and made sure he had solid eye contact with Lorrie Ann before saying anything else. "Again, I want to thank you for keeping Celeste. She can be a bit high-strung, and some people find her energy level overwhelming."

"I deal with musicians and agents on a daily basis. Handling high energy and mood swings is my specialty."

Her sweet smile was at odds with the image he had of

a music-industry insider from California. As she walked out of the cabin, John followed her. "You must be exhausted driving in from California today. Have you spoken to your mother yet?"

She stopped at the steps with her hand on the railing, turning back to him. "My mother? How do you know Sonia? I haven't heard from her in over three years."

"Oh." He didn't know what to say. Sonia had wanted to be sure of her sobriety before talking to Lorrie Ann. She should have contacted her by now. If she hadn't, he had just opened a nasty can of night crawlers. "She visits Maggie."

Lorrie Ann's eyes went wide. "Really? Do you know where she's living?"

"Have you asked Maggie?" He needed to talk to Maggie and find out what was going on. He had promised Sonia to keep their talks private. Did that include her daughter? He knew she struggled with guilt over her past with Lorrie Ann, and guilt did weird things to people, led to bad decisions. Was she still avoiding Lorrie Ann?

"I'll do that." She paused for a minute, her lips tight. Glancing down, she broke eye contact.

John waited, and when she brought her gaze back to his, she smiled and whispered, "Good night, Pastor Levi."

"Please, call me John."

He watched as she made her way back to the ranch house. An unfamiliar loss at her departure settled softly in his chest.

He wanted to spend more time with her, hear her laughter and watch her smile. He shook his head and turned back to the cabin.

It had been thirteen years since he had asked some-one out on a date, and he had ended up married to her.

He stopped. Where had that thought come from? Un-wanted memories surfaced, and John closed and locked the door, both physically and mentally. Even contem-plating a relationship with Lorrie Ann needed to stop.

He felt confident in his work for God and tried hard to be a good father, but he had made a lousy husband. He wished he could close the door on the hurt in Carol's eyes as he locked the door behind Lorrie Ann.

His wife had deserved a better husband, but by the time he'd realized that, it had been too late.

Chapter Five

Tuesday slipped by quietly into Wednesday morning.
The sun slid through Lorrie Ann's window, and she just
lay there. A slow smile eased across her face when she
realized she had nowhere to be, no appointment to make
and no people to mollify or manipulate. She could lie
in bed all day if she wanted.

Her forehead creased. She did have one thing she
needed to do. Quick thumbs and the text to Melissa,
the lead singer of the band, was sent. With a satisfying
thump, she closed the drawer with the cell phone inside.
She had a few weeks to hide.

Shoving the guilt aside, Lorrie Ann reminded herself that everyone deserved a holiday, and hers would
be in the Lone Star State this year.

She sighed. What she really needed was a new job.
There was no way she and Brent could work together.
If her boss, Melissa, had to pick between the talented
but troubled drummer and the band's manager, Lorrie
Ann figured she would be the one to go.

Once dressed, she headed outside. Bible in hand, her
other hand trailed over the smooth worn cedar railing of

the zigzag stairs leading to the river below the cabins. The cool October breeze ruffled her hair as she made her way to the edge of the Frio. The flow of the river had changed since she'd left.

With her hand on one of the large cypress trees, she slipped off her shoes and stepped into cold, clear water. In California, she'd been so focused on being successful she'd misplaced her love for the outdoors.

"Miss Lorrie Ann, Miss Lorrie Ann. Hello!" Celeste's excited voice drifted down from the top of the cliff.

Lorrie Ann cupped her hand over her eyes to block the sun as she turned to find the six-year-old hanging over the edge of their balcony. "Hi to you, Celeste. Hear you're coming over today for a visit."

"Daddy has to take Rachel in to get casted. Can we cut some more grapes?"

"Sure. Thought we could make some cookies, too."

The little girl started to jump up and down. "Yeah! We can take some to Amy." Celeste leaned over the railing, suspended over the cliff.

"Celeste Rebecca Levi, put your feet on the floor right now!" John's stern voice came from the cabin door behind Celeste.

She looked back to the cabin and pointed down to the river. "Sorry, Daddy. Miss Lorrie Ann's in the river."

A few seconds later he appeared next to his daughter, one arm wrapped around the precocious six-year-old. "Hey there, Lorrie Ann. Hope you're well rested." His mussed hair fell across his forehead as he looked down at her. "Isn't the river cold?" The sun emphasized the highlights streaked in his dark blond hair. She knew men who paid hundreds of dollars to get coloring like his. Without a doubt, nature created his color.

"Maybe, but it feels good." She shrugged and smiled up at them, placing her hand over her heart. "I believe I should be reciting from *Romeo and Juliet*."

His laughter soothed her as much as the clear water running over the rocks.

Nose wrinkled, Celeste leaned over and asked, "What's Romeo and Julie?"

"Juliet," John corrected.

Lorrie Ann threw her arms wide. "A love story with a tragic ending. Poor Romeo stood under Juliet's balcony and professed his undying love."

"Then Daddy should be Romeo and you, the beautiful princess. Is Juliet a princess?"

"Monkey, I think Lorrie Ann wanted quiet time, not a literary discussion." He picked her up and swung her onto his hip.

"Quiet time? But that's boring." One small arm wrapped around her father's neck, Celeste slanted over the edge with a puzzled look on her face. "Miss Lorrie Ann, were you really wanting quiet time?"

"Well, I was thinking about finding a place to pray and think."

"Oh, I'm sorry. Daddy likes quiet time, too. But he does it at the church. Maybe you can go to the church with Daddy."

Even from the river, she could see the lines around John's eyes deepen with his smile. "Come on, monkey. Let's leave her to her solitude." He patted her back. "Sorry about the interruption, Lorrie Ann."

"Oh, please, don't apologize. I'll see you in a little bit, rug rat."

"Bye, Miss Lorrie Ann. Tell God hi for me." She waved as John turned them toward the door. "Daddy, what does *literinary* mean?"

Lorrie Ann couldn't stop the smile as she looked down at her toes beneath the water. Curious little minnows started checking out her feet.

In a few hours, the family would be eating dinner together before heading to Prayer Night at the church. The smile slipped away. Thinking of her cousin, Yolanda, caused old hurts to boil up from the deep places she thought buried.

Back then she had been afraid Aunt Maggie would side with her real daughter. Lorrie Ann remembered living for the day she would leave this small town, proving to everyone she mattered. Truth be told, she was still a little afraid what would happen if Aunt Maggie had to choose between them.

With a deep breath she closed her eyes, focusing on the sounds around her: the water, the wind dancing through the trees and the leaves floating to the ground.

"God, I've come back to find You. I know it's been a long time, and I'm not sure what to do. I've messed up so much I need You to show me the way to go." She stepped farther into the river. "I don't want Aunt Maggie to be hurt. Please show me what to say to my cousin, Yolanda."

She waded down the riverbank to a little platform. On the other side a ladder dropped down to a swimming hole with a long flat rock creating a natural edge. Above it hung a thick corded rope.

Climbing to the platform, she sat and dangled her legs in the water. Running her fingers along the pages, she opened her Bible to the prayer in Ephesians and read how much God loved her.

A noise on the steps alerted her to someone's presence. Turning, she raised her eyebrows at the sight of Celeste hopping down the stairs with one hand on the railing.

When the little girl spotted Lorrie Ann looking at her, she crouched on the step and whispered, "Are you finished with your quiet time?"

Lorrie Ann closed the Bible and grinned. Who knew a child could be so entertaining? "Yes, rug rat. Does your father know you're down here?" She glanced up to the cabins.

"He sent me over to Aunt Maggie's house." She skipped the rest of the way to Lorrie Ann and sat down, crisscrossing her legs. With her elbows on her knees, she rested her chin on her intertwined fingers. "Are we still talking to God or the fish?" She intently stared into the water.

"Um…well, I kind of ran out of things to say to God, and I've never talked to fish before. You talk to fish?"

Celeste rolled her legs around and flopped onto her tummy. With one hand under her chin, she dipped the other in the water.

"Yes." She looked up at Lorrie Ann with a big smile. "It tickles when they nibble on you. They're my pets." She moved her gaze back to the water. "Shh…there's Rainbow—he's the biggest." They both sat still staring at the fish underwater as he stared back at them. They waited in silence. Lorrie Ann smiled when she realized she was in a staring contest with a fish.

"Celeste Rebecca Levi!" They both jumped at the sound of John's voice. "I told you to go to Aunt Maggie's house. You are not allowed down by the river." His long strides had him by their side in seconds. "You can't be interrupting Lorrie Ann's prayer time."

He stood over them, hands on his hips. Lorrie Ann arched her neck back to look up at him. It just seemed wrong that a man of God would look so good. Wasn't there some rule about pastors being old grandfatherly types?

His cotton polo shirt fit just right over his broad shoulders and tucked neatly into his jeans. In silence, he stared down at them. Celeste jumped to her feet, her small body mirroring her father's stance as she fisted both hands on her hips.

Lorrie Ann squirmed, feeling like a kid caught skipping school. "Oh, it's all right. I saw her and called her down. I…um…finished—" she waved her hand in circles "—you know…praying."

He raised one eyebrow and grinned at her, probably amused about her stumbling over words he used all the time.

"Daddy, Rainbow almost came to me. You scared him away." She looked back into the river, searching the clear deep water for the fish.

He crouched down, balancing on his heels. He rested one hand on Celeste's shoulder and brought his gaze to rest on Lorrie Ann's face. "Are you sure she's not bothering you?"

For a minute she couldn't breathe, feeling lost in his eyes, but she managed to shake her head.

"Well, then I'm heading out. Are y'all good for the day? Need anything before I leave?"

Lorrie Ann gave a quick nod, still unable to speak.

"Give me a hug, monkey." He held his arms open.

Celeste leaped at him, kissing his cheek. "Love you, Daddy. Hurry back."

"We'll be back for dinner. See you then, Lorrie Ann." He flashed another heart-stopping smile and then headed up the stairs. Her gaze stayed locked on him as he bounded up the steps, two at a time.

"Do you like Daddy?" Celeste had flopped back on her belly, hanging her chin over the edge of the platform.

Lorrie Ann shot a startled frown at the back of the little girl's head. "What do you mean?"

Celeste twisted back around and wrinkled her nose. "A lot of ladies at the church look funny at Daddy, the way you just did." She threw a small rock into the water. "Some of them said I need a mom." She threw another rock. "Rachel says they're just busybodies wanting to marry Daddy and we don't like them." Jumping to her feet, she started gathering some more small rocks. "You're fun. If you wanted to be my mommy I wouldn't be mad. Rachel might be, though."

The bottom of her stomach fell. The thought of being anyone's mother horrified her.

Celeste started tossing the rocks sideways. "Rachel knows how to skip rocks. Daddy told me to keep practicing and I'd get it." She wrapped her fingers around another rock, her tongue sticking out between her teeth.

Lorrie Ann held her breath as she watched the rock fly. With a slight skip, it bounced back up once before dropping under the water. A huge smile filled her face.

Screaming, Celeste turned to Lorrie Ann, jumping up and down. "I did it! I did it! Did you see?"

Lorrie Ann laughed and clapped her hands. "Yeah! That was awesome, Celeste!"

As she twirled in circles, the little girl's ponytail swung out. "I skipped a rock!"

Out of breath, Maggie appeared at the top of the stairs. "Lorrie Ann? Celeste? Is everyone all right? What happened?"

Lorrie Ann laughed aloud, her smile feeling too large for her face. "Celeste skipped a rock!"

"I did! I did, Aunt Maggie! It skipped right over the water just like Rachel's and Daddy's." She squeezed her hands together in front of her, her body trembling.

"Celeste, you scared me half to death. If you two are going to make cookies for tonight, you had better get up here. No more lollygagging." With those words, she turned and disappeared.

"What do you say? Ready to go up and make those cookies?" Lorrie Ann dusted off a bit of gravel and leaves from her black cropped pants.

"Please don't tell Daddy. I want to surprise him."

"No problem, rug rat. Um…and you won't mention anything about the funny way I looked at him, right? I don't want him or Rachel to worry." She didn't know whether to laugh or cry at the thought of her, married to a small-town pastor.

Celeste pulled her out of the altered universe when she grabbed her hand, looking at her as if she'd gone crazy. She snorted. *Crazy* was a good word for her life.

"It's okay, Miss Lorrie Ann. Daddy says gossiping about people is hurtful. I won't tell your secret."

With that, the rug rat skipped up the stairs.

Great—the only thing between her and complete humiliation was a precocious six-year-old.

Chapter Six

As Lorrie Ann approached the kitchen later that evening, she faltered a moment and took a deep breath, willing the knot in her stomach to ease. With her best let's-do-lunch smile, she tossed her hair back and stepped through the archway, one high-heeled boot at a time.

She had spent thirty minutes changing into and out of clothes. In the end, she'd put on her Los Angeles armor.

Reaching out with both hands, she greeted her cousin. "Yolanda! It's been so long."

Yolanda's dark green eyes widened and for a second her mouth dropped open as her gaze took in the burgundy leggings and the silk blouse. But then again, Lorrie Ann thought, her cousin's surprise might have something to do with the five-inch brown leather boots that covered her knees.

Yolanda pushed the loose ends of her hair from her face, trying to adjust her ponytail.

Yolanda had taken after her dad in height and stood about seven inches taller than Lorrie Ann. Because of the boots, they almost met eye to eye.

"Oh, wow, L.A., you look—" Yolanda stepped forward into a quick hug "—great. It's been so long."

Maggie joined them. "Now, Lorrie Ann, I told you this was a casual family dinner." Her gentle voice had an unusual sharp edge. "Why did you get all dressed up?"

"This?" Lorrie Ann ran her hand over her silk shirt. "It's my first family dinner in twelve years." She gave Yolanda a tight smile.

Yolanda bit her lip. "Excuse me. I need to clean up." With a glare to Lorrie Ann, she brushed past her and headed down the hallway to her old room.

Turning back to the kitchen, Lorrie Ann met Aunt Maggie's dark eyes. The smirk fell from her face, and she felt as if she had been caught stealing Uncle Billy's last cookie.

"What?" With her arms crossed, Lorrie Ann suppressed the need to squirm under her aunt's scrutiny. "I didn't do anything." She gave a heavy sigh and rolled her eyes. *Okay, so I have officially reverted to an insecure teenage girl.* "People expect me to be a certain way, you know, coming from Los Angeles and all."

"*Mija,* if you give people a chance, they will like the real you."

Lorrie Ann turned away from the gentle look in Aunt Maggie's eyes. Why did guilt feel so heavy and ugly?

She moved to the stove. "I'll finish warming the tortillas." As she flipped the tortillas, she heard a vehicle pull into the driveway. Celeste came rushing into the kitchen from outside.

The screen door slammed back as the hurricane of energy swirled into the room. "Lorrie Ann! Aunt Maggie! Rachel has her cast! It's purple."

"Hey, rug rat. Slow down."

"Rachel's so slow because she has to walk on the crutches and won't let Daddy help her. Aunt Maggie, Uncle Billy said to bring him the veggies."

Maggie grabbed the bowl and headed to the grill, ordering Lorrie Ann to make the tea while rubbing Celeste's head. A few breaths later, a knock on the door announced the arrival of John and Rachel.

"Hello?" John walked through the screen door then stood with his back holding it open and flashed a grin. "She insists on walking without my help."

The sound of Rachel's shuffling feet and the thump of the crutches came with agonizing slowness as they waited for her to make an appearance. When she finally made it to the door, John reached out to help her over the threshold.

"I have it, Daddy." With an awkward movement, she adjusted the crutch and managed to step up as her tongue stuck out in concentration.

John turned his face to Lorrie Ann, rolled his eyes and shook his head. "She can be a bit stubborn." He shot her a wink. "Gets it from her mom."

Celeste scooted a red step stool by the sink and started pulling out plates from overhead. "I'm stubborn, too, just like Mom. Grandpa says so."

"Celeste, get down from there! Wait until I can help you." One of John's hands stayed on the door as he tried to reach for his younger daughter with the other.

Lorrie Ann moved to Celeste. "Here, let me help you."

"Rachel always sets the table, but now I get to do it." The stack of thick milk-glass plates wobbled over her head.

Lorrie Ann reached up behind her to balance the plates and lower them to the counter.

Rachel twisted toward her father. "She can't do my job."

"Rachel, she just wants to help." His large hand covered her entire shoulder. "With the crutches, how would you carry the plates?"

"How about setting the silverware?" Lorrie Ann pointed to the table. "The basket's already there."

"Thanks," John whispered close to her ear as he walked past her to help Celeste carry plates and glasses. "I see you're back to your L.A. gear and artificial height?"

Standing in the kitchen with John, her decision to change made her feel shallow. She gave him the same weak line. "I wanted to wear something special for my first family dinner."

With his arms braced behind him, John leaned against the sink and watched the girls set the long table. "You looked nice this morning."

She shrugged and flipped another tortilla.

"Oh, you look so pretty, Miss Yolanda," Rachel suddenly called out.

Lorrie Ann turned and saw the perfect example of feminine refinement walk into the kitchen. Her cousin wore a soft green dress with a faint floral print. It swirled around her knees and complemented the low-heeled sandals on her feet. Her thick brown hair now floated in waves just below her shoulders. Lorrie Ann straightened her spine and repeated her mantra, *Smile, stand tall, fake it if you have to.*

"Daddy, I want to dress up!" Celeste jumped up and

down, clapping her hands. "Can I have some pirate boots like Miss Lorrie Ann?"

He laughed as he caught the six-year-old up in his arms. "I'm not sure a ranch is the best place for pirate boots."

Yolanda opened the cabinet door next to John. "L.A. did always love costumes."

Lorrie Ann felt like growling as she watched her cousin bat those incredibly long lashes at John. Instead, she repeated her mantra a few more times.

Yolanda continued in her soft Texas drawl, "Good evening, Pastor John. How did the trip to the doctor go today?"

"All went well. It was a clean break."

Celeste slipped out of his arms and ran off to get the napkins. Turning back to Lorrie Ann, he reached for the sugar as she poured boiling water over the tea bags.

He held out the container for her. "I want to thank you again for keeping Celeste. She went on and on about the plans you had today."

Taking the sugar from him, Lorrie Ann smiled. "To tell you the truth, I looked forward to it myself." She looked up and was struck by the gentleness in his light brown eyes. For a moment she studied the gold flakes that radiated warmth. Oh, what had she been saying? "Um…she's a great kid."

"Please, let me know if she becomes too much."

Yolanda came up and laid her hand on his sleeve. "You know I can watch the girls whenever you need help."

Before he could reply, Aunt Maggie and Uncle Billy brought in the fajitas and grilled vegetables.

"Is the table set? Ice in the glasses?" Maggie set the

platter of meat and bell peppers on the table and smiled. "Looks nice, girls."

"I got the plates and glasses, Aunt Maggie." Celeste ran from the table to the refrigerator. "I can get the ice, too!"

In a voice too prim for a young girl, Rachel yelled after her sister. "Celeste Rebecca Levi, you need to sit down." She lowered her voice and squinted. "You're going to give Daddy a headache."

John's rich laughter filled the room as he lightly pulled Rachel close to his side. "Thank you, sweetheart, but I think I'll survive."

Uncle Billy got the ice instead. After bringing out the rest of the food, Aunt Maggie sat down next to her husband. "Come on, everyone. Let's eat before it gets cold."

Lorrie Ann reached for her old chair and collided with John's hand. They both yanked back.

"That's Daddy's chair," Rachel informed her. "He always sits there next to me."

"Oh, I'm so sorry."

"No, you take it." His now-familiar grin made her forget about dinner. "We don't have assigned seating— just creatures of habit." He looked over at Rachel. "It's good to shake up our routine."

Uncle Billy's gruff voice snapped the air. "Can y'all sit down so I can pray?"

"Yes, sir," they answered at the same time. She slid a glance to her right and found Rachel glaring at her. To the left, John had his head bowed. Everyone joined hands. The words of her uncle's prayer slid into her heart. She had missed being part of this family worship.

As soon as the prayer finished, Aunt Maggie jumped right in. "So, Pastor John, have you had any ideas about the Christmas pageant? With Martha out of town, I don't know how we're going to get it all done. It is the hundredth anniversary, so it needs to be big."

Dread slipped through Lorrie Ann. She carefully put her filled tortilla back on her plate. "Aunt Maggie, please don't."

"Oh, *mija,* it's perfect." She handed a warm tortilla to her husband, never taking her gaze off John. "What about Lorrie Ann?"

She had to stop her aunt before she went any further. "No way."

John raised an eyebrow. "I don't think she's interested, Maggie." Filling his tortilla with meat and avocado, he shrugged his shoulders. "Vickie said she'd do it."

Yolanda snorted "Vickie? She's an awesome seamstress, but organizing and directing? She doesn't know the first thing about music."

Lorrie Ann thought of any suggestions she could make. "What about Mrs. Callaway, the high-school drama teacher? I remember her directing the pageant when I sang."

"That *is* Martha." Yolanda made it sound as if she should have known Mrs. Callaway's first name. "Her sister's having health problems, so she went to Houston to stay with her."

Aunt Maggie pointed her knife at Lorrie Ann. "Someone with the experience of organizing big music events is sitting right at this table."

Lorrie Ann gripped the knife, beating down the frustration. Disappointing her aunt seemed to be her forte. "No one in this town would want me anywhere near the pageant."

"Oh, pish-posh, that is just nonsense. The committee has been praying for someone to step up and lead the pageant." She looked at John as she poured Yolanda more iced tea. "Don't you think God is at work here?"

He took the opportunity to fill his mouth with his fajita. She watched his throat as it moved with each swallow.

The poor man needed to be rescued. "Aunt Maggie, I organized rock concerts not…church plays," Lorrie Ann tried to explain one more time.

"I can do it," Yolanda offered. "I've helped with the set and props for the last few years."

"You've done a great job, *mija,* but we need someone with a big vision. It is the pageant's hundredth-year anniversary."

Yolanda's salad became an innocent victim, each stab fiercer than the last. Her eyes stayed focused on her plate.

"Lorrie Ann played Mary when she was eleven. Remember?" Aunt Maggie looked back at John. "She's gifted with a voice so sweet." Her hands waved upward. "Her singing brought everyone to tears. You know she went to Los Angeles to start a singing career."

John smiled at her, eyebrows raised. "So that's how you got into the music industry."

Under his gaze heat slipped up her neck. "During college I discovered Hollywood was full of good singers waiting tables." She shrugged. "On the other hand, people who could organize musicians, not as common."

Yolanda pushed her beans around, talking to her plate. "I played Mary the following year." Another stab. "But Martha didn't let me sing."

"Oh, *mija,* you were born with your daddy's voice."

Maggie patted Yolanda on the arm before looking back to John. "You might have noticed in church, he couldn't carry a note if I stitched a handle on it." She chuckled at her own joke.

Uncle Billy shook his head and took another bite of his fajita.

"Aunt Maggie!"

"I don't think she wants to—" John started.

"Daddy, I'm supposed to be Mary this year!" Rachel interrupted. "But with my leg I can't walk with Joseph."

John took a deep breath before answering. "Sweetheart, we'll find something for you to do."

Now Lorrie Ann wished she had let him sit next to his daughter.

Celeste bounced in her chair next to Yolanda. "Can I be Mary? Can I?"

"No! You can't—you're too young," Rachel bit at her sister. "Daddy, I've been waiting to be Mary all year!"

Lorrie Ann struggled with placing an arm around Rachel's shoulders. Maybe she should just talk to her. "There are other parts just as important to the story."

Lorrie Ann's heart broke at the sight of the girl fighting back tears.

The ponytail bounced with a nod. "I can be in the choir again." She leaned forward to see her father and blinked her eyes before forcing a smile on her face.

Lorrie Ann gave in and placed her hand on Rachel's arm. "What about a narrating angel? Talk to the shepherds and warn the wise men. We could use one of the farm's cherry pickers to lift you above the audience. Then you wouldn't even have to walk—you'd be flying." She gave Rachel a tentative smile. "You'd make a perfect angel."

Aunt Maggie flashed an I-told-you-so grin. "Look, she is a natural—already solving problems."

Lorrie Ann rolled her head back. "No, I just—"

Celeste sat on her knees and clapped her hands. "Please, Miss Lorrie Ann. I want to be in the play."

Rachel snapped at Celeste again. "You're too young."

Lorrie Ann softened at the sight of the small drooping shoulders. Her tiny kindred spirit pulled at her. Against her better judgment, she threw out another idea. "Maybe the kinder group can open the pageant with candles."

John's sharp intake of breath gave her the first clue that this might not be her best idea, the look on his face her second.

"Celeste with fire…real fire?"

The tiny shoulders popped up and the clapping started again. "I could do it." She practically stood in her chair. "Oh… Oh… What about Jenny, Mark and Carlos? We could all do it!" She threw her arms over her head. Yolanda encouraged her to sit back down and glared at Lorrie Ann.

"See, I can't do this."

Rachel looked at Lorrie Ann with steel in her eyes. "Kindergartners are too young to be in the pageant."

Lorrie Ann turned back to John. "Sorry."

His warm smile made her feel worse. "We'll work it out. God has a plan."

"What about you, Pastor John? You could lead the music part."

Rachel glared at her again. "Daddy doesn't do music anymore."

Uncle Billy tapped his watch, drawing all their attention.

Aunt Maggie jumped up from the table. "Oh, my, look at the time. We need to head over to the church for the prayer meeting. Pastor John, you're going to be late."

Lorrie Ann started gathering dishes.

"Oh, don't worry about those. Lorrie Ann, you go with Pastor John. Yolanda, we have to pick up Dolly." Without another word, she followed her husband out the door.

Chapter Seven

Lorrie Ann watched the screen door bounce shut with Aunt Maggie's quick exit. She sighed.

A heavy trepidation fell on her shoulders. The thought of going to the church and facing all the people from her past made her want to curl up under her quilt and never come out.

Her hands had a slight shake to them as she carried bowls to the counter and started covering them with foil.

She closed her eyes and drew in a slow deep breath. Feeling calmer, she turned back to the table and gathered more dishes. "I'm not going. I'll stay here with the girls and clean up." She focused on her voice sounding casual and nonchalant, throwing a smile over her shoulder for good measure.

John had started to scrape the dishes, and his light chuckle caused her to think she wasn't as successful as she imagined.

"Oh, no, you don't. After the Wednesday-night prayer meeting, the girls have choir. The committee meets while they're singing." He leaned a hip against the counter. "You can get information on the pageant. No commitment just information. I promise."

John took the glasses out of her hands and placed them in the sink.

"Someone once told me, we always do what Aunt Maggie says." He ended that sentence with a wink.

"Smart man." Unable to resist his charm, she smiled.

Celeste giggled while she held the door open for Rachel. "Lorrie Ann, you get to ride with us."

She needed a way out. "I can bring the girls home for you." She opened her eyes wide. "Don't you have some kind of vow to help damsels in distress? Come on. Please, give me an excuse to leave the committee meeting early. You would be rescuing me from the dragons roaming the streets of Clear Water."

His laughter rumbled deep from his chest.

"I think you're confusing me with a fairy-tale hero. Besides, the dragons aren't bad. Their intentions are good, even if a bit meddlesome at times." He looked her straight in the eyes. "Anyway, *helpless* is not a word I would associate with you."

A grateful smile eased across her face. "It's nice that you think that of me."

John cleared his throat and moved to the door. "We need to leave." She ran across his mind more than he would ever admit.

"Come on, Pastor John—taking the girls home will give me a good way out. Please?" She placed a hand on his sleeve.

He focused on her face. "Okay. You bring the girls home." He held the door open. "Come on, Lorrie Ann.

Rachel's beating us to the truck. Can you manage in those boots or do you need help?"

With a flip of her hair, she rolled her eyes and passed him to walk through the door.

John tried not to be aware of the exotic-smelling perfume mixed with sunshine. It had danced through his dreams all night. He popped a green Jolly Rancher in his mouth and followed her to the truck.

Sliding behind the steering wheel, he noticed Lorrie Ann as she glanced over her left shoulder at the girls in the backseat. She then leaned toward him and whispered in a hushed voice, "I just want to warn you, taking me to the church is asking for a disaster in your chapel. Don't be surprised if lightning strikes."

He felt one eyebrow pop up as he bit back another laugh. Man, she was fun. Leaning in, he winked at her and whispered back, "God never actually struck anyone down with lightning, not in the Bible, anyway." That was so lame. He had to stop himself from groaning aloud.

It had been years since he'd flirted, but really, was that the best he could do? How had he ever managed to get Carol's attention?

He closed his eyes briefly. The images of his wife sitting on the floor and listening to him sing flashed in his mind. She had loved his music. Up until the point his music had become more important than her or God. Opening his eyes, he stared at the hand that used to wear his gold band. He had put those mistakes behind him along with any thought of starting another relationship.

With locked jaws he put his truck in gear and headed to the church. He needed to focus on his daughters and work.

* * *

Pulling into an empty parking spot on the main street, John slipped out the door with just a smile and wink. Lorrie Ann sat frozen as she watched him trot across the small manicured lawn in front of the town's picturesque church, complete with white clapboard, steeple and beautiful stained-glass windows. He greeted people at the large double doors that stood open.

If she had her way, she would have stayed in the truck. Instead, Celeste grabbed her hand and dragged her out of the safe cocoon of the cab. So with a deep breath, she reminded herself to smile, stand tall and fake it as long as she needed to.

Rachel, already out, swung her crutches and looked back with a scowl. "Hurry, we're late."

Lorrie Ann decided to ignore the curious and shocked faces as Celeste led her through the doors and to the front pew.

"This is where we sit," Celeste whispered. She turned and waved to a little boy a few pews over.

Rachel gritted her teeth and pulled her sister down. "We're already late, so behave."

Lorrie Ann closed her eyes. *Great—a few days in my company and the pastor shows up late to his own prayer meeting.*

Sitting up front worked out well because she could focus on God and ignore the peering eyes behind her.

The prayer meeting only lasted about thirty minutes. People took turns reading assigned scriptures. Requests and praises were shared, and finally John led the group in one last prayer.

As people started moving around, Lorrie Ann saw her aunt slide out the back door of the church.

Lorrie Ann looked down at the girls, not sure where to go. "What now?"

Rachel rolled her eyes and started pulling herself up. "We go to the children's building for choir. You need to head to the fellowship hall for the committee meeting."

Celeste grabbed her hand. "Come on. I'll show you."

John joined them as they passed the back doors. "Hey, thought you three beautiful gals could use an escort." He winked at Lorrie Ann.

"Daddy, you're so silly." Celeste giggled as he tickled her. They moved out the back door and walked across the small courtyard. Celeste held her father's hand then reached over and grabbed Lorrie Ann's fingers.

She relaxed when Katy Norton, now Buchanan, opened the door for them. It had been nice to reconnect with her friend from high school. Now Katy corralled a group of boys into the next room. "Rhody! Paul! Take these boys outside." She turned to Lorrie Ann with an all-encompassing hug. "I didn't get to greet you earlier. I'm so glad you came. Maggie came by the store and said you would be taking charge of the annual pageant."

John gave Katy a quick hug. "Well, we got her here, but no agreements yet."

Katy patted Lorrie Ann's arm. "Oh, it'll be good. I was so excited when Maggie told me you might do the pageant. I love the mysterious ways God works." She hugged her again. "I've got to go. Poor Abby has all eighteen girls by herself. I'll introduce you to my boys later."

Together she and John headed to the fellowship hall. Lorrie Ann's knees started to feel rubbery, and it had nothing to do with the stone walkway or her high heels.

As they approached the back door, nausea rolled down to the pit of her stomach. She stopped.

Lorrie Ann could already feel the heavy judgmental stares like stones thrown at her soul. Why had she let them convince her going to church would be okay?

Whispers screamed her unworthiness. She didn't belong in this community. She could be a Christian without going to church.

"Lorrie Ann?" John's fingers gently braced her wrist, bringing her back to the present. The concern in his voice mirrored the worry in his eyes. "Are you okay?"

She turned from him to study the moths fluttering in the security light at the corner of the building. She could march in there with all the confidence she carried in L.A., but she didn't feel like pretending tonight. She'd made a huge mistake coming here.

Moving away from John, she shook her head. "I'm fine. I'm going to the car." She closed her eyes. No car...trapped. "I'll...help the girls. Katy...um...had a roomful of kids."

"She has Rhody, Abby and Paul to help with the children's choir." He grinned at her. "Man, you must really be scared if you'd rather spend the next hour with a bunch of kids than face the adults."

His words triggered a flash fire of outrage through her body. Her hands fisted at her hips. "Scared? I'll have you know there is nothing these people can say or do to me—"

Stepping back, he threw his hands up, palms out. "Just a little joke." He tilted his head and looked her straight in the eye. "A vein looks like it's about to derail from your neck." He gently put his hand on her shoulder. His smile faded and compassion filled his gaze.

"Don't go in if it upsets you this much. But you could also focus on God instead of these doubts and fears."

He offered his strength, and she wished she could accept. She pulled back and wrapped her arms around her ribs. The blue door leading to the fellowship hall taunted her. "The last youth night I attended, Vickie told everyone I had parked under Hammond Bridge with Tommy Miller, the quarterback. I knew they had gone to the prom together, but I always thought she and Jake Torres liked each other. I know Jake liked her. I thought Jake and I were friends, but…" She bit down hard on her tongue.

She glanced again at the moths dancing around the light. It looked welcoming and safe, but she knew how it burned if you got too close. "Then she started a rumor that I left with Jake. I can't believe he's a state trooper now."

She twisted her silver bracelets around her wrist. "Both those guys seemed to follow her around every-where, so I never understood why she lied about me being with them. Jake and I were friends, but Tommy never even gave me the time of day until the rumors started. I should have ignored them, but everyone be-lieved her." She couldn't bring herself to tell him what had hurt the most. She stood alone while Yolanda walked past her to join Vickie's group. They turned their backs to her, giggling and whispering.

The old pain felt just as fresh as it did then. She had become the outsider again. Unable to comfort the sev-enteen-year-old girl she had been, she closed her eyes.

John approached her, his fingers warm and strong as he squeezed her shoulder. She turned her head away, not wanting him to see the weakness of her stupid tears burning her lids.

She shrugged. "Without knowing why, I had been exiled from the group." Her eyes burned and her voice sounded harsh to her own ears.

How could something from twelve years ago hurt so much? This was why she never talked about the past.

"Lorrie Ann, fear will stop us from living the life God meant for us to live." He kept his gaze on her. "You don't have to go in with me, but I think you'll find it friendlier than your teenage memories."

The sincere concern in his golden-brown eyes jabbed at her self-pity.

She forced a smile. "Truthfully, I had some very unchristian experiences in that building." She tossed her hair and stretched her spine until she stood an inch taller. "But I'm a grown-up now and need to act like one." Maybe this was why God had brought her back. With a firm nod of her head, she placed her other hand over his.

John moved in front of her and waited until she made eye contact. "Lorrie Ann, people will hurt us. It's unfortunate but true. We all have our weaknesses and insecurities." He smiled. "God's always true. You have to trust in Him…with all things."

"I just don't want you to get caught in the cross fire. You're a very nice man."

He rolled his head back and groaned. "Oh, no." He fixed his stare back on her face.

She stared back with a blank expression. What was he talking about?

The corner of his mouth pulled to one side, giving her a lopsided grin.

From inside the fellowship hall, Aunt Maggie tapped on the kitchen window. Sliding it open, she called to them. "Lorrie Ann! Pastor John! What is taking you two so long? Come on in. Everyone is waiting."

Leaning in close, he looked her directly in the eyes. "Are you sure you're ready?" He held his arm out to her.

She smiled at John's gallant gesture. She had asked God for a sign, and now she walked back into a church on the arm of its pastor. Maybe now she should start trusting God. She had already waited twelve years. Nodding, she placed her hand on John's arm and walked through the blue door by his side.

Chapter Eight

Like dominoes falling, silence moved from person to person as each became aware of Lorrie Ann's entrance with John. Memories connected to the smell of lemon beeswax and coffee filled her head.

Aunt Maggie stood at the counter making fresh coffee, a broad smile on her face. "Lorrie Ann, come over here."

Avoiding eye contact with everyone, she headed straight to the safe harbor. Maybe if Aunt Maggie had been there twelve years ago it would have ended differently.

She had Lorrie Ann unwrap the homemade desserts and arrange them next to the coffee. People started milling around, pouring coffee and filling small plates with cookies, cake and pies. Many even greeted her, welcoming her back. Tension eased. Everyone had a smile for her.

Lorrie Ann made a quick glance around the small crowd, looking for Yolanda. She spotted her at a table on the far side of the room, next to Vickie. *Great!* Her warm-and-fuzzy feeling might have been a bit premature.

Vickie glared at Lorrie Ann with her arms crossed over her chest.

Please stay over there, please, please. Vickie moved toward her. Lorrie Ann's spine deflated for a moment.

With bold strides, Vickie headed straight to the dessert bar. Lorrie Ann fought back the somersaults that started low in her belly. Tossing her hair over her shoulder, she took a slow sip of her coffee, never taking her eyes off Vickie's sour face.

"What are you doing here?" The sugar-sweet tone of Vickie's voice didn't hide the malice puckering her mouth.

Lorrie Ann allowed the silence to linger. Her gaze traveled around the room until it landed back on Yolanda, still sitting at the far end of the room. Her cousin twisted a strand of dark hair around her fingers as she chewed on her bottom lip. The whole time Yolanda's crossed leg jerked up and down.

Vickie started squirming, stretching her neck. "So?"

Keeping a bored look on her face, Lorrie Ann shrugged and took a bite of a snicker-doodle Celeste and she had made earlier. "Aunt Maggie thought my expertise could help, and Pastor John offered me a ride." Taking another bite of the cookie and a sip of her heavily creamed coffee, she paused before asking her own question. "What are you doing here?"

Vickie leaned in and whispered, "I belong here."

John stood at the head of a group of tables pushed together and called for the meeting to start. After commanding everyone's attention, he called Lorrie Ann over to him.

She smiled at Vickie. "Excuse me. Pastor John needs me."

Her smile fell a bit when she noticed all eyes on her. Nevertheless, she moved to the front and sat down in the empty chair next to John. She squirmed a bit in the metal chair, feeling guilty for the pettiness of her last thought about Vickie. She really needed to grow up.

"First, I want to thank each of you for being here. The giving of your time and talents makes this annual event a special testimony to God's love." He turned to Lorrie Ann and smiled.

The bottom of her stomach fell out, but she made sure her own smile hid any discomfort and anxiety. *Fake it, girl.*

"Many of you know Lorrie Ann Ortega as Billy and Maggie's niece. She also happens to have experience managing and organizing large musical events. Fortunately for us, she's visiting for the holidays, and Maggie, Katy and I are working on her to lend a hand in the absence of Martha. She's come tonight to see what we have and what we need. So, please share any information you have that might convince her to assist us."

Applause filled the old fellowship hall. Lorrie Ann relaxed.

Maggie started handing out packets. The rest of the meeting ran smoothly, and, keeping an eye on the clock, Lorrie Ann jumped up to get the girls. Her goal: reach the back door without talking to anyone.

She stopped breathing as Jake Torres made his way toward her. Being a state trooper fit him. In high school, he had walked across campus with purpose and power. All the girls loved him, and she had counted him as a friend. When he'd remained silent in the face of the horrible rumors, it was clear who was more important to him. Vickie was part of his crowd, and they reminded her she would always be the outsider. Of course, Lorrie Ann had heard Vickie had ended up married to Tommy, so he had been on the losing end also.

She remained stiff as Jake pulled her into a quick bear hug. "Let me officially welcome you back."

Even with her heels on, she only reached his upper chest. In her silence he continued. They were all adults now; she really needed to get over the old hurts.

"I wanted to thank you. Not everyone can keep calm at an accident site. You helped the girls and John. I imagine it wasn't easy for him."

Lorrie Ann smiled and nodded as she waited for something ugly to enter the conversation. How could he talk to her as if he didn't know his silence had destroyed her life in Clear Water? It was twelve years ago; maybe he forgot.

He just smiled and kept talking as if they were long-lost friends. She knew if she wanted to grow in her faith, she'd have to let go of some of this bitterness. But really? Not even one small *sorry?*

"You should help out with the pageant. I'm the construction chair this year. There's about twelve of us on the committee, and basically we can build anything you throw at us."

John joined them. The men greeted each other before he turned his attention to her. "I have a financial-committee meeting, and it'll probably go late." He glanced back to Jake with a wary grin. "JoAnn and the ladies want to buy a new vacuum cleaner, and George and his boys think it's a waste of money."

Jake laughed, patting John on the back. "It's good seeing you, Lorrie Ann. I'm outta here before someone needs a peace officer."

She managed to nod. Once alone, John tilted his head slightly to the right. "Are you good?" He spoke softly.

"The church is still standing. I'd call it a victory." She grinned and tucked her hair behind her ear. "But I'm still not sure I want to take on the pageant."

"Maggie'll have all the information you'll need." He handed her the keys. "Ready to take the girls home?"

She smiled as relief flooded her body. "That's the plan. I'll go get them." She paused. "Thank you, John."

She slipped out of the door, heading to the children's building. Her steps were light, feeling as if she had conquered some childhood fear, but her celebration might have come a little too early.

Vickie ambushed her halfway down the curved sidewalk.

"Hey, don't walk away from me." Vickie grabbed Lorrie Ann's arm and spun her around.

Too tired to put up with the attitude, Lorrie Ann pulled her arm free and kept walking.

"The way you throw yourself at Pastor John is wrong," Vickie hissed at her back, following her. "You're pathetic in your cheap boots and L.A. ways. You stay away from those little girls. They need a real mother."

Lorrie Ann froze then slowly turned and faced her high-school nemesis. Silence filled the air between them, the minutes stretching out. Lorrie Ann prayed for the right words, to harness her anger. Her pulse raced as her breathing grew heavy.

The past twelve years disappeared. Inside, Lorrie Ann felt like the seventeen-year-old girl that never stood up for herself. She put her fisted hands on her hips and opened her mouth to give it all to her. "Vickie, you need to…" Lorrie Ann paused.

Anger and bitterness radiated off Vickie, her chest raising up and down in quick motion. Vickie stood alone. Lorrie Ann thought about her living in a trailer on her parents' property and working at the local grocery store, the one-time prom queen divorced by her perfect quarterback sweetheart, Tommy Miller.

Immediately Lorrie Ann pulled back her words. They came from her anger, not God. She turned her back and went to collect the girls.

Vickie, Jake and Tommy still seemed to have some left-over issues. She refused to be pulled into high-school drama again. She had her own problems to deal with in order to figure out her own future.

Lorrie Ann rested her hand on the light switch in John's bedroom. He'd thought with Rachel's hurt leg they should sleep downstairs, and he would sleep on the sofa. Growing up with her mom, Lorrie Ann's only bed had been the sofa in whatever apartment they'd stayed in. No adult had ever given up their bed for her.

She had tucked the sheets around his daughters, and now they looked so little in his big bed. "Good night, girls. Lights out. I'll be in the living room until your dad gets here. Okay?"

Celeste popped up. "No, we're not done!"

Lorrie Ann paused to think what she might have missed. Nothing came to mind. "Well, let's go over the list." She touched one finger. "Bath?"

"Check." Celeste bobbed her head.

Lorrie Ann smiled and added a second finger. "Pajamas on."

"Check."

"Teeth brushed."

"Check."

"Backpack ready for school?"

"Check."

"I can't think of anything else."

"You forgot something." Celeste giggled and sat with her legs folded under her.

"Um...a drink?"

"Nope."

"Uh...let's see." She racked her brain trying to figure out what she had missed. "A good-night kiss?"

"Nope." She bounced her legs. "Silly, Daddy does that."

"We got the pillow and blankets out for your dad." Lorrie Ann looked from Celeste to her older sister. "Rachel, can you give me some help here?" A slight shrug was the only response. The silent treatment had pretty much held up all night.

"Let me think." Pinching her nose, she closed her eyes and a new thought occurred. "Oh, I have it." She snapped her fingers. "Your prayers."

"You're closer." The six-year-old stretched out the two words. "We do those after the next thing."

Lorrie Ann drew her brows down in confusion. "After what, Celeste? Please just tell me."

Celeste crossed her arms over her small chest and pouted. "You have to guess."

"Celeste, your father told me you would drag out bedtime, so I can just turn off the lights and go to the living room."

With a heavy sigh, Rachel flopped to her back. "Celeste, give it up." She looked back to Lorrie Ann. "She wants a story. Daddy and Amy always read us a story before we turn out the lights. You don't have to." Twisting her back to them again, she pulled the covers over her head.

"Oh. Sorry, your dad didn't say anything about a story, and I'm kind of new to this bedtime-ritual thing." Lorrie Ann realized this was the sort of stuff she had missed growing up. What a surprise that these two girls could teach her so much.

Celeste looked confused. "Your mom didn't read you stories at bedtime when you were little?"

"Well, she was busy, so I just went to bed." She didn't think it was appropriate to tell them her mom was either passed out drunk or partying with her latest boyfriend.

She patted Celeste's leg under the quilt. "I would love to read you a story." Glancing around the room, she didn't see any children's books. "I could make up a story. I did that a lot growing up. I didn't have any books, so I would make up my own stories."

Celeste clapped and bounced in the bed.

Lorrie Ann laid her hands on Celeste's shoulder. "Careful of Rachel's leg."

"Oh, sorry. Can you make up a story about a princess?"

Lorrie Ann tapped her finger on her lips. "I do happen to know about one princess, but she didn't know she came from a royal family. A jealous duke wanted revenge on his brother, the king. So, he stole the king's most precious treasure. Do you know what he took?" Lorrie Ann noticed Rachel had turned back to them.

"His golden crown?" Celeste whispered.

"Good guess." Lorrie Ann smoothed Celeste's hair from her face. "But it wasn't gold or jewels. His newborn daughter slept in a basinet laced with colorful ribbons. The duke hired a villain to steal the infant and kill her. But when he went to strike her, he stopped. Her innocent face looked up at him, and his black heart melted. So, instead he took her to the woods where coyotes roamed and left her nestled in the roots of a giant oak tree."

Celeste wiggled under the covers and pulled her stuffed animal closer.

"Hearing the soft whimpers, the mother coyote came to investigate the strange noise in her forest. She curled her body around the babe, giving her warmth through the night. Close by, an isolated cabin stood. Rumors about the old lady who lived there swirled in town."

"Did she find the baby?" Celeste yawned.

"Maybe." Lorrie Ann stopped the story when Celeste's lids fluttered down. She ran her hand over the child's wayward curls.

"More story." The two words came out slurred as her eyes fluttered shut again.

"Next time, rug rat." She smoothed Celeste's hair away from her face. Looking across the big bed, she found Rachel watching her. "Night, Rachel."

"Good night, Miss Lorrie Ann." The soft reply gave Lorrie Ann a strange and unexpected sense of peace.

Stepping out into the living room, she checked the time. Eight forty-five. John said he'd be home before ten. She plugged her laptop in and opened her emails.

She touched base with Melissa, who told her Brent had gone into rehab and reassured her that after the holidays they would talk. It didn't matter how much Brent apologized or if he got sober, she was not going to have that drama in her life. Lorrie Ann refused to become her mother.

She sent and replied to a long list of emails then followed up with some texts. Glancing at the time, she finally shut her laptop down. It was almost ten.

Anticipation fluttered across her nerves. Lorrie Ann looked at the front door, imagining John walking through it. Standing, she moved to the glass doors at the back of the cabin.

Her mind drifted back to the conversation she and John had been having before going into the fellowship hall.

The room became too small. She stepped out onto the deck and left the door open so she could hear the girls.

John walked into his quiet house. Lorrie Ann's presence lingered in the air. The idea of her waiting for him to return home felt good. He immediately pushed that thought out. Carol, his wife, should be the one he wanted here. With her death he had made a conscious decision to stay out of any romantic relationship. Lorrie Ann was someone new and just making him aware of his loneliness. The girls needed all of his focus; he would remain strong in this choice to remain single.

After checking on the girls, he made his way to the back of the living room toward the sliding glass door. He noticed a pillow and extra blankets folded neatly on the sofa. He had told Lorrie Ann to put the girls in his room. He smiled. It was nice of her to set those out for him.

He stepped through the open door to the back deck. Somewhere a bonfire burned. The breeze carried the smoldering scent of mesquite and cedar through the air.

At the edge of the deck, Lorrie Ann stood with her fingers wrapped around the worn-smooth wood railing.

"Lorrie Ann?" He spoke softly, not wanting to disturb the mood of the night.

Lorrie Ann sighed, her fingers relaxed. She kept her eyes closed.

He walked across the deck but made sure to keep his distance from her. "How did the girls do? Celeste give you any problems?"

"No, they were great, and I actually got a good bit of work done after they went to sleep."

She would not make eye contact with him. He studied her profile. He could see Sonia, her mother, in her bone structure. Had she made some of the same mistakes as her mother while living in L.A.? Well, she was here now and seemed to be looking for answers. He would treat her like any member of his congregation in need of help.

"Good. Thank you for helping. I'm sure this has been a rough week for you." He moved to stand next to her. He turned to the side, his left hip resting against the railing as he crossed his arms.

After a few moments of silence he continued. "I know your aunt means well, but she can have the tenacity of a pit bull when she gets an idea in her head." He tucked his hands into his front pockets. "I don't want you to feel obligated to help. Guilt can be a strong motivation, but it's not the right one." Turning parallel to her, he braced both arms on the cedar railing. "Your aunt is so excited about you being home she might miss the point of you being here."

He loved Maggie's passion, but he also knew she

could steamroller people into what she thought was the right thing for them whether they agreed or not.

His fear now was that she had decided to play matchmaker. He rubbed his eyes. That was all he needed. Forcing a smile on his face, he looked back to Lorrie Ann.

John gave Lorrie Ann a half grin that made her want to melt against him and tuck her head over his heartbeat. She had to wonder, how did the women of his congregation concentrate on his sermons? She shook her head and looked back at the landscape. Maybe it would be better if Yolanda had brought the girls home.

Silence stretched out between them. She struggled with her thoughts and what she wanted or what she should do. *Stick to the plan, girl. Get your life in order and head back to California.*

His calm voice pulled her out of the vicious cycle of her thoughts. "Just take your time and please don't let your aunt blackmail you into doing anything."

The tension eased a bit. She rolled her shoulders and twisted her neck, forcing her body to relax. "Thanks. It's not that I don't want to help. I just don't have anything to give right now." She could make out his nod in the dark.

With his encouragement, she continued, "I'm the last person anyone wants at the church." She rubbed the back of her neck and gave a halfhearted snort. "I'm way too flawed to be directing anyone about the birth of Christ."

"See now, there's where you're wrong. Sometimes it's the imperfections in our lives that make us the perfect choice to help others."

She snorted. "I have never been the type to help others. I'm pretty much a look-out-for-myself type of girl."

He grinned. "Yeah, I can see that."

Turning away, Lorrie Ann focused on the outline of the surrounding hills. After what seemed like an eternity of silence, she could not resist a glimpse back at John, but the moment she made eye contact, her muscles froze. He had set a trap, and like an experienced hunter, waited for her to enter. The warmth of his eyes held her in place as strongly as an iron cage. Heavy stillness sparked the air around them.

He took a step closer, his right hand wrapped around the smooth wood, a butterfly's touch from her fingers. She tried to swallow, but her mouth had gone sand dry.

"I..." She what? Shouldn't be here, had already fallen in love with his girls, needed to go back to L.A.... wanted to kiss him. She felt her skin tighten and heat up. "I...um." She needed the ground to open and pull her under, that's what she needed.

This gorgeous, perfect man standing in front of her had two little girls and he worked for God. A few steps and she would be safe on the other side of the door. Focused on the escape, she willed her feet to move.

His hand left the railing and gently touched her arm. "Lorrie Ann, it's okay. You don't have to volunteer for the Christmas pageant. But if you could help me with the girls while you're in town I would appreciate the time."

An invisible hand guided her gaze back to his face. That was her excuse, anyway.

"This might be hard to believe, but most people find Celeste just a bit overwhelming." He pushed his hair away from his forehead and stared at the surrounding hills. "Rachel can be so closed off and reserved. She has a hard time with new people in our lives. They both love Amy, but she's out for a couple weeks while she recovers." He turned back to her. "They seem comfortable with you."

Rachel…liked her? He had to be joking or blind. After a long pause, she decided he must be blind. "You know they see Amy as safe. They don't have to protect you from her."

"Safe? Protect me from what?"

She saw confusion on his face. Poor man. "The women in this town who want to either marry you or set you up with someone in their family."

"That's ridiculous." He jammed his hands in his front pockets.

"Rachel told Celeste to be careful when the ladies are nice to her because they want to date you." She smiled. "According to Rachel, you have to be protected from the ladies because you're busy doing God's work and saving people."

"Celeste told you this?" His words, slow and pronounced, came one at a time.

"Yes. They don't worry about Amy. You're too old for her, and she doesn't have any family members they have to worry about."

John turned from her and leaned his forearms on the top railing with his fingers entwined. One polished burgundy boot rested on the bottom. The mesmerizing eyes that had held her now contemplated the night sky.

She had tried to be funny, but her efforts seemed to have fallen flat.

"Every decision I made after Carol's death was for

the girls' sake. How did I miss this?" His low voice sent
an arrow straight to her heart.

"You're a great father. Some parents never give a
thought to how their decisions affect their children.
Don't beat yourself up over this."

Once again, his full attention fell on her face. His
eyes moved over every inch, resting on her left check.
"You told Maggie you got the bruise from the accident.
But you had it earlier in the day."

She turned away from him. He didn't seem to care
about what had happened twelve years ago, but how
would he feel if he knew the truth of her choices in the
past two years?

She flashed him a full smile. "That's my story and
I'm sticking to it."

"Okay, we'll leave it at that for now. So what about
the girls—will you help me out for the next few weeks?"

She shrugged. "Are you sure you want me?"

He gave her a simple nod.

"Okay, how can I be of service?"

"I take them to school in the morning, but I need
someone to pick them up other than Monday. I get them
on Monday. They get out of school at three-fifteen. I'm
usually home by five, unless there is an emergency.
Wednesday night I'd need you to bring them home like
tonight. Get them tucked into bed. That's it."

"I think I can handle that. I really like them. You've
done a great job."

"Thanks. I paid Amy…"

"Oh, I'm not taking your money. I'm just helping out.
Use the money for something more…I don't know…
useful, like a vacuum cleaner."

With a low chuckle, he turned sideways, leaning

on the railing, and smiled. "So you don't have use for money? Independently wealthy, are you?"

A flash fire surged through her body. "I'll have you know, I have worked hard for every penny. I..." She paused at the sight of his raised brow and smirking lips.

Taking a deep breath, Lorrie Ann calmed herself before continuing, "Sorry, I can get a bit defensive." She glanced at her watch. "Oh, I need to go. You have to get up early and I'm keeping you."

"Let me check on the girls, and I'll walk you home."

Following him into the cabin, she stopped at the bedroom door, allowing him to go in alone. She felt like an intruder as she watched him whisper something to Rachel. His daughter settled back into her pillow, and he kissed her forehead before moving to the other side. He straightened the sheets Celeste had kicked off, her small body sprawled across the king-size bed. The thought of the little girl not even remaining still in sleep melted her heart a bit, and it scared her.

In a few weeks she would be back in L.A., and attachments led to hurt. She was already regretting her agreement to help out. She needed to get better at saying no.

She moved away from the bedroom door to lean against the hallway wall. She pushed her tongue hard against her teeth and wrapped an arm around her stomach. She had to get out, away from John and his girls. Her hand grasped the handle.

"Lorrie Ann?" He moved beside her, his arm reaching across her to open the door.

For a second she imagined those arms embracing her. His voice brought her back to reality.

"Thanks again for helping. It's a huge worry off my shoulders."

John's presence warmed her insides with each step across the wooden planks of the deck. She longed to stay next to him, but those thoughts were dangerous.

Biting her lip, Lorrie Ann reminded herself of all the reasons she needed to remain distant from him. It was hard when just walking silently next to him comforted her. The spark of anticipation kept her wanting to know him more.

But she wasn't what he needed. Without a doubt, he would not like what he found. People didn't stay; it was best to be the first to go.

His voice yanked her from the spiral of depressing thoughts. "Um…Lorrie Ann, I was wondering what you were doing Saturday night. I have a friend from Houston who's an artist, and he's having an opening in Kerrville. It's his first solo show in Texas. I told him I'd be there. Would you join me? It won't be like anything in L.A., but he's an incredible artist."

She froze. Excitement, doubt and fear battled it out in her brain. She stared at him, unable to make a decision. Had he just asked her out on a real date?

The silence became awkward. His hand moved to the back of his neck and his eyes darted, glancing everywhere but at her. She had no idea what words to form. She felt her mouth open, but no sound came out. He finally broke the agonizing stillness.

"Listen, don't worry about it. It's just…I never invite anyone in town because it could lead to misunderstandings and assumptions. With you leaving soon, I just… It's no big deal."

"I'll think about it." Lorrie Ann's eyes went wide

in surprise. *Don't overreact.* She shrugged and played with her bracelets. "I'll check to see if I'm busy." Lame. "Night, John." She turned away from him and walked as briskly as possible without actually running. Even though running did seem the best plan of action.

Chapter Nine

John hit the razor on the side of the sink and rotated his face around to check for any missed spots. He looked himself in the eye and berated the man in the mirror again. What possessed him to invite Lorrie Ann to Gary's art opening? He just got her to agree to watch the girls, so why did he feel the need to push himself into her life even more? After wiping the sink, John stepped out of the bathroom.

The startled look on Lorrie Ann's face when he'd asked had caused him to regret his impulse the minute the words left his mouth. Her hesitation and polite *maybe* didn't do much for a man's ego. He might have well said, "I'm asking you because I can't ask anyone else." *That was smooth.*

"Celeste, you're not helping!" Rachel's frustrated voice shrieked, derailing John's contemplation. With a sigh, John gave up all hope of a peaceful morning.

He shook his head and forced his thoughts back to the moment at hand and away from his new neighbor. Walking into the living room, he grabbed a green Jolly Rancher from a handmade ceramic bowl and popped it in his mouth. He needed coffee and real food, but this would do for now.

"Daddy, I can't wear the yellow socks with this skirt!" Rachel struggled to get off the sofa.

"I like it!" Celeste opened the refrigerator door.

"That's because you're six and don't care what people say about you."

The offended six-year-old stuck her tongue out.

John set Rachel's painkillers on the counter and turned to Celeste. "No breakfast until you're dressed and hair brushed. Go up and get another pair of socks for your sister."

Standing in a purple shirt with yellow polka dots two sizes too big and red mud boots, she looked down with a puzzled expression. "I am dressed, Daddy."

A dramatic sigh came from the living room. "See what I mean, Daddy? And you want her to pick out my socks!"

A knock on the door saved him from answering. Quickly turning to the entryway, he saw Lorrie Ann standing on the other side of the cut-glass door. He couldn't stop the grin from spreading across his face. Man, he felt like a twelve-year-old with his first crush.

"Mornin', Lorrie Ann." He stepped back so she could enter. "I wasn't expecting to see you until this afternoon."

"Good morning. I come bearing gifts from Aunt Maggie's kitchen." She lifted the plate up.

"Lorrie Ann! You brought…" Celeste sniffed the air. "Cinnamon rolls!"

"And coffee for your dad." She gave him a half-hearted smile. "Sorry about intruding, but Aunt Maggie worried it might be hard to get everyone ready this morning."

"Who would have thought one broken leg could knock a normal routine so out of whack." He sighed and looked back over his shoulder. "They're not finished dressing, and I still haven't made breakfast." He followed her to the kitchen. "Please, make yourself at home." As he slid past, the clean smell of her hair distracted him for a moment.

She looked up when he paused, and her brows rose.

He cleared his dry throat and lowered his voice. "Did you think about Saturday?" He jerked back when he realized he had his nose almost pressed into her hair. He looked down and found his youngest daughter in a wide-eyed stare. "Celeste, go upstairs and get the socks."

Lorrie Ann handed him the thermos and unwrapped the warm rolls. The rich smell filled the air, and his mouth watered. He adored fresh cinnamon rolls.

"I want the green ones." Rachel twisted around to face the adults.

John scowled. She wanted a green cinnamon roll?

"Daddy, please tell me you're not going to let her wear that outfit to school. I would be *soooo* mortified." She flopped her head against the back of the sofa.

John raised an eyebrow and paused in the process of pouring coffee into a mug. "Ah...you want the green socks." He closed his eyes and took a slow sip of the dark drink. "Why are you so upset over Celeste's clothes?"

She glared at Lorrie Ann. "It's her fault. She's trying to look like you."

"Me?"

"Rachel!" John's shocked voice over his daughter's rudeness joined Lorrie Ann's.

Celeste came to the railing. "I can't find the green ones!"

"They are in the closet in the basket on my dresser." Rachel hit her casted leg. "I hate having a broken leg."

"Rachel, you owe Miss Lorrie Ann an apology, and I don't see the problem with the yellow ones." John placed a roll on a small plate and carried it over to her, sitting on the edge of the ottoman. "What about white? They go with everything." He sighed as he watched her roll her eyes. When did she become a drama queen, and how did the color of her socks become so important?

He noticed Lorrie Ann moving to the stairs and raised his brow in a silent question.

With a flick of her hand, she pointed to the loft. "I'm going to retrieve the green socks and see what I can do to help Celeste's outfit choice. You and Rachel eat your breakfast—Aunt Maggie's orders." Her voice pitched higher on the last three words as she reached the top.

Rachel picked at her icing.

"You know you shouldn't let other people make you feel ashamed of your sister, and a broken leg is no excuse for being rude."

"I'm sorry." Glancing up from her plate, she looked into his face. "She doesn't get it, Daddy. They watch us, and if we do anything wrong they say it's because we need a mother."

Lorrie Ann's words from last night flew back to him.

He patted her knee. "Sweetheart, I love you." He paused, asking God for the right words. "You know people talk—that's just part of human nature. For the most part, they just want to help, and unfortunately, everyone has an opinion on what that looks like. You can't let them change you or your sister." He smiled at her. "That's my job."

"But you have a big job already, and Celeste doesn't make it easier."

Pounding on the steps brought his attention up.

"We found your green socks! And Miss Lorrie Ann pulled my outfit together!" She jumped down the stairs.

"Well, what do you think, Rachel?" Celeste twirled in front of them. The necklace Lorrie Ann wore this morning now worked as a loose belt with the large silver loops wrapped twice around the small waist, making the shirt look like a dress. A black turtleneck and tights actually looked good, and John grinned at the zebra-striped boots. He remembered the argument he'd had with his father-in-law over buying the pricey boots for a six-year-old.

Lorrie Ann pulled Celeste's newly done braid to the front. "We even found yellow ribbons to match."

"She could braid your hair, too. I brought green ribbons for you to match your socks." Celeste held out the sock and ribbons to her older sister.

"No, thank you. I like doing the ponytails Daddy taught me to do. I fix Celeste's hair and mine each morning." She took the sock and started struggling to get it to her foot.

"Rachel?" John sighed. Had she always been this defensive?

After a few heartbeats, Rachel responded, "I'm sorry for earlier, Miss Lorrie Ann."

He stood and kissed Celeste on the forehead. "You look great." Meeting Lorrie Ann's gaze, he smiled at her, surprised by the rightness of having her here.

"Thank you, Lorrie Ann." He touched Rachel's shoulder. "Sweetheart, why don't you let Lorrie Ann braid your hair, so I can feed our monkey, okay? Then we will be off, and Miss Lorrie Ann can report back to the admiral that her mission was completed."

His oldest daughter nodded. She gave him a tentative smile as she pulled herself forward. Lorrie Ann moved behind Rachel and started weaving her hair.

His heart tightened. The older Rachel got, the more she looked like her mom.

What had he been thinking when he'd asked Lorrie Ann on a date? One look in his daughters' eyes should remind him that his selfishness had cost them their mother. In the past five years he had created a balanced life for his girls. Why would he risk that for any woman, especially one who would be leaving in a few weeks? He snorted at the thought as he poured milk for Celeste.

"What is it, Daddy?"

"Oh, it seems your dad forgot he's not nineteen anymore. Got things to do, places to go and girls to raise." He winked at her and tugged her hair.

"You must be getting old if you forgot all that."

The laughter burst from his gut. The other two females looked at him in surprise. He just smiled back.

John whistled as he stepped through the side door of the church leading to the offices in the back. Lorrie Ann kept invading his thoughts when he needed to focus on the message for Sunday.

"Pastor Levi, welcome back! Hope our girl is on the mend. We've been praying for her." JoAnn, the secretary he'd inherited four years ago, greeted him from her large oak desk.

He smiled and thanked her. No matter what time he arrived, she was always waiting for him with coffee and a schedule for the day.

"Here are your messages. With you being out, they got a little backed up. Mostly calls about Rachel and sending you prayers." She handed him a neat stack of white note cards. He knew each one would be precise and detailed. "Here is a list of activities. I rescheduled the meeting with the other pastors. Raymond Hill is back in the Uvalde hospital, so you might want to visit him. You and the girls have been invited to the Campbells' and the Lawsons' for Sunday dinner. I told the Lawsons you were already eating at the Campbells'. I knew you would want to spend some time with Amy."

He nodded, knowing better than to interrupt her morning drill. He played with the Jolly Rancher in his pocket and wondered what she would do if he popped it in his mouth. She had several rules for him, and life was easier when he followed them.

"We do need to talk about the Relay For Life fundraisers when you get a chance. The building committee has given you three dates for the picnic at the pecan farm. Let me know which one works for you, and I'll work with Maggie to get that set."

He tuned out, and his brain shifted to something more interesting—Lorrie Ann. He should treat Saturday like a date, including dinner. Oh, man, he hadn't thought of taking her to dinner. He didn't even know what she liked. He squinted and flexed his jaw. She liked Mexican food, so Mamasita's would be a good choice.

JoAnn startled him from his thoughts, her glare telling him she was fully aware he had not been listening to her. Her four-eleven frame now stood firm in the doorway with hands on her hips.

"Sorry, JoAnn." He flashed an innocent smile, or tried to, anyway. By the look on her face, she wasn't buying the act. "What were you saying?"

She shook her head in disappointment then looked completely to the left and slowly to the right. Even though they were alone, she lowered her voice and became even smaller. John had to step in to hear her.

"Rhody and Katy Buchanan are in your office."

He gave the closed door to his office a puzzled frown and whispered back, "I didn't see any of their vehicles."

"They're needin' some marriage advice, but they don't want anyone to know."

Closing his eyes, he sighed deeply. The one thing he'd tried to avoid the past four years was marriage counseling.

JoAnn moved back to her desk. "Here are the business cards you always give out." Handing him three cards, she marched to the coffee and filled his favorite mug. "Such a shame. Young people just don't know how lucky they are to have someone to love, and those four boys..." She shook her head.

"They came for help, JoAnn, not a divorce. That's a good sign."

Pointing her finger to his chest, she looked him sternly in the eyes. "Yes, and a testimony to their trust in you."

Sometimes she acted more like a mother than an employee.

"Are you going to help them or send them away like you always do?" She thrust her sharp chin to the cards he had tucked into his shirt pocket.

With a crooked grin and soft sigh, he took the warm cup from her hands. "I *am* helping them, by sending them to a trained professional." If they knew the truth, he would be the last person they'd seek out for marriage advice.

"I'll pray for them." She moved to her desk. "And you."

"Thank you, JoAnn." He turned to the door and paused with his hand on the knob. He closed his eyes for a quick prayer, asking for the right words to give the couple he considered good friends.

Rhody stood and held out his hand in greeting when he entered. "Pastor Levi." Stiff voice, not the usual easygoing one John enjoyed.

"Sit, sit. Hi, Katy." He smiled and noted the framed photo she held.

"Oh, sorry. I was just telling Rhody what a great family picture. We've never been to the beach. You should've had someone else take it so you could be in the photo, too."

He nodded and watched her place the picture of Carol and the girls back on his desk, bracing for what always came next.

"It looks like Celeste is about one. This must have been right before the accident." The deep sadness glistened in the moisture of her eyes.

He nodded again as he took his seat, hoping to put her at ease. "It happened two weeks later. I keep it on my desk to remind me how fast life can change and the blessings we take for granted. Both the girls talk about that weekend at the beach as if they remember. They've watched the video a million times."

"That's nice." She swallowed and reached for her husband's hand beside her.

John took a deep breath and pulled out the cards in his chest pocket. "So what brings you in this morning?"

Alone, John sat at his desk, the earmarked Bible lying open under his hands. His thoughts turned to Lorrie Ann again. He glanced at his sermon. It needed a bit more polishing, but he couldn't focus.

Rachel seemed to be more on edge lately, or maybe it had just been brought to his attention. He needed to add a daughter-father lunch date to his schedule.

In the process of reaching for his detailed itinerary, the framed photo Katy had moved earlier caught his attention. The only framed photo he kept on his desk always created conversation.

The soft sunset surrounded Carol's golden hair as she held a chubby Celeste on her hip. At her feet, Rachel smiled up at the camera as she tried to catch waves in her bucket. It showed the perfect family on a summer beach vacation. Katy had made the same comment many others had while smiling at the beautiful picture. "John, you should have had someone else take the picture so you could be with them instead of hiding behind the camera." He would chuckle, letting them assume he agreed.

He never corrected anyone, but he hadn't been the lucky one to take the picture.

When they'd been invited to go with some friends to the coast, he'd once again declined. He needed to finish a song and had meetings to attend. With his music career about to launch, he couldn't afford to take off. Upset, Carol insisted on taking the girls without him.

He traced a finger along the edge of her face. She'd begged him to go, but he'd believed at the time his music career needed him more.

After Carol's death, Julie, the photographer and friend, brought him the pictures and video. A reminder of the beautiful gift he'd taken for granted.

Lunch with Rachel sounded like a great idea right now. He went to call JoAnn, but before he picked up the phone, it rang.

"Mornin', John." The familiar voice came boldly over the line.

"Hey, Chuck," John greeted his mentor from the past fifteen years. "Good to hear from you. What's up?"

"Not much. Just going over my prayer list and realized we haven't spoken in a few weeks."

John chuckled. "So you're checking up on me?"

"Figured someone has to. No telling what goes on in that small town of yours."

"You'd be surprised. How're Jill and the girls?"

"Everyone's good. We found out that Karen and Eric are making us grandparents. One minute you're holding a baby girl in your arms, then you wake up one morning and she's having her own." Chuck sighed. "Speaking of daughters, how are your little ones?"

"Actually, right now we're dealing with a broken leg." John went on to tell him about the accident. He even admitted to the concerns he had in getting everything done, along with the fundraiser for the youth building.

"I didn't realize how much I needed to talk, Chuck. God's timing is as faithful as always."

"Call me anytime. In a small town, you have a bigger threat of feeling isolated. Tell me, how's the music coming along?"

John spun his chair until he faced the window behind him. "I haven't found the time between my ministry, the girls, remodeling the house and all the community events."

"It's a talent you've been given. I remember you always sitting at the piano or with a guitar in your hand. You were never without music. I know it helped through your parents' deaths."

John couldn't help but snort. "Yeah, look where it got me with my family. A wife I didn't get to spend enough time with and two little girls who didn't know me."

"John, stop punishing yourself. It's all about balance and sharing that gift with your girls. Do either of the girls show any musical talent?"

John smiled. "Rachel loves singing. She has a very mature voice for her age. Celeste will try any instrument she can get her hands on." He grinned. "Not that she can actually play any of them." He frowned and pulled in his lips. In his vow to keep music from his life, had he also deprived the girls? He rubbed his hand over his jaw and looked up to the clear sky outside.

"John? You there?"

He thought about the guitars and violins he had boxed up and locked away. "Yeah. I get a bit overwhelmed at times."

"Hey, that's why you need someone to talk to." His friend chuckled. "Even Jesus gathered twelve friends around Him. No one expects you to go it alone. We all need help."

John picked up a pencil and started tapping it off his knee. Leaning his head back, he smiled at the ceiling.

"Now you sound like some of the women around here. They all seem to think I need a wife. My girls, on the other hand, have gotten it into their heads they need to save me from the women."

"Do the girls have someone safe to talk to?"

John froze in his chair. "What do you mean? They have me."

"Yes, but they also want to protect you."

"Now you sound like Lorrie Ann."

John closed his eyes, not able to take back the words. He could see the graying eyebrows arch in question. Like all the times he sat across from him.

"Lorrie Ann? Not to make this a big deal, John, but this is the first time I've heard a woman's name other than JoAnn's or Maggie's."

"Then don't make it a big deal. She's Maggie's niece from California and is visiting for a couple weeks. With Amy's injuries, Lorrie Ann is helping out since she's right next door."

"How old is she?"

"Really, Chuck? You're going to go there?"

"Hey, just because you're a father and pastor doesn't mean you can't have a social life. When was the last time you went out for fun with adults?"

"I don't need to have fun." John heard Chuck grunt. "Well, that didn't sound right."

"You didn't answer my question. When was the last time you went on a date?"

Silence.

"John, don't tell me in over five years you have not gone out once."

"I live in a small town, and when I say *small* I'm talking population four hundred and six, and that includes the horses. I don't know. It'd be more complicated than it's worth, and until now I've had no desire to go out. I didn't set out *not* to date. I just haven't met anyone worth the risk."

"Until now, huh? So, is she worth the risk?"

He spun the chair back around to face the sweet faces of his wife and girls. "Maybe."

"So, have you asked Lorrie Ann out?"

Silence, longer and heavier this time.

"Oh, boy, you have, and you don't know what to do next!" Chuck went into full laughter.

"I'm glad you're finding this amusing, mentor of mine."

Chuck coughed. "Sorry. Listen, I know it's hard to balance a personal life between church and family. Being a single dad makes it even harder, but really, you need to relax. Do I need to remind you God's in charge of all the days of your life? You have always been a bit of a control freak. Besides, the only way you'll find out if she's worth it is by spending some time with her."

"That's why you're my mentor, Chuck." He let out a heavy sigh and noticed the time ticking away by the minute on his clock. "I've got to be going, but this call could not have come at a better time. Thanks, Chuck."

"God is good, John. How about we close in prayer?"

John closed his eyes and focused on the words in Chuck's prayer, and he asked for his own heart to be open to God's will.

Lorrie Ann watched the SUVs line up behind her in the school driveway as she leaned against the BMW's silver hood, her brown leather boots crossed at the ankles. A few people waved at her, some stared, trying to figure out who she was, and others just glared. She smiled at them all, enjoying the irony of her, Wild Child L.A., in the soccer-mom line.

Worried about being late, she had been the first to arrive. She now stood where Aunt Maggie used to wait for her and Yolanda. Not much had changed. Everyone from preschool to high school attended the same campus, with the gym in the center of the buildings.

A few minutes after the bell rang, doors burst open and kids ran everywhere. Lorrie Ann thought about Rachel moving with this rambunctious crowd. Maybe she should have signed her out earlier.

"Miss Lorrie Ann! Miss Lorrie Ann!" Celeste ran across the playground with her backpack dragging behind her, stirring up the dirt. A small group of little people followed, and much to her horror, they all stopped in front of the BMW.

"See, I told you she had pirate boots! And she plays in a rock band, and she's going to let us be in the Christmas pageant." Celeste aimed her big smile straight at Lorrie Ann.

"I manage a rock band—I don't play in one—and—"

"Are you a real pirate?"

"She can't be a pirate, stupid—she's a girl."

"Girls can be pirates."

"Hold on, guys. Girls can be pirates if—"

"The car's top goes down into the trunk."

A chorus of aahs followed Celeste's announcement.

"Did you steal this car?"

"No!" How did one control a conversation with six-year-olds? They managed to make musicians look docile. She gave them her best stern look. "Celeste, would you please introduce me to your friends?"

"Oh, I'm sorry. This is Bethany, Daviana, Carlos, Colt, Jenny and Rey."

She sat on her heels to greet the short creatures eye to eye. "Nice to meet you. To answer your questions, I am not a pirate—I just like tall boots. Even though girls can be pirates, it's wrong to steal. I manage a band. I don't play in it."

"But you're going to direct the play and let us be in it, right?" Celeste wrapped her arms around Lorrie Ann's shoulders.

"Maybe." She shrugged. "I haven't decided yet." Another decision she had avoided since coming to town. The list kept getting longer.

"Please, please!" The chorus of high-pitched voices surrounded her.

"You look like you could use some help." Katy approached from behind her car. "Colt, are you causing problems?"

"No, Momma. We're helpin' Celeste to get Miss Lorrie Ann to run the Christmas play so we can be in it."

"Yeah, we want a rock star to help the play so it'll rock!" The kids laughed at Carlos's air-guitar jam and started jumping and cheering.

Katy laughed. "I think you have your own fan club. So, you're helping Pastor John with the girls?"

"Just for a week or so."

"You might as well agree to help with the play, too. I personally think it's a God thing. I know your aunt would be over the moon with glee." Katy winked at Lorrie Ann. "The people in this town could use a shot of something new. Pastor John, well, that poor man just needs a social life. You would be good for him."

Lorrie Ann stood and frowned at Katy. Why did everyone think they knew what that man needed?

"Come on, Colt. We need to find your brothers." Katy grabbed her son's arm. "Bye, L.A. I'm sure I'll see you soon."

The short people still stared at her. "Um...don't you have people waiting for you?" As the little ones started running off, she turned to Celeste. "Where would Rachel be? Do you think she needs help?" She searched the buildings and playground. No Rachel. Great—first day on the job and she'd already lost one of the girls.

"She's probably just talking with her boyfriend and doesn't want our help. Are you going to date Daddy?" She took Lorrie Ann by the hand and started leading her to the small courtyard outside the fourth- and fifth-grade buildings. Lorrie Ann didn't really hear any of the girl's words after "boyfriend." Oh, that didn't sound good.

"Why do some people call you L.A.?" Celeste asked as she led her to the tennis courts.

"It's my initials for *Lorrie Ann,* and all I talked about in high school was going to California and becoming a big star. So people started calling me L.A. I liked it at the time."

"Do you like it now?"

"Not as much. It just doesn't feel like me anymore."

Celeste broke free and started running to her sister. "Rachel! We've been looking for you."

"I'm right where Amy always picks me up." Her glare darted from Celeste to Lorrie Ann. She was going to make a textbook teenager at this rate.

She motioned to the boy next to her. "This is Seth Miller."

"So you're the new babysitter," the boy snarled, flipping the long hair out of his eyes. He slumped next to Rachel, holding her hand, his hoodie and jeans looking two sizes too big for his slender frame.

Rachel hit him in the arm. "I don't need a babysitter."

"I'm not a baby either! And you're not supposed to be holding a boy's hand." Celeste crossed her arms over her chest, glaring at Seth.

"Maybe you should move to the other side of the table, young man." Lorrie Ann grimaced. Did she just use the term *young man?* "You're Vickie's son, right?"

He shrugged his skinny shoulders, dropping Rachel's hand and moving over. "I hear you drive a real sick car."

Lorrie Ann looked back the way they had walked. "Would it be easier if I just drove around to the tennis courts? You need to elevate your leg, Rachel."

Celeste scooted next to Seth, looking in his notebook. "What you writing?"

"Celeste, you come with me." Much to her surprise, she caught a grateful smile from Rachel. She felt way in over her head when it came to dealing with children and wondered what crazy bug had gotten in her brain that had made her agree to take care of these two.

"Seth is Rachel's boyfriend."

"Uh...does your dad know about them?"

"Nope." And with that one loaded word, Celeste skipped ahead.

Chapter Ten

A shirt landed on Lorrie Ann's head, blinding her for a moment. Raising her face to the loft, she caught the next piece of flying clothing before it hit her. "Hey!"

Rachel laughed as she sat with her leg high on pillows. "That's Celeste's idea of gathering up the laundry." She turned her face to the loft. "Don't forget my purple shirt with the black threading. I want to wear it for Spirit Day."

Lorrie Ann opened the closet with the stacked washer and dryer and started the water. "What about your dad's clothes?"

Rachel shrugged but kept her face in the book she read. The sky opened up and a downpour of girls' clothes flooded the living space.

"When was the last time you did your laundry?" Lorrie Ann asked as she picked up the small shirts, jeans and socks mixed with towels and sheets. "We're not going to get all this in one load."

She looked up to see Celeste swing from the top of the stairs.

"Celeste Rebecca Levi, walk down those stairs!" Rachel yelled before Lorrie Ann could say anything.

"I'm going to Jenny's pj party this weekend. We're going to sing and practice for the play." Celeste brought a basket over by the washing machine and started putting the sheets and towels in a pile.

"You can't go this weekend," Rachel said. "I'm going to Kendal's bowling party. It's a sleepover."

"Why can't you both go to your parties?" Lorrie Ann closed the lid and faced Rachel, puzzled over the girl's concern.

"I don't want to leave Daddy alone for a whole weekend."

"Oh, that's sweet, but I'm sure your dad can handle it. He's a grown man, and sometimes adults like to have their own time."

"Not Daddy. He told me he loves having us home with him and it's too quiet when we are both gone. Anyways, some of the ladies in town might use it as an excuse to bother him."

She thought of his invitation for Saturday. Maybe it wasn't a date so much as him wanting company. But why her?

"Well, he did ask me to go to Kerrville with him."

"You?" Rachel's voice sounded alarmed. Lorrie Ann decided not to take offense. Rachel cared about her father and wanted the best for him. She agreed. A wild child from L.A. was not it.

"We're just friends, Rachel. I'll be heading back to California soon." She put water in the kettle to make tea. "It sounds like you both have great plans for the weekend. Your dad would feel bad if you canceled because of him."

Celeste took her hand and led her to the other side of the L-shaped couch. "I told everyone you put my outfit together and did my hair. They liked it." She jumped and clapped her hands together. "I have a great idea. We can have a sleepover here, with you. You can do our hair and help us dress up. It would be fun."

"Daddy won't allow it. You know that."

"But if Miss Lorrie Ann stays then it's okay." She looked back to Lorrie Ann. "Daddy doesn't think it's smart to have our friends overnight because we don't have a mom. But if you stayed it would be okay."

"No, we have a mom. She's just not here," Rachel snapped. "She can't spend the night. It would cause even more gossip. You're such a baby."

Celeste planted her fists on her small hips and stomped a zebra-striped boot. "Am not."

It never occurred to Lorrie Ann all the land mines a single father had to step around, and being the local pastor just made it worse.

"I'm sorry, Celeste. I don't think it would be a good idea. Most of the moms don't really know me either."

Celeste crossed her arms. "You could still help with the pageant."

"You know what? I think I will. It's not as if I have anything better to do while I'm here. Sitting around will drive me crazy."

Clapping, Celeste jumped up and down. "Yay!" With a shout, she threw herself at Lorrie Ann and wrapped her small arms around her neck.

"But *she* will drive you crazy." Rachel shook her head and grinned at her little sister.

Turning back to sit down, Celeste stuck her tongue out. "I will not."

Lorrie Ann sat in the corner with a throw pillow under one arm. Celeste quickly crawled next to her as if it was the most natural thing in the world to curl up in Lorrie Ann's lap.

"Will you tell us more of your story?"

"My story?" Her forehead wrinkled between her eyes. She couldn't imagine Pastor John being happy with her telling them stories from her past.

"Yeah, the one about the lost baby princess." Celeste nestled deeper into Lorrie Ann. "The mother wolf protected her in the forest."

"Oh, that one. Well, let's see. We were deep in the forest, right? Far away from the village, an old lady lived by a river. The people in town whispered about her weird behavior, evidence of her craziness." Lorrie Ann ran her hand through Celeste's silky strands. Glancing over at Rachel, she smiled. The girl's book lay open, but Rachel had her head back, gazing into the heavy rafters.

"Is she a scary old lady?" Celeste whispered.

"Oh, no, but because she was different, people stayed away. She wore every piece of jewelry she had collected over the years. The gold and silver rattled every time she moved."

"She didn't have a sister or husband?" Celeste asked.

"No, she lived alone. When she found the baby lying in the tangled roots of her favorite tree, she thanked God for the precious gift of a child she thought to never have. The old lady loved the baby but feared someone would hurt her, so they stayed deep in the woods. The secret princess grew strong. Her only playmates were wild animals of the forest."

"Didn't she want to play with other kids?" Rachel asked without ever looking at Lorrie Ann.

"Yes, she did, and as she got older she would ask about the world beyond their little cabin. She loved the woman she called Grandmamma, but in her heart she knew there was more."

Celeste turned so she could look up at her. "What about her daddy? Was he looking for her?"

"Celeste, if you would stop asking questions Lorrie Ann could finish the story."

The younger sister stuck out her tongue at Rachel. "You asked a question, too."

Lorrie Ann couldn't hold back the laughter. "You girls fight over the silliest things." A high-pitched whistle filled the cabin. "Come on, Celeste. You can help me make tea."

Celeste jumped up. "But what about her daddy—was he sad?"

"Of course. Every day people would come from far and wide to report sightings of his daughter. Many even brought in little girls, claiming they had found the lost princess. However, he knew a secret that would prove to him his precious jewel had been found. With each proving false, his heart would grow a little tighter. But every year on the day of her birth he sent out five hundred doves, each with a message to her."

Celeste opened the refrigerator door, and Lorrie Ann put the iced tea in to keep cold. She added the garlic bread to the oven and took off the foil lid to the lasagna.

When they finished, Celeste pulled her back to the sofa. "Did a dove ever find her?"

"A few found their way to the forest, but the old lady chased them off. By now, almost twenty years had passed and the girl no longer wanted to wait to discover the world. Late one night she packed a bag and climbed out her window."

"Wait—if she was twenty, why did she have to sneak away?" This time Rachel turned to her and frowned. "She's old enough to live on her own."

"But the old lady wouldn't let her leave, right?" Celeste rubbed her hands together. "She was afraid of being alone."

"That's part of it. She also knew someone wanted to hurt the princess. She wanted to protect her from the dangers of the world."

The door opened, and all three turned their heads.

"Daddy!" both girls said at once.

Celeste ran to her father. The little girl's unguarded joy gave Lorrie Ann images of what she had missed as a young child.

John swung his more energetic greeter to his hip and kissed her on the cheek as she tangled her arms around his neck. "Hey, monkey. Mmm…the kitchen smells good."

"I helped Miss Lorrie Ann make dinner."

He slid his daughter to the floor. "You didn't need to start supper."

His gaze focused on Lorrie Ann. She made herself stop chewing on her upper lip and smiled. "You have enough casseroles in your refrigerator and freezer to feed a family for three months. We just threw one in the oven with the garlic bread. You want some tea?" She moved to get the pitcher, avoiding his probing eyes.

He chuckled and moved into the living room to check on Rachel. "A blessing or a curse of being a single dad in a small town? Every female in the area has a desire to feed us."

"Poor you. Well, I'll be going home. Rachel did her homework, and Celeste started a load in the washer."

John gave his daughter a quizzical stare. "You did a load of laundry?"

"Yes, I did! Miss Lorrie Ann helped me. But I separated the towels and whites like Rachel told me."

"Good job." With a smile that created a long dimple on his left cheek, he turned his attention to Lorrie Ann. "Why don't you eat with us." He hung up his jacket in the closet and pulled his tie loose. "I'm sorry. I told you I'd be home by five and it's almost five-thirty. You're probably ready to get outta here."

"Stay, Lorrie Ann!" Celeste grabbed her hand and started jumping up and down. "Tonight's game night. We can have four!"

"Stop embarrassing yourself, Celeste," Rachel scolded from the living area.

"Settle down. Lorrie Ann might have other business to take care of." John mouthed a *sorry* to her.

"No, no. It's okay. The smell of warm garlic butter has my mouth watering." Maybe it wasn't the food as much as the man.

"Good. We always seem to be the guest. We never get to serve from our table." He headed to the kitchen. "If I ever get our house on the ranch finished, we'll get to invite everyone to our home. I'll make the salad."

"Um…" All of a sudden, she felt as if she was playing house with Pastor John Levi, but instead of the dolls Yolanda used to have, this was with real children. A family of her own had always seemed out of her grasp. She'd tried to force it with Brent, but look where that had gotten her.

Did God want her to see what she had given up? Lorrie Ann looked around for something to do so she wouldn't feel awkward. "I can chop something."

"Too late—all done." He held up an empty bag of precut salad mix. "What does it say about a society when we are too busy to cut some carrots and lettuce?"

The timer went off, and Rachel started making her way to the kitchen table.

Once seated, they joined hands and prayed. The feel of John's strong hand wrapped around her smaller one, while Celeste held her other, gave her a lump in her throat. She repeated each word of the family prayer and stored them in her heart.

After the prayer, easy chatter about their day filled the room. Lorrie Ann remained silent. She didn't want to destroy the warm, cozy ambience at the family table. For a moment in time, she was the mom of this beautiful family. Then guilt snaked its way up to her stomach. She wasn't their mom, and she had no right pretending even for a minute. This was the dream she never even knew lay buried in her heart, the dream she'd sacrificed at the altar of fame and success.

John laughed at something the girls said then turned his attention to her.

"What do you think, Lorrie Ann?"

"I, um…wasn't listening. Sorry."

"That's okay. So, how did the first day of pickup duty go?" he asked with a friendly smile as he took another bite of lasagna.

Oh, with everything else she had forgotten, she needed to talk to him about Rachel's boyfriend. She had wanted to speak to him privately so as not to embarrass Rachel. She looked at both girls. They suddenly concentrated on their food.

"This isn't good. Who's going to tell me what happened? Celeste, did you cause problems?"

"It wasn't me. It was Rachel. She has a boyfriend!"

A frown creased his forehead. "Rachel? That can't be true."

The preteen had her hands under the table, her face focused on her plate.

John moved his glare to Lorrie Ann.

With a sigh, Lorrie Ann answered the question in John's eyes. "It wasn't that big a deal. After the playground cleared we couldn't find her. She was waiting on the other side of the school, sitting at the picnic tables."

Rachel picked her head up and looked at her dad. "That's where Amy always picks me up. Every day after school. Then we get Celeste off the playground. Celeste gets to play for a while, and the traffic clears out. It's what we did. I forgot to go to the car lineup today." She turned to Lorrie Ann and gave her a glare that rated off the charts. "That's all."

Celeste popped up on her knees. "No, that's not all. She was sitting with Seth Miller."

John tilted his head and raised his eyebrow.

"He's her boyfriend." In a singsong voice, Celeste chimed loudly. "K-I-S-S-I-N-G."

The shock on John's face would have been comical if not for the tension in the cabin.

"They were holding hands." Celeste made kissy faces at her big sister, unaware of their father's mood change.

"You're a baby!" Rachel yelled, leaning forward.

"Well, you were!" Arms crossed over her chest, Celeste flopped back in her chair.

"You're eleven years old." John's strong voice silenced the room.

"I'm almost twelve," she whispered after a period of quietness.

He looked at Lorrie Ann as if he somehow wanted to blame her.

"You know the rules about boyfriends." He covered his plate with the dinner napkin.

"We aren't dating, Daddy. We were just…holding hands." She buried her chin into her chest, which muffled her last words.

"How long has this been going on?" His jaw flexed.

"He asked her Wednesday night." Celeste provided the answer.

"At church? You're grounded." His sharp reply came fast.

"Why?" Tears hung in her eyes now. "I haven't done anything wrong. We…we…just held hands. He asked me to the homecoming dance."

"You're not going." John stood, taking his empty plate to the sink.

"Daddy, you already said I could go!"

"With your friends, not Seth."

"He *is* my friend."

Lorrie Ann felt like crying. Everything had been so perfect until she'd ruined the night. "I'm sorry." She started gathering the leftovers. "They were just sitting on the bench writing in a notebook."

"We were doing our English homework," Rachel mumbled. "May I go—" she looked up to the loft then around the cabin "—to your room? Please." She wiped her eyes with the back of her hand.

"Yes." John sighed and reached his hand out to cup his daughter's face. "I love you, but you're too young to date. We'll talk about this later. From now on, you will go straight to Lorrie Ann's car."

"Yes, sir."

Lorrie Ann started running water in the sink. "I ruined the family dinner."

He carried the remaining dishes to the counter. "No, you didn't. That's what families do. We laugh, love, fight, work it out and start all over." John braced his arms on the tile edge next to her. "Actually, this might be the first time Rachel has broken any of my rules." John started drying the dishes as she washed.

The domestic job had her feeling warm inside.

He set the towel down and turned to her, one hip rested on the edge. "Man, she's almost a teenager. I don't think I'm ready for a teenage daughter. I don't know how I'm going to do this without Carol. If I had my way, I'd just lock the girls away. What do I know about teenagers? Carol was the only girl I ever dated. I didn't even have a sister."

"You'll be fine. I personally think dads are the key to raising a self-confident girl."

He leaned in closer, about to say something. Her gaze stayed on his eyes, waiting.

"Daddy, tonight's game night. Can Lorrie Ann play with us?"

They both pulled back.

"Oh, no. I think I've done enough damage for one night. I'm going to be heading home."

John's golden eyes pierced her. "Why don't you play with us. You can pick the game."

Lorrie Ann wanted to linger, but what frightened her most was the desire to stay forever. He needed a stable woman in his life, not a walking disaster.

"Good night, rug rat." She kissed Celeste on the cheek. "I'm sure Aunt Maggie will be sending me over with breakfast again."

"Good night."

"I'll walk you out." He opened the door and waited for her to walk through. "Dinner was nice, thanks. I don't remember the last time I came home to dinner on the table."

"Up until the middle-school drama." She stopped on the front porch. As much as her brain screamed for her to run as fast as she could, something else wanted to hang on and never leave. "Sorry about the boyfriend thing." She bit her lip and debated if she had a right to make the next statement. "About the dance—you should still let her go. I'm sure they would love to have you as a chaperone. My aunt and uncle attended all our dances when I was in school."

"You're probably right. Lorrie Ann, it's not your fault. She's growing up, and I'm going to have to find a way to deal with it." He shuffled his feet, his hands fisted deep in his pockets as he looked over the driveway toward the pecan orchard. He cleared his throat. "About Saturday…?"

She smiled. He reminded her of a middle-school boy asking a girl for his first dance. "I would love to."

His face turned back to her. "Really?"

"Yeah. The girls said they had plans with their friends and you didn't like being alone."

"Oh." Something crossed his face she hadn't seen before, but it disappeared quickly, and he flashed her his heartwarming grin. "I'll be working on the house until about two or three. I'm trying to get the remodeling done before spring. We can head to Kerrville about five. That should give us time to eat dinner then head out to the art gallery."

"Sounds good." *Back away, girl. Put one foot in front of the other.* She moved to the steps.

He followed her down. His boots crunched the red gravel walkway. She could hear the wind whispering through the branches as insects chirped and sang. The urge to hold John's hand caused her fingers to clench. She kept a safe distance between them. More important, she needed to keep her heart at a safe distance. A bad feeling washed over her that she would spend most of the night wondering what it would be like to kiss a pastor. Well, not any pastor—just Pastor John Levi.

John lingered on the edge of the porch, even after hearing the screen door close behind Lorrie Ann. Sometimes life changed so fast he felt out of control, but he couldn't remember ever feeling so alone. Walking to the front railing, he scanned the rows of pecan trees that stretched into the darkness. The stars appeared anchored in the velvet night sky, but under his feet it felt as if his world was shifting.

He didn't like this edgy, restless feeling that had been hounding him. Was it an awareness of Lorrie Ann as a woman or the idea that Rachel inched closer to growing up each day?

Both thoughts made him uncomfortable. It didn't

matter how nice it felt having Lorrie Ann at the dinner table. He couldn't let his heart go there.

His head dropped between his shoulders. How could he raise two girls without Carol's insight and wisdom? Just the thought of Rachel dating... No, he couldn't let his mind wander down that path. Despite his love for Carol, he had neglected and hurt her. If he couldn't prevent that from happening, how could he allow himself to trust some kid with his daughter's heart?

"Daddy?" Celeste had her head poking out the door. "Can we play a game? Rachel is already asleep."

What he could do right now was hold his little girl and let her know he loved her.

"Come on, monkey. How about a story instead of a game tonight?" He led her into the living room.

"Sure!" She headed up the stairs and returned with a large hardcover book. With one arm wrapped around the children's story Bible, Celeste jumped onto the sofa next to him.

One thing he knew with certainty—there was no promise of a second chance. He pushed a few loose strands of hair from her face and kissed her forehead. "Which story do you want tonight?"

"The one about Joseph and Mary with baby Jesus."

She curled into his lap, her head on his chest. He took the time to feel the rhythm of her heart and hear her soft breathing. He forced himself to live in the moment and the incredible gift curled up in his lap.

Chapter Eleven

A late-October front had blown in and dropped the temperature. Wrapped up in Aunt Maggie's poncho, Lorrie Ann felt like Little Red Riding Hood as she followed the dirt road along the fence. Pulling the heavy wool closer, she grinned. Well, more like Purple Riding Hood. Sent to the Childress Ranch, Lorrie Ann carried a basket heavy with hot coffee and cinnamon rolls.

She slipped through the gate that divided the two properties and continued on the road until she saw the grand two-story limestone home. She remembered hiding in the huge house when she was little and recalled the broken boards leading to the sagging porch and the ugly carpet that gave the house a moldy smell.

Now, standing out against the majestic hills in the background, the porch and upper-level deck gleamed with newly replaced rich wood, taking the home back to the pride of the first Childress that had settled here.

As she moved closer, she saw John's truck parked at the side of the house, breaking the illusion of days gone by.

Taking a deep breath, she moved up the recently re-

built steps. At the door, she hesitated with disappointment when she spotted two other vehicles. She shook
her head. She should be relieved John had company.
The less time they spent alone the better.

"Hello?" Stepping into the house was a shock. The
place stood gutted; only a few of the old columns remained. From the front door, she could see all the way
through the house to the French doors and huge window covering the back wall. Clear plastic covered old
wood floors. Jake and two other men she recognized
from church worked in the far left corner.

"Lorrie Ann." Jake turned off the power tool and
walked toward her. "Let me guess—you're looking for
John?"

She felt her face heat up, and she glanced to the grand
staircase. John appeared at the top and paused when he
spotted her. Then a grin filled his face, bringing out his
dimple. She forgot all about Jake and the others.

"John! You have company, and I think she brought
gifts from Maggie's kitchen." Jake took the loaded basket from her and peeked inside.

Now she knew why Aunt Maggie had packed so
much. "With the front moving in so fast, she thought
you might want some warm coffee. And of course,
being Aunt Maggie, she had to send food, too."

In a few seconds, the guys pulled together makeshift
chairs and passed around the basket. She found herself
sitting on the foot of the curved stairs next to John.

There was no talking as the men ate the cinnamon
rolls, just a few moans of appreciation. When George
wiped his hands on paint-stained work jeans, she remembered the wipes in the basket and handed them out.

"This is why we work for you, John—the off chance

your neighbor will feed us." Jake winked at her as he stood. "I guess that's good for a bit more work. We're going to finish the drywall in the kitchen, then it'll be ready for the cabinets." He nodded to Lorrie Ann and grinned. "Thanks for the delivery. It hit the spot."

"Want a tour?" John stood and offered his hand to her.

"It looks a little different from the last time I was here." She put her hand in his, enjoying the feel of his warmth and strength.

Her feminist friends in L.A. would be appalled at the way she liked feeling feminine and a bit fragile. Even though she knew safe and protected was an illusion. She sighed. Yep, she definitely needed to get back to California.

He led her to the area where the guys hung drywall. The nail gun punctured the wall with a loud thud.

"This is obviously the kitchen. We're putting a large island here that has a curved countertop raised on that side." He swung his arms, showing the layout. "It'll be large enough to fit five people. The stove will be here so you can face the living area while cooking. I thought about putting the sink there, too." He turned to face the back wall, where a giant window framed a view of the hills. "But I decided to keep it under the window looking out back. We're using local granite." He patted Jake on the back as they passed him. "Good work, guys. I can't thank you enough for helping me on your day off."

"Make sure to put in a good word for us with the man upstairs," Adrian said, wrapping a cord around another power tool as he started packing them up. "I love restoring the old homes around here."

John nodded. "I can't wait until we get started on the

cabinets." He looked at Lorrie Ann. "We're using the old wood from the carriage house.

"Over in the far corner, where the large bay window sits, is a new room and bath." He placed his hand under her elbow. "For now, I'm going to use it as an office, but I wanted to have a bedroom on the ground floor if we ever need it." He gave her a lopsided grin. "I was thinking more along the lines of Dub moving in with us, but with Rachel's leg I think it's a good idea to have the bedroom option down here."

She nodded. When she and Brent had looked at houses, it had never crossed their minds to think of the future or the needs of others. "That's a smart plan."

"This whole floor will remain open from the kitchen to the living room, with a large dining-room table along those windows joining the two." His words created an image of the perfect family living space. "A little like Maggie's." He winked at her. "I love her big table and the idea of family and friends always having a seat."

Lorrie Ann couldn't help comparing it against her life with Brent. The large glass-and-steel table at his house had such a different purpose, to impress and intimidate.

"That's perfect. Are you going to have it made out of the old wood?"

"No, I already have the table. On a mission trip to Mexico, we came across some furniture makers. They had this twelve-foot table. The legs are a foot thick and hand carved. They're incredible. The wood was saved from an old mission. The men were so proud of their work." He laughed. "We had to tie it down on the top of the bus with ropes running across the roof, crisscrossing from window to window."

His hand slipped from her elbow to her hand as he pulled her up the staircase. "The stairs and front porch were the first structures we repaired. It was amazing no one was hurt."

She laughed. "I used to hide here. The stairs scared me."

"No one's lived here for over twenty years. We had to evict a family of raccoons." With his last words, they reached the second floor. To the right, the large bay seating area drew her to step into the open space. The floor-to-ceiling window gave a panoramic view. From up here she could see her uncle's pecan orchard. The river curved below the bluff behind the house. She turned to John. "This is beautiful. You have a million-dollar view here."

He looked to the hallway behind him. "This floor had six small rooms and one bathroom. We reframed it as four rooms with larger closets and two-and-a-half baths. The front is the master."

She poked her head into each room. "Have the girls picked out their rooms yet?"

"Oh, yes. Celeste wants the room with the box-seat window. She likes the idea of hiding things in the seat, and it's next to my room. Rachel took the room with its own half bath."

She smiled, picturing Celeste with clothes, books and toys all over the floor and every piece of furniture. Rachel would have a place for everything and everything in its place.

"This is going to be a wonderful home for the girls."

"I'm hoping to get enough done that we can move in before May so Maggie can have her biggest cabin back for the summer tourists. Plus, it'll be nice to have our own place. Only one floor left." Going back to the large bay window, he led the way up a narrow staircase taking them to the once-upon-a-time attic.

"This is my favorite room." The large half-circle windows at the end of the room were breathtaking. "I won't be able to finish it out anytime soon, but I want the basics in place." He stood at the window that looked across the ranch. "From here you can see Dub's stables and arena."

He turned back to her, the sun highlighting his bone structure. She put her hand in her pocket to keep it from running along his jaw. The dark shadow of a beard gave him the look of a rugged workingman, the kind of man who took care of his family.

"I thought about making this floor the master suite, but it's a bit disconnected from the rest of the house, and all this room would be wasted on one person."

"Do you think you'll ever remarry?" Did she just blurt that out? "Sorry, that was really personal."

"You take care of my girls, and I've given you the first tour of my home. Hopefully, we're friends enough to ask personal questions." He glanced at his watch. "If we're going to eat dinner before the art opening, we need to close up shop." He held his arm out to her.

As they headed out of the house, she realized he never answered her question.

Standing in front of the mirror, Lorrie Ann twisted back and forth. Maybe she should change. The heels might be a bit much for an art opening in Kerrville. But she loved the way the black velvet straps laced up her calves. She wore a knee-length wraparound skirt and a blue-and-green-marbled silk shirt with a bit of a Southwest look to it. She glanced back in her closet. Maybe the shirt with a pair of jeans and a pair of Aunt Maggie's designer cowboy boots would be better.

A knock on the door interrupted her thoughts.

"Lorrie Ann?" Aunt Maggie's voice drifted through the door. "Pastor John's here."

Lorrie Ann's eyes flew to the clock by her bedside. Ugh, where had the time gone? She crossed the room and opened the door.

"Are the shoes too much?"

"You're asking me after what you wore to the Wednesday-night prayer meeting?" Laughter laced her voice. "Come on. You're beautiful, and that poor man looks nervous."

"Oh, Aunt Maggie, I'm sorry I didn't even think about how my choices affect you."

"Don't be silly. I don't let what others do or think bother me. Anyways, this is Texas. You can wear stilettos or torn jeans, as long as you walk with enough confidence. Now, hurry on with you."

Lorrie Ann took a deep breath and walked down the hallway, keeping her back straight. *Smile, stand tall and fake it as long as you have to.*

John stood with his back to them, looking at the photos lining the shelves.

Uncle Billy put the newspaper down and smiled at her. "Lorrie Ann, you look downright pretty."

John spun on his heels. "Wow, you always seem to surprise me."

"Is that a good thing?" She held her smile, trying to read him. "I wasn't sure what kind of art gallery we were going to, so if I need—"

"No, it's perfect. He does contemporary Western

type of stuff, so I think you're perfect. I mean your out-fit is perfect. Well, you are, too, but I…"

Her smile became real as her heart jumped around a little.

"Have her home by nine o'clock." Uncle Billy's stern voice startled them both.

A panicked look flashed across John's face. "The show doesn't end until—"

Uncle Billy laughed. "I'm just kidding. It's been a long time since I got to say that for one of my girls. Y'all be careful."

"Yes, sir." John shook his hand.

Lorrie Ann bit her lip as they headed out the door. The words *one of my girls* hit her heart hard and caused strange emotions to bubble up.

John tilted his head and gave her a questioning look. She managed to nod. "He… I don't think he's ever called me his girl before."

John's concern melted into a slow smile. "He loves you."

"I'm not even related to him by blood, and he's so quiet I never really knew how he felt. My mother dumped me on them and left." She crossed her arms around her waist and took in the pale yellows and pinks settling over the endless rows of pecan trees. She had never told anyone how she had come to live with her aunt. "I was in and out of their house growing up. My mom…well, she had issues. Whenever it got too rough or she got in over her head with the latest boyfriend, we would come here to hide." She looked up at John, and the warmth in his eyes pushed at the cold that had been in her heart for so long. No other man had ever listened to her the way he did. In a way, it scared her to find she might actually trust him. He didn't know the real Lorrie Ann. "When I was twelve she decided I got in her way and took off without a backward glance. That was the last time I saw her. Uncle Billy and Aunt Maggie didn't have a choice. They were stuck with me." She paused. "All these years later and they are still stuck with me. No one seems to know where my mom is—" she gave a half laugh "—or they're just not telling me."

Silence hung between them for a moment as John intently studied her face, his lips tight.

Finally he smiled. "That's not the story they tell. You were a blessing to a couple that had dreamed of having a house full of kids but were only able to have one. William's the kind of man who shows his love through action. Giving you a place to live, feeding you and taking care of you... That's him saying he loves you."

She used the tip of her finger to wipe away the tear before it fell and messed up her makeup. "I thought he just tolerated me because of Aunt Maggie."

"He may be quiet, but he loves his family deeply, and you are his family."

He paused at the end of the patio. "So, do we go in my well-loved, well-worn truck or your fancy city-slicker car?"

"I love your truck, but have you ever driven a BMW?"

With his eyes on the car, he gave a shake of his head.

She pulled the keys from her small clutch purse and held them up. "She's all yours tonight."

"Really?" Another smile slowly eased its way across his face, and she knew then and there she would do anything just to see his smile.

He sat behind the wheel and ran his hands over the

leather steering wheel. She shook her head. What was it about men and cars?

Starting the engine, he eased the Beemer out of the driveway and winked at her. "I've never sat in, let alone driven, a machine worth more than I could make in three or more years as a country preacher."

"Well, enjoy. I'm trading it in for something more practical. It was a birthday gift from Brent. He said it would look good parked in front of our house when we got married." She watched the trees flash by as they climbed higher into the hills. "Since I won't be moving back I should get rid of the car, too."

"When do you plan on going back?"

"I'm not sure. A few things have to be cleared before I return. If it doesn't work out, I might just stay here for a while."

"A great deal of people would love for you to stay."

She laughed and made a face at him. "Yeah, right. Everything I worked for is back in L.A. It would be like…I don't know…letting Brent win."

"If you're happy, you win no matter where you live."

"I just can't imagine my life without everything I have in L.A. It's who I am now." She studied the sun setting behind the hills. Spots of red and yellow fall foliage mixed with the evergreens that covered the rocky slopes.

What scared her most? She could see herself in John's house, at his dinner table, watching the girls as they did their homework, hosting an all-girls sleepover while he hid upstairs in the master bedroom. She could see it so clearly and knew it was wrong. She didn't belong in his home, playing mother to his children. The sooner she got back to her real life the better for everyone.

"Is it safe to go back?"

She bit her lip. "You mean Brent? He's in rehab right now, and I won't go back unless I know he won't be around. If he stays in the band, I'll find another band to manage. I have enough connections and already have some people contacting me."

His jaw flexed, and he nodded, giving her a stiff smile before looking back to the road. "Good."

Good. That was all he could come up with to say? He shook his head. Just the thought of her being anywhere near that guy raised his blood pressure.

He knew the bruise on her eye didn't have anything to do with the accident. He took a deep breath and focused on the road, sliding the car around a sharp curve that hugged the hillside. This road had never felt so smooth.

Which just took his thoughts right back to Lorrie Ann, causing him to smile. She would have been just fine coming in his truck or her little show car. She might like to think of herself as all L.A., but she was also one of the most down-to-earth women he knew. He really enjoyed being in her company.

He cut a glance at his passenger, who stared out the window. He had gotten too personal earlier. *God, help me here. I haven't been on a date in a long time.* He tightened his fingers around the leather as they hugged another curve.

"Have you eaten at Mamasita's?"

She turned her head and smiled back at him. "Uncle Billy took us there anytime we had something to celebrate. It's his favorite restaurant." She gave a small laugh. "I love watching them make the tortillas."

"That always keeps Celeste entertained for a good fifteen minutes."

The conversation moved from the girls to his plans for the ranch house. A couple times he wanted to bring up her mother but wasn't sure how without breaking Sonia's trust. By the time they pulled into the parking lot of the restaurant, they had started discussing the Christmas pageant and ideas Lorrie Ann wanted to try.

Through dinner, they continued talking about pleasant things, when he really wanted to ask why she was going back to a life that made her miserable. He sighed and reminded himself he didn't want a long-term relationship. It was just one date.

As they left the restaurant and headed to the gallery, Lorrie Ann reminded herself she had been invited to come along tonight because he didn't want to go alone.

This was not a real date.

A man like John would only invite her because she made an uncomplicated companion. She grunted at the idea of her being uncomplicated. A better word would be *convenient*.

By the time they arrived at the art gallery, she had any wild idea of a romantic relationship firmly locked down. They were friends. God sent her to Clear Water to reconnect with her faith. What better friend than John, a man of God, to guide her?

He held out his arm as they approached the steps to a large Victorian mansion. A hand-carved sign proclaimed the establishment as J. K. West's Fine Art Gallery and Studio.

The deep porch wrapped around the entire house. Elaborate iron lanterns hung from each column, and more light blazed from the windows, welcoming them into its historical splendor.

The glass-and-wood door swung open as soon as her heels clicked on the polished wooden boards. The well-dressed hostess handed them a brochure about the artist and escorted them to a buffet table full of hors d'oeuvres and desserts. With a big smile, she offered them something to drink then headed back to the door.

John leaned in close to her ear. "Between your car and fancy shoes, I think they believe we're buyers."

She saluted him with her glass of ice water and gave him a cheeky grin. "Maybe we are."

"Yeah, right." He glanced at a price listed next to a large canvas. "Do you know how many vacuum cleaners I could buy for the price of one of Gary's paintings?"

Lorrie Ann gave a soft laugh. This man would be so easy to love. They moved through the rooms connected by large archways, each wall displaying another canvas.

"These are brilliant." Taking her gaze off the painting in front of them, she turned to John. "How do you know the artist?"

"We grew up playing football together until my grandparents took me to Houston my junior year. He moved in with me while he attended the Art Institute of Houston."

A hand grasped John's shoulder. They both turned quickly. "*I* played football. He just wanted to talk to the cheerleaders."

"Gary!" The men hugged and gave each other a pounding on the shoulder. "Where have you been hiding?"

"Some collectors wanted a tour of the studio upstairs." He turned to Lorrie Ann. She could not imagine this tall, lean man playing football. *Beautiful* came to mind with his dark hair framing perfect skin and teeth. His thick lashes gave the illusion of eyeliner, making his coffee-dark eyes riveting.

John moved into her line of vision, drawing her attention back to him. "Lorrie Ann, this is Gary Sanchez. Gary, Lorrie Ann is my neighbor's niece. She's visiting from Los Angeles."

He held out his hand to her. "Thank you so much for coming."

Lorrie Ann could not shake the feeling she had seen him somewhere before. "This sounds lame—" she smiled "—but have you done print work or TV? You look very familiar."

He shook his head, but John interrupted before he could speak.

"You've seen him in the wedding picture in the cabin."

Gary then shot a quick glance to Lorrie Ann with brows raised.

Lorrie Ann felt her face grow warm. "I'm watching the girls." She swallowed, suddenly feeling nervous. "Rachel broke her leg."

Gary laughed and slapped John on the back again. "Yeah, John told me what happened. So, you're the one who's helping out?" His beautiful smile showed off perfect teeth.

Lorrie Ann smiled back.

John took a sip of his water. "Gary *was* my best man."

"I'm still your best man."

"This summer Gary's moving into the former maids' quarters. He's turning it into a studio."

"I prefer to call it the guesthouse." He glanced around the room and smiled at a couple studying his work. "I'm excited about living in the Hill Country." He nodded toward the archway to their right. "Have you been to the front parlor yet?"

"No, we were heading that way."

"Your work is breathtaking. The strokes of colors are so packed with emotion and energy they pull me into the painting."

"Thank you."

As they stepped into the room, a four-by-six canvas pulled her closer. "Wow. This is…" She stared at the painting. "It's so uplifting, like there's music coming right off the image."

John turned to Gary. "Is this what you did with the pictures of Celeste and me?"

"This is *Joy* number 3. I listened to your CD while I painted. A total of five paintings came from those photos and drawings from that day."

Lorrie Ann tilted her head and squinted. In the swirl of vibrant colors, she could see a larger figure swinging a smaller one through the space above him, each brushstroke sweeping her along. "You and Celeste posed for this painting?"

John grinned. "Not really. Gary came out to visit last summer to do some landscape studies."

Gary chuckled. "While I worked on sketches, Celeste grew a little bored, so John started spinning her in circles. I ended up taking more pictures of them than the landscape. By the time I got back to the studio, I knew I had to capture that joy on canvas." He turned back to the painting. "I've already sold two. They've become my favorites."

"Celeste will love to see this."

"They're on my website. Numbers 2 and 5 are in New Mexico." He placed his hand on John's shoulder. "I'm so glad you made it. I've got to play host and sell some of my babies. Very nice meeting you, Lorrie Ann, and I hope to see you again before you head back to L.A."

They moved to another room, studying a collection of smaller paintings grouped on one wall.

Lorrie Ann chuckled. John raised an eyebrow. "What's so funny?"

"Only in Texas would two high-school football players become an artist and a preacher." Her gaze met his. "How did you end up a pastor?"

What she really wanted to ask him? How did a drop-dead-gorgeous hunk become a country pastor in the middle of nowhere? But she knew that would come across as shallow.

"In the church I attended as a teenager there were two youth ministers that changed my life. I knew my purpose by the time I finished high school. I was called to serve God."

"Wow, it was that clear and easy?" She followed him to the next painting.

He looked down at the glass of water he held between his hands. Raising his eyes back to her, he pulled one corner of his mouth to give her a lopsided grin.

"I have to admit it's a bit more complicated. I grew up in Flower Mound, outside Dallas. That's where Gary and I played football. My junior year I lost my parents. They were flying to an air show with my uncle and aunt when their plane went down."

Lorrie Ann moved closer to John, no longer interested in the artwork surrounding them. She laid her hand on his arm.

"I found myself living with my grandparents in Houston." He gave a grunt and took another drink of his ice water. "Grieving four family members, they didn't know what to do for a confused sixteen-year-old. They dropped me off in the youth building at their church, a megachurch with programs that kept me busy day and night. I joined the worship band and found a place I belonged."

She knew what it felt like to be dumped and alone. Of course, her mother had had a choice. His focus stayed on the painting in front of them, but Lorrie Ann wondered if he even saw the room. After a few minutes of silence, she searched for a safe topic.

"You played in a band? Gary mentioned a CD." She grinned. "Now, that sounds right up my alley. Do you write? What instrument did you play?"

He started walking to the next wall display. "If it had strings I played it, guitar being my favorite. The music is part of my past. Chuck and Cody, my youth ministers, had a huge impact on my life and growing my relationship with God. When I graduated, there was never a doubt that I wanted to serve God and join the ministry."

"I wish I had that kind of faith."

"You can. We're designed to worship, but with free will we get to choose who or what we worship."

"I think I might have been at the wrong altar for the past twelve years."

He leaned into her, lightly bumping her shoulder. "It happens to the best of us. I understand how easy it is to have the wrong god on your altar and not even know it." He sat on a flat cushioned bench in the middle of the room and contemplated a landscape that covered the wall from floor to ceiling.

"Don't let guilt or fear stop you from living a full life." His eyes never moved from the painting.

How did he sound so confident and nonjudgmental at the same time? "You make it sound so easy." She slid down next to him.

"Oh, it's not easy." He turned to gaze into her eyes. "It can be so hard sometimes you just want to hide."

"I can see you leading a huge congregation, so how did you end up in little ol' Clear Water?"

"God knew what my family needed before I did. Carol had talked about moving back before she died." His hands braced on the edge of the bench, he dropped his head and paused for a minute. After a deep breath, he continued, "After we lost her, it became difficult to be around our friends, the sad looks and the awkwardness when they celebrated good news. Dub had been trying to get me to his church for about a year. The old pastor wanted to retire, and they couldn't find a full-time replacement."

"Pastor Kemp." She snapped her fingers and smiled as she remembered the old man. "He baptized me. I thought he was in his eighties back then."

"Yeah, that's him. He's incredible."

She thought about how she had lived her life, but she couldn't imagine what she had to offer. "I don't know how God could use me."

He smiled at her and winked. "He already has. Like organizing a Christmas pageant?"

She nudged him in the arm. "No fair."

"As Katy and Maggie have said over and over again,

you came to us because God knew we needed you." He paused, tilted his head and looked her straight in the eye. "I think you needed us also."

She sighed, and her smile felt a little wobbly. "Oh, I know I needed all of you much more than you'll ever need me."

Lorrie Ann glanced at the large clock on the wall, surprised by the time. "It's late. We should be heading home. You're not going to be late for church in the morning. Everyone will blame me." She looked around the gallery and noticed most of the people had already left.

John took her arm to slow her down and laughed. "You act like the clock's about to strike midnight and your car will turn into a pumpkin." He looked around. "Let's say goodbye to Gary."

Lorrie Ann felt a flush cover her face. What was it about this man that caused her to act like a sixteen-year-old?

As they neared the front, she spotted Gary talking to a couple. John lightly touched his arm and said goodbye. Gary gave her a light hug and thanked them for coming.

With her hand on John's arm, they walked to her car. Lorrie Ann settled into the leather seat and studied John as the light from the dashboard reflected on his face. He had a purpose for his life and he knew it. His girls, the church, even his late wife knew the purpose. How did she ever think she could fit into his life?

Chapter Twelve

Wednesday night, sitting in the second pew, Lorrie Ann couldn't believe she had been back in Clear Water for over a week now. After Saturday's nondate, she'd been careful to keep it all business with John. She declined invitations to stay for dinner when he arrived home and avoided any contact with him.

Not that it stopped her from thinking of him. The affection she felt for the girls surprised her the most. Just the thought of saying goodbye to them already tore at her heart.

Lorrie Ann looked at the scriptures being read: *Don't let your hearts be troubled. Trust in God, and trust also in me. For our present troubles are small and won't last very long. Yet they produce for us a glory that vastly outweighs them and will last forever!*

She smiled as Celeste squirmed next to her, causing Rachel to shoot her little sister a warning look.

As people started sharing prayer requests and praises, Celeste raised her hand and waved it until her dad acknowledged her. "I would like to thank God for bringing Miss Lorrie Ann to us and pray that she stays."

She looked at Lorrie Ann before adding, "God willing." With a nod, she folded her hands in her lap and lowered her head.

Lorrie Ann put her hand on Celeste's back and could feel her heart beat. Her chest tightened at the little girl's prayer. Rachel rolled her eyes. Lorrie Ann found herself smiling and adding her own prayers silently to the list. Soon, everyone stood and joined hands to finish the meeting in prayer.

Taking a deep breath, Lorrie Ann slung her bag over her shoulder. The people working with the pageant would meet in the fellowship hall tonight.

"Lorrie Ann!" Katy ran up to her, interlocking their arms. She pulled her close and kept walking toward the back door. "I'm so excited you are doing this. Martha was good, but it was the same thing for the past twenty years. If there is anything I can do, anything at all, please let me know."

Lorrie Ann smiled. Katy's enthusiasm gave her a shot of confidence. "Since you know the kids, I really need your help with them. Picking out the music, casting, that sort of thing."

"Oh, sure, that will be fun. I have some ideas I would love to run by you. Martha had the same songs every year."

As they walked into the hall, the smell of coffee already filled the air. Maggie once again stood behind the counter with a couple other women sorting the desserts.

Lorrie Ann organized the packets Aunt Maggie and Yolanda had helped her create. The room filled with adults, teens and children. She groaned when she saw Rachel sitting with Seth. "Rachel, come here, please."

With a heavy sigh and a roll of the eyes, Rachel stomped over to her. "We're just sitting there talking."

"Yes, but do you think your father would be okay with you sitting in the corner, alone with Seth?" She handed her a stack of color-coded folders. "Maybe Seth can help me pass these out? And I recommend you and Seth sit with your other friends."

John entered the room with Vickie by his side. She touched his arm and laughed. Lorrie Ann opened her computer and focused on the screen. She had no right to be angry about another woman talking with him. Her tongue started pushing back and forth against her teeth.

When she looked over the room, Vickie flashed a smile and leaned closer to John. He cleared his throat and stepped away, moving toward Lorrie Ann.

Oh, that felt good, even though she knew pettiness should be above her. She turned to smile at Vickie's narrowing eyes. Yes, she could be the bigger person.

John stood next to her. "Are you ready?"

She nodded to the people gathering around the tables. "Not sure if they're ready for me."

"They'll be fine." He gave her the slow smile that melted her heart. "Once this meeting gets started, I'll be taking the missionary committee to my office. Tonight shouldn't last as long. I might even get to take the girls home tonight."

Disappointment inundated her. She had started looking forward to the bedtime ritual. As a child, she'd never had a routine of any kind. She had been too busy staying out of the way.

John called for everyone's attention. "Welcome. First, I'm excited to announce that the play has been moved to the unfinished youth building."

Mutters and mumbles filled the room.

Vickie spoke up first. "Pastor John, that doesn't make any sense. There are no walls."

"We don't have electricity run to the building yet," someone else yelled from the back.

John grinned. "That's right. We're scheduled to have utilities in by the end of next week. As far as no walls, that works perfectly for the ideas Lorrie Ann has shared with me." He smiled at her. "Now, if you'll excuse me, I have another meeting. I leave you in capable hands."

Her stomach dropped a bit when he left. She scanned the room. Everyone had turned their attention to her. It surprised her a bit when she realized how many friendly faces sat in the crowd. Maybe her memories had painted the town much darker than it deserved.

Stretching her spine, she filled her lungs with oxygen and put her best smile on her face. Lorrie Ann slowly rose from her chair. "This year we will be using live animals and a cherry picker to hoist an angel in the air. The concrete floor with the metal poles will be a perfect stage for our setting."

Mrs. Miller, the Dragon Lady, hit her cane on the floor. "Live animals with kids and an audience? Sounds dangerous to me."

"What if it's cold or rains?" someone else shouted out.

Lorrie Ann continued to smile and made eye contact with the people gathered. It was a mix of people from six years old to eighty. "That's why I need help from you. We will need an animal wrangler. We'll also come up with an alternate plan in case of bad weather. When I asked Pastor John about the problems with the plan, he gave me some great advice. He said to proceed with faith." Lorrie Ann held up her green folder. "Based on the information Aunt Maggie gave me last week, I've created folders for each person by committee."

Rachel handed out the last folder and sat at the table with the other girls.

Lorrie Ann soaked in the level of excitement she heard in the conversation.

"I have ideas and drawings included in your folder, but please feel free to come up with your own."

"Wow, Lorrie Ann, this appears ambitious." Jake leafed through his folder and then smiled at her. "It looks great."

"The costumes are awesome."

Vickie stood with arms crossed. "We usually just redo and alter the ones we already have. Your plan will need new costumes. Who's paying for all this material?"

"We do have a small budget, and donations have already been made to cover the costs."

"I have some leftover panels we can use for the set design."

"Thank you, Adrian. Now, if you look at the first pages you'll see a calendar with rehearsal dates and deadlines. It's color coded to your folder. There's no need for everyone to be at every meeting or practice. Not until we start full run-throughs, anyway. And as groups you can set your times to meet as often as you need. We're going to need the youth group and children's choir to meet Saturday to confirm parts. There are twenty roles, plus the two choirs and band."

As they separated into groups, Katy, Rhody, Abby and Paul took the teens and children in order to assign roles.

Separated from the groups, a dark-haired boy sat

alone in the far corner. He pounded out a beat on his legs with a pair of drumsticks. The piercings alone screamed *back off,* but with the black clothes and spiked hair he made sure everyone saw his contempt. Lorrie Ann smiled, thinking of the rebellious teen she had been. She approached him carefully and sat down, not talking to him at first. After a few minutes, she held out her hand to him. "Hello, I'm Lorrie Ann Ortega. Are you here to play in the band?"

"Nope. I brought Carlos." He stuck the sticks into his heavy army boots.

"Do you play?"

"Are you the lady that works with a band in L.A.?"

"Yep, that's me." She winked. "So, the hair and piercings are the norm where I come from."

He snorted. "They don't much like it here."

"Are you good with the drums, or do you just mess around?"

He shrugged.

"Well, I have an idea, but to make it work I need a really good drummer."

He pointed his chin toward the adult committees working on their piece of the show. "They would have a fit if you used me."

Lorrie Ann laughed. "Funny, I used those words myself just a few days ago. I haven't been run out yet." She leaned closer to him. "I have it on good authority God does not love us based on our clothes or hairstyle."

He didn't respond.

"Thursday night, the band is getting together to go over the music. It'll only be the teens and their leaders. You should come by, and I can tell you more about my vision for a drum solo. The drummer will be the backbone of the whole show, so he has to do more than keep a beat."

"Kyle's not too bad. He's the only one with any skill. Don't know if he could carry a solo."

"It's not a part with the band."

One pierced eyebrow arched up, and she thought she might have seen a slight nod.

"I expect to see you." With the final word, she walked away, smiling.

Lorrie Ann moved through each group to answer questions and hear ideas. She loved the planning stage, seeing all the different parts coming together to make one great event. Jake and his crew had some plans of building a village with storefronts leading into a three-level platform she had drawn out.

The only group that seemed a little cold to the ideas was the sewing crew. Vickie kept complaining, but with Maggie on the committee, Lorrie Ann didn't have to deal with her directly, even though she kept trying to pull Lorrie Ann into an argument. Lorrie Ann just smiled and finally excused herself after giving them the amount donated to purchase new fabric. The look on Vickie's face brought a shallow pleasure to Lorrie Ann's inner teen.

John tried to stay focused on the missionary work and funds, but his thoughts kept floating back to Lorrie Ann. Saturday had been fun, and he got the impression she had enjoyed herself, too.

However, when he got home Tuesday after work, she had been out the door before he removed his jacket. Tonight, at the family dinner, she had made a point of sitting at the opposite end of the table. He should be happy about the distance she put between them, but it had irritated him.

He knew she needed to heal and he…well, he didn't have anything to give to a personal relationship. He couldn't even be completely honest with her because of his promise to Sonia, her mother. Maybe he would get Sonia's number from Maggie.

He leaned back in his chair. Lorrie Ann made it so easy to talk. He couldn't remember the last time he had talked about his parents' deaths and the path that had brought him to the ministry.

Looking down at his notes, he tried to refocus and saw little swirls and stick people. At least he hadn't been reduced to doodling hearts and Lorrie Ann's name. He shook his head and checked his watch. The budget meeting would be over soon. He had started looking forward to his Wednesday-night chats with Lorrie Ann on the back porch.

An hour and a half later people started leaving.

The door suddenly swung open, and for a moment Lorrie Ann's brain couldn't comprehend what she saw. She looked around for help. Maggie and Yolanda worked the kitchen. Rachel, Seth and Celeste still sat at the table with Vickie. They all stopped to stare at the stranger.

Brent couldn't be here; he just couldn't. "You're in rehab" was all her brain could manage. How had Brent ended up in her church?

"Hello, Lorrie Ann." His Irish accent completed the charming facade of bright blue eyes and rumpled blond hair. "It was stupid. I don't have a problem like those other blokes."

"How did you find me?" She had to get him out of here.

"GPS on the Beemer. Had it installed, case it was stolen." He walked toward her, ignoring the people in the room. "Never dreamed I'd use it to track down my own sweetheart."

Maggie came across the room and stood in front of the six-foot Irishman, her hands on her hips. "I'm Margarita Ortega-Schultz, Lorrie Ann's aunt."

"Pleasure to meet ya." His brogue rolled off his tongue as his hand hung in the air, ignored. He stuffed it back in his jeans pocket and cleared his throat. "Well, I came to make things right."

Lorrie Ann found her voice. "You shouldn't have driven all this way. I don't want to talk to you."

Both of John's girls sat wide-eyed, glued to the drama in front of them. She saw Rachel stand, gripping her crutch. She had to get this ugliness away from them. She put her hands on Aunt Maggie's shoulders. "Could you take the girls home for me?"

She narrowed her eyes at Brent. "Yes." Her small frame stood tall as she took a step closer to Lorrie Ann's ex. "She has family here and friends to take care of her. Come, girls, I'll drive you home tonight." She waited for the girls to join her, and with them tucked under her arms she headed to the door.

Brent watched Maggie leave before turning back to Lorrie Ann. "Well, that was unpleasant. What did ya tell her?"

"Nothing, except I ended the engagement. You need to leave." She gathered her paperwork and prayed to have the right words and actions to send him away.

"You'll have to go to Kerrville in order to find a hotel at this time of night."

"I'm not leaving until we talk about this."

Lorrie Ann stopped and glared at him. She stared at the man she had dreamed of building a life with in California. He didn't get it. For him it was all about money and fame. She had been caught up in that lifestyle, too. Now she looked at him and saw her past, a past she would no longer allow to weigh her down. "There is nothing to talk about, Brent. Now leave." She shoved her folders into her bag.

"I called, texted and emailed." Desperation edged his voice. "You wouldn't return any of them. I had to talk to you."

"I didn't return them because I *don't* want to talk to you. It's over. Go back to rehab and get your life straightened out."

He moved to her and fell to one knee. "Lorrie Ann, I know what I did was unforgivable, but it was the drugs, not me. I would never do that to you. In the past two years I have never raised a hand to ya."

She stood straight and looked him in the eye. "Leave, Brent. It's over."

"No, I'm not giving up until you agree to come home with me." He reached up to touch her face.

She stepped back and bit hard on her lip. "We're not together anymore, Brent, and it's more than just what happened that night. It's more than the drugs and partying. I don't want that lifestyle. I want more."

"More!" He shot up from the floor and grabbed her arms, pulling her against him. "The houses, the cars, all the clothes and parties aren't enough for you?"

Lorrie Ann tried to pull away from him, but he was

Lone Star Holiday

too strong. She looked him in the eye. How did she ever think she loved this man? Without a doubt, she'd made the right decision leaving California. Fear started paralyzing her; she knew that would be the worst thing to let happen. How could she get him out of here without anyone getting hurt?

Chapter Thirteen

John glanced at his watch. The Christmas meeting should be over. He prayed for open hearts and minds to hear Lorrie Ann's ideas.

She had shared a great vision with him of how the pageant could look. With a sigh, he thought of all the times people fought him over change just because it was change.

"They've been running for a year now and doing well. I move we increase the monthly funds sent to Peru by fifty dollars."

John raised his eyebrows. He had missed the whole discussion. Everyone voted in agreement, and Deacon Copeland adjourned.

At a light knock on the door, they all turned. Vickie poked her head in the room.

"Pardon the intrusion, but there's trouble in the fellowship hall."

"Is someone hurt?" John moved to the door, his heart jumping a beat faster, thinking of Celeste and Rachel.

"Oh, no, it's an unexpected guest." She bit the corner of her mouth. "Brent Krieger, Lorrie Ann's fiancé."

He rushed down the hall not hearing anything else Vickie said. He needed to get to Lorrie Ann. The thought of her ex in the same room with her sent unfamiliar anger surging through his bloodstream.

Barging into the room, he didn't see anything but Lorrie Ann being pinned against a stranger, his large hands wrapped around her small arms.

"Get your hands off her!" John's voice was sharp and demanding.

The other man released her and took a step back. His glare moved back and forth between John and Lorrie Ann.

John noticed Yolanda outside the kitchen area with a frying pan clasped tightly in two hands. Seth stood, his fist clenched tight, a cell phone in one hand. Tension filled the room.

"I suggest you leave now."

"I don't know who you are, but she's mine, and this is between us."

"She is *not* your anything," John snarled, moving to stand next to Lorrie Ann. He was ready to physically remove this jerk if needed. He felt her hand softly lie against his arm and looked down. Her straight back and smile reassured him she could handle the situation.

Brent's accented voice broke their contact. "Lorrie Ann, come back with me. I don't want to lose the life we have there."

"You don't get it, Brent. I don't want more of what we had. I want more family, community, a real purpose for my life. I need God in my life."

The door eased open, and Jake, in his uniform, slipped into the room.

Brent's gaze darted from person to person, and his

hands started to shake. "I promise to stay in rehab, Lorrie Ann. I'm getting better. I realized how important you are in my life. I want to fix us. I want to go back to what we had. I need your forgiveness so we can start over."

John watched her intensely, tracking the emotions that fluttered across her features one at a time. He prayed, without taking his eyes off her face, that God would wrap her tightly in His love and let her know she didn't stand alone.

Lorrie Ann squeezed his arm with a barely there touch. Her soft low voice broke the profound silence. "Thank you, Brent." A gentle smile eased its way to her eyes. "I do forgive you."

A big smile covered the Irishman's face as he took a step toward her. John stiffened.

Lorrie Ann raised her hands, palms out. "No, Brent, I forgive you because I need to in order to move forward. We're finished. You need to leave now. Everything that needed to be said has been said." Chin up, she took a step back, closer to John. "Goodbye."

John didn't like the man's clenched fists. Brent tried to loom over Lorrie Ann and brought one hand up to point a finger at her. "You will regret this. You'll lose your job, and no one will hire you. Your career will be over. See where your God is then."

Hand resting on his gun, Jake opened the door wide and stepped back with one brow raised. Brent shot a heated glare around the room before he stomped out and slammed the door.

Silence fell heavily in the fellowship hall. John slid an arm over her shoulders. "Are you all right?"

She took a deep breath and nodded. Her small frame trembled.

From the corner, Vickie demanded everyone's attention. "I told you she doesn't belong. Her history with men has reared its ugly head. Deacons, Pastor John—" she edged closer to Lorrie Ann, jabbing the air with her finger "—I'm asking that you ban her. I'll direct the pageant."

The three older men shuffled and looked to John with uncomfortable expressions.

Yolanda crossed the room to block Vickie's path. "She doesn't have a history. You made it up. You lied, and I let you. This time I'm not going to let you chase her out of town. This is her home, too."

Vickie gasped, her mouth opening and closing. Her heavy breathing filled the air. "But she…"

Jake positioned himself next to Vickie. "That's enough. In high school we all stayed silent. It stops tonight, Vickie. We're adults now. It's time to grow up." He looked Lorrie Ann in the eye. "I'm sorry for not speaking up when the rumors grew."

Seth left the corner and grabbed his mother's hand. "Mom, let's go, please."

"But I… She…" Vickie pointed to Lorrie Ann. "She doesn't have a right to be here. I didn't…"

John stepped toward Vickie and prayed for the right way to handle the situation. He forced his jaw to relax, wanting to defend Lorrie Ann but knowing he also had to be Vickie's pastor. Anger and bitterness surrounded Vickie.

"Vickie, gossip and rumors have no place in the church." He stopped a few feet away from her and put his hand on Seth's shoulder. The boy's face burned red, and he kept his eyes down. "I know this has been a brutal year for you, but turning on others isn't the answer."

Seth glanced at him from under long bangs. He turned to his mother. "Mom. Please, can we just leave?"

Jake held out his arm. "Come on. I'll make sure you get home safe." He glanced at Lorrie Ann. "I'll call the sheriff and see that Brent gets all the way out of town."

With a glance filled with resentment, Vickie allowed her son and Jake to pull her from the room.

The three deacons lingered by the opposite door, ready to make a quick exit. "Well, um…it's late. We should be going. Call us if you need anything, Pastor." They each nodded to the women. "Night, Yolanda. Lorrie Ann."

Yolanda's gentle voice bid them a good night.

Lorrie Ann sat alone, her bag pulled close, not saying a word.

As soon as the men closed the door behind them, she turned to Yolanda. "Yolanda, thank you. After dealing with Brent, I didn't know what to say to Vickie. Thanks for standing up for me."

Yolanda rushed to her side, sitting next to her. "Oh, Lorrie Ann, I'm so sorry it was twelve years too late. I should've done that back in high school. I was so afraid of her, and, well, jealousy is just ugly."

Lorrie Ann's forehead went into deep wrinkles, and her gaze jumped to Yolanda's face. "Jealousy? Why would *you* be jealous of me?"

The younger woman laughed and pulled Lorrie Ann close. In that moment, she resembled her mother. "It's really lame, but I thought my mom loved you more. At school, you were so cool, and the teachers would always compare my work to yours. Then there was your singing."

"How sad are we? I always felt like an intruder." Lorrie Ann tucked her hair behind her ears. "Remember when we were little and told each other all our secrets?"

Yolanda took her cousin's hand in hers. Her voice dropped to a whisper. "I'm so sorry I wasn't there for you. Especially when Vickie spread those ugly lies. You couldn't even trust me enough to let me know what's been going on the past few weeks."

"I've handled everything wrong." Lorrie Ann used the pad of her thumb to wipe a tear off Yolanda's cheek. "Tell you what. I'll forgive our teenage drama if you forgive me for discounting our friendship all these years."

Yolanda pulled Lorrie Ann close again. "I don't deserve your forgiveness."

"The stories Vickie told about me in high school might have been lies, but the choices I've made since are all mine." Lorrie Ann pulled away from Yolanda.

John watched her move across the room to gather up supplies. With his elbows on his knees, he rested his chin in the palm of his hand. He still needed to battle down his own anger at the attacks both Brent and Vickie had brought into the church. He didn't trust himself to speak right now, so he continued to listen and pray.

With her back turned to him, her voice sounded muffled, but he could still hear the uncertainty. "Coming here might have been a mistake. Church has never seemed like a good place for me to be."

John sat up, unable to allow that comment to go unchallenged. "Lorrie Ann, the church should be a place of refuge, a safe corner in a world of devastating storms. What happened here tonight had nothing to do with God, but you handled both with grace. This church belongs to you as much as anyone else. You belong to

God. Can you forgive us?" He stood in front of her now, wanting to take her in his arms.

"Us? You didn't have anything to do with it." Her eyes looked huge as she gazed up at him.

"You've had so many arrows thrown at your heart. I shouldn't have allowed it to happen tonight."

Lorrie Ann smiled. "You can't be everywhere all the time. I'm thinking about the scripture you gave Aunt Maggie to read tonight. It said our troubles are small and won't last forever. But they give us glory in the long run." Lorrie Ann reached for Yolanda's hand. "I faced my monsters tonight and realized they are just hurt people. For twelve years I've been running. No more."

Yolanda hugged her. "I've missed you." A cell phone went off in the kitchen. "Oh, that's Mom's ringtone." Yolanda rushed to answer her phone. "Hey, Mom, Lorrie Ann's fine. Yeah, he's gone." She looked to John and Lorrie Ann. "I'm with John and Lorrie Ann now." She smiled and nodded to whatever Maggie said on the other end. "Okay, I'll tell her. Love you."

"So what did Aunt Maggie say?" Lorrie Ann asked.

"Apparently, Rachel and Celeste are worried about you and waiting for their story."

John had his phone out to call the girls.

"I came with Mom, so I need a ride to my place."

Pulling the keys from her bag, Lorrie Ann handed them to Yolanda. "Here, take my car, and I'll ride to the house with John."

John walked to the door. "Sounds like a plan. The girls are anxious to see Lorrie Ann."

Yolanda followed them out and waited as John locked the building.

"I'll see you tomorrow. I love you, Yolanda."

"Yeah, me, too." Yolanda wrapped her in a hug before getting in the little sports car.

John held open his passenger door and waited for Lorrie Ann to buckle up. They watched as the BMW backed out and drove down Main Street before heading home.

Driving over Second Crossing, John's thoughts were still centered around Lorrie Ann. She came across as strong, but there was vulnerability at her core that made him want to protect her. She had not had many people to trust in her life, starting with her mother. To be that man for her scared him. He had let Carol down. She had deserved a better husband than the one he was to her. He hadn't been able to protect his wife. What worm in his brain made him think he could do any better for Lorrie Ann?

He thought of Lorrie Ann's mother. Sonia was afraid of disappointing her daughter after years of struggling with alcohol and drugs. She had made Maggie and him promise not to tell Lorrie Ann about her going through rehab in San Antonio. She was just an hour away and afraid to see her daughter. Maybe he had something in common with her. They both were cowards. He gave a short laugh.

"What?"

He shook his head and grinned at her. "Nothing. Just thinking."

John pulled in front of his cabin and cut the engine, but instead of getting out, they both stared at the dark landscape surrounding the cabin in silence. He wanted to give her some extra time to calm her nerves. To be honest, he really wanted to wrap her in his arms and protect her from the ugliness of the world.

"Thank you, John. I like to pretend I'm strong and independent, but I felt much safer when you charged into the room." She looked out the side window, her fingers playing with the handle but not opening the door.

"You *are* strong and independent. Doesn't mean you don't need support."

The porch light came on, and Aunt Maggie stepped outside, peering into the darkness.

John laughed. "I feel like a teenager bringing home his date." He turned to her. "Ready?"

With a nod, she climbed out of his truck. He followed her, grinning as she marched straight to his room, where the girls waited. She barely stopped for a quick hug with her aunt.

Maggie laid a hand on his arm. "Is she okay? I've been praying nonstop since I left with the girls."

He nodded. "You'd be proud." He smiled down at the fierce prayer warrior. "God works in strange ways."

"Yes, He does."

John leaned against the railing. "Have you told her about her mother yet?"

"No." She sighed and shook her head. "Sonia's afraid. I told her Lorrie Ann could handle it, but you know how guilt eats at people."

"The longer we keep it from her, the more betrayed she's going to feel."

Maggie laid a hand on his shoulder. "I know. I'll talk to Sonia again. With Lorrie Ann in town, there is no excuse." She sighed and patted him on the shoulder. "It's been a long day. Good night."

"Night, Maggie."

A little bit later, the door eased open, and Lorrie Ann's head poked through. "Ah, there you are. Not sure if you had gone to bed yet."

He spent a moment just watching her move next to him before speaking. The cool breeze pushed her dark curls from her face. "The girls got their princess story?"

She cut her gaze to him for a quick second before going back to the stars. "Yeah, thanks for letting me tuck them in. Who would have guessed the highlight of my week would be a bedtime fairy tale?"

"The smallest things in life can be the biggest blessings."

"I think I'm starting to see that." She rubbed her hands together and tucked them under her arms. "I'll come by in the morning and help with breakfast." She raised her eyebrows and smiled. "Give you time to shave in peace."

"Ah, yes, the little things." He walked her across the graveled path to Maggie's back door.

She paused as she reached for the screen door and looked up at him. "Well, good night."

John swallowed hard and stared into her large eyes, the color dancing from gray to green. Then he remembered to mumble, "Good night."

He wanted to lean in and kiss her, but he took a step back instead and shoved his hands in his pockets. With one last smile, she turned and disappeared into the dark kitchen. John really needed a distraction. Tossing a green Jolly Rancher into his mouth, he headed back to the cabin.

Chapter Fourteen

John frowned as he thought about the unused guitars and violins he had in storage. For a Saturday, the church teemed with an unusual number of people. Music poured from the sanctuary. Now the loud enthusiastic chords filled the church with joy, even the misplaced and out-of-tune ones. They could use some good instruments.

"Um…Pastor John, I…um…" Rhody scratched the back of his neck as he stepped out of one of the small rooms, blocking John's path. "I was wondering if I could ask you something."

"Sure, Rhody, how can I help you?" John bit back a smile as he watched the other man fidget and look everywhere else to avoid eye contact.

"Well, the other day Katy…um, wanted to talk to you about our marriage. Do you remember?"

"I remember. Have y'all gone to one of the counselors I told you about?" Dread filled John. He didn't want to give out marriage advice.

"No, I don't think… Well, they don't know us…." Rhody made a sound in his throat. "I just want to make her happy. She seems fine one moment, and then she's sad. She's always moping over these travel magazines, and I think about the crazy stories of women just taking off, no warning. I'm...I'm afraid one day she's gonna leave."

"Maybe she just wants to travel. Where have y'all gone on vacation?" Regret swamped him as John thought of the vacation Carol had taken without him.

"Vacation? With the store open seven days a week, I don't have time."

John closed his eyes. The same excuse he'd given Carol every time she'd planned time together. *God, You know I hate giving marriage advice. Please help me say what he needs to hear.* "What about your honeymoon? Where did you take her?"

"We went to San Antonio. It was the Stockshow and Rodeo. My brother got Grand Champion Steer that year."

Stopping himself from rolling his eyes, John put his hand on Rhody's shoulder. "Listen, she wants to share an adventure with you. Let her pick a place to go then take her. Enjoy the gift God's given you."

"You think that's all it is? She wants a vacation with me?"

"She loves you. Those four boys are her world. But sometimes we can feel our world is too small."

Rhody smiled. "I can do that. It'll be hard covering the store, but maybe my parents can step in for a bit, or Vickie. Yeah, I can do this." He clasped John's shoulder. "Thank you."

John took a deep breath as he watched his friend head out the church door with a new joy in his step. He thought of the simple things he'd never get to do for Carol. Regret made his shoulders heavy.

He continued to the sanctuary, hoping to hear the band practice. As he walked through the doors, only silence filled the space. Checking his watch, he frowned. He had missed them.

Walking up front to the stage, he saw one of the old church guitars resting on its stand. He picked it up and played a few chords.

He thought of Rhody and the store. It was so easy to let people down. The hours he had put into his music had destroyed his marriage. Putting the guitar down, he walked to the piano and sat, looking over the sheet music.

Without thought, his fingers started dancing across the keys. Lorrie Ann brought the best out in the kids. Images of Lorrie Ann faded into memories of Carol working with the youth at his old church. He flinched when his fingers hit the wrong chord.

He had taken Carol and his family for granted. His jaw locked. Worse, he had avoided responsibility by blaming the music God had given him. He had told Rhody to savor the gift of love. What a hypocrite.

Did he deserve another chance at love? Muscle memory took over, and his fingers flew across the keys. The music he had kept locked up poured out of each individual cell inside him, and he surrounded himself in the emotions emptied from every note.

As Lorrie Ann headed back to the sanctuary, it surprised her to hear a piano. The carpeted hall silenced her footsteps. As she approached, the music started soft, drifting down the hall. The tone changed, and passion filled the air, rising high and swirling in a storm of chaos and fear. Then it quieted down again, a feeling of sweet hope in each note. That could not be one of the kids; it sounded too professional even on the ancient piano. She froze in the doorway.

John sat, fingers on the worn keys, absorbed in the music he created. Locks of hair moved as his head dipped down then thrust back, eyes closed tight.

The composition compelled her to move toward him. Energy and worship filled the empty pews. The disappearing sun reached through the colored glass, highlighting the man at the piano in a wave of rich color.

It all came to a sudden crash when John slammed his fist on the white ivories and lowered his forehead to the top ledge of the piano. Heavy breaths rushed out of his lungs as if he had just finished a race.

"John?"

With a sharp jerk, he brought his face up, glaring at her.

"What are you doing here?" The harsh voice did not sound like the man she had come to know.

She took a step back. One thing she knew for a fact— men were unpredictable, especially if they felt threatened.

"I'm sorry." She stepped back to make her exit. "I wanted you to know that Uncle Billy said we can use the cherry picker." She started to turn but paused. An overwhelming longing made her tell him what she had just experienced. "You just played the most beautiful, compelling piece of music I have ever heard."

"Thank you." The words came from a still jaw. He looked back at the piano, his fingers casually running over the ivory keys and tickling little notes out of the old upright.

She swallowed. *Just leave, girl.* Instead, she heard herself speaking again. "Can I ask a question?"

Without looking up, he gave a half grin. "Sure."

"Do you ever play in church? I've never heard you."

He tilted his head back and combed his fingers through his hair, pushing the strands off his forehead. He shook his head.

Lorrie Ann moved closer, pausing at the base of the three steps leading to the platform. "I don't understand. You play music like that, but you don't share with your congregation?"

He sighed. "Nope." He started playing with the keys again. "I was hired to preach, not make music."

"Um…I think they'd be okay with it. Have you ever played in front of people?"

He laughed, closing the lid to the piano. John rested his elbows on the wood and intertwined his fingers. "A few thousand."

"Really?" This man always surprised her. "I don't know a great deal about the Christian-music industry, but I think you're very marketable." She crossed the stage and laid her hand on the top of the piano. She knew music, and his was incredible.

"It's not what I want."

She knew people in the business that would give anything for a sound like his. "I don't understand. If you don't want to market your music, the least you could do is share with your church. Isn't there some verse about it being a sin when you waste a talent God gave you?"

"So, you're going to come from L.A. and give me Bible lessons?" Anger edged his voice.

She took a step back and closed her eyes for a moment. "You're right. I'm way out of line. Sorry I bothered you." She turned sharply to leave, acid burning in her throat. She was so stupid.

"Lorrie Ann, wait, please." John's voice followed her.

Before she got to the last pew, the tips of John's fingers touched her lower arm. She stopped but kept her back to him.

This man made her so weak. She didn't know who she hated more—him or herself.

"You have every right to speak the truth." His grip became a bit firmer as he silently urged her back to him. "We all need the truth. I've been hiding my music for five years now. Today, I couldn't keep it buried."

She focused on the tiny pattern weaved into the blue carpet under his boots. "I'm sorry I interrupted," she whispered. "It's not any of my business."

"I've played to crowds of thousands. Tears running down their faces, hands raised high as they sang the words. All that attention can be a bit intoxicating." John dropped his hand and stepped back, but his gaze never left her.

"You don't owe me an explanation."

"The truth has been locked up with the music for too long." He reached into his jacket and popped a Jolly Rancher into his mouth. "I didn't see my girls unless Carol brought them to the youth building. Ironically, the music became a stumbling block in my relationship with God. It ruined my marriage." He took a deep breath. "*I* ruined my marriage. I hurt Carol, who had given me nothing but love and support."

"John…" She had no clue what to say.

Moving away from her, he sat on the nearest pew. "I

was lost, but being wrapped in a Christian label, no one knew it…" He swallowed and bit down the raw emotion that boiled up in his brain. "Other than Carol." He looked up to the cross. "When I saw her at the accident site, covered in the yellow sheet, I knew her death was my fault. My sin."

"Oh, John." She stepped closer, wrapping her warm fingers around the coldness of his hand. "It was an accident. You weren't even in the car. You know it's not your fault, right?"

He squeezed her hand. "In my head, yeah. But I also know I had pretended to be a man of God, while living for myself in complete and utter selfishness." He turned her hand over, running the calloused pad of his thumb across her palm before letting go.

He twisted the finger on his left hand, playing with a wedding ring that he no longer wore. "Carol knew and had called me out."

He looked back up and gave her a lopsided grin. "Like you just did. She was good at speaking the truth."

The sorrow in his eyes pierced her soul. "I didn't have the right to tell any—"

He shook his head, stopping her from finishing. "I've never told this to anyone. I'd missed our monthly date night. Again. So Carol left the girls with the babysitter and tracked me down in the music building." He took a deep breath, and his jaw flexed. "There was no yelling or crying. She calmly informed me she'd prayed while waiting and decided to move back to Clear Water. When I got my priorities right, she'd be waiting for me. Then she left." He sat up and ran his fingers through his mussed hair. "I went brain-dead." He snorted and cut a look to her. "Know what my first thought was?"

Lorrie Ann shook her head and bit her teeth. She didn't want to hear any more. "I can't imagine." Her right hand reached out and took hold of his.

"I panicked at how others would react. The negative image it would create for me." He stood. "My wife was so hurt. She'd just left me, and all I cared about? How it would look to others." He moved to the piano.

Lorrie Ann followed him. Her cracked heart completely shattered.

"I knew right then I hadn't been living to God's glory but my own. I rushed out to follow her, to tell her I'd been wrong. To fix the mess I'd made. But I came up to the accident."

Her heart seized. "Oh, no, John. Don't. It's not your fault. Do you really believe God punished you by killing Carol?"

John stood before the stained-glass cross. His throat worked, trying to swallow. "No, but..." He walked back to the piano, running his hand along the top. "I blamed the music." He gave her a sad grin that pulled at her heart. "I guess it's my self-imposed punishment—no music and no love."

She moved to stand with him. "John, that's crazy. You managed to cut music from your life, but love? You're the most loving man I know. I've seen you with your girls, the people of this town, even the dragon ladies. The love you have for God is in everything you do." She smiled at him, wishing he could see the hope he had given her. "You seem to have an endless amount of love."

He grunted. "*Love* is a loaded word. I *do* love my girls. I love the Lord, love my life here in this small country town." He picked up a guitar and sat down on a stool. His fingers softly strummed the strings. "But a wife? I've destroyed one woman's life because of my selfishness. My heart can't risk it again. I can't risk someone loving me like that again."

Between his stark words and lonely chords, sadness covered her like a humid, sticky fog. This man deserved to be loved by someone who would share his burdens. That wasn't her. "What made you play today?"

"In the hall, a friend ambushed me, wanting advice about his wife." He paused. "No one knows Carol was leaving me. People talk about what a perfect couple we made." He focused on the strings for a moment. "I don't give marriage advice. It makes me feel a little hypocritical. I told him not to take love for granted."

"Not long ago you told me it is our imperfection that enables God to use us to help others." She sat on the piano bench, careful not to touch him but wanting to be close.

He shook his head, and a halfhearted grin pulled at the corners of his mouth. "No fair. I turned to music when I lost my parents. Playing was my conversation with God. I could write about emotions and fears. They would pour through the instruments."

"The music I heard earlier moved me. I felt God."

"Actually, an old friend recently pointed out the selfishness of not sharing with my girls and the church."

"He's right. Rachel has the most amazing voice. Do you sing?"

He gave a slight nod, and she suspected his voice was as spectacular as his playing.

She continued, "Have you seen Celeste? She's already learned some basic chords just from watching

Kenny on the piano. You have to share your talent with them, John."

"Yes, ma'am." He focused on his hands for a moment and once again changed the tempo of the song.

She sat back and enjoyed the music, his music.

He whispered low, "Thank you. Carol had no problem setting me straight either. It can be difficult in Cold Water. Everybody knew her from the time she was born. I didn't want them to know how I'd failed her."

"You weren't a bad husband, just a man, a very young one." She felt a little jealous of Carol knowing this man's love. How pathetic was that?

He snorted. "Thanks for that vote of confidence. Why do I get the feeling that's not a compliment?"

"Hey!" She threw a wadded piece of paper at him. Her heart melted when he chuckled. She watched his fingers drift back to the strings. This man deserved to be loved with a whole heart. Not the tarnished, damaged one that beat in her chest.

"You play?" Mrs. Miller's voice suddenly boomed from the double doors, a fierce scowl puckering her face. The disapproving energy crushed the fragile mood.

"Yes, ma'am," John answered with a heavy sigh.

Her cane thumped the floor with each step. "Why haven't you led the worship music?" her voice snapped.

"I was hired to preach." He gave her a gentle smile.

Lorrie Ann loved how he treated everyone with respect and tenderness, even the dragons. She didn't have the tolerance, another reason she didn't belong with him.

"Pish!" The old Dragon Queen gave a final stomp of

her cane. "Pastor Levi, this is not your highfalutin big-city church. You have more than one job."

"Yes, ma'am. Miss Ortega just suggested the same thing. Great minds must think alike." He dared to wink at her.

Mrs. Miller's frown went deeper into her wrinkles. "I heard a rumor. You need to know, I will remove my support if that Puente boy, with all the things on his face, is in the band." She glared at John. "This is what happens when you let people like her run things." Her nose went higher. "Their kind corrupts."

Lorrie Ann bit her lip and battled to keep the ire locked down. Not trusting herself to speak, she focused on John. He moved closer to the old lady.

"Mrs. Miller, I appreciate your concern, but we do represent the body of Christ, and our doors are open to everyone." John patted her arm and led her back to the foyer.

Lorrie Ann collected herself and joined them. *Please, Lord, give me the right thing to say. I need words from You and not my anger.*

"Please let me reassure you." She used her best smile. "Derrick will not be playing with the band. I hope you attend. Please keep us in your prayers. I believe it will be a special night of worship."

"Humph…we'll see." She stood tall and glared at John for a while. "Young man, you need to stay focused and not become distracted by things that glitter."

"You're not giving me dating advice, now, are you?"

"Humph! Better men than you have been led down the wrong path because of a woman."

"And hearts have been touched because of a woman, Mrs. Miller."

She narrowed her eyes. "Maybe." She cut her glare back to Lorrie Ann.

Lorrie Ann watched as John escorted the Queen Dragon to her car. He did love unconditionally.

With a sigh, she wondered what it would feel like to have someone love her that way.

She shook her head, disgusted with herself. All her life, Aunt Maggie had loved her, but because of old hurts, she had pushed her away. Just like Uncle Billy and Yolanda. They hadn't made her an outsider; she had done that to herself.

John returned with a big smile on his face. She sighed. Man, did she love that smile.

"Did I hear you lie to that poor woman?" he whispered.

"Poor? Right. Anyway, I didn't lie." She dramatically laid her palm over her heart. "I promise he won't be playing *with* the band." She winked. "We have other plans for Derrick."

John laughed. "You are exactly what this town needed."

She smiled back. "God knew, I needed this town."

"Yeah, He's good that way."

She sent a word of thanks to God. Life was good—better than she'd ever dreamed.

Chapter Fifteen

Lorrie's life turned into a nightmare. In the morning, Melissa called from L.A. and informed her that due to the recent incidents they would be looking for a new manager. Apparently, some so-called friends had forwarded a couple gossip blogs about her and Brent's little scandal.

Oh, well, so went life in the entertainment business. She had already received some messages from other groups interested in her but hadn't returned any of the calls or emails just yet. What surprised her most? She didn't really care enough about it to be upset.

All her energy was focused on the current disaster heading straight at her. The locals liked to call it the One Hundredth Annual Christmas Pageant.

She now referred to it as her pending nightmare.

With coffee in hand, she looked over her list. She heard a truck pull into the driveway but didn't bother looking up. Uncle Billy must have come in early for lunch.

It surprised her to see John's boots stopping in front of her. Putting her laptop and coffee on the little table next to the rocking chair, Lorrie Ann stood. "Is everything all right?"

John nodded, his face grim. "I need your help."

"Sure, what is it? The girls?"

"The girls are fine." His throat locked up. This had been a mistake. He couldn't do this.

He glanced away from her, not really seeing the trees and birds past the patio but instead…all the time he had spent in the studio, away from his wife and family.

He needed to do this. *God, give me the strength to turn it all over to You.* "I need help with something." He turned back to Lorrie Ann. She stood with a concerned expression on her face. Her dark hair was pulled back into a ponytail, and she had no makeup on. She really had no idea how beautiful she looked without all the extras.

Sighing, he forced himself to focus on the reason he'd come to her. "Do you have some free time now? If not I can come back later."

"Oh, no, it's fine. I can help you now."

He found he couldn't talk, so he settled for nodding and heading back to his truck. Her steps quickly followed behind him. Holding the passenger door open, he waited for her to settle in before closing the door and getting into the driver's side. The journey began.

After a few minutes of engine-rumbling silence, she turned to him. "You should know I'm not in the habit of jumping into a car without knowing where I'm going." Silence sat between them. "Any hint as to where you're taking me?"

"I have to get something, and I don't think I can do it alone." His knuckles turned white on the steering wheel.

She sat silently again, waiting as they continued the drive. He finally veered through the big gates of his father-in-law's ranch. Taking the winding road past the main house, John pulled up to one of the bunkhouses in the back.

More silence as they sat there. He ran his hands over the worn steering wheel, feeling the cracks. Fear and guilt choked him. *Okay, God, I know those feelings aren't from You.*

Lorrie Ann reached across the bench seat and touched his arm. "John, you're starting to make me nervous. Why are we here? What do you need me to do?"

She trusted him, and he knew that didn't come easy for her. He was suffused with more guilt as he thought about her mother. He couldn't even think of any type of relationship with her while that hung over them.

Taking the keys out of the ignition, John separated one of them and handed it to her. "I need you to unlock the door for me."

"Okay. Can you tell me why?"

He didn't look at her, shaking his head as he climbed out and walked toward the porch. Pausing at the bottom step, he rested his hand on the rough railing. It was past time to unlock the door. Once the decision was made he thought it would have been easier. Did it make him weak that he needed her here, to get him over the threshold?

Lorrie Ann walked past, pausing before going up the steps. She looked up at him. "Are you sure everything's all right?"

He nodded, not even bothering to try to speak. His heart pounded against his chest, and his hands started to shake a bit. It had been over four years since he'd taken the walk down these steps.

Lorrie Ann stood at the door, and after a few seconds of wrestling with the lock, she pushed it open. Turning back to him, she waited.

"Thank you." His voice croaked, raw with emotion. Easing through the door, he focused on Lorrie Ann's presence.

Musical equipment covered the wood floor, carefully boxed and stacked against the bare walls. He watched her walk through the dust particles that floated in the beams of sunlight.

Following her, he brushed calloused fingertips over the amps, drums and boxed-up soundboards. John tried to swallow, but his throat didn't seem to work.

"You have enough equipment to start a band." She pivoted around.

John couldn't speak. This was the right thing, and he was glad they were doing it together. With a sigh, he picked up one of the smaller boxes and handed it to Lorrie Ann.

Clearing his throat, he managed to get some words out. "Thanks for unlocking the door. I didn't think I could do it by myself. I'm taking all this stuff to the church."

She nodded and followed him. In silence they loaded one box after another. He stopped after the fourth trip. Seeing each box placed in the bed of his truck, he felt the tension begin to ease. Now for the big one. "I'll get the rest of these. Would you start pulling the instruments from the room over there?"

"Sure." She smiled at him before heading to the other door, not asking a single question.

While taking another load to the truck, he heard Lorrie Ann gasp.

John found himself smiling. He figured she'd appreciate what she found. As he crossed the room, his footsteps echoed off the walls.

At the open door, he saw her holding a black lid, the hard case containing one of his many guitars. Her eyes wide, she met his gaze. "Is this a 1958 Les Paul?"

He moved closer to her. "Yeah. I should take that one to the house."

She just nodded before heading to the quilt-covered grand piano. Lorrie Ann looked back at him. "Is this a Steinway?"

He grinned. "The one in the back is a newer Steinway." He joined her, lifting the custom-quilted cover off the baby grand. He played a few keys. "This is a 1970 Baldwin. It was a gift. It needs to be tuned. I'll probably get George to help me move them to the church. When the youth building's finished, I'll take them all over there."

He closed his eyes and listened to the sweet notes. A lightness settled across his shoulders. A weight he'd carried for so long he hadn't even noticed it, dissipated.

"Oh, John, this baby grand would be perfect in the corner of your new living room. I can see it right next to the office."

The vision flashed across his mind's eye: his girls sitting side by side, on a bench, playing music. "I always kept my music at the church. I didn't want the music to interfere with family time."

"So you spent all your time at the church." Lorrie paused. "Instead of isolating that part of you, maybe the music should become a part of your family."

He stepped away from the Baldwin without responding.

She followed him, her gaze roaming over his old life. "This collection of quality instruments tells me a great deal about the owner. Music is not just a hobby but in every fiber of your DNA. How could you cut it out of your life completely?"

Opening a violin case, he ran his fingers over the dark glossy wood. "Guilt. Easier to lock it away than deal with it." Raising his head, he looked into her sweet eyes. "Ephesians tells us, 'For by grace you have been saved through faith. And this is not your own doing; it is the gift of God, not a result of works.' When I cut music from my life I wasn't completely trusting God." He walked over to her. "The other day you said I wasn't sharing my gifts. I'd like to thank you for that, Lorrie Ann. I know you think God brought you here because you needed us, but God also brought you into my life. Because we need you just as much."

"Oh, John." Tears started beading up before she spun away from him. "I'll put these in your backseat. The kids are going to fall in love with them."

Yeah, and he seemed to be falling in love with her. But he kept that to himself, grabbing a couple violins and following her out.

Lorrie Ann looked across the field. Everywhere she turned, people were working. She glanced down at her list, so much still undone.

The donkey, Alfredo, only moved if you gave him a banana, but it disagreed with him, causing foul odors to fill the air around him, every time. Her fingers went to her forehead when she saw Celeste and her group rolling around like puppies again. The pressure pounded against her temple.

She looked down at her notes once more, hoping for answers. The lights guy still didn't understand stage cues, and Vickie argued over every costume idea. As of yet, Lorrie Ann had not seen one completed outfit.

She walked toward the band. Her solo drummer had pulled a disappearing act again.

Stopping at the edge of the stage, she waited for John to finish showing Kenny how to place his fingers on the strings of the new Gibson.

"Excuse me, guys. Have you seen Derrick?"

They both looked up at her, smiles on their faces. "No, ma'am, but I saw Carlos, so he should be around somewhere," Kenny answered.

She hated when they called her ma'am, but they couldn't seem to help themselves.

Humor flooded John's eyes as he smiled at her. "Your special project gone AWOL again?"

There seemed to be a new lightness in John since they had pulled his instruments out of storage. Sharing his music skills with the kids came so naturally to him.

Last Sunday in church, he had led a worship song. His voice had hit every note perfectly with so much emotion, everyone had stood in awe, forgetting to sing along.

With his influence, the quality of their sound would improve greatly by the night of the show.

That was the only thing going right. She looked down at her notes yet again. More question marks and concerns shadowed her script.

She reluctantly looked back to the stage. The worst part of her life right now? She was totally falling in love with a man that could never be hers.

She checked her phone. She didn't have even half the

to-do list done, and everyone was already packing up. Mothers arrived to pick up the younger ones, and she finally saw Derrick sitting in a truck waiting for Carlos.

She hurried over and smiled at him. "Hey, missed you. Have you been practicing?"

He nodded. "I had work to do for my uncle."

"That's fine. Your part is a solo. Just keep practicing. You'll make it for the full rehearsal, right?"

He shrugged.

"Derrick, if you need any help, all you have to do is ask. It's okay. People want to help."

He nodded but kept his face straight ahead.

"Well, okay." She patted the door. "Oh, look, here comes Carlos."

"Hello, Miss Lorrie Ann. Dare has been practicing every minute at home. Momma yells, but he just keeps practicing."

Derrick rolled his eyes and waited for Carlos to buckle up before starting the old work truck.

"Bye, Carlos. Bye, Derrick."

Carlos leaned out as far as the seat belt would allow and waved. "Bye, Miss Lorrie Ann. Bye, Celeste."

Lorrie Ann looked behind her and found Celeste standing there. "Hey, girl. You ready to go home? Your father has meetings tonight at the church."

"Yeah. Rachel is talking to Seth."

Lorrie Ann frantically scanned the area, tracking down Rachel and Seth. They sat at the piano, laughing. She grabbed Celeste's hand and rushed toward them. A groan escaped her throat when she saw John make his way to the pair.

He laughed at something Seth said, causing Rachel to glare at her father. Seth slid off the bench and shook

John's hand. He moved away from them, walking backward. With a silly smile on his face, Seth missed the step and lost his balance. Rachel gasped and jumped up, reaching for her crutch.

Vickie stood by the storage door. "Seth, stop being an idiot and get to the car." She stomped off without another word.

John stood over Seth with his hand out. "Are you okay, Seth?"

"Yes, sir." He took the offered hand, his face redder than a fresh strawberry.

"Welcome to the man club. Beautiful girls turn us all into goofs." John patted him on the shoulder.

"Daddy!" Horror filled Rachel's face.

John laughed and rubbed the top of her head. "Sweetheart, it's time for y'all to head home. I have a building meeting tonight." He hugged Celeste and winked at Lorrie Ann. "I'll see you when I get home."

She raised her eyebrows. His mood seemed different tonight.

"See ya." She reached for Celeste's hand and headed to her car. Rachel pouted as she climbed into the front seat.

Lorrie Ann sighed as she headed home.

Home. Oh, man. When had John and his girls so completely slipped into her heart? When had the cabin become home?

She thought about the contacts in California, waiting for her reply. Time had run out. She couldn't afford to play house with John any longer.

John's boots hit the top step. If anyone asked him about his faith, he told them he'd turned his life completely over to God. For the past week his eyes and heart had been open to the punishment he'd inflicted on himself.

Lorrie was right, but he didn't know if he wanted to tell her. He smiled. She already seemed a bit bossy.

Working with the youth and music brought another worship experience back into his life. Threading his fingers through his hair, John interlocked them on the top of his head and gazed at the stars shimmering in the deep purple sky.

He should know by now God's timing was beyond his understanding but always virtuous. He needed to trust God's plans for him were good.

With a deep breath, John gave the stars one last look before turning to the cabin. He stopped and laid his palms flat against the rough cedar wood of the door. He pictured her waiting for him on the back porch and the two precious girls sleeping in his bed. He took a deep breath and prayed.

"God, give me courage to deal with what's in my heart. Lord, You know my soul and the fear I harbor. Release me from that burden so I can serve You more completely."

He put his hands on the doorknob and eased it open. Stepping into the hall, he checked on the girls. The night had turned cool, and he fixed two cups of hot chocolate before heading to the deck. He paused at the door and let his eyes drift over her. The soft light of the moon washed her in warmth as she leaned against the railing, face turned up to the stars.

"Hello."

She jumped.

"Sorry." He stepped through the door and handed her a cup with steam still swirling upward.

She grasped it with both hands and took a deep breath, pulling the warmth into her. "You read my mind." Sitting in the other rocking chair, she looked at him over the cup and smiled. "Thank you."

Smiling back, he took a sip before saying anything. "You were deep in thought when I got here. Girls give you any problems? Rachel still mad at me?"

She laughed, the kind that reminded him of softly playing Christmas bells. "I told her to get used to it. A father that loves his daughter should take every opportunity to torture the boys around her."

"Yeah, I thought about installing a rifle over the front door. Dub has an old twenty-two. I remember the first time I met him, he was cleaning it." Laughing, he leaned back in the rocker and took another sip. "Carol got so mad at him. Later I learned he never kept bullets in it."

Her laughter became louder before she covered her mouth and twisted to see if she had wakened the girls. "Sorry, that's just too funny. They'll appreciate your efforts one day, I promise."

He tried picturing his girls old enough to date and couldn't do it. He looked back at Lorrie Ann. She had one leg tucked under her as she rocked with the other one. She stared at the black-outlined hills while taking sips of the hot cocoa. Below the deck a deer snorted.

"So, if it wasn't the girls, what had you lost in thought?" The only sound she made in response was a deep sigh. Amazing how much a single sigh said while at the same time saying nothing at all. "Anyone giving you problems with the play?"

She shook her head. He knew sharing didn't come easy to her, so he waited.

Setting her cup on the deck, she pulled her knees to her chest. She wrapped her arms around her legs, making herself into a tight ball. He wanted to haul her up against him and promise her he'd fix it, but his own fears kept him out of arm's reach.

She finally turned to him, her cheek resting on her knee. "I got a call this morning from Melissa. The band has decided to hire a new manager."

"Oh, Lorrie Ann, I'm sorry."

She gave him a heartbreaking grin, the kind he now recognized Rachel used when she didn't want him to worry.

"Surprisingly, I think I'm okay with it. The whole messy drama with Brent had me concerned anyway."

Hope flared in John's chest. If she stayed here longer, he could take more time to figure out what they had. They could also settle the issue with her mother. She needed the truth, but Maggie had told him to hang on a little longer.

She faced out again, chin on her denim-clad knee. "With the rumors of the breakup, I'd already received a few inquiries." She smiled back at him. "In this business, you never know when you have to move on, so having options keeps you relevant. I'm thinking of taking an offer in Nashville."

With those words his hope died. *God, why can't something in life come easy?* Well, that was not true. His relationship with Carol had been easy, up until the point he had taken her for granted.

"As soon as the play is over I need to get back to my life. I thought it had to be in L.A., but I realized there are other options, like Nashville. Either way, I'm getting too comfortable here."

"What's wrong with here?"

"This isn't real life."

"It's real to me." He tried to keep the bitterness out of his tone.

"I'm not a part of this life. I'm just a guest."

John didn't know the details of her past, but talking with Sonia he could surmise it had been one atrocious event after another. He thought about that little girl, scared and alone, and he wanted to give her a home of her own, a place where love and safety lived in abundance. The question: Would she give up her music career to move here, permanently?

"You could be a part. Live here." He leaned forward.

She shook her head.

He had to convince her that the dream of a family was waiting to become a reality. He might not be telling her the truth about her mother, but he could tell her what was in his heart. "I'd like the opportunity to know you better."

She turned to him, eyes wide. Profound silence filled the space between them.

"No, you don't. I'm…" She gave a loathe-filled snort. "Stupid. I thought Brent would stop the late-night parties and take our relationship to the next level. We'd been drifting apart, not really connected. I thought if we got married… Well, classic female naïveté. I should have known better." She bit her lip and turned away.

John let the silence hang between them. His fist clenched, wanting to hold her.

"Man, was my timing off. He flew into a rage, one of the worst I've ever seen. He'd been mad at me before, but only when I nagged about his partying." She buried her face in her hands. A sob escaped. "In my head that sounded normal. I sound like a battered-women cliché."

"Lorrie Ann, your life is not a cliché." John couldn't hold back any longer. He moved his chair toward her until their knees touched. His fingers wrapped around her smaller hands.

Lorrie Ann studied the calloused hands in contrast with the tender touch John gave so naturally, making her want to curl up in his lap and hide from the world. He had to know the ugly truth about her. "His drug use had gotten worse. He was missing rehearsals and studio times, messing up onstage. I thought if we got married, started a family, he'd straighten out. He screamed at me that I wanted to ruin his life. I don't remember much of anything after he started hitting me and threw me into the kitchen counter. I pulled up tight into a ball and waited for him to stop. He kicked me a few times then left."

Somewhere during the retelling, John had moved next to her. His arms created a warm cocoon as he pulled her against him.

She rubbed the tears off her cheeks with the backs of her hands and pulled away, ashamed to look John in the face. From the corner of her sight, she saw him comb his fingers through his hair and take in a deep breath.

Reluctantly, she turned to him, shocked to see a tear run down his cheek. She cupped his face with her hands. "Oh, John, don't cry for me. I put myself there. When he left, I lay on the floor, and you know what I did?"

His lips pulled tight in an angry line. With a slight

movement of his head, he encouraged her to go on with her story.

She swallowed the lump in her throat, and her voice dropped low. "I prayed. In twelve, thirteen years, I hadn't talked to God once, but huddled on the ground, I asked for His help." She turned her face to the sky, unable to look at him as he heard the truth. "I realized I had become my mother. I had somehow become just like her. I checked for broken bones. I cleaned up and filled my car with clothes. I asked God to take me somewhere safe. There wasn't a single person in L.A. that I trusted." He took her hand and pulled her back into his warmth, giving her the courage to continue. Her face pressed against his neck, and she could feel his blood coursing through his veins.

"I was almost thirty years old, nowhere to go, hiding in a public restroom." A self-deprecating laugh escaped her lips. "You could say I'd hit rock bottom. And it wasn't anyone's fault but my own. Bible in hand, all I could think about was this purple-and-black afghan that Aunt Maggie made me for my thirteenth birthday. I wanted to pull it over my head and hide from the world." She rolled her eyes and snorted. "I thought I was too cool to take it to L.A. Stupid, huh?" She wiped her face with the back of her arm.

"No, I think God uses people and items to lead us. You'd need a reason to come home."

"Well, there you go. I'm sure you can find at least ten reasons the local pastor shouldn't date me." She stood up and moved to the railing. "So half the wild stories about me are lies, but it doesn't change the facts of my life the past twelve years." She took a deep breath, clenched her hands in the soft fabric of her skirt and slid a sideways glance at his beautiful face. She feared seeing loathing, or worse, pity. "I'm not the woman you need, John."

"Let God and me decide what I need in my life, Lorrie Ann. Especially what I want."

She leaned over the railing, listening to the water move over the rocks and around the roots of the century-old cypress. "The people of this church will never accept me, and if we date, everyone would think we're moving toward marriage."

"For me, marriage would be the goal."

"I can't be a preacher's wife." Her voice went a pitch higher. "People would stop coming to your church. They…would think you had lost your mind."

He snorted. Actually snorted at her.

"Maybe I have. Or at least my heart."

Her own heart twisted at his words. "Don't laugh at me. I'm serious."

"God knows you. You can't allow others to tell you who you are as a person."

"I know who I am, and more important, what I'm not. I've no clue how to be a mother. My own mother gave the world's worst example."

Guilt twisted his stomach. Maybe he should tell her now. He closed his eyes. It wasn't his secret to tell. He gazed at her, studying the outline of her profile in the moonlight. "My girls lost their mother, and I'm not looking for a replacement. She can't be replaced, but that doesn't mean they don't need mothering. Just as Maggie stepped in when your mother couldn't take care of you." He moved next to her, gently forcing her to look at him. "I want them to be around women of character and courage. You, Lorrie Ann Ortega, are a woman of character and courage. In spite of how your mom raised you—" he put a single bent finger under her chin "—or maybe because of her choices." He moved in close. His face hovered within inches of hers.

Lorrie Ann could feel his warm breath on her skin. Her gaze locked with his.

"My girls already adore you. You've brought silliness and tenderness to their lives. I tried so hard to be the perfect parent that I didn't see Rachel trying to be the perfect mom to Celeste."

She bit her lips and pressed her fist against her mouth. Swallowing hard, Lorrie Ann refused to let the cry escape. Despite her best efforts, she heard a pathetic sound slip past.

The worst part? She was sure John heard it, too. Her knuckles became wet with silent tears. She wanted to scream, but she knew that wouldn't ease the pain. In a last-ditch effort to stop a full-on sob, she squeezed her eyes shut. *God, please just make the pain stop.* "This is why I never, ever talked about the past. It can't be changed, so why relive the stupid heartache?"

John pulled her back into his arms. She couldn't stop the unleashing of emotion. The weak whimpering sounds became painful sobs, stuck in her throat, causing her to take large gulps of air.

"I hate this." *Breathe.* "I hate being weak. And I'm getting you all wet. Sorry."

"Hey, that's why I'm here."

She wiped at his shirt. "Being a pastor, you probably have to deal with people's emotions all the time."

"Is that how you see me? As your pastor?"

She laughed at the frustration in his voice. "You're so much more than just a pastor. I never dreamed I'd have a pastor as a friend. God knows what we need before we do, right? God knew no ordinary Christian could help me. My life needed a full-time professional."

His jaw flexed. "Lorrie Ann, I want to be more."

She shook her head. "I can't, sorry." Pulling herself away from his warmth, she forced herself to walk slowly through the cabin and out his door. This night he didn't follow her.

Chapter Sixteen

Lorrie Ann watched John lift a faux roof panel on one of the storefronts as Jake drilled the pieces together.

After she left his cabin three days ago, he stayed on her mind. The idea of being loved by a man like him seemed unreal. Then she imagined how his church would react and that was very real.

"Hello, anyone home?" Katy waved her hand.

"Sorry, I got distracted." She put her autosmile in place.

"Yeah, right." Katy laughed. "Pastor John seems more...I don't know, relaxed? Would you know anything about that?"

"I think music..." Before she finished, Katy swiped at Lorrie Ann's arm.

"I've seen the way he looks at you." She sighed. "He's such a good man, and being a small-town preacher has got to be tough." Katy looked over to the men assembling the stage. "It has to be a bit lonely. He can't really talk to anyone."

"He needs someone the community can trust, too."

Lorrie Ann bit the corner of her lip. By leaving, she would be doing the right thing.

"They don't know you. Anyway—" Katy shrugged her shoulders "—God is the One we need to trust."

Lorrie Ann rubbed the palms of her hands into her eye sockets. All this thinking formed a major headache. She needed to change the subject.

"What I need is a clean run-through. Why didn't someone stop me when I told Celeste she and a small herd of six-year-olds could open the play?" Ugh, another headache.

"I think we did." Katy laughed. "I'd be more worried about the foul odor your mood-setting donkey might bring to the manger." She wrinkled her nose.

"Oh, don't remind me." Lorrie Ann groaned then, taking a minute to look around at the unfinished youth building. "At least the building committee outdid themselves. If nothing else we'll have a great setting."

Three teenage girls giggled as they wrapped the metal poles in white icicle lights. In Lorrie Ann's mind, the jury was still out on tacky versus beautiful. It had been Katy's initiative, so she was willing to explore the idea. She glanced down at her clipboard. "Have you seen Vickie, or a hint of a costume?"

"No, but as much as she can be pigheaded about you, she would never do anything to hurt the play or the kids. You just gotta have some trust."

Lorrie Ann stopped herself from rolling her eyes. If she heard that word one more time, she might throw something.

Her gaze found John again. He had moved to stage left to erect the manger.

She smiled. She did trust him and her aunt Maggie.

Maybe there was hope for her. She sighed and loosened her grip on her to-do list. She needed to trust God in all things.

"You're staring again." Katy bumped her and laughed. "You're worse than a high-school girl with her first crush." She took a sharp intake of breath before breaking into a giggle. "Don't look now, but guess who's headin' our way?"

Lorrie Ann felt her skin getting warm. She needed to get away from him. Fear of giving up her dream for him caused her throat to close up.

"Hey, ladies, I can't believe how well it's coming together." The devastating smile that wiped out all good intentions flashed her way. Did he even know what kind of weapon he carried?

Katy laughed. "Lorrie Ann's list of problems is still longer than her 'done' list."

Lorrie Ann glared at Katy and reevaluated the best-friend status she had given her.

"Just a little trust, Lorrie Ann." He winked at her.

How dare he wink when everything was falling apart, including her life as she knew it.

"We're so far ahead compared to years past, and this is the most ambitious show we've ever attempted. The setting is incredible, Lorrie Ann. You and Jake have outdone yourselves."

Katy looked around. "It's beautiful, isn't it?"

John bent his neck to watch the girls above them hanging the lights. "At night, all the white lights will be spectacular. Great idea, Lorrie Ann."

"Katy's idea, not mine."

Katy wrinkled her nose. "Are you sure it's not too home-fried?"

Lorrie Ann hugged her. "Nope, John's right. They're perfect."

Katy raised her eyebrows and mouthed John's name while batting her eyes.

Lorrie Ann cleared her throat, which to her horror brought his attention back to her.

"Are you all right, Lorrie Ann?" He stepped closer to her.

"Um…Pastor John, do you think we can have a full dress rehearsal next Saturday?"

He narrowed his eyes at her and tilted his head. "That's the plan, Miss Ortega."

Katy touched Lorrie Ann's arm. "I have to go. Rhody is taking me to a movie in Kerrville, *without* the boys. He says he has a surprise." She made a face. "Hope it's good."

John smiled. "I'm sure it is. Enjoy your evening." He glanced over to the stage, where Jake, Adrian and Rhody stood putting the last pieces together. "I'll make sure he gets home."

"Thanks, Pastor John." She waved.

"Lorrie Ann, about the other night. I—"

She held her hands up to stop his words, took a deep breath and forced her eyes to look at him.

"Right now I need to stay focused on the play. But your words have planted themselves in my brain. I just don't know what to do about them."

He stepped closer. His fresh, masculine scent filled her senses. She closed her eyes.

"Maybe you should put them in your heart instead of your brain."

Her eyes popped open, and she moved back. "Maybe

you should tell Rhody it's time to go home. Katy's been talking about their date nonstop."

"Yes, ma'am."

He leaned in, not allowing her to escape. The smell of his apple candy excited her senses as his lips fluttered close to her ear. "This isn't over." Then he turned, leaving her.

She watched him walk away. When she left town, a part of her heart would be staying here forever.

Lorrie Ann looked at her notes but didn't see them. Maybe she could stay here and see what happened.

"Lorrie Ann!" Aunt Maggie's voice broke into her musings.

"Aunt Maggie, hey, did you get a chance to talk to Vickie?"

"Yes, yes, yes, but that's not why I'm here." A huge smile covered her aunt's face. "I have a big surprise for you."

Lorrie Ann sighed. She hoped the great revelation would be a new donkey.

"Close your eyes." Her aunt disappeared behind a line of SUVs. "Are your eyes closed?"

Lorrie Ann rested her face in the palms of her hands. "Yes."

"Surprise!"

Bringing her face up, Lorrie Ann blinked in confusion. "Mother?"

The slim woman standing in front of her should look to be in her mid-forties; instead, she looked older than Maggie, who was fifty-two.

Lorrie Ann had to be in shock, because she felt nothing. More than fifteen years had passed since she'd seen her mother, and now, out of nowhere, she appeared. No anger, no happiness, nothing.

Lorrie Ann gave a small laugh. Last week, she had decided to forgive her mother for all the bad decisions, for putting men and drugs ahead of her daughter. What did God do? Plant the woman right in front of her.

Sonia crossed her arms over her chest and rubbed her hands up and down her bone-thin biceps, as if to ward off the cold that no one else felt. Lorrie Ann could see purple and pink streaks of color on the underside of her dark ponytail.

She darted her gaze to Maggie then back to Lorrie Ann. "Hello. I'm sure you don't want to see me. I… Um…my, you're beautiful."

A million thoughts ran through Lorrie Ann's mind; questions ricocheted across her skull. "Where have you been?" She noticed her mom looked clear-eyed. It was like trying to start a conversation with a stranger.

"I live in San Antonio. I've been sober for two years now." She gave Lorrie Ann a lopsided smile.

In shock, Lorrie Ann stared at the two women. "You've been in San Antonio this whole time? Sober?"

She nodded. "When I made the decision to get sober, I called Maggie, and with Pastor Levi's help, they found a rehab center in the Hill Country. I spent six months there, then eight months in a sober house. Now I have my own apartment and a job." She bit her bottom lip.

"I don't understand. Why didn't you call me?" She turned to Maggie. "You knew? The whole time you knew!" Shock flashed into hurt, but Lorrie Ann preferred anger. She glared at the women who had raised her.

"Hey, ladies." John's voice interrupted the scene.

It gave Lorrie Ann time to collect the pieces of her thoughts and put them back together in some sort of order.

She watched as he swallowed Sonia in a bear hug. "How have you been?" He then moved to Maggie and kissed her on the cheek. "So, you finally convinced her to come up and see Lorrie Ann?"

Lorrie Ann looked at him. She had let her guard down and trusted him. She should have known better. He had known all along. This was what happened when you trusted people. They betrayed you.

He looked uncomfortable. *Good.*

Maggie broke the silence that had started to linger. "I thought we'd surprise Lorrie Ann."

John's eyebrows shot up as he jerked around to Lorrie Ann. He opened his mouth, sure to say something wise. Lorrie Ann didn't want to hear it.

"Can we go to the farm and talk? If that's okay." Sonia's voice was hesitant.

Lorrie Ann wanted to get away, to get a chance to clear her thoughts. "Sure."

They moved to the car, away from the only two people she had trusted the most. Sonia continued talking. "I just need to say I'm sorry. There's no way to make up for the mess I made of your childhood, but…"

Lorrie Ann stopped at her door and looked over the car to the woman who had abandoned her to Aunt Maggie's care.

"Listen, I've lived in L.A. for ten years. I've seen what drugs and alcohol do to a person. That you've been sober two years is great." Taking a deep breath, she forced a smile, for now one of her practiced smiles. They both slid into the BMW.

"You know God's timing is…well…so God." Lorrie Ann backed the car out and paused. "A few weeks ago, I probably would have screamed at you or just stomped away in anger." She shifted gears and made eye contact with her mother.

Tears hovered on the bottom of Sonia's lashes, and in a raspy voice she whispered, "I deserve it."

John and Maggie still stood in the same spot she had left them. They stopped talking and watched her drive past, but Lorrie Ann kept her eyes facing forward. Silence filled the car.

For three hours she sat on the back patio talking with her mother. As a teenager, she'd dreamed about this. She might even accept God had put her here at the right place and the right time. Why fifteen years later?

"Mother, I have one question." She swallowed, trying to get past the dryness. "Why did you leave me?"

Sonia stood. Wrapping her delicate arms around her middle, she looked out over the hills. "You were getting older, and I feared that I would be too…messed up to protect you. Your aunt and uncle had asked to take custody of you from the time you were a baby. I knew they would give you a safe place to live, a loving home, school."

"Why didn't you say goodbye?"

"Oh, sweetheart, I had tried to leave you with Maggie and Billy before, but you would cry and beg to go with me. I always gave in, so I knew I would have to sneak out and not come back. I'm so sorry. You've treated me better than I deserve."

Lorrie Ann shrugged. "You're my mom." She had

her answer to the question that had hounded her for fifteen years, and it didn't change anything inside her.

"Lorrie Ann, I know the hurt I caused you will not go away overnight. Thank you for giving me another chance to know you."

They both turned at the sound of boots on the gravel path. John stepped into the light. He cleared his throat and fisted his hands in his front pockets. "Ladies."

Sonia gave him a quick hug and said good-night before slipping through the screen door.

Silence hung in the air. John moved to stand next to Lorrie Ann and reached for her hand. "Lorrie Ann..."

She snatched her arm away. "You knew. This whole time, you knew about my mother being sober and in San Antonio, but you didn't think I needed to know?"

"Lorrie Ann, it wasn't up to me. Your mom was scared of giving in to the addiction again and didn't want you to know until she felt it was safe."

She crossed her arms over her waist. "I trusted you, and Aunt Maggie...Yolanda...you all knew!"

"Lorrie Ann." He reached for her.

"Don't. Stop saying my name. I trusted you and you lied to me."

"It wasn't our—"

"I don't want to hear excuses." She sat down hard and stared at the landscape but didn't actually see the beauty around her. In L.A., people lied, but you expected it. You worked with the knowledge everyone had his or her own agenda. "I've decided to take the new job in Nashville. They need me there in two weeks."

"You're just looking for an excuse to push me away. Don't do this, Lorrie Ann."

"Why?" She turned to glare at him. She had gotten

too close and had made the mistake of falling in love. "There is nothing for me here."

She moved away from him and opened the door. Turning back, she forced herself to meet him eye to eye and waited for him to say something, anything that would convince her to stay.

After what seemed like hours of silence, she turned her back to him.

Before she started crying or did something else just as stupid, like rush into his arms, she snapped her body around and marched to the kitchen door. She didn't stop until she collapsed on her bed and sobbed herself to sleep.

Chapter Seventeen

"Lorrie Ann!" Celeste ran full blast and threw all her weight onto Lorrie Ann's torso, nearly causing them both to go over on the ground. "I missed you at our Wednesday-night dinner."

"Me, too, rug rat. I just had too much to do here." *Plus, I can't bear to be in the same room as your father.* "Are you ready to head home? You did a great job leading your group down to light the lanterns tonight."

"Rachel's in back with Uncle Billy and Aunt Maggie. They're decorating the bucket that'll lift Rachel."

"Let's go get her. You have school tomorrow, and this has been a long day." Lorrie Ann took Celeste by the hand and headed to the back of the stage.

From there, it didn't take long to get home and go through the bedtime ritual. Several times, Lorrie Ann caught herself wanting to hug the girls and never let them go. If she thought about it being the last time, she'd start crying.

Rachel wore a small brace now and could move much easier, so the girls slept in the loft again.

Slipping to the edge of Celeste's bed, Lorrie Ann

pulled the cover up to her little chin and stroked her hair. "Well, you get the end of the story tonight." She swallowed the lump that suddenly clogged her throat.

Rachel surprised her by swinging her leg out from under the covers and sitting up. "No, Lorrie Ann, please don't stop tonight."

"But tonight the princess is reunited with her father. She gets to go back to his kingdom," Lorrie Ann whispered, praying she could get through this without crying.

Celeste clapped her hands. "Yeah, the bad duke is banished." She threw her arms wide, causing the covers to slip off her.

"Celeste, you are such a baby. Don't you know what this means? She *is* the princess. She's going back to L.A." Rachel crossed her arms and glared. "She's leaving us."

A sharp intake of breath made Celeste's mouth open, and her eyes went even larger. "No. You…you have to stay."

Lorrie Ann closed her eyes against the pain she saw in the innocent eyes. Maybe it was her own guilt she tried to hide. "Sweetheart, we always knew I wasn't staying forever. I have a new job in Nashville."

"But we're here. You can't leave us."

"Grow up, Celeste. People leave all the time. Momma left." Rachel's harsh voice became muffled as she threw herself back and jerked the sheet over her face.

Celeste cried out, "But Momma died." Her tear-stained face turned back to Lorrie Ann. "God's not taking you away, is He?"

"Oh, Celeste, I'm just going to Nashville. We can still talk on the phone, and I can even write stories and email them to you. I'm not leaving *you*. I just have to get back to my real life."

Rachel snorted under her sheet before she flipped her back to them.

Lorrie Ann sighed and drew the precious six-year-old into her arms.

"I promise I'll email or call every day if that's what you want. And I'll be back to visit."

"What about the play? You have to be here to see me light the way."

A hiccup from the small chest created the most heart-twisting sound Lorrie Ann had ever heard. She kissed the top of the small head as she stroked the silky baby-fine hair. "I'll be here for the play, then I leave for Tennessee. I'm so sorry, rug rat."

"You need to get over it. People move on. It's just life. Stop crying and go to bed."

Celeste looked at her older sister. "But you said that her and Daddy liked each other." She placed her little hands on each side of Lorrie Ann's face. "Don't you like Daddy? If he did something wrong, I'll talk to him. You don't have to leave." Her bowed lips pushed out in the saddest pout Lorrie Ann had ever seen.

"I do like your daddy. It's not his fault." How did you tell a six-year-old the problem was you liked her daddy too much?

Maybe for the girls she could do it. She closed her eyes. *Dear God, please show me what to do.*

She laid her cheek against Celeste and pulled her closer, smelling the fresh shampoo John used with the girls.

No, she needed to stop this. Once she returned to the music world, her life would fall back into place.

Soft sniffles created a pattern in Celeste's breathing. Glancing down, she realized the child had fallen asleep.

She slid the small body under the covers and stood as she pulled the blankets around her.

She bent down to kiss her and froze, remembering the first night she had seen John tuck the girls in. That seemed like a lifetime ago. With a light touch of her lips to Celeste's forehead, she asked God to keep the girls tucked in His arms and whispered, "Sweet dreams."

Standing, she put her hand on her lower back and arched.

"Good night, Rachel." She waited for a reply, but only silence followed. "Rachel, I'm sor—"

"Don't worry about it. I understand you have more important things to do than hang out in this middle-of-nowhere town."

Lorrie Ann didn't think she could have felt worse than holding a crying rug rat. Rachel proved her wrong. She moved to the door, stopping at the frame when she thought she heard a sniffle. "Rachel?"

"Night." A clear and decisive dismissal.

Lorrie Ann went straight to the deck, leaving the door open. Tilting her head back, she absorbed the sounds and scents of the night air. The water running over the rocks below calmed her. When she left, she wouldn't wait another twelve years to come back home.

Having a place to call home made her smile. She couldn't remember all the places her mom had dragged her to. Even in California, she'd bounced from hotels to apartments. She'd helped Brent decorate his beach house. It had never felt like a real home, no matter how much she tried.

John's little temporary cabin felt more like a home than all the steel and glass ever did.

She lifted her arms over her head and stretched. Bringing them down, she curled up in the giant rocker and pulled her knees to her chest.

Hearing the door, she twisted around to greet John but didn't see him. He'd probably gone upstairs first. She settled back in and waited.

What was taking John so long? Anxiety crawled up her spine. Were the girls still upset? She slipped her shoes back on and walked to the base of the staircase.

The moonlight cut through the darkness. Pausing, she tilted her head to listen. She didn't hear John or the girls. Scanning the room, she whispered John's name and waited. Lorrie Ann moved to his bedroom door and softly knocked. "John?"

Looking toward the entryway, she noticed the front door slightly open. She had heard the door. Stepping through it and onto the porch, she scanned the driveway. John's parking space remained empty. Her stomach got tight, and she rushed back inside.

Breathe, Lorrie Ann. You're getting worked up over nothing. Nervousness pulled her skin tighter as she climbed the spiral staircase.

When she saw Celeste sitting up in her bed and Rachel still bundled under her covers, a rush of relief left her legs weak.

Celeste clutched her floppy rabbit to her chest.

"Celeste, sweetheart, what's wrong?" she whispered so as not to bother Rachel. Celeste's wide eyes darted to her sister's bed.

Her stomach started coiling again. Under closer scrutiny, Lorrie Ann noticed the form under the blankets didn't look quite right. Heart pumping against her throat, Lorrie Ann pulled back the covers, finding nothing but pillows and stuffed animals.

Her eyes flew to Celeste. Horror stories of children stolen from their beds flooded her mind. She reached for her phone to call John but realized she had left it downstairs.

"Celeste." She grabbed the girl by her shoulders. "Do you know where Rachel is?"

"She made me promise not to say anything." Tears welled up in her eyes. "She made me promise on the Bible."

"Come on—we need to call your dad." She took Celeste by the hand and headed down the stairs. As she reached for her phone, the door opened.

Hope surged through every fiber in Lorrie Ann's DNA. Instead of the missing eleven-year-old girl, John walked into the kitchen.

"Hey, guys. What's going on? Why is Celeste—"

"I'm sorry.... I was on the deck."

"It's my fault, Daddy." Their words overlapped.

"Rachel left."

"Left? What do you mean 'left'? An eleven-year-old doesn't just leave her house at ten o'clock at night."

"I put them to bed and then went on the deck to wait for you. I told the girls about me going to Nashville. They were upset. Rachel seemed angry, but I didn't think she'd run away. Where would she go?"

His face had lost all color as he ran his hands through his hair. He turned and looked around the room as if lost.

Then he pulled out his cell and called Maggie, asking her to start calling people on the phone tree. They would be meeting here with floodlights.

"How did she get out without you knowing?" All his words came between clenched teeth. "When did you discover she was missing?"

"I had my phone to call you. She must have left about ten minutes ago. She can't be far."

He opened his phone again and called Dub, the whole time pacing. This conversation was shorter than the one with Maggie.

He braced his hands on the granite bar, closing his eyes. "Please, God, be with her. Keep her safe and lead us to her quickly." He rubbed his palm over the back of his neck. "The thought of her out there alone…" He turned and headed to the front entrance.

"She's not alone, Daddy. She's with Seth."

He froze and turned to Celeste. Then his glare darted to Lorrie Ann. "Anything else I should know?"

"This is the first I've heard of her being with Seth." Celeste buried her face in Lorrie Ann's neck while she strangled the poor bunny in a death grip.

"Apparently, Rachel made Celeste promise not to tell anyone."

He walked over and stopped in front of them. Taking Celeste from Lorrie Ann, he gently sat her on one of the barstools and leaned in until father and daughter were face-to-face. His voice stayed low and tender.

"Sweetheart, someone can't make you promise to lie to your father using the Bible."

She reached up and wrapped her soft fingers around his stubbled jaw. "Daddy, please don't cry." She bumped her forehead against his. "And don't be mad at Miss Lorrie Ann. It's my fault."

He covered her tiny hands in his large ones. "I just want to get Rachel home. What do you know, monkey?"

"Seth threw some twigs at our window right after Miss Lorrie Ann tucked us into bed. Rachel went to the window. I couldn't hear what they said, but she told me to stay quiet and made me promise on the Bible. She said she'd be back soon. She wanted to talk to Seth, but he couldn't come in our room."

"Thank you, sweetheart." He kissed her on the forehead then stepped back. "I'll call Vickie." He already had the phone to his ear. Lorrie Ann blinked as each ring lasted an eternity. *Please, please, God, let Rachel be there.*

"Hello, Vickie. I'm looking for Rachel. We think she might be with Seth."

Lorrie Ann could hear the woman's voice, but the words sounded muffled.

"Would you check to see if he knows where she is, then?" He dropped his chin and rubbed the bridge of his nose with his free hand.

His head suddenly shot up, and she could hear yelling in the background.

"Vickie, calm down. Do you know where he might have gone?"

All Lorrie Ann could make out was something about his father.

"Maggie's already started calling on the phone tree. People are going to be meeting here to walk the area. I'll call Jake and have him and his group meet at your house. We'll start walking. They should be somewhere in between."

Lorrie Ann heard Vickie's voice pitch higher.

"Florida? Why would he try to—" His sentence got

interrupted. "Vickie, I don't think Rachel would run away to Florida, but she would probably try to stop him. They've been gone from here less than—" he looked down at his watch "—twenty minutes. We'll find them.... Okay. Call your parents. I'll touch base in a little bit."

He headed for the front door. "Will you stay here with Celeste?"

She nodded, not knowing what to say.

"I think Dub's just pulled up." With that, he disappeared out the door.

She hugged Celeste one more time. The little girl looked so miserable. It ripped into her heart.

"Can you think of anywhere they might have gone, a favorite place?"

The petite face twisted in deep thought. "They like to hang out at the swimming hole behind the big house." Her teardrops hung to her thick lashes, making her eyes look bigger than normal. "But it's dark, so why would they go there? We aren't allowed to go to the river without an adult."

Lorrie Ann didn't bother pointing out they weren't allowed outside without an adult and that hadn't stopped Rachel. She hit John's number on her phone.

"Lorrie Ann?" She heard a mix of hope and irritation in his voice.

"Is anyone heading to the big house?"

"No. Why?"

"Celeste says they might be at the swimming hole."

He gave a frustrated growl. "We just got lines of people walking the area between the Lawsons' ranch and the pecan farm. That's the opposite direction."

"I can take the dirt road through the orchard and

check it out. Can I take your truck?" She needed to do something. Sitting here frayed her nerves.

"Okay, call me when you get there." The distress in his voice made him sound harsh.

"I will." He had already disconnected.

"Come on, rug rat. We're going to the swimming hole."

Seat belts locked in place. She made her way down the rut-filled dirt road that ran along the back side of the pecan orchards. When they arrived at the gate that joined the two properties, Lorrie Ann was surprised to find it open.

Going as fast as she dared, she finally saw the two-story limestone home standing sturdy in the moonlight. She put the truck in Park by the old stone barbecue pit and picnic tables.

Grabbing the flashlight, she slid out of the truck. Celeste followed suit on the other side. Lorrie Ann paused. What to do with her charge? Leaving her alone in the truck sounded dangerous.

Before she could decide, Rachel's desperate voice came from the river below.

"Rachel!" She yelled as loud as she could to make sure the girl heard her. The blood in her veins slammed into her skull while leaving her legs empty and weak. "It's Lorrie Ann." She broke into a run. "I'm coming, sweetheart."

God, please be with me. Breathe, girl. You can't panic now. Just breathe. Pulling her phone out, she hit John's number.

John answered before the first ring finished. "Is she there?"

"Yes, she just called up from the riverbed. There's

a problem, so I'm calling 911." She ended the call and started hitting the next numbers.

"Lorrie Ann? Please, help me! Seth's hurt!" Gasps for air punched periods in the middle of her sentences. She sounded as if she'd been crying for hours.

"I'm coming, Rachel." Hurling herself down the old rusty metal stairs, Lorrie Ann prayed.

She swept the area with the flashlight until she found Rachel on her knees with Seth draped over her lap. His lower body disappeared in the water, and they were both wet.

"What is your emergency?"

"This is Lorrie Ann Ortega. I've found Rachel Levi and Seth Miller. We're at the old Childress ranch house down beside the swimming hole. I just got here. They're both wet, and he appears unconscious."

"I don't think he's breathing," Rachel cried, her panic-filled eyes begging Lorrie Ann to fix him. "I told him not to jump." She slumped over him and sobbed.

Lorrie Ann fell to her knees on the other side of Seth. She ignored the river rocks biting into her shins.

She handed the phone to Rachel. "Tell them what happened. I think we need to get him flat, but move him as little as possible."

She started checking for his pulse and any signs of breathing. Fear gripped her. Nothing. She couldn't find a thing.

Oh, God, please, please let him live. Please, please, please.

She pushed back the hair that clung to his forehead and looked up at Rachel. She spotted Celeste standing behind her sister, the stuffed rabbit held tight against her chest.

"Celeste, I need you to go to the picnic tables and watch for your dad and the ambulance. Okay?"

"Okay." She turned and headed up the steps.

"We have to start CPR." Lorrie Ann's heart pounded in her ears, and her limbs went numb as she pinched his nose and blew into his mouth. Meanwhile, she prayed frantically that someone who knew what they were doing got here fast.

A couple more breaths then she pressed on his chest, remembering the "Staying Alive" song the way her instructor had taught her. Her prayers to God never stopped. She knew His power and strength kept her focused because there was no way she could do this on her own.

"Daddy!" Rachel's high-pitched cry broke through Lorrie Ann's focus.

Seth started coughing. Hope surged through Lorrie Ann as John came into her line of vision. He grabbed Rachel, kissing her on the ear.

"How is he?"

"He just coughed up some water. That's good, right? Should I breathe into his mouth again?"

"Have you checked his breathing and pulse?"

"I forgot." She moved back to Seth's face and bent over him.

John pulled Rachel to her feet. "Go up to Celeste."

"No! Daddy, I have to stay with Seth…"

"Go! Your sister's up there alone."

As she turned, the EMTs were heading down the stairs. Brenda led the group, and two others followed with a backboard.

Lorrie Ann had never been more relieved in her entire life. She stepped back as she answered their questions.

John's arm wrapped around her, and she pressed her back into his chest, the warmth of his body making her realize how cold she felt. His other arm held Rachel against his side. All three watched silently as the medics worked on Seth. He coughed up more water before they eased him on the flat surface of the board. With practiced skill, they moved him up the stairs, not one time jostling or bumping him.

Brenda approached the small group huddled together. "Are you all right, Rachel?" Her professional tone sounded calm and reassuring.

Rachel nodded. "Is Seth going to be okay?"

"We're taking him into town to be airlifted to Children's Methodist in San Antonio. You and Lorrie Ann did a great job. You gave him the best chance he can have."

Brenda led the small group up the stairs. At the top, they found Vickie in pajama bottoms and a large T-shirt, her tall frame swallowed in Jake's large arms as she tried to reach her son. Brenda rushed to them and quietly talked to the distraught mother.

Vickie closed her eyes and nodded to whatever Brenda told her. Jake's powerful arms slipped away, and the EMT led the subdued woman to the back of the ambulance. With the closing of the doors, they were gone.

Lorrie Ann turned to find Celeste and realized her whole body shook. Both girls now clung to John, and for a moment, she felt like an outsider that desperately wanted to be part of his family.

A stupid tear slipped down her cheek. She had no

right to his family after the way she'd messed up tonight. She had no business trying to be a mother.

Maybe she should book a flight out sooner. They didn't need her here. Jake's authoritative strides cut the distance between them.

"Lorrie Ann, you need to sit before you fall down." Jake's command left no room for argument, but that didn't mean Lorrie Ann couldn't find any. With what she hoped was a defiant glare, she looked him in the eye and…collapsed.

John quit breathing and rushed to her side, pulling her from Jake's arms. He eased her onto the picnic-table bench.

"What's wrong?" Rachel's worried stare didn't leave Lorrie Ann.

The moan Lorrie Ann released twisted his spirit. She leaned forward, resting her forehead in her hands. Her fingers threaded through her hair, screening her face from view. He moved his hand to her back, needing to keep some sort of contact.

With the other hand, he pulled Rachel closer. She looked so lost. Celeste squeezed between and crawled into his lap, pressing her small body next to his heart.

For a moment, he closed his eyes and thanked God for them all being safe in his arms. He prayed for Seth and Vickie.

"Daddy, I didn't mean for anyone to get hurt. I'm sorry." More tears ran down Rachel's already red and swollen eyes. "Lorrie Ann?"

Lorrie Ann raised her head. "It's okay, sweetheart. I just feel so stupid. I've never fainted before."

Jake took one step closer and sat on his heels. "It's

a crash from the adrenaline rush. It's common." The trooper moved his gaze from Lorrie Ann to John. "They're airlifting Seth to Methodist. I called Vickie's parents. She won't be able to ride in the helicopter. Are you going? She needs someone with her, and I'm pretty sure that useless ex-husband of hers can't make it." He sneered the last sentence.

John sighed. They needed to head to the hospital. Vickie had a long night ahead of her, and she needed all the physical and spiritual support they could give her.

"First, Lorrie Ann and Rachel need a change of clothes before we go to San Antonio." He realized he assumed Lorrie Ann would come with him. She might just want to go home and burrow in her bed deep under her quilt.

He felt Lorrie Ann straighten. "Yes, we need to get Rachel out of those wet clothes. I…um…apologize for my little bit of drama." She rubbed her palm across her forehead, and he noticed it still shook.

"Lorrie Ann, thank you." His throat tightened. "I shouldn't have gotten upset earlier. I was—"

"You were worried." Lorrie Ann finished his thought for him. "It's okay."

"Well, I'll be going. Good night, and please let me know if Vickie needs anything. She won't call me."

John watched as the state trooper backed out and drove down the graveled driveway of the old limestone house.

"I'd planned to put a fence around the stairs to the river when we moved in here. I should have done it already." What he would like to do was build a twelve-foot fence around his girls.

"Daddy, I'm going to the hospital with you, right?" Rachel asked.

"Wouldn't dream of leaving you behind." When he stood, Celeste clung so tightly he didn't need to hold her to him, but he did. With a slight smile, he kissed the top of her head and moved to the truck. He had driven Maggie's golf cart, but he could have one of Dub's boys take it back in the morning.

"Daddy, is Seth going to be okay?" Rachel's whisper could barely be heard over the night sounds.

"All we can do is pray and trust in God."

A flash of anger crossed her face as she sent a glare his way. "You can pray all you want, Daddy, but sometimes bad things still happen." Her young voice sounded old beyond its years.

He focused on buckling Celeste into the backseat of the truck and prayed for the right words to say.

As he slid in behind the steering wheel, he found his daughter in the rearview mirror. Her face turned away from him and pressed against the window.

"Prayer and faith doesn't mean a life without trouble and loss, sweetheart. But it does mean you're never alone, even if the people in your life can't be there." He took a deep sigh and glanced over at Lorrie Ann. She had her arm stretched over the seat with her hand resting on Celeste's leg. He faced the front, looking over the hood at the trees in his headlights. "Rachel, life has brought me to my knees many times, but God is my strength."

He made eye contact with her in the rearview mirror. In her short eleven years, his little girl had experienced too many harsh realities of life. He knew a pat on the head and a reassurance that everything would be all right would insult her. "The hardest and most fearful prayer I've ever spoken was to ask for God's will to be done. I've never regretted following God. I have questioned many things in my life but never God's love for us."

She sat alone in the backseat, huddled in a ball. "Daddy, I'm so afraid."

"Let's pray." He twisted, and with his right hand, he entwined his finger with hers. He took his left and invited Lorrie Ann to join the family circle.

Her hand still had a slight tremble. He noticed Rachel's also shook as she reached for Celeste. He closed his eyes. "Dear Father, we turn our fear over to You. For we know You are with us. We lift Seth up to You. Your love will strengthen us and help us. Thank You, God, for holding us in Your hands. Amen."

Once at the pecan farm, it didn't take long to get Celeste settled in and find a change of clothes for everyone before they headed to San Antonio. He bent down to give Celeste a kiss.

"Daddy, can I go?"

"No, you stay with Aunt Maggie, but I need you to pray."

"Like the disciples in the garden? I can do that. Miss Martha said they fell asleep. I won't, Daddy. I'll pray for Seth."

John smiled and pulled the blanket over her shoulder. "Pray as long as you can then sleep. You promise to sleep? I don't want to worry about you."

"Faith means not to worry, Daddy."

He shook his head at the wisdom of innocence.

Chapter Eighteen

John's hand controlled the steering wheel as he eased the truck off IH-10 and onto the Medical Drive exit.

Lorrie Ann sighed. "Maybe I shouldn't have come."

He hated the doubt in her voice.

"It'd be an understatement to say Vickie and I weren't friends. I might be the last person she wants around her right now."

"You gave her son a fighting chance to survive." He reached over and took her hand. "It's a big hospital. If it becomes a problem, there're plenty of other waiting rooms."

She weaved her fingers through his hand and held tight. "I guess you're a bit familiar with hospitals. I don't know what to say."

"From experience, I can tell you there's nothing you can say. It's just about being there, so no pressure to find the perfect words of wisdom." He tightened his grip for a second before putting his hand back to the job of driving.

With a deep breath, Lorrie Ann tilted her head back and combed her fingers through her hair.

"That was a loaded sigh if I ever heard one. Want to share what's going on in that brain of yours?"

"I'm thinking your family would be much better off without me. Since my arrival, your girls have been in a car accident, the drama in the pageant, and I let Rachel just two-step right out the front door."

"Wow, I didn't know you were all-powerful." He found the energy to give a half smile as she rolled her eyes at him.

He pulled into a parking space and shut off the engine. "Lorrie Ann, God puts people in our path when He knows we're going to need them." He turned to make sure he had her full attention. "Did it occur to you that you didn't bring the bad, but you're the gift God sent to help us through these events?" He pulled her hand into his. "I know you can't wait to get back to your old life, but you've been a godsend. Don't ever forget you've impacted the lives of my family and others."

He moved in a little closer, their noses inches apart. "You got that?"

Her eyes turned a strange shade of grayish-green surrounded by the moisture gathered in the black lashes. She nodded.

"Good." He reached over the seat and gently nudged his sleeping daughter. "Rachel, sweetheart, we're at the hospital."

Climbing out of the truck, both girls followed John across the parking lot. As they walked through the sliding doors, John grabbed Rachel's left hand. He watched his daughter reach out to Lorrie Ann with her free hand. Joined, the threesome entered the children's wing, prepared for the worst, praying for the best.

Entering the waiting room, Lorrie Ann saw Vickie

with her parents on either side of her. She tried to duck behind John and Rachel, but the girl wouldn't let go of her hand. She licked her lips and swallowed the knot in her dry throat.

Vickie looked up and, with a gasp, rushed them. She headed straight to Lorrie Ann and wrapped her in a death grip.

"Thank you, oh, thank you." Vickie started sobbing. "They said you saved him. If not for you we would have lost him."

Huge gulps of air filled Lorrie Ann's ear.

Not knowing what to do, she brought her arms around Vickie's shoulders. She made eye contact with John and gave him a *help me* look.

He moved in and gently touched Vickie's arm. "How's he doing?"

She turned and sniffed, wiping her eyes with the back of her hand. "Oh, Rachel." She grabbed the girl's face, cradling it in her hands before pulling her into her arms.

"How…how is he?" Rachel asked.

"He's alive." Vickie held Rachel at arm's length and brushed her hair behind her ear. "Thanks to you and L.A., he made it here."

Vickie pulled Rachel back into her chest and looked at John. "They're running tests on his brain and spine."

"Is there anything we can do?" John's hand gripped Vickie's shoulder.

"No." She shook her head. "We're just waiting and praying."

A doctor walked in, and Vickie's mother led her to meet with him.

Lorrie Ann found a lone chair in the corner. She

leaned back, causing the vinyl chair to squeak. With eyes closed, she tilted back her head. The strong smell of disinfectant faded as she focused on the images of people, events, words and decisions that swirled in her brain, creating a whirlpool of thoughts. Her mother, Aunt Maggie, John, the girls and Vickie, the list went around and around until she felt the pressure suck her under.

John knew the truth to a life well lived. She didn't fully trust God, not with her heart.

Bowing her head in prayer, she asked for guidance. "God, please show me what You have planned for me." She waited. Opening her eyes, she studied her hands. *How do I know what to do, God?*

More silence. With a deep sigh, she closed her eyes. So, what if she went to Nashville?

Quiet, she waited and listened to her heart's response. The sounds of the hospital faded as the beat of her heart rushed in her ears. The girls—she'd miss Rachel and Celeste. She bit her lip at the thought of leaving John's daughters. They had taken a permanent place in her heart. She nodded.

Okay, what else? Images filled the darkness behind her eyelids: the river, the trees, Aunt Maggie's smile, Yolanda. With a sigh, she waded deeper into her consciousness and found her mother's sober eyes. A woman she didn't even know yet. Then the youth and all their music and laughter entered her thoughts. That surprised her. She'd discovered an unexpected purpose working with the youth group. A purpose she'd just found.

John. She bit down on her top lip. He felt like home. A home she never allowed herself to even dream about in her most secret desires.

Lorrie Ann thought of the new job in Nashville. She searched for anything positive. Nothing.

Opening her eyes, she scanned the waiting room and recalled her life in L.A. She had been spiritually dead. God had brought her here so John could give her CPR.

"Lorrie Ann?"

She jumped, surprised by the nearness of John's voice. She opened her eyes to look up at him.

"Can I sit?" He motioned to the empty chair next to her.

She nodded. "How is he?" *Please, God, let it be good.*

John smiled. "It looks like he'll be fine. Vickie took Rachel to see him."

"Oh, thank You, God." She reached out and placed her fingers on John's arm. The warmth shot through her. She pulled her hand back into her lap and hoped to give the impression of being unaffected.

She stared across the waiting room, not wanting to risk the rejection she might see in his eyes if she declared her change of plan. Would he even care if she stayed?

"I'm thinking of sticking around for a while."

John's eyes widened. "Really? Why have you decided to stay?"

She bit her lip, twisting her fingers together in her lap. "I'm thinking it might be nice to get to know my mom."

His stubbled chin rested on his fist. Cutting a side glance at her, he nodded. "She'd like that."

"And I'd love to keep working with the youth, after the pageant's over. I mean, if it's all right with you."

He gave her a lopsided grin. "I think it's a good idea. How about—"

Rachel burst through the doors and ran straight to John. Wrapping her arms around her father, she buried her face in his chest. "He talked to me, Daddy, and made a lame joke."

John pulled her closer and smiled at Lorrie Ann over his daughter's head. "That's good news, sweetheart. Let's talk to Vickie, and then we can head home."

Lorrie Ann smiled back and followed as they walked toward Vickie and her parents.

She felt lighter. With the decision to remain, a burden lifted. She was home to stay. *Now, God, what do I do about John?*

Chapter Nineteen

The day of the play had finally arrived. Unlike Lorrie Ann, John had no doubt the Christmas pageant would be successful. He had other reasons to be nervous. He pushed the sour-apple-flavored candy around in his mouth.

He looked at his girls, sitting in front of him. Rachel, wise beyond her years, reminded him so much of Carol—not just her looks, but her mannerisms, too. He smiled at Celeste. Less than a minute of sitting and she already wiggled in her chair.

"Girls, you know I like spending time with Lorrie Ann, right?"

They nodded. Rachel's face became tight. "Just as friends, right?"

"I love Lorrie Ann, Daddy." Celeste kicked her feet.

Rachel turned on her little sister. "Can you sit still for five minutes?"

He pulled Celeste into his lap and, with his other hand, settled Rachel against his side. She grumbled, but nestled in close and laid her head on his shoulder. For a moment he savored having them close.

"After the play—" he took a deep breath "—I'm going to ask her to stay with us."

Rachel picked her head up. "But, Daddy, she's already decided to stay in Clear Water."

"No, I'm going to ask her to marry me and live with us at the ranch house."

Celeste jumped off his lap and wrapped her arms around his neck. "Oh, Daddy, she'll be my mom, and we can have sleepovers!"

Rachel pulled back and yelled, "We already have a mom, Celeste!"

Celeste looked at her sister in confusion. "But she's not here."

"Rachel, it's okay to love more than one mother." He knew she would have a harder time than her sister. Tucking Rachel's hair behind one ear, he brought her face up to look him in the eye. "I love Lorrie Ann, and I want to share my life with her. You're part of that life."

The tears hanging on her lower lashes sliced at his heart. "But, Daddy, I love Momma and I don't want to forget her."

"Oh, sweetheart, the human heart is phenomenal when it comes to loving. It doesn't kick people out. It just gets bigger. Your mom will always be a part of us, living in our hearts." He squeezed Rachel with his arm and laid his cheek against the top of her head. "You know what your mom is doing right now?" He felt her shake her head against his chest with her nose pressed flat. "She's scooting over to make an empty space right next to her. I can see her patting the seat as she invites Lorrie Ann to join her. That's what your mother always did, at every opportunity. She pulled people in and loved them."

"You think Momma would like Lorrie Ann?"

"Yes, and just because I love Lorrie Ann doesn't take away any of the love I have for you or your mother. It's just more love."

"I think Lorrie Ann would be good for Celeste." Rachel pulled away a little and sat straighter. "You'll have more help. It's nice to have a woman to talk to about things."

John laughed. "Yes, it is." He kissed her forehead and pulled both girls tight within the circle of his arms. He flexed his jaw and sent a prayer out. Now he had to convince Lorrie Ann.

Chapter Twenty

The unfinished youth building had become a biblical village. Red-and-green Christmas sweaters filled the seats. Lorrie Ann nodded and smiled as people greeted her. A gentle breeze mixed the fresh outdoor smell with the aroma of the cinnamon snicker-doodles set out for the audience.

She glanced at the entrance and saw John shaking hands with each person coming in to watch the pageant. He looked over the crowd, stopping and smiling when he made eye contact with her.

He sent a slow wink that melted her spine and demolished all the tight nerves. She felt her smile reach her ears. *Oh, God, please wrap Your love so tightly around every heart here tonight, so all they see is the hard work the kids have put into the play.*

Mrs. Miller moved next to John, and the look she sent Lorrie Ann's way did not include a smile. Acid burned her throat as monkeys flipped wild somersaults low in her belly, pulling every nerve taut.

The list of things that could go wrong flashed through her brain. *We shouldn't have used the donkey.*

What if he does something embarrassing? The cherry picker might get stuck again. Uncle Billy sat at the controls, so he would handle any malfunctions.

She glanced at John and wished she could stare at him all night, but her list called. Looking at her cell phone, she realized the kindergarten group should be lined up and ready by now. Lorrie Ann moved to the large panel off to the left, hoping to find them prepared.

Only fifteen minutes to showtime. The checklist scrolled through her mind's eye: the horsemen were in place; Mary and Joseph had Alfredo, the donkey; the choir stood to the right, their robes detailed beautifully; the innkeepers mingled with the crowd, passing out programs and offering hot cider. Pride filled her as they worked hard to set the mood.

Off to her left, the shepherds watched over their small flock. Some of the audience members had walked over to see what was going on with the herd of sheep. The band filled the night air with soft background music. Her blood rushed with the excitement of all the parts coming together.

Then her eyes went wide. She hadn't seen Derrick. She scanned the area, and her mouth went dry.

John had put so much faith in her. She had to make this right.

Behind one of the faux buildings, Lorrie Ann found Katy. Celeste and her classmates stood quietly, waiting for their cue to start the events of the night. She couldn't stop the grin.

Now she needed to find her drummer boy. "Katy, have you seen Derrick? I can't find him."

Katy shook her head. "He brought Carlos, but I haven't seen him since."

John walked over to her. "Everything looks great, Lorrie Ann." He smiled down at the short angels.

She skimmed the area. "I don't know where Derrick is. He should be here with the kindergartners, but I haven't seen him."

Carlos stood in front of them, tugging on John's blazer. "Pastor John, I think he's hiding in the shed." He pointed to the storage shed next to the fence. His big dark eyes looked up to Lorrie Ann. "Sorry, he made me promise not to tell you."

She gave him a relieved smile and ruffled his curly hair. "It's okay. Thank you for telling Pastor John."

She headed toward the shed, covering ground in double time. John kept pace with her. She glanced at him. "We only have about ten minutes before you need to be onstage with the opening prayer."

He dared to laugh and moved closer to her. "In a hundred years, I don't think it has ever started on time."

She narrowed her eyes at him. Did he not realize how serious she took her job? "Not on my watch. I've never had an event start late. We *will* start on time."

His grin caused her to take a deep breath to calm her nerves.

"Yes, ma'am." He flipped his hand from his forehead in a small salute.

She didn't have time to reply as they came face-to-face with Derrick, sitting on a gray wooden bench. Knees pulled to his chest, he had his head against the rough wood of the storage shed.

"Hey, Derrick."

He jumped.

"Pastor John, Miss Lorrie Ann. I…um…I was looking for my drumsticks." He jumped to his feet.

John raised an eyebrow. "Really? You sure it's not a case of stage fright?" John sat on the bench and picked up the drumsticks. "The first few times I got up in front of people, I almost got sick."

"You?" The youth's lanky body folded back down on the bench.

John nodded his head and handed the wooden sticks to Derrick.

Misery and doubt clouded Derrick's dark eyes as he looked up at Lorrie Ann. Her irritation fled, and her heart went out to the vulnerability she saw in this teenage rebel.

"What if I mess up?" He looked down at his hands. "Some of the old folks don't like me. They think I don't belong here."

"They're not the ones to decide if you belong here or not." She cupped his face and brought his eyes up to meet hers again. "You belong."

John placed a hand on Derrick's slumped shoulder. "You need to remember you're not performing for the people in the chairs, not even for Lorrie Ann or me. You're using your music tonight to praise and worship God." John gave the teen's shoulder one last squeeze before standing to leave. "He knows none of us are perfect, Derrick. Just give Him one hundred percent of you. If you decide not to do this, we understand. One night doesn't make who you are." He looked at Lorrie Ann and winked. "Well, it's time to get this thing started." He turned back and handed Derrick a green hard candy. "These have always helped me."

Lorrie Ann watched as he headed for the stage.

"He's right, you know." Derrick's voice carried softly across the night. "Tonight won't make or break you. It's not your fault if we make a mess of the pageant." He popped the Jolly Rancher in his mouth.

A supple laugh escaped her lips. "Now you're giving me advice?" She smiled at him. "Good advice at that." She sat on the bench where John had just been. "By the way, I like your haircut. You have beautiful eyes. You also took out the piercing. Why?"

He shrugged and picked up the drum, running his fingers along the stretched top. "Didn't want to give them any more reasons to be mad at you."

Her heart melted. "Oh, Derrick, thank you, but you didn't need to change for me. I've been taking care of myself for a long time."

"Yeah, maybe you should let someone else help you every now and then." He flashed his seldom-used smile. "Someone told me that not long ago."

She heard John's strong voice quiet the crowd, and the monkeys in her stomach started jumping around again. She gave Derrick one last look. "Are you good?"

He nodded and picked up his drumsticks.

With a thumbs-up, she went off to find Katy and Celeste.

As she drew closer, Celeste waved at her, the long white drape of her sleeve flying with enthusiasm. No stage fright for this one.

Lorrie Ann smiled at Katy as she hugged Celeste and mouthed, *They look ready.* Ten little six-year-olds smiled back at her, their battery-powered candles ready to light the way.

Katy nodded and signaled them to turn on their candles. John said his final words, and as he stepped offstage, the overhead light went dark, leaving the kindergartners' candles as the only light.

Celeste led her group down the aisle, singing "The First Noel." Each student stopped at their assigned lantern that hung along the rows of chairs and in front of the buildings of the village. One by one, the lamps came to life as the children's sweet voices filled the air. They slowly disappeared behind the storefronts that made up stage left. Their song faded out.

Surprised at the overwhelming sense of pride, Lorrie Ann bit her bottom lip.

"They did great!"

John's whisper caused her to jump. She placed her hand over her rapidly beating heart.

He leaned in again. "Sorry, didn't mean to scare you."

Apple candy filled her senses. She smiled at him, and her heart soared, loving that he chose to be next to her as their little production unfolded.

In the heavy silence, people started shifting in their chairs. Anticipation of the unknown filled the atmosphere.

From the front entrance, hooves hit the concrete floor. People turned to see Alfredo the donkey led by Seth, playing Joseph. Sarah Garcia, a fourteen-year-old middle schooler, had been transformed into Mary, tired and miserable.

"Hang on, Mary. I'll find us a place to rest." Seth opened with the first line.

They made their way through the audience, stopping at each facade. Each time they were turned away. Finally they made it to the last inn, next to the stage. Alfredo, the sweet little donkey, plodded along without a fuss or rude odors. Lorrie Ann couldn't contain her smile.

They made their way up to the stage. The lights dimmed as the band and choir started "Hark! The Herald Angels Sing."

A spotlight found Rachel with large golden wings above the crowd. The audience gasped in surprise as they watched the cherry picker rise above them, cloaked as a white cloud.

Lorrie glanced at John and nodded with a full grin. His eyes glowed with pride, and he draped his arm over Lorrie Ann's shoulder and gave her a quick hug while staring up at his daughter.

The music faded, and Rachel spoke to the shepherds in a strong voice that brought good news and joy. As the light faded, the band and choir started "O Holy Night."

Horses' hooves pounded the ground from the outdoor area. People turned, and some stood as light flooded the right side of the grounds. Three riders, all from the high-school roping team, brought their horses to a sudden stop.

Bobby Gresham pointed to the east, toward the stage. "Magi, look! There is the Eastern Star we have been waiting for."

Kevin, his brother, removed his cowboy hat. "Where is the newborn King of the Jews? We see his star, and we'll go worship him."

The youngest of the trio and a cousin of Lorrie Ann, Rafe Ortega, swung his hand over his head, spinning his horse around. "Let us ride!"

Some of the spectators chuckled at Rafe's enthusiasm. All clapped as the three wise men rode out and the spotlight shut down.

The shepherds came and worshipped. The Magi brought gifts while the choir and band went through their songs. Rachel stayed overhead, leading the voices in praise.

The music stopped and the actors froze. Once again, the audience started murmuring. Whispers grew louder. Anticipation stirred the cool air.

Lorrie Ann bit her lip and reached for John. Would Derrick come through, or was it too much for him?

She looked up at John. His fingers interlocked with hers and squeezed. Then she heard it, the light tapping. It built as the drum moved closer.

As one, the audience turned to the front doors. Derrick stood still, playing a steady beat on his drum. The rebel teen's eyes remained glued to the stage, on the baby.

One boot at a time, he moved down the aisle. With each step, the beat became stronger. His voice joined the cadence, giving his only gift, the gift of his music.

Not another sound could be heard; even the animals remained silent. Derrick stopped in front of Mary and the baby. When his song came to an end, he bowed his head. The baby reached out to him, touching his hair. Derrick looked up to see the tears on Mary's face.

"Thank you for your song." Her soft voice carried throughout the silent building.

Lorrie Ann wiped the wetness from her face and realized many of the audience members had tears in their own eyes, including Mrs. Miller, the Dragon Queen.

Rachel raised her arms. "In the highest heaven, glory to God! And on earth, peace among people of goodwill!"

All stage lights went out, and the actors exited backstage as the choir sang "Joy to the World."

Lorrie Ann's heart burst with pride and happiness.

She watched John make his way to the stage, giving credit to the members of the band and choir. He called the kinder group up and introduced each as they waved to family members. The actors came onstage, and he called their names. Derrick hung back, but John motioned him forward, and as he nervously stood center stage, the audience surged to their feet with applause.

Lorrie Ann clasped her hands together and brought them to her mouth. Her throat tightened as she tried to swallow. Derrick shifted his weight from one foot to the other, gripping the drumsticks tightly. She smiled and waved at him. He sent back a crooked grin.

John had the committees stand and acknowledged everyone who'd worked on the pageant. Celeste and her friend Carlos brought flowers to John, giggling the whole time. The pastor smiled at Lorrie Ann and waved her over. She shook her head, her muscles suddenly going numb. Could she refuse? She felt over two hundred pairs of eyes turn to her.

"There is one last person we would like to thank before we leave for the night."

Celeste jumped up and down. John laughed as he placed his hands on her small shoulders.

Swallowing, Lorrie Ann made her way to the stage, one slow step at a time. She battled a strong desire to run the opposite direction as fast as possible. Her skin felt too tight for her muscles as blood ran a furious race throughout her body.

She made sure to stay focused on John in order to avoid the stares of the townspeople.

He took her hand. "Lorrie Ann, you have brought so many gifts to our town and its people. But mostly to me."

To her horror, he dropped to one knee. She became immobilized; the crowd froze.

"Lorrie Ann Ortega, I love you."

The townspeople gasped as one.

"You have brought more joy and happiness than I thought possible. You already have my heart. Will you do me the honor of sharing my life and becoming my wife?" He held a ring up to her.

Her eyes went wide when she realized it wasn't just any ring but her grandmother Ortega's ring. Her gaze shot up to find Aunt Maggie standing with Sonia, off-stage behind John. They had known? The sisters, both her mothers, stood in identical stances with hands clasped over their chests and tears in their eyes.

She forced air back into her lungs and looked down at John, still holding his pose. She saw his throat work as he kept his gaze locked on her.

She smiled.

He raised his eyebrow.

"At one time, you asked me if I could trust God," she whispered, leaning down. "Yes, I do. I love you and—" she swallowed the tears back and said the words that came the hardest "—I trust you." Pulling him up, she gave him a huge smile and cried. "Yes, I'll marry you—" Her words cut off when John grabbed her and swung her around.

"You scared me." He laughed.

The girls ran to them, Celeste's flowers losing petals as she squeezed tight. "We can have sleepovers now."

Her aunt, mother and cousin joined them, surrounding her in family love.

The audience stood on their feet, clapping and whistling. Some chanted, "Kiss her!"

John cradled her face in his hands and gently touched her lips with his. She closed her eyes, feeling cherished.

Someone else broke the spell by yelling, "None of that until the wedding!" Everyone laughed.

John rested his forehead on hers. "Are you sure you want to be a preacher's wife?"

"I'm sure I want to be your wife." She smiled at the rightness of the words. "I'll leave everything else up to God, including the dragons."

* * * * *

Dear Reader,

Thank you for taking the time to visit my small town of Clear Water in the beautiful Texas Hill Country. I'm thrilled to share it with you. Even though the little town is fictional, the Frio River is very real. Much of the landscape and a few of the places fill my own memories from childhood.

To share Clear Water's hundredth Christmas pageant with you has been a pleasure. I adore the Christmas season and all the traditions that go along with it. Between spending time with friends and family, baking the classic holiday treats and singing my favorite Christmas songs, I can feel the very creation of joy that makes the holidays something to remember.

In *Lone Star Holiday,* John and Lorrie Ann both have to accept God's forgiveness and people's love even when they don't think they deserve it. I enjoyed my time with them while they discovered the power of complete trust along the path to a new love.

I would also like to thank all first responders for their dedication and hard work, especially Brenda Gonzalez for answering all my questions about water accidents and airlift.

Stop by for a visit at jolenenavarrowriter.com. I would love to hear from you. The teacher in me would appreciate your opinions and answers to the discussion questions. Everyone gets an A!

You can also track me down on Facebook or Twitter.

Jolene Navarro

Love Inspired®

Save $1.00

on the purchase of any
Love Inspired® or Love Inspired®
Suspense book.

Available wherever books are sold,
including most bookstores, supermarkets,
drugstores and discount stores.

Save $1.00

**on the purchase of any Love Inspired® or
Love Inspired® Suspense book.**

Coupon valid until April 30, 2019. Redeemable at participating retail outlets in the
U.S. and Canada only. Limit one coupon per customer.

52616033

Canadian Retailers: Harlequin Enterprises Limited will pay the face value of
this coupon plus 10.25¢ if submitted by customer for this product only. Any
other use constitutes fraud. Coupon is nonassignable. Void if taxed, prohibited
or restricted by law. Consumer must pay any government taxes. Void if copied.
Inmar Promotional Services ("IPS") customers submit coupons and proof of sales
to Harlequin Enterprises Limited, P.O. Box 31000, Scarborough, ON M1R 0E7,
Canada. Non-IPS retailer—for reimbursement submit coupons and proof of
sales directly to Harlequin Enterprises Limited, Retail Marketing Department,
Bay Adelaide Centre, East Tower, 22 Adelaide Street West, 40th Floor, Toronto,
Ontario M5H 4E3, Canada.

U.S. Retailers: Harlequin Enterprises
Limited will pay the face value of
this coupon plus 8¢ if submitted by
customer for this product only. Any
other use constitutes fraud. Coupon is
nonassignable. Void if taxed, prohibited
or restricted by law. Consumer must pay
any government taxes. Void if copied.
For reimbursement submit coupons
and proof of sales directly to Harlequin
Enterprises, Ltd 482, NCH Marketing
Services, P.O. Box 880001, El Paso,
TX 88588-0001, U.S.A. Cash value
1/100 cents.

5 65373 00076 2 (8100)0 12391

® and ™ are trademarks owned and used by the trademark owner and/or its licensee.

© 2018 Harlequin Enterprises Limited

LICOUP44816

*With her family in danger of being separated,
could marriage to a newcomer in town
keep them together for the holidays?*

Read on for a sneak preview of
An Amish Wife for Christmas *by Patricia Davids,
available in November 2018 from Love Inspired!*

"I've got trouble, Clarabelle."

The cow didn't answer her. Bethany pitched a forkful of hay to the family's placid brown-and-white Guernsey. "The bishop has decided to send Ivan to Bird-in-Hand to live with Onkel Harvey. It's not right. It's not fair. I can't bear the idea of sending my little brother away. We belong together."

Clarabelle munched a mouthful of hay as she regarded Bethany with soulful deep brown eyes.

"Advice is what I need, Clarabelle. The bishop said Ivan could stay if I had a husband. Someone to discipline and guide the boy. Any idea where I can get a husband before Christmas?"

"I doubt your cow has the answers you seek, but if she does I have a few questions for her about my own problems," a man said.

Bethany spun around. A stranger stood in the open barn door. He wore a black Amish hat pulled low on his forehead and a dark blue woolen coat with the collar turned up against the cold.

The mirth sparkling in his eyes sent a flush of heat to her cheeks. How humiliating. To be caught talking to a cow about matrimonial prospects made her look ridiculous.

She struggled to hide her embarrassment. "It's rude to eavesdrop on a private conversation."

"I'm not sure talking to a cow qualifies as a private conversation, but I am sorry to intrude."

He didn't look sorry. He looked like he was struggling not to laugh at her.

"I'm Michael Shetler."

She considered not giving him her name. The less he knew to repeat the better.

"I am Bethany Martin," she admitted, hoping she wasn't making a mistake.

"Nice to meet you, Bethany. Once I've had a rest I'll step outside if you want to finish your private conversation." He winked. One corner of his mouth twitched, revealing a dimple in his cheek.

"I'm glad I could supply you with some amusement today."

"It's been a long time since I've had something to smile about."

Don't miss
An Amish Wife for Christmas *by Patricia Davids,*
available November 2018 wherever
Love Inspired® books and ebooks are sold.

www.LoveInspired.com